TWO LEFT FEET

TWO LEFT FEET

A Novel

Kallie Emblidge

DELL
NEW YORK

Dell
An imprint of Random House
A division of Penguin Random House LLC
1745 Broadway, New York, NY 10019
randomhousebooks.com
randomhousebookclub.com
penguinrandomhouse.com

A Dell Trade Paperback Original

ISBN 979-8-217-09275-8
Ebook ISBN 979-8-217-09276-5

Printed in the United States of America

1st Printing

BOOK TEAM: Production editor: Kelly Chian •
Managing editor: Saige Francis • Production manager: Jane Haas Sankner •
Proofreaders: Kathryn Jones, Frieda Duggan, Deborah Bader

Book design by Caroline Cunningham

Title page illustration: efks/Adobe Stock

The authorized representative in the EU for product safety and compliance is Penguin Random House Ireland, Morrison Chambers, 32 Nassau Street, Dublin D02 YH68, Ireland. https://eu-contact.penguin.ie

For Wes,

who hates football and loves me.

It's all for you.

“Some people believe football is a matter of life and death. I am disappointed with that attitude. I can assure you it is much, much more important than that.”

—BILL SHANKLY, manager of Liverpool Football Club from 1959 to 1974

CAMDEN FOOTBALL CLUB ROSTER, 2016–2017

NAME	NUMBER	AGE	NATIONAL TEAM
GOALKEEPERS			
Joseph Adamou	1	26	Cameroon
Nicholas Butler	23	22	England
DEFENDERS			
Anthony Moss	2	35	England
Kendrick Woods	12	25	England
Ahmed Haji	5	24	Morocco
Matthew Kelly	3	26	Scotland
Arturo Carda	22	31	Spain
Ji-Hoon Choi	4	29	South Korea
Henri Dupont	24	27	France
MIDFIELDERS			
Oliver Harris	6	26	England
Gavin Johnson	15	33	Wales
Charles Kerr	10	34	England
Lukas Weber	18	28	Germany
Noah Maes	20	29	Belgium
Alberto Garcia	8	29	Colombia
FORWARDS			
Marcos Santos	11	24	Brazil
George Allen	7	25	England

Trevor Keita	9	26	England
Emmanuel Asante	21	29	Ghana
Finn Bakker	19	25	Netherlands
STAFF			
Willem de Boer	Manager		
Sebastian Carr	Fitness Manager		
Anna Zhang	Head Physician		
ON LOAN			
Scott Hutchinson	27	23	Wales
Leonardo Davies-Villanueva	16	23	Undeclared

TWO LEFT FEET

Sunday, January 1, 2017: West Bromwich Albion at Camden

MATCHDAY 19

Blink and you'd miss it—a *whoosh* and then a sickening *thunk*.

And there he is: suddenly and involuntarily sprawled at the base of the freezing stairs, clutching his upper leg, pain radiating down to his toes. Oliver Harris is beginning to suspect that 2017 might not be his year.

"Ah, *Christ*," someone, probably Garcia, shouts from behind him. The remainder of the squad follows suit, bellowing and cursing as they converge in a protective ring around Oliver's prone form. He feels as if he's looking up at the chief mourners from his own grave.

It falls to Anthony Moss, center back and team captain, to make sense of the chaos. It always does. He assumes a crouch beside Oliver, stern in the face.

"Easy, lad, sit up now. What did you do?"

"Careful, it's slippery," Oliver jokes weakly, before he's hit with another queasy wave of pain. "Oh fuck, that hurts." He scrabbles his way to sitting, but finds it impossible to shift his left leg, his good leg, at all.

"We're getting Sebastian and Willem," Anthony says. "You stupid bastard." His tone brooks no argument, even if Oliver were inclined to disagree with the assessment. He nods resignedly, trying to regulate his labored breathing as it puffs into clouds in the cold air.

Anthony motions the rest of the men out into the stadium so only the two of them are left in the mouth of the tunnel. The squad can't wait for a diagnosis; there's a match to start, though Oliver won't be playing in it. The massive lights of Regent Road cut through the rain, streaming over the crowd, across the pitch, and down the tunnel to the changing room, a beacon for forty thousand witnesses to Oliver's private despair.

The sheen of the damp grass paired with the guttural roar of the crowd can make a man larger than he really is. Oliver doesn't believe in magic, yet he can't deny he's felt the air in the stadium fill his lungs with something more than oxygen. Now the familiar surge of adrenaline has turned poisonously inward, flooding his veins with anxiety and a stabbing in his hamstring. He lets his head fall back again as the medics swoop in to stretcher him away.

Hours later, he's still horizontal and he's still not alone, on a cot in Anna's office at the training grounds, Camden Crossing. It's only ten minutes in the car, with traffic, between Regent Road and here, but the small complex of brick buildings and manicured grass where Oliver's spent the better part of his life feels a million miles away from where his New Year's Day began.

Sebastian Carr had cheerfully stuck his head in around three to tell him Camden Football Club beat West Bromwich Albion decisively, and that Henri Dupont of all people had scored in the thirtieth minute to put them ahead. Oliver had tried to ask to see a clip of the goal before Anna shooed Sebastian from the room, telling him that he's not to bother patients in her care, no matter how many times he gets promoted. Oliver had felt vaguely smug at the dismissal; a few months ago, Sebastian had been a good-looking physiotherapist and his genuine friend, but since his elevation to the role of fitness manager and assistant coach, right-hand man under the reign of new manager Willem de Boer, he is no longer to be trusted.

Dr. Anna Zhang is a different story. It's not the fact that she's a brilliant physician—although she is, of course, specializing in orthopedics, plus a background in internal medicine, and some expertise in psychology; that would be true of any doctor at any club. It's that each of her patients is a sportsman, with all the money and the ego that comes with and yet when they're submitting themselves to treatment, they know for certain none of them are a match for her.

"All right, Mr. Harris," she says, smoothly sliding next to him on a rolling stool. She's sharp in wool trousers and a crisp blouse, only the sloppiness of her plait and a slight smudge on her glasses' lens betraying her day of work. "I've finished with the imaging. Shall we have a chat about where we are?"

"Start with the good news, please."

"I didn't say there was any," she warns, but she touches his knee with a gentle hand while she says it. The MRI reveals a barely visible tear, tiny fragments of splintered white muscle glinting against the glossy black of the photograph. He'd like to think there's been some kind of mistake, but even without a medical degree he can sense that the swelling matches what's looking up at him from his leg. "It could be much worse. Hamstrings bounce right back, and yours nearly held itself together," Anna continues briskly, taking the picture out of his hands and cutting his questions off at the pass. She rattles on in doctor-speak without missing a beat. "I'm more worried about recurrence than initial recovery. If you listen to me and we have just a bit of luck, you'll play again before the season's over. Late March, maybe April. And you'll certainly be able to keep fit—this won't preclude cross-training exercises. A couple days off your feet to start, all right? Just to be safe. I'll give you a pamphlet." She always gives them the damn pamphlets, and they never say what's actually going on, which is, of course, *You're screwed*. "I know this is a bad time of year to get this kind of news," she adds, more softly.

"Mate, any time of year is a bad time to get this kind of news," he says. He's still afraid they might try to make him go to a hospital.

"Don't call me that. Oliver, people get injured in this line of work, even you. And I won't prescribe anything for your mood unless you see a therapist, so do try to meet me halfway."

He slumps back and rubs irritably at his tired eyes with the flat of his palms. Even though he knows that she wouldn't talk to him this way if she didn't care about him, it still rankles. Oliver hates being hurt, forced to stop moving. Until recently, he considered himself someone who always takes painstaking care at terminal velocity. He doesn't go for the stupid challenge. He won't let a defender catch him unaware. Recently, though, he can't stop taking himself down—and he's never learned how to account for that.

• • •

Anna releases Oliver with crutches in hand, making him ring for a cab in front of her and swear on his life he won't walk back home. He's done it before.

There's something deeply undignified about the process of shoving oneself into the back of a stranger's car in a full football kit on a frigid January evening, toting two massive aluminum sticks and a bad attitude. Despite his wish for the earth to swallow him whole, or at the very least grant him a moment's peace, the cabbie recognizes him immediately. The whole of Camden, anyone born and bred in its borders, always does: if he's nothing else, Oliver Harris is their golden boy.

The man is sorry for such a tough break. He doesn't ask if the injury is serious, or how things are going with Willem, or for a selfie, just if Oliver might sign something for his nephew. The driver even has a Camden scarf at the ready, draped around the rearview mirror like a talisman. Oliver can't bring himself not to, circumstances aside. Even now, there's a tenderness to the recognition, a kinship in it. A pen is unearthed from the glove compartment with one hand as they snake their way through the honking cars and the spitting rain, so he scrawls his messy, practiced signature and adds a tiny number 6 for good measure.

When they pull up to the elegant, narrow townhouse, the cabbie shoots Oliver a look.

"A lot of stairs," he says leadingly. "You'll be all right?"

Whether or not he will be all right feels immaterial—he'll crawl up to the landing and sleep on a sofa if he has to, but he needs to be at home, alone, expeditiously.

"I've got it, mate," Oliver replies. "Appreciate your help." He stuffs sixty quid of crumpled banknotes from his wallet in the seatback pocket as he exits, in thanks and in penance.

He stumbles his way up to the front door, punches the keycode, and immediately begins shedding: crutches, training jacket, backpack, and the rubber slides Anna's PA fetched from the changing room each hit the floor in rapid succession. Oliver hobbles to the bay window and collapses onto the padded bench. Lights across the canal glimmer in the rippling water, an array of jewels tumbling in a box of velvet: breathtaking, no matter how many times he claims the view as his own, his city winking back up at him. Eventually, his reflection in the glass takes enough shape to remind him he's still wearing his shirt from the match, the Christmas-tree-green home kit he knows so well: color that echoes his eyes, an intricately stitched white rose resting right over his heart. It feels foolish to be wearing it in his house, like a supporter might. He hasn't been a fan of Camden since he was a child; his role in the club has been something heavier and more pressurized since the moment he hit puberty.

Enough self-pity for one day, he thinks. He's getting the sense he'll have to ration it for the next few months, which means it's far too early to be brooding and staring wistfully out the window—that one he'll save for later, after he's missed another match or two. Oliver limps back to the mess he's made and carefully returns things to their right places before beginning the slow trek up the stairwell, left leg aflame: step, pause, rest, step, pause, rest. The second floor will have to do for the evening's domain; there's the kitchen and a shower at least, and the guest bed has just as fancy a mattress.

He feels more human after he's rinsed off, with a glass of water in one hand and a much-needed carton of chocolate milk in the other. Not quite human enough to recover his phone from his bag and see what's awaiting him there, but enough to know it's time to do it anyway. Oliver's a dutiful person, on and off the pitch.

The team WhatsApp is conciliatory about his leg and jubilant about the win. He's been strongly encouraged to meet them out or let them come to his place. Just left seeing Anna. Can't drink on painkillers, he lies in response. Georgie and Noah, predictably, each react with a thumbs-down almost as soon as he hits send.

There are other texts and calls, an email from his agent, queries blinking up at him from the iPhone, but he shrinks from the lit-up screen as if the afternoon's injury was a concussion. In the guest suite, he flops face-first onto the bed and allows himself a groan, pouring his hurt and exhaustion and frustration into the down-alternative, handspun linen pillow sham.

When he'd bought the house, he'd still felt like Maggie's boyfriend in most of the ways that mattered, and she'd delighted in having an unlimited budget for a decorator. Oliver had let her loose, wild and spendy, and she'd gone on to commission an army of well-dressed designers to bring him local artisan pieces that were properly Feng Shuied for the space. Two years ago, barely twenty-four, it felt surreal enough to own a home, let alone a massive one next to the park, sillier still to care about the thread count on the spare sheets (seven hundred) and whether or not there should be stems on the wineglasses (there are). Now, he can appreciate that Maggie, bless her, knew exactly what kind of place would feel like home to him, so she'd spent his money and given it to him. Even this room, rarely occupied, emulates his favorite sort of off-season boutique hotel, all dark woods and warm beiges, an amber glass sconce on the wall and a weathered photo floating above the bed of his grandparents minding the bookstall.

From within the nest of pillows, Oliver asks Siri to call his mother. Nicola Harris answers on the fifth ring, sounding harried.

"Ollie?"

"Mum, hi. You on shift?" he asks, already knowing she is.

"I'm due for a break, they can cover. I didn't think I'd hear from you until late."

Without the senior Oliver Harris, Mum and Oliver the younger have both developed the tendency to conduct life squarely within the bounds of their work and their responsibilities, which makes them equally hard to reach. As a child without a father and a wife without a husband, this clarity of focus has kept them both afloat: Nicola cares for Camden's bodies; Oliver is meant to feed their souls. It also means that grief still thickens the air between them, catching Oliver unawares when it rears its head. He can't blame either of them for it; they've both just tried to survive, with every pressure heightened and only half of themselves free to meet it. He doesn't think he'd know how to safeguard his heart and his place in the starting eleven if he hadn't learned from watching her. Still, he hopes her bedside manner might give her care to spare for him tonight.

"Sorry, sorry, I don't mean to interrupt at work. It's just . . ." He trails off. "I'm not sure if you caught the match highlights or not? But I had a fall earlier. I . . . I tore a muscle in my hamstring," he rambles, knowing she hasn't watched anything if she's been at work, probably hadn't even known the kickoff time if she'd left before the crowds materialized.

"My love," she murmurs, just as he'd wished she might. Then she hops into crisis mode. He can see her transforming into who she really is: someone who handles injuries far greater than this every night without blinking an eye. "What happened? Where are you? Why don't you come round to the hospital right now?"

"No, no," he says. Oliver hates the hospital and the memories it evokes; hates any helpless, sick, or injured feeling. Instead, he rolls over to lie on his back and assess his leg, which looks the same as it has for hours, hurts the same too. "I slipped in the rain, it was my own fault. Daft, clumsy move. I've been with the doctor and now I'm home. She's got me sorted for now. I just wanted you to know."

"You've always been so lucky, so healthy . . ." she frets. Oliver has been lucky, his whole career, but he's also been careful, to the degree of paranoia, and he's been secretive, to the point of untruth, about anything that could slow him down or take him off the pitch. "I suppose everyone trips sometimes, but not everyone's legs are worth as much as yours. This is the last thing you needed. Goodness. How are you now?"

"Like you'd expect—I mean, it's fine. I'm relieved it's not worse," he says. "I just thought you ought to hear from me and not on TV."

She hums down the line, the swirl of the hospital playing out in the background. Oliver regrets giving her another thing to worry about, but her concern feels good, even as he hates causing it.

"You were right to ring me," she says firmly, hearing him without words. Any distance he's ever felt from her is always swallowed up in moments like this, when he tries to let the space open up and she chases him down. "Ollie. You know I wish I could be there now. Are you sure you don't want to stay at home with me? I could nip down and pick you up when I finish, as soon as I can."

Nicola lives just up the road, essentially, in the same flat on Hawley Road where Oliver grew up, where his parents did too. Despite his offering to get her a proper house or cut back her hours at work, she refuses anything extravagant. He owns the flat now, and he'd convinced her to let it be remodeled within an inch of its life—no builder grade left to speak of, fitting right in with the shiny new Camden they're both bewildered by—but Nicola still wakes up in the same place where she and Oliver Senior first lived and takes the number 1 bus to the Royal Free Hospital in her scrubs. Oliver could take her up on it, sleep in his childhood room and have breakfast brought in on a tray, but he doesn't feel he's earned it.

"I think you do enough nursing as it is, Mum. I should only be on crutches for a few days. I promise you, it's not a big deal."

She sighs, knowingly and a bit sadly. He wouldn't have called her if that was the truth.

"You'll get some rest?"

"I already am," he promises, meaning this one.

"We'll talk tomorrow," she says, half a warning. He can hear she's on her way back into the thick of it as she hangs up. His phone screen stays lit up after the call ends. When he cranes his neck, he sees the opening line of an email from Sebastian.

He audibly grumbles as he swipes to read the whole missive.

Oliver,
Hope you're getting some rest and feeling as well as you can. Anna assures me we've got a plan in place and will be making progress before we know it. I've passed along some info from her to Willem, and he likewise is relieved to hear things are well in hand.

He'd like to speak with you about the rest of the season. I know you're meant to start rehab in the next few days, but if you could come to the Crossing tomorrow and meet with him for tea, we'd be grateful. He'll be in his office from noon onward. Let me know if there's anything you need from me, recovery-wise. Here to help.
All best,
Sebastian

Oliver rolls his eyes at the insipid, formal business-speak and chucks the phone back on the side table without replying, rolling over again, for the long haul.

For the last six weeks, after Willem de Boer arrived from the Netherlands with his extended stares and his inscrutable advice, everything in Oliver's life has felt tenuous, right at the edge of shattering.

Back in 1987, James Finch had bought Camden Football Club with a notable chunk of his first billion pounds and has had, frankly, fuck all to show for his efforts since. So, on a Sunday morning last November, he'd called the team in—from Anthony Moss to the newest nutrition intern—after a dismal showing away at Everton, after they'd already gotten kicked out of England's interleague tournament. Over conference room tea service, he'd announced, grandly, that even a patient man must have his limits. He'd said this with Willem, former star of Atlético de Madrid and Manchester United and current steward of the

Dutch national outfit, standing indomitable at his side, with Camden's former manager conspicuously absent. Willem's job, Finch had said, was to make sure the coming year went better than the previous one. Since then, the changing room has changed very much and the scoresheets have changed not a whit.

Oliver has no doubt Willem is a genius on the pitch. There's that one goal from 2006 against Real Madrid, the one where he controlled a loose cross and flicked the ball past the goalkeeper without it ever touching the ground, and it loops in Oliver's mind whenever he's on the treadmill. But his arrival, his first big shot at the Premier League, was an open warning to every person at Camden Crossing: *Everything is about to be remade. If you don't get with the program soon, there will be no program for you to get with.*

There's not a great history of championship runs beginning with ultimatums. So it's obvious what Willem was hired to do, with his business degree and his chilly Dutchness: fuck the season in front of them, build something for himself and for Finch next year with a clean slate. He's given to long silences during tactical meetings and enigmatic looks at training. Sebastian was given a dream promotion; Oliver got himself expelled from the pitch with a two-match ban in December that de Boer didn't even bother to appeal. It doesn't seem to bother Willem when they lose or please him when they win. But Oliver can't afford to be patient or to be injured in the second half of a season when it feels like a lot more than their rank in the Premier League is on the line. Camden is in his blood and his heart and his ruined hamstring. Where is it to Willem, save for his pay stubs?

Oliver wants to fight him on it, to storm into the office, high on his newly volatile reputation, and tell Willem exactly what he thinks: that he can get in the long line of people who think they can do better. He knows he won't. The only thing in this world he loves too much to ever risk losing is the patch of grass a few streets over, so he'll go to that meeting and he'll listen, he'll smile, he'll nod, and then he'll go to physiotherapy.

• • •

Monday arrives with a sense of reassuring normalcy, a frosty gray London dawn alight with the bustle of everyone returning to work for the first real day of the new year. Camden is alive when the low tide of tourist season rolls out, friendlier and less frantic, all Christmas decorations without anyone crowding around the tree. Oliver loves it best this way, when the cold air is warmed by the smell of Indo-Chinese takeaway mingling with chip oil and lock water, somehow impossibly pleasantly.

He stays sacked out until he wakes without an alarm. Off days are the only times that belong to him alone; sometimes he sees Maggie or his mother or his teammates, but just as often he passes them happily alone. They're even better in the winter, when he can tuck away into long coats and knit hats and plaid scarves, hiding his form and his features just enough to ride the tube unnoticed and go for a bite or to the cinema without anyone tweeting about it. Well, without *too* many people tweeting about it.

Today, dread sets in anyway, from something bigger than the traffic. It sticks in his ribs as he parks and fetches the crutches, makes his way into the building. It sits thick in his stomach down the main hall toward Willem's office. No one else is around the day after a win to distract him or waylay his progress, so he limps up the stairs to the manager's office and knocks with his crutch on the heavy oak door that's sitting slightly ajar.

Despite the turmoil he's wrought, Oliver can't deny that Willem looks perfectly at home reading from his tactical notebook at the old writing desk, a Dutch philosopher king in luxury athleisure. He's strong and well-built even as he gets closer to fifty than forty, and frankly still rather handsome. Willem sets down his notebook and steeples his fingers, regarding Oliver intently for an arduous, silent moment.

"Well, how are we?" Willem asks, an eternity later.

"It's uncomfortable, but I trust Anna when she says that it won't be too long a recovery," Oliver says, quickly and with what he hopes is assuredness: a media soundbite. Willem dips his head once and waits for a beat, expecting more. He tries again when Oliver doesn't go on speaking.

"And how do you *feel*?" he probes. "A new year is the time to take stock of things. To be introspective. So that one doesn't make the same mistakes."

Oliver freezes. Willem said *one* but he meant *you*, Oliver is certain. There are going to be consequences for the last month, for his injury and his red card. The last thing he wants is to be introspective—to be vulnerable, in reach of the past. He might as well be nine years old, haunting the cancer ward with his dying father, or seventeen, standing in the first team changing room alone, or newly eighteen, explaining to Maggie why he's breaking up with her.

"I won't make the same mistakes this year," he murmurs.

"Oh, I'm sure you won't," Willem replies. "You've never struck me as careless, Harris, recent events aside." Oliver's leg twinges in acknowledgment. "Listen: I know my presence here is unsettling. I've seen how it's affected the dressing room. And I've been in your boots. I've been in Anthony's and now I'm in the manager's chair. There's much to do and precious little time to do it, especially without you . . . but we do have an opportunity to finish well in the Prem, and perhaps it's a silver lining that we have nothing else to focus on. So let's focus, shall we?"

"I am," Oliver mutters, still stung by *recent events* and all the different things Willem might have meant by saying it.

"I'm certain you are, and I'm glad to hear it," Willem says

evenly. "Now, before you go—I'm going to take advantage of the transfer window and recall one of our players on loan while you're recuperating. He came up through the academy, younger than you are, and he's been wasted ever since. Excellent potential, deployed ineffectively. You can show him the ropes, help him adjust, get in fighting shape. Let's give him a good debut and find a place for him to be of use, instead of abroad and on our pay sheets."

The other shoe drops, studs up, right into the tender flesh of Oliver's wounded leg. He won't even get the chance to avoid repeating last year's mistakes, because Willem wants to make use of Oliver just enough to sell tickets and prepare someone to supplant him. The whole meeting has been a pretense for Oliver learning this, without Willem ever having to say it aloud.

"You want me to . . . train my replacement?" Oliver asks, working to keep his voice level. He's a footballer, he can play dumb. The manager will have to spell it out for him. "I know I've been off my game, out of line, sir, but I'll fix it. There's no need to threaten me."

Willem appears surprised at this wording but furrows his brow thoughtfully.

"In a sense, he'll be your replacement, that's true, in the short term," he responds. "But more than that, I want you to have a hand in his career here, and I want you to have a partner in the midfield. You're the best example of promotion from within that this club's ever had. Your trajectory is seen as more a novelty than a priority. That's a colossal waste. There's far too much talent languishing in the academy and across the sea on loan, particularly when results are wanting at home. I'd like to set a new precedent. None of this is a threat, Harris."

That's absolute shit, Oliver thinks savagely. He can't be buttered up. If Willem wants a new midfielder, he should train one himself, or actually use one of the ones he has. He's not ever been in any of their boots, he won a goddamned Ballon d'Or. Oliver, meanwhile, has been injured less than twenty-four hours and is already relegated to a babysitter, when he should really only be thinking about returning to the kind of form he knows is still somewhere inside him. There's not a chance in hell Willem is seriously trying to win the Prem this year. They're barely clinging to sixth place and even that feels like luck. He'll keep Oliver around just until he's shaped a new starting eleven in his own image, and then he'll be on the chopping block too.

"Right," Oliver mutters, fight gone out of him like a deflating balloon, as he picks at the fraying maroon thread at the edge of his chair. "If that's what you want."

"It is," Willem says, almost gently, acting as though the atmosphere in the room hasn't changed at all. "This should be fruitful for both of you."

"Hutchinson, is it?" Oliver asks, already hating the idea of him.

"Oh, no," Willem replies. "Davies-Villanueva. Poor boy has been bouncing around, at Valencia, then Getafe, then Valencia again. He's a born playmaker, but they keep trying to make him play defensively, do the holding. It's not done him any favors—he's been all right in Spain, but it's time to bring him home and see if he can play for Camden, finally put some shots on goal. He certainly wants to try."

The name rings a bell—he remembers a skinny teen at academy events, years ago, with a wisp of an accent. He can picture Davies-Villanueva's face. He's got to be just aging out of the under-23s now, floating between loan spells until he can get himself a proper contract.

Maybe he will, by taking it from Oliver.

Tuesday, January 3, 2017: Camden at Bournemouth

MATCHDAY 20

You give up your life of athletic prowess and move somewhere without phone service? CALL ME BACK! reads the text from Maggie on Tuesday morning. His leg is much less swollen today, so Oliver had been planning to go to great lengths to re-create his precious free-day routine, as a treat. Now he thinks longingly of the butter croissant and flat white he'd planned on enjoying in a corner booth with his headphones in, mixing himself into anonymity with all the hungover punk rockers and bleary-eyed, jet-lagged tourists.

Did you give up on your life of artistic integrity and move somewhere without the internet? he snarks back. I'm wrecked. Tear in my hamstring, flying dutchman is making me spend recovery babysitting. Respect the mourning period.

It's always something with you, Oliver. Please ring anyway. A moment passes, then the phone buzzes a second time. When you're free and want to talk, I mean. Obviously.

He cracks a grin. In this world, few things are certain except hating Kilburn Rovers and adoring Margaret Corbyn. If he hurries, Oliver will still have time to get his breakfast after all, before he's due at the Crossing.

After being put through his paces on stretches and then what he thought was an hour of strain on the stationary bike, but, with the benefit of hindsight, might have in fact been closer to twenty minutes of light pedaling—his leg really does still hurt—Oliver's turned loose once more for hydrotherapy. He loves the frigid bite of the first dip into the plunge pool, and he especially loves that it's followed by a much longer stretch of luxuriating in what's basically a huge, fancy hot tub.

He's seen neither hide nor tail of Willem's ward in the nearly three hours he's been at the Crossing, so his guard is down when he lets himself into the unfortunately named Water Lounge. The shock of an ice bath is nothing compared to what he finds inside: Davies-Villanueva is there, all right, and he doesn't resemble the spotty tween of Oliver's memories. The young man standing in front of him, waist deep in the freezing water, is just that: a man. He's slight but well-built, several inches shorter and shades darker than Oliver's perma-fairness, dotted with freckles all over.

Davies-Villanueva looks up, gleaming white teeth chattering, at the sound of the changing room door.

"Hiya," he says, waving and trotting toward the edge of the pool, pushing deep brown curls out of his face. *Oh God,* Oliver thinks, helplessly. *He got fucking cute.*

"Hey, Leo," Oliver says, shooting for blasé and landing somewhere daft.

"It's Leonardo. Lay-oh," he enunciates; Oliver can hear Spanish sunshine peeking through the London accent. *Leo,* he remembers now. Spelled like Messi. Lucky him—his whole life, even if he's rubbish, people are going to keep thinking he must be destined for something because he shares this proximity (bears a resemblance, even) to greatness.

"Sorry, mate—been a while."

"Not a problem," Leo laughs, hoisting himself up onto the deck and shaking himself off like a wet dog. "I was never brave enough to correct anyone, when we were younger."

Oliver's not sure what to say to that, so he gingerly hops into the water Leo just vacated and hopes that will be that. But even after he gets his bearings, Leo remains there, sitting cross-legged on the concrete and watching him shiver.

"Going to get warm?" he asks.

"I don't mind the cold, actually," Leo says. "Reminds me I'm home. I'll wait for you."

"The water's shallow, I don't need a lifeguard," Oliver replies, snidely, immediately nasty before he can even think to be otherwise. "There's a TV here, above the therma-pool. And another in the changing room, or in the canteen, or in the lounge. Take your pick."

Leo looks bewildered, both at the tone and at the list of options. He nods in the direction of the heated pool and finally stands, moving out of Oliver's line of sight. He doesn't try to talk again throughout the length of the ice bath, seemingly solely focused on the echoey television audio, but when the fifteen minutes of cold are finished and Oliver joins him in the heat, Leo can't resist.

He tears his eyes away from the pre-match coverage and says: "It's weird to watch Camden play without you. I feel like you've started every match since I was, like, a kid."

If he tries to bond with me, Oliver vows solemnly, thinking bitterly of the recent matches he *hasn't* started, *I will drown him.*

He shrugs in response, even though Leo's right: Oliver's held down the midfield by himself for going on a decade. He feels unmoored when he can't play, four of his limbs missing instead of just the one with an injury. He wishes, fervently, he could be there, running drills in the chilly mist, making Joe work for his warmup shots, trying to emulate Emmanuel's pre-match Zen. All of those rituals make him who he is: competitive, superstitious, a lonely only child awed by the luck of spending his life with two dozen brothers.

Leo interprets his contemplation as companionable silence, which he ruins immediately.

"I was watching the match with my family last week," he says. "My dad was, like . . ." Davies-Villanueva trails off anxiously and Oliver flinches when he realizes why.

Everyone knows the origin story of Camden's boy wonder, wee Oliver Harris spotted by a scout in Regent's Park playing kickabout with his grandfather, already wearing a little green kit. He's just old enough to secure a tryout for Camden Football Club's new academy the next week and never looks back until he's the best player on the first team. A veritable English rose, firstborn son of Camden come alive at Regent Road. But, it's said in whispers, he almost didn't join the academy at all, after what happened with his father . . . and the rest is history, except for how it hasn't ever ended.

Oliver Harris, Sr.: inexplicable Oxford graduate, bookseller, Camden native, beloved husband, local tragedy. He'd wasted away before everyone's eyes, increasingly weak-limbed all over Camden Market, then dead six months after Nicola's colleagues at the hospital discovered that his worsening fatigue had come from a tumor, already spread to his liver.

He was gone before Oliver really knew him or was really known by him, but he's missed him fiercely every day, regardless. Sometimes he wonders if he should feel abandoned, or maybe angry, but even when he plumbs the most ungenerous parts of his soul, he's only bereft and nostalgic. Dad hadn't even liked football that much, too literary and introverted for team sports. He wanted Oliver to focus on school. He would have been disappointed that he didn't, that his son had gone to live in the academy instead and barely made time to study between training sessions. Their first and only fight had been about whether he might go. But Oliver remembers long afternoons organizing stacks of books into tunnels to crawl through, conducting dubious baking experiments while Nicola was on night shifts, watching old movies in the hospital toward the end—his dad was *fun*. He'd have been in the Camden box at every match, hollering himself hoarse, cheering for the younger Oliver.

He believes that, but he won't ever know. If he'd been better at football a few years younger, had more time to prove himself, he might have found out, but he wasn't and he didn't. What Oliver does know is that his parents had loved Camden. No other place in the world could hold their attention; they only wanted to stay here. So, Oliver can't leave—big clubs, people with money and titles, have asked—but his place is this one. This is the only place he'll ever be at home. Injured, in sixth place, statistics plateauing, whispers that he's lost a touch, inscrutable new manager, it doesn't matter. Harris means Camden, through and through, from the shirt on his back to the rose sprig tattooed down his rib cage. His grandparents lost their business and their son on Camden High Street; Nicola became a widow there too. All Oliver has to do is kick the football and do it loyally.

None of this private agony is for Leo Davies-Villanueva to share in. Oliver barely understands it himself.

"It was a long time ago," Oliver says. "I'm fine. People have dads, you know? I don't mind hearing about them."

Leo meets his eyes head-on—his are a Cadbury shade of brown, fringed by impossibly long, dark lashes.

"You're brave about it. You always were. But I probably should have said a couple more sentences to you before I brought it up right away."

This, for some reason, is the thing that rankles. Oliver's not brave about anything. What does Leo know about it? They barely know each other. They're not friends.

"Anyway, your dad was, like, what?" Oliver asks. Leo seems appropriately chastened by the change in subject.

"Oh, when you fell, he said that it might finally be my lucky day. I was so pissed at him—I mean, you were hurt and nobody knew how bad it was. But I guess he was right, in a way? I've been waiting and waiting, wondering if I might get a real shot here. I hoped, maybe, when Willem arrived, but you know, that came and went. Then he rings me, all serious, telling me it's time to move back to London. You'll have to tell me how I'm doing, because I've been bricking it."

Leo shrugs, dusting off those lingering nerves, and grins at Oliver.

Where to even begin? The happily hyphenated Davies-Villanueva clan *jajaja*-ing it up at Oliver's suffering? Leo praying for some long-awaited big break, like it's his to lose and not to earn? Oliver wonders, distantly, how much trouble he might be in if he took Leo out to the practice grounds and stomped right on his ankle. He needs to get out of here.

"I'm going to change," Oliver says, even as he's already halfway up and toward the door.

"Do you want to watch somewhere else?" Leo queries, somewhat meekly.

Oliver doesn't reply, only lets the silence speak for him, but ten minutes later when he's sitting in the canteen with a second coffee and a scrambled egg on toast, right ahead of kickoff, Leo reappears. A few admin staff, an academy kid, and Marcos, who didn't make the match squad, are all sitting at other tables, but Leo takes the seat next to Oliver without a word, both of them clad in matching black joggers and team hoodies—Leo's are creased with newness, never worn before.

They watch Finn kick it off to Trevor, who swiftly loses possession to Bournemouth, one of their big hulking strikers playing aggressively from the jump.

Silence isn't awkward during a football match. Sometimes, Oliver yells along with the best of them, cursing the ref and the opponents and God himself, but when he's really watching, with his head and not just his heart, he's quiet. He observes the footwork, picks out the upcoming passes before they happen, and because he's not made of stone, touches the rose on his chest and prays Camden will score. Leo seems to innately grasp this, sitting stock-still with his chin in his palm, tracking the ball back and forth like a cartoon character at Wimbledon. They spend forty-five minutes plus stoppage time this way, nary a sound or reaction passed between them. It probably helps that the match is a disastrous, scoreless slog that never leaves the very center of the pitch. The shrill pierce of the halftime whistle brings Oliver back to the present time and place, coming up for a gulp of air after a deep dive underwater. Leo looks at him and grimaces—even pulling faces, he has perfectly symmetrical features.

"What did you think?" he asks Oliver, who just shrugs again. Whatever de Boer asked of him, Oliver didn't promise to obey the spirit of the law rather than the letter. And he isn't particularly eager to reveal any useful information or thoughtful commentary. "If you were playing, would you do anything differently?" Leo tries again.

"Score, maybe," Oliver snaps. Leo's pretty face turns downcast; for the first time, he seems to understand that Oliver's responses are short and sullen on purpose.

"Did I say something wrong? Or have you always been such a dick?" Leo asks, hotly, a touch sulkily.

"Oh no, you're grand. I'm super thrilled to be taking care of your fledgling career instead of focusing on, I don't know, the Premier League."

They're sizing each other up across the table now, bristling and glowering. Oliver notices for the first time that Leo has a stupid gold hoop in his nose. It's a miracle no one has yanked it out of him yet.

"Well," Leo hisses back. "You're doing a great job. You've said ten words to me and been supremely unwelcoming. I guess I should be flattered that you're so threatened by me."

Oliver laughs sharply, all teeth and no smile.

"Listen, mate—"

Leo cuts him off before he can say anything further.

"I'm not your *mate,* but I am your fucking teammate, okay?"

Oliver takes a deep breath. He's going to get up and walk out of here and hopefully never have this lengthy of a conversation with Leonardo Davies-Villanueva again. He leans in and lets his voice drop to a whisper, carefully enunciating every syllable while looking squarely, unblinking, into a pair of furious, enormous eyes.

"Tell the gaffer whatever you want, but this"—he waves a dismissive hand between them—"isn't my job. If you're still in the picture in a couple months—which, for the record, I highly doubt you will be—I look forward to working with you. Otherwise, get back to Spain in one piece, yeah?"

• • •

Even once he gets home, Oliver's skin still prickles like he'll have to choose between fight or flight at any minute and he can't even properly pace the house with one working leg. He'd listened to the second half of the match from his phone in the shower. It was as bad as the first, the team limping to a scoreless draw and looking dead on their feet for the entire hour and a half. Now he's sitting on the sofa in his media room (a fancy name for where the big TV lives), ostensibly watching the news but actually frowning up at the ceiling.

What is it about Leo that makes him want to earn himself

another red card? One hour around this guy and he's seriously considering fisticuffs. It's kind of embarrassing—he *is* threatened, but he shouldn't be.

Usually, he loves having an academy graduate around, having been one himself. Camden FC produces clever and precocious footballers, roses to their very core. There's something to Leo, though, that makes Oliver's blood pressure rise. Does he think a triumphant homecoming to the first team and a once-in-a-generation playmaker for a mentor were his destiny and not an extremely rare combination of hard work, skill, luck, desire? And his whole vibe! The nose ring and the tan and the fluffy hair. What a complete prick. Leo doesn't look like a footballer; he looks like he did a master's at the Royal College of Art with Maggie—oh, he should call Maggie.

Seconds later, her flatmate answers, chirping brightly down the phone.

"Oliver! Oliver Harris! How are you? Coming by anytime soon? My boyfriend literally cannot wait to meet you, you know, everyone always thinks it's just *brill* that I know you," she barrels along cheerfully. The last time Oliver saw her, when he'd come to meet Maggie for dinner just before Christmas, she'd recently sworn off men forever and was courting a beauty from the artisan candle shoppe in the Maltby Street market. Talking to Millie is not unlike experiencing whiplash, but pleasantly.

"Mills," someone calls from the background. "That's my phone! Let him go!"

"We're catching up! Wait, give me that!" she says, but clearly Maggie has recovered the phone because now it's her voice saying, "Hi, hi, Ollie."

"Maaaaaaaagssss," he whines, drawing her name out into many syllables.

"Lay it on me," she says promptly.

"Do you think I'm, like, fundamentally a bad person who deserves cosmic punishment?"

"Yes. I've been saying that for years."

He snorts and slides partway off the couch, contorting his back in a way that only an extremely fit professional athlete could ever really manage and which almost definitely won't help his recovery.

"Willem wants me to teach this guy—some academy burnout, a no-name—how to be Camden's new favorite midfielder," he says, realizing as he speaks just how much that hurts to hear. "He's more interested in me showing it to someone else than he is in the fact that I'm still here."

Maggie hums thoughtfully, but not unsympathetically.

"Don't you think, maybe, that him asking you means he knows what he's got with you?"

"If I trusted him, I might think that." Oliver had suspected this reasoning from her and he rejects it. "But I don't trust him. I think he's punishing me for losing my cool last month and then getting injured right after. And catching up with this guy didn't give me a lot of confidence in his judgment."

"Okay, oof," she says. "What's his deal? Do you know him?"

"Hardly. He's been on loan in Spain, so he's never played in the Prem, he clearly thinks he should have been called up sooner, he has *so* much energy, and he was extremely upset that I do not want to be his best friend."

Oliver counts the reasons on his fingers as he lists them off to be sure he doesn't miss anything.

"Name?"

"Leo Davies-Villanueva," he says, adopting a Spanish lisp to say the name as dramatically as possible. Almost as soon as he gets the words out, Maggie lets out a soft "Oh." From the background, Millie shrieks and wolf-whistles.

"Ollie, he's so *handsome*," Maggie says. "We can't hate him!"

"Wait, how did you even do that? Did you have Instagram open this whole time? And yes, we can hate him! We do hate him!"

"Maybe I hate you! The cutest boy in London is vying to hang out with you, and you loathe him. This is criminal. What a waste," she sniffs. She's joking, but Oliver winces. Recently, everything has been sitting so close to the surface, liable to pop up and knock the wind out of him with no warning.

Maggie was his first girlfriend—his first real best friend too. They'd met in primary school and been inseparable until the night of his eighteenth birthday. They still are now, but differently so. By eighteen, Maggie was an absolute knockout, all thrifted blazers and silky hair, as well as an art history student and budding sculptor, while he was just getting used to keeping all his things in the first team changing room. And Oliver couldn't keep lying to her. He wanted to keep her close, to hold on to the Camden of his childhood and to her wonderful company, and he loved her, of course, he loves her still, loves her loud laugh and her calloused small hands, but he knows now he wasn't ever really *in love* with her. He was in love with football, and maybe with the famous names who transformed from his idols to his co-workers before his eyes.

There were no gay men in the Premier League when Oliver's career began, nor in any other top flight in any country, and *technically* there aren't any now either, because he's not telling. Someone tried once, in the nineties, but he never made a team sheet again. One guy in America came out and the day the news broke Oliver cried in the shower until he felt woozy from the steam, partially because it was a huge deal, but mostly because it still felt like it hardly counted—not when it happened somewhere where they call it *soccer*.

It's a different kind of serious in England. The stakes are

higher—too high—for him. Oliver wants to believe he can't be the only one, that he's not totally alone in the life he chose, but he is. *There's no one like him,* Camden fans like to say, *no one like Harris.* And it sure feels like there isn't. All his life he's taken the pitch with ten other teammates and thousands of screaming people in the stadium, but he's always been alone.

Even when he hasn't wanted to be, or hasn't wanted to believe he is, something—some*one*—always reminds him. In December, it was a midfielder from Southampton, who Oliver had snapped at, told him to stop tugging his shirt. *Yeah, all right,* he'd said back to Oliver, almost conspiratorially. *Don't get yourself in such a fucking strop. Acting like a faggot, you are.* The way he'd said it, so casual, like they might have a laugh about it together after the match was over, tore Oliver in two. He'd gotten himself into a bigger strop, and he'd shoved him down, hard, right to the pitch, unprovoked in the eyes of anyone standing more than a foot away from them. He couldn't defend himself, to the referee or his teammates, nor to Willem later. To admit why he'd done it would reveal why it bothered him so much—so Oliver accepted his suspension, watched Camden lose the match and then the two he was forbidden to play in, and read all the headlines, all of them right but none of them knowing why: HARRIS LOSES HIS COOL. CAMDEN'S ROSE HAS ITS THORNS. IS OLIVER HARRIS WHAT HE USED TO BE?

"Ground control to Major Harris," Maggie says, drawing him back from the memories. "Sorry, shouldn't have said that. I'm only teasing."

"I know you are, Mags. But it's not . . . that's not why," Oliver says vaguely, afraid of what Millie might hear.

"I believe you. But I also believe this kind of thing will solve itself. Try not to resent him too much."

Maggie's right, but Oliver will allow himself the dignity of not admitting that to her.

"You're running late to the studio, aren't you?" he asks, pleased when it comes out airily, as if it just occurred to him.

"Someone called in a crisis and kept me," she replies. "Goodbye, Ollie. I love you," she reminds him as they hang up.

• • •

Oliver dreams about the World Cup. It's in England and the final is at Wembley, a misty night with stars somehow visible overhead. There are the three lions on his chest and it's the seventy-fifth minute, but his uniform is starchy white. His hair isn't sweaty at all, still neatly sweeping across his brow. He's not tired, either, tracking the whole massive length of the pitch faster than he's ever run before, the ball fairly glued to his left foot. The team scores again and again and again. When he finds the stands, he sees his parents and Maggie all together, dancing and shouting with face paint on their cheeks. His own face aches from smiling—he's so happy, so incredibly happy, he's going to be a world champion. He scores *again,* a chip from outside the box, such a sexy little thing. He wants to run to the nearest teammate, wants to jump into their arms. Then he spins around toward his left and standing there laughing brightly, curls askew under a headband, hands reaching for him, is Leo.

Oliver sits bolt upright in bed, chest heaving. His bedroom is meant to be calming, with crisp white sheets and a smattering of tapered candles lining a deep-set window. Somehow his whole body is thrumming anyway, gasping for each breath. When was the last time he dreamt of his parents like that? Why on earth would he be celebrating the World Cup with Leo Davies-Sodding-Villanueva, even subconsciously? How is 2017 already so weird and cursed and awful, just four days in?

He works his way up, registers the stiffness in his left leg, and immediately sits back down at the foot of the bed, rubbing at his throbbing forehead. He wants to skip training, an urge that's unfamiliar and unwelcome to him. Of course he won't, of course he *can't*, especially because Joe is picking him up and that means he's already late.

Joe is the Premier League's most underrated goalkeeper and Oliver's best football friend, since they were the only first team players too young to go out drinking. He is also always two things: overdressed and ten minutes early. When Oliver limps down the icy stoop, Joe is leaning out the window, wearing a freshly pressed shirt and shaking his head at Oliver's running leggings and ratty old team hoodie, mismatched under his calf-length winter coat.

"You didn't need to come get me," Oliver grumbles, once he's gingerly climbed into the passenger seat. "I'm doing great, as you can see."

"Are you?" Joe says. "I was actually going to say I have a New Year's resolution for you: cheer up."

"It doesn't feel like a new year," he replies. "It feels like the end of an era. Every time we get to the Crossing I wonder if it'll be the last time. I worry we might never play together again. I'm perfectly cheery, under the circumstances."

"Is that it, then?" Joe asks, sounding shocked. He reaches over to jostle him—Oliver bats him away and points insistently at the road. "De Boer is in your head, man. I'm not going anywhere, I swear to you, neither of us are. You've been stringing Camden along by the laces of your boots since you were a kid. They'll not let go of you."

"Willem might."

"No, he won't. He just wants to see what we're made of. What we had wasn't working for anyone, so he's trying something new."

It's a generous read, and Oliver has never had a reason not to trust Joe's judgment before, but he doesn't buy it.

"He called back Davies-Villanueva, the one on loan in Spain.

He asked me to mentor him. He's coming to training and he'll probably debut before I'm back," Oliver says. "I think Willem wants me to shape him up to take my spot. I have this horrible feeling, like I'm actually finished here." His voice is tight and hoarse with the effort of holding back tears, which embarrasses and infuriates him.

Joe regains his grip on Oliver's biceps and gives him another shake.

"Ollie, you beautiful fool. You're missing the forest for the trees. Why would Willem want anyone to learn from you if he thought you were shit? This is a gift. He's finally giving you a midfield partner. No more having to do it all alone." Oliver shakes his head, still not looking at Joe, chewing on his lower lip. Since his arrival, Willem's piercing looks seem to see all the weakness in him, the stuff worth punishing, not preserving. Joe, bless him, loves Oliver too much to see that, but *he* can feel it in his gut. Willem is testing him, first with playing time and now with an unbearable boy. Oliver doesn't think he can handle it. He's always coasted on being young and healthy in addition to being talented, but now he knows that you can only ever see the light of a dying star, and he has no idea if he might be about to burn out. And if he's not a footballer, he's not sure who he is. He's given everything up for the sake of being one. He thought it would be worth it, for Camden; he never anticipated it would mean this. "I wouldn't lie to you, mate," Joe insists, less forcefully.

"Christ, Joe, of course not," Oliver says quietly. "I know you wouldn't."

"So do you believe me?"

"I believe that you believe it, sure."

"You're not going anywhere. We're gonna get old and retire here and then they're going to bury us under the pitch," Joe says as he pulls into his parking spot.

"Speak for yourself." He turns to face Joe. "I'm getting cremated and the urn is going on your bloody mantel. Now leave me to brood, would you?"

"Yeah, yeah," Joe says, ruffling Oliver's sandy brown head as he exits. "Lock it behind you. And if you're not inside in five minutes, don't think I won't send Charles to get you."

It's no idle threat—Charles is built like a bulldog and about as friendly—so Oliver only waits three minutes before getting out of the car. He wasn't expecting Leo to be skulking in the fog, blocking the players' entrance to Camden Crossing from beneath a bundle of hat and gloves and scarf. The newcomer looks decidedly chagrined; somehow, even the way he lifts a hand to wave feels passive-aggressive.

As they stand across the car park appraising each other, Oliver feels a sweeping shame that someone could witness him glowering at a new teammate. It's accompanied by continued annoyance at Leo, who seems to always appear when he's least welcome and ruin even the best of feelings.

Oliver takes his time walking to the door, both to delay the inevitable and to demonstrate some kind of masculine mastery of the chilly air. When he reaches the building, Leo still hasn't moved or spoken, so Oliver raises his eyebrows in an approximation of a question, hoping they communicate something along the lines of, *Well, you'll have to go first, because I could stand here comfortably all day.*

"I shouldn't have snapped at you," Leo says sorrowfully, by way of greeting. "I'm sorry."

Oliver bites back a laugh. He's not ever seen a person look colder or more begrudging. If it were anyone else, it would be truly kind of him to wait outside, clearly miserable, nearly late for his first day in the Premier League, just for the sake of delivering an apology.

"And don't you look it," he replies, saccharine-sweet, then

feels like an arsehole for it. He relents, sighing and nodding an acknowledgment, then yanks the door open, indicating Leo should step through first. Reluctantly, he chucks an olive branch at the back of his head. "Go on and start getting ready. I'll introduce you to the lads."

The changing room itself is pure, unmitigated chaos: twenty-two men under the age of forty in varying states of undress, hollering over each other in a not-uncramped space with strangely excellent acoustics. It's loud, colorful, and truthfully a bit smelly. Oliver loves it. When he steps in, the whole room unifies into the bedlam of hellos and he's buffeted by a rush of Camden-home-team love, better than any drug could ever feel.

"All right, you animals," Oliver shouts from under the crush of a group hug he's receiving from Garcia, and Joe, and Ji-Hoon, and Trevor.

Anthony, leader of men, gets his voice to rise above the crowd.

"If you fuck his leg up more, he'll just be gone longer," Anthony calls out, and Oliver gratefully claps his captain's hand in greeting as he extricates himself from the tangle of limbs. "And who's that you've got with you?" he continues, gesturing to where Leo is hovering in the doorway, looking unsure. Oliver wills himself to come off as welcoming, polite, mentorly.

"Okay, boys," he announces, though he's certain he's got everyone's attention already. "Some of you might remember Leo. He's back from loan, courtesy of the gaffer and my bum hamstring, fresh from Valencia. Everyone, meet Leo. Leo, meet everyone." He probably should have more to say—about Leo's career or about his potential as a teammate—but he's only exchanged a handful of noncombative words with the guy and couldn't be arsed to watch the scouting report Willem foisted on him, so this will have to do.

Luckily, the equipment staff has put Leo's things in an open locker next to Ahmed Haji, who came up through the academy the year above Leo and was called up to the first team three months ago. The two of them gravitate together to start an excited, whispered conversation that also seems to involve taking selfies. Oliver's work here is done. He starts changing at his own stall, which is both tidy and long inhabited, with a number of pictures taped to the green metal and an extensive, expensive skincare routine in his shower caddy.

He's about to strip down to his swimming gear, preparing for the ceaseless pattern of laps back and forth in the water instead of around the pitch, when Willem and Sebastian enter the fray, descending the stairs from the main building. The room silences and pivots all attention to the two of them, but rather than speaking, Sebastian begins drawing an intricate, many-colored diagram on the whiteboard. Standing beside him, pale and cryptic under the fluorescent lights, Willem surveys the team placidly. After a beat, he speaks—Oliver isn't sure if his tone is ominous or if it's just what he's saying that's so unsettling:

"Harris, a word?"

Joe shoots him a panicked look. Henri visibly winces. Oliver doesn't respond, just rises from beside his locker and follows Willem into the small meeting room next door with the feel of a man walking the plank. He shuts the door behind him, conscious that the upper half of the room is windowed and that Gavin is a strangely talented lip-reader. Willem, predictably, only sits across from him in one of the scattered plastic office chairs and says nothing at all.

"Something up, coach?" Oliver asks grimly, resentful to be made to initiate his own punishment.

"I've heard your meeting with our young Leo was a disaster."

Oliver blanches, lightning fast, before schooling his expression to blankness and forcing out a questioning hum.

"Spare me the particulars," Willem sighs, before turning his full focus on him with something more forceful in his face than Oliver's ever seen. "What did I miss, Oliver? Everything I've read about you, everything I heard before I took this job, led me to believe that anything I might wish to accomplish in Camden led back to you. I thought you were the beating heart of this club."

Willem sounds almost plaintive, but his eyes are angry. Oliver waits for his own anger to come, defensiveness even, but only fear and a deep well of sadness rise up to meet him. He *wants* to be those things. He thinks he can be. If he isn't—who is he at all, then? That's what all this has been for, the whole sum of his life.

"Come on, sir. You might have thought that, but you didn't ask anything of me, until you wanted me to train someone else," he says desperately, before it occurs to him to attempt guardedness. "Why didn't you tell me to play harder? Train me to score more? Appeal the match ban?"

Willem, somewhat distressingly, leans forward and rests a heavy hand on his shoulder. Oliver starts to move, intending to shove him off, but in the nick of time he thinks better of it and stays in place, right fist clenched in his lap.

"Oliver, I fully expect you will always score often and train hard. You are a remarkable footballer. And last month you were clearly in over your head. I could see why. I wanted you to take a beat, and I didn't want to start my tenure here by provoking the officials," de Boer tells him, sincerely, looking him right in the eye. "What I want to know now is if you'll be our next captain. If someday you'll be on this side of the room talking to someone sitting where you are now." Oliver feels his heart drop into his stomach in a churning mixture of relief and the gnawing sensation he can't seem to shake lately, whatever he does. He nods jerkily, but Willem is already continuing on. "We're on the same side, Harris, but you need to understand something. No matter how he talks to the media, James Finch does not understand the delicate balance of power a new manager has. He lacks the patience or the vision to wait out a careful rebuild."

That Finch is behind this approach is news to Oliver, who only ever suspected Willem to have such an agenda, eager to begin razing and reconstruction. As an institution, Camden Football Club has always been resigned to mediocrity, regardless of the flashes of brilliance. Clearly something has shifted without him noticing.

"What does that mean for you, then?" Oliver asks, while he's on the streak of earnest questions.

"For *us,* Harris. If we don't finish at least fourth, if we don't qualify for the Champions League, I'll be sacked. Likely they'll try to get as much money as they can for you, then they'll give it a go with someone else."

"Jesus fucking Christ—ah, sorry, sir." Even in his darkest fantasies about what this change in management might mean, he didn't realize it was his head so specifically on the platter, or what he'd have to do to keep it off of it. All those big contracts he's said no to, for all these years—none of it will matter if Finch decides to sell him.

"I don't disagree. It was not an ideal set of terms for a job, I admit. But to coach in the Premier League . . ." Willem says, smiling wryly. Oliver gets it. He'd take that kind of risk too. He has taken it, over and over. "I wouldn't be here if I didn't think it was more than possible, and if we can do it—" He falters slightly, then regains course and composure. "I'm keen to manage this team for longer than a few months. To manage you."

Against his will, Oliver feels himself resigning to a truce. He can't—no, he *won't* leave Camden. He doesn't care how much money Finch could wring out of selling Harris to the highest bidder, he'll stay here and play for pennies if he has to. And if he needs Willem, of all people, to help him stay, then so be it. Apparently, they both need all the help they can get. He forces his body to unclench, and exhales forcefully.

"I'm warning you, we'll never be as good as you were. But I'll give it my best shot, as soon as I can. We all will," Oliver says vehemently. Then, less enthusiastically, "And I'll talk to Leo."

"That's all I ask, Harris. I think you, at least, might have given me a run for my money." Willem claps him on the shoulder again, then once more for good measure. Oliver bravely doesn't roll his eyes at the comparison, assuming his best imitation of a loose, cheery demeanor when he returns to the main room. Casually, as if it just occurred to him, he saunters over to lean against Leo's newly acquired locker. The younger man looks up from a concentrated stare at Sebastian's whiteboard. Oliver beams, which unfortunately but hilariously seems to frighten him.

"Come on, time to meet everyone properly," he says briskly. Leo doesn't move.

"I've met some of them," Leo replies, like he thinks it's a trap.

"What, you think Ahmed is better company than I am? No offense, mate," Oliver assures Ahmed, who is a good sport and merely throws a sock at him. "Come on, Davies. Ugh, no. Davies-Villanueva? What do they call you, with fewer syllables?"

"Davito," Ahmed supplies. "Little Davies." Leo looks betrayed and murderous, but he doesn't protest.

"Davito," Oliver says definitively, and tosses the offending sock back. "With me, then." He ushers him over toward the center of the room, to his own locker, and plops him down. Ignoring the painful twang of resistance from his hamstring, he crouches next to Leo. "Brace yourself," he warns. "There are, as you can see, rather a lot of us."

"You really don't have to do this," Leo replies. "I got the message. I know you're not, like, volunteering to be my tour guide."

Oliver is tempted to take the out, offered up so easily, but it's too late—he's gotten it into his head that this is what he needs to do, so there will be no stopping him now. Willem won't question who the beating heart of this operation is when he's through. He can be winsome, and charming, and all the other things too.

"We got off on the wrong foot," Oliver says, understatement of the century. "If you'll let me help, I'd like to."

Now Leo is the one seeming tempted.

"Go on, then, mate," Leo confirms, only a bit of a challenge in his voice. "Let's have it."

"Cracking right on. First up: there's Joe and there's Nick—" Oliver points to the corner of the room where the keepers hold court, both of them lanky and big-handed and currently silent. "You know how they can be—they have to get to an entirely different headspace than the rest of us. Let them keep their headphones in and don't bother them now, and then try to make them smile when you get on the pitch. Joe is all laughs, but Nick can be a nervous wreck." Leo nods in time with each sentence, giving the distinct impression he wishes he could take notes. On some level, Oliver respects the attentiveness, but a larger part of him wants to watch him squirm. He's a footballer, not a saint. "Could I get the back line to join us for a moment?" he calls, and a swarm of defensemen materialize in front of Oliver's locker. Leo doesn't waver, but some of the color leaves his cheeks. They're each about twice his size. "Captain, tell us about these fine young men," Oliver continues. Anthony grins.

"Well, Leo, you know me and you know Ahmed," Anthony says, waving his hand between the two of them. "So that covers that."

Henri curses incomprehensibly in French.

"You will make him sick with your wretched English humor," he sniffs. Everyone boos and summarily drags him to the back of the crowd ("Oh, sod *off*, Henri," Georgie adds from across the room, guffawing). Leo looks shell-shocked at the new, rapid flow of banter and overlapping chatter, in a different language than he's probably used to, but he chuckles along with them.

Anthony gets them back on track and presents the others in a single breath:

"Kendrick Woods, Matty Kelly, Arturo Carda, Ji-Hoon Choi, Henri Dupont," Anthony pronounces, each of them bowing in turn. They're a magazine-cover bunch, with Woodsy's high cheekbones and Ji-Hoon's glossy, inkblot hair. Carda is from Galicia, so he pulls Leo away to gossip in Spanish while the others mill around Oliver, who reclaims his locker seat. Matty good-naturedly kicks at Oliver's healthy leg.

"Nannying looks terrible on you," Matty says in his thick Scottish brogue. Oliver sighs and kicks him back.

"Don't you start," he replies glumly. Matty chortles and joins Henri in raiding Oliver's stash of moisturizer. Leo catches his eye from where he's standing down the aisle and half his mouth curls up into a shy half-smile. Only because Oliver is already looking at him does he catch the barest flutter of Leo's hand from where it's dangling at his side, a whisper of a wave. Oliver must have some of that English humor in him, because he responds by saluting him back with a crisp, exaggerated snap of his elbow.

Sebastian has at last finished his scribble of practice plays and shouts an "Oi oi" that they all echo, a well-worn call-and-response. They assemble in a haphazard circle around the board, squashed up against each other and leaning into each other's space with easy, practiced intimacy. Oliver loses sight of Leo, then spots him on the periphery sandwiched between Carda and Garcia. The other members of the team will meet him naturally, he supposes, so in a way he's gotten off easy, despite the significant look from Joe that he's pretending to not see.

"We're running five-a-side today," Sebastian says. "Nothing

cheeky, let's see how you move. We've got a week's break with a full squad, I don't want to waste a moment of it."

"Off we go," Willem adds, if only to have the last word.

Woodsy is nursing a bone bruise on his ankle from a nasty challenge in Bournemouth, so he hangs back as the others jog out toward the foggy training ground.

"Shall we get some laps in, then, Woodsy?" Oliver asks him. Before he answers, Noah Maes comes down the stairs with an arm in a sling.

"Fuckin' hell, you too?" Woodsy asks. Noah waves sadly with his left hand.

"I've been sent for lifeguard duty," he says.

"Fat lot of guarding lives you'll be doing one-armed," Oliver notes. "If I go under, I'll tell you right now, just let me go, mate. Don't strain yourself." Woodsy gets him in a headlock for that and starts dragging them off toward the pool, mussing his coiffed head in a way that's only allowable before it's about to get wet anyway.

"I'd save you, man," Woodsy says. "And they'd probably knight me for it."

Oliver hoots as he finally pushes himself free. The water looks much more inviting than last time he was here, with Noah and Woodsy and the faint sounds of training filtering in and echoing through the cavernous space. He leaps off his right leg into the lap pool, flopping headfirst into the chlorine-scented water and breaking into a powerful stroke, too fast for anyone to reach him.

• • •

He's shaking droplets out of his fringe in the shower when Anthony crops up in the doorframe, earlier than Oliver would've expected.

"Captain's privilege," Anthony says by way of explanation,

but he winces and Oliver knows that means his knee is troubling him.

"Steady on," Oliver replies. "Can't lose you too."

Anthony scrubs at his salty face and steps under an adjacent spray.

"Don't I know it," he gargles around the stream of water. "Bad fucking time for it." There's something jagged lodged in his throat—it's not like Captain Anthony, always so present and resolved. Oliver surmises he might not be the only one caught in a whorl of resentment and exhaustion recently. "When you're young, you want to be in every match, every season, right until the last second. But then you get old and you hurt all the time, so sometime in January you're ready to throw in the towel until it warms up, and you hate yourself for wanting to."

Oliver can't imagine it. Sometimes he feels old for his years, but in this way he's absolutely still in his twenties. Everything else hurts: it's the game that feels good and he's aching without it. Anthony meets his gaze for the first time, then shrugs and continues in his normal, level tone.

"Maybe you'll get it someday, but I wouldn't be surprised if you stay young and spry forever. You've got the temperament. The new lad does too," Anthony concludes. He shuts off the water and starts to leave. Oliver glares at his retreating back. He slams his own shower off and stomps after him, naked and outraged. Anthony, infuriatingly, has crinkles around the corners of his eyes and wicked amusement on his face.

"Oh, come off it. He's that good?" Oliver asks, rumbling with indignation.

"He's a little pocket rocket, all right," Anthony replies. "Very quick on his feet." Oliver, who currently cannot run at all, finds this deeply offensive. He roughly towels his hair rather than answering, but Anthony carries on. "I don't know why you're so pissed about this. If I were you, I would be sodding thrilled. You two could be Charles and Gavin, but, you know, *something*. Xavi and Iniesta in London."

"Yeah, only Xavi and Iniesta like each other," Oliver scoffs from beneath his towel.

"Then you better put on that famous Harris smile and go be his buddy," Anthony says. "Don't you want to ever see Camden's name on a trophy? Stop looking a gift horse in the mouth."

"I'm being perfectly pleasant, and I've not once looked in his mouth, all right?"

Anthony flings his head back and cackles, like a cartoon villain.

"I'm sure you haven't," he replies. "We're going to watch the end of training, so cover up your arse."

Watching everyone practice without him, fawning over the shiny new Leo, does not sound like a particularly fun or mentally healthy activity, but he can't see a way out of it. He wouldn't put it past Anthony to fine him five hundred pounds for leaving early. Reluctantly, Oliver puts his clothes back on and slinks outside, crunching the frosty grass under his trainers as he makes his way to Noah and Woodsy. They're sitting in the first row of Camden Crossing's small cluster of stands and observing the ongoing five-a-side. Oliver leans against the railing, all the weight on his good leg, arms crossed for warmth, and tries to size things up.

"What's the verdict?" he asks.

"Trevor's on a hot streak," Noah says. "But Davito nutmegged Ahmed and tackled Charles."

"You're leaving out the part where Nick accidentally stepped on Marcos's foot and then he called him a bastard," Woodsy adds. Oliver whistles lowly.

"Bet Willem loved that."

"He said something about how we should always endeavor to act with trust and respect, but I'd wager my car he swore in Dutch first," Woodsy reckons.

Oliver surveys the scene enviously. Aside from Marcos, who looks pissed, and Garcia, knackered, everyone appears to be in good spirits. The ball is whipping to and fro between the two miniature squads and the men on the sidelines are shouting encouragement between substitutions. Trev is moving so fast that the ubiquitous Tourism New Zealand and Nike logos are a blur of white on his training kit. Oliver wishes he could run down and join them, even leap onto Joe's back and earn himself a booking for goalkeeper interference.

"Golden goal!" Willem announces from where he's standing and watching at the edge of the pitch. "Next one wins, gentlemen." Everyone, save the ten lads in the fray, whoops and shouts. Georgie digs out a challenge on Finn and scrambles up to pass to Leo. Unexpectedly, Oliver finds himself calling out to him.

"Come on, take us home!" he yells, accidentally.

As if Leo's heard him, he stumbles, startled, yet manages to keep the ball in his possession. He takes a sloppy extra touch, but regains control and suddenly whacks a sharp, hard shot with his left foot, right past Joe's outstretched fingertips. The whole team erupts.

Glittery-eyed and open-mouthed with joy, Leo keeps running, turning a jubilant circle back toward the squad. He spots Oliver and points toward him gleefully, once, twice, thrice, like he's dedicating the goal. Somewhat bashfully, Oliver returns the gesture with a bow.

Even Willem's ending whistle somehow sounds pleased as punch.

• • •

While the others finish slapping each other on the back and singing about needing a one dance (so badly it must be purposefully off-key), Oliver and the rest of the wayward injured orphans lounge around the sofas in the canteen. Halfway through his second cup of tea, people start to trickle in, everyone appearing distinct for the first time all day in their street clothes and smelling of a hundred different colognes. The sofa is full to bursting with Joe and Trevor shoving in alongside the three of them, but Oliver keeps his armrest open and waves Leo over so he can perch on the end, because he's a nice lad and not a dickhead. This is the first time he's gotten a good look at Leo in repose, wearing beat-up black skinnies and an absurd, color-blocked windbreaker. His damp curls and big jacket make him look tiny, and young, and much less threatening. When Leo brings one leg into his chest, resting his chin on his knee, Oliver can see that someone's drawn a little sunburst in black ink on the rubbery side of his shoe.

"What happens next?" Leo asks, more eager than anxious. Trevor speaks before Oliver can.

"Your guess is as good as ours," he says. "Willem is a man of mystery."

"And he grew up in The Hague, man," Joe adds. "That's where he'll send us if we can't hack it."

"Stop it, we talked about this. You know The Hague is, like, a fully normal city," Oliver tries to assure him, and himself as well. "This is just the first big break we've had with him around. Not sure how he'll handle it."

"Probably with sprinting drills," Noah predicts gloomily.

"And heart rate monitoring," Joe adds.

Leo has the look of someone whose own heart rate monitor would currently be beeping wildly. Furtively, Oliver jabs him with his arm, just enough to make himself felt without disturbing Leo's edge-of-the-couch balance. They make tentative eye contact and, in the relative privacy between them, Leo gives him a look somewhere between a grin and a grimace.

They're still pulling faces at each other when Willem clears his throat from behind them. The rest of the team is clearly already at attention, looking at the manager. Leo erupts in scarlet and Oliver's sure he looks the same. Willem is as stoic as ever, not saying a thing about it.

"I won't keep us," de Boer tells the full group. "Only to say that this was a great session. We need to have more of them. You're all very fit and you've been so for months. I want you to think of our next meeting in terms of refinement and commitment."

There's definitely going to be sprints, then. Or they're bound for The Hague after all.

"What I mean," their coach continues, "is that we have an opportunity to hone our techniques. For precision. And we have an opportunity to hone our *connections*. You will learn to trust yourselves and each other. For the rest of the season, I want you to be able to look at the man next to you, see him and acknowledge his strength, knowing he thinks the same of you." Willem talks like a cult leader sometimes, but it also works. Everyone is meeting his eyes with rapt focus, like he's talking directly to them—Oliver included. Leo's forearm is radiating heat where it's still making the lightest contact with Oliver's own upper arm. "We'll go through the specifics during tomorrow's session. Also, we'll only have morning training all week. Light time in the gym. When we play Swansea, I want your legs fresh and your minds hungry. Have a good evening."

The energy in the room is pleasantly sparking with electricity as Willem ambles off and everyone else makes moves toward departing. Oliver is nobody's private detective, but even he can sense what some of this spare time might be meant for. He steels himself, then catches the sleeve of Leo's jacket in his hand before he can stand up.

"Okay workout? You feel okay?" Oliver asks, inanely.

"I'm buzzing," Leo says—and he looks it. He has such an expressive face, the kind that's impossible to keep secrets with. Oliver surprises himself by smiling back.

"That's how it's meant to be," he replies. "Good on you. I know I'm missing your first couple go-rounds, but if you have questions, or you just want to talk, I'm here." The words feel weighty and clumsy in his mouth, but he finds that he means the offer genuinely. Leo is wary, his eyebrows scrunching into two puffs. Oliver goes for broke. "I'm sorry too, while we're at it," he confesses. "I was upset about a lot of things the other day, not just you."

"And you're not upset now?"

"Not with you," Oliver hedges.

Leo runs his index finger across his lower lip. Oliver dutifully maintains eye contact.

"Will you drive me home?" he asks. "I don't have a car yet."

Oliver flashes an affirmative thumbs-up. "I can do that. Let's go." Leo gives him an address in Marylebone, just as close to Regent's Park as his own home, only a little ways south. The drive is short and silent—when he agreed, Oliver hadn't considered how claustrophobic it would feel for them to cram into a sports car with only each other for company. He responsibly keeps his eyes trained directly in front of him as they glide down the outer edge of the park and then across Baker Street, before Leo directs him to a side street and a chic building that might pass for a boutique hotel. A shiny-capped doorman is holding the front door ajar for a man in a three-piece suit talking animatedly into an earpiece, displaying a polished marble lobby visible even from the car.

"You have expensive taste," Oliver tells Leo, who blushes again.

"Give it a rest, I needed a quick lease. I've barely unpacked," he replies. "I'm not fancy." Oliver can't really argue, what with his own almost-mansion.

"No one said that," Oliver chides. "Not in that jacket. Expensive, maybe. Fancy, no."

Leo's mouth forms a moue, but jokingly—the pout doesn't reach his eyes.

"You're teasing me," he says matter-of-factly. "Like friends do." It lands with a wallop.

"Maybe we're going to be friends, then," Oliver suggests. They aren't looking at each other, but he can feel the hot weight of Leo's attention like a physical thing.

"I tried that already," Leo reminds him. "Now it's your turn."

Oliver makes a concerted effort to turn his whole body, so that they're facing each other over the center console the same way they did across the car park this morning.

"Fair play," he says. "Should we shake on it?" Leo rolls his eyes and starts for the door handle, but for the second time in twenty minutes, Oliver grabs for his arm. "I mean it," he insists, sincerely. "You were right, before. We're teammates. No one could accuse me of being a mentor, but I'll try that too, if you want."

Maddeningly, Leo leans into the touch, leaving Oliver gripping the muscle of his biceps and resisting the urge to squeeze.

"No one could accuse you of anything, Harris." Leo puts his hand on top of Oliver's to detach it from his arm, letting his forearm flop back into his own lap. "Thanks for the ride. I'll see you." He closes the door and Oliver puts the car in gear, wondering if he'll ever have an interaction with Leo that doesn't leave him driving home in a fugue state afterward.

• • •

The next few days are less emotionally charged, infrequently eventful. Oliver gets his medical treatment but feels about the same, spins or swims till his mind goes blank, then freezes his arse off in the stands while everyone else does strange bonding activities. They take Sunday off and that's as close to normal as anything's been in weeks. Oliver shows off by making his mother a chicken korma before she brings him back down to earth when she mercilessly thrashes him at Scrabble, then lets him fall asleep on her sofa under the ancient wool afghan like he's a teenager again. *You look like your dad, more and more every day,* she tells him when they're saying good night, and it's more than they usually talk about him, and hearing it sounds like the highest compliment. All the racking turbulence in his heart settles down to a gentler rocking motion, one that doesn't make him nauseous.

Monday rolls around in a liminal space—the week is fresh but there's still five more days without a match. If Oliver were healthy, he'd be restless and itching for competition; while he's injured, he just feels marginally achy and listless. Everyone else seems to be enjoying the break, though. It's actually quite discomfiting to have your doctor smile while they make you stretch your torn hamstring until it throbs in pain.

Inevitably, the wanton destruction of the relative peace in his life and routine comes from Willem, delivered via Sebastian. It's downright balmy for London in January; Oliver's vantage on the sidelines could almost be sunbathing. He's tipping his head up to the sky and hearing the city rumble just beyond the fence line, drinking in the cloudless blue, when someone calls his name. When he comes back down to earth, Sebastian is standing above him with an air of impatience.

"Join us, Ollie. No legs required."

He's of the mind that nothing with no legs required is quite worth doing, but it wasn't phrased as a question, so he clambers to his feet over the protestations of his hamstring.

"Trust ball," Sebastian announces to the larger gathering. Everyone is appropriately confused by that nonsense, but he continues on regardless. "Stand across from your partner, put a meter between you. Pass the ball back and forth, heads only. I want to see you maintain a rhythm."

"There's a twist," Willem shouts from the edge of the pitch. Of course there fucking is. There's a groan, in unison, from every man over the age of twenty-six. Oliver bites back his own dissent. "By the end of the exercise, I want you to be able to tell the squad something about your partner we don't already know." Everyone mutters apprehensively, the musty scent of mutiny lingering in the air. The manager is unperturbed and continues what must be a prepared monologue. "The game," Willem says, undeterred, "is to hear each other over all the noise. You each could make these passes asleep and blindfolded. But for *this,* you have to listen. Strive to allow your partner's words in. Shut out other noise. Be someone they can count on. Put all of your energy into this moment, on being part of this team. Talk to each other, not to yourselves. Let's begin."

It's some business-degree nonsense, Oliver can tell, better fit for primary school than the Prem. *Team-building.* It's extremely undignified but intuitive enough; the squad starts to assemble themselves and Oliver tests his weight on each leg, feeling out his range of movement.

"Going to tell me all your secrets, Harris?" Finn asks, moving to stand across from Oliver and raising one eyebrow suggestively.

"You couldn't handle them, Finny," Oliver warns, but he throws him the ball regardless.

The drill is less exciting than Willem tried to make it—there's not much the team doesn't know about each other, and the only things left to tell are the pieces Oliver guards close to his heart.

Every other pass, when Oliver tries to share a fun fact, Finn replies, "Duh."

Finally, Sebastian calls them off, neither satisfied nor upset with their performance. Oliver fears they're about to be quizzed on what they've learned, but he only tells them to switch the lines up and go again. When Oliver looks up from tying his shoelace, Leo is hesitant at his side, clearly having been directed there by Willem and probably also by Joe.

"You need a new partner?" Oliver asks, feeling irresistibly like he's back in primary school. Leo nods, biting one corner of his lips anxiously. "Then you go first," Oliver mutters, lobbing the ball over to Leo, who bops it neatly into the air with his forehead. While it hovers above him, he shouts back to Oliver in the panicked tone of someone confessing to a crime.

"I have three passports," Leo says. Before Oliver can process or react, the ball is flying back to him. He nudges it skyward and immediately becomes aware this game is more difficult than it looks.

"Try again, we could've guessed that."

"I'm allergic to shellfish," Leo offers, somewhat feebly.

"Not good enough."

"Why don't you give it a go, if it's so easy?"

"Oh no, you keep at it."

At last, Leo's pass strays off target and when Oliver turns to go and fetch, he sees the rest of the squad in awkward silence, futilely resetting after each quiet pass. Gavin has given up completely and is instead watching everything with a glimmer of mirth in his eyes—Oliver flashes him a deeply sarcastic thumbs-up as he passes by.

"I like to draw," Leo offers, as they start again, which explains the doodle on his shoe. Oliver has a sudden vision of Leo as an artist, instead of an artistic midfielder—he can see him in a beret, holding a painter's palette, cigarette behind his ear.

"Draw fouls, maybe," Oliver replies, laughing at the image in his head, which for some reason makes him kind of shivery.

They continue like this until he knows that Leo once shoplifted a Kinder Bueno and his dad made him go back and return it, the only time he ever snuck out of the academy was to go cumbia dancing, and that he broke Oliver's own record for passes completed in a season for Camden's under-18 squad. Oliver keeps his own mouth shut, but the more he listens, he has to admit, Willem maybe had a point about staying present in the moment—it would be useful, in a match, to be able to hear the calls of his teammates so clearly.

• • •

Oliver hasn't driven Leo home since that first day—he's been preferring to call a cab or catch a ride with Garcia, but Oliver extends the offer anyway as they're walking out of the changing room. Leo hesitates.

"I was going for a glass of wine with some of the others—catching up, you know, with some of the guys from my year," Leo says.

Oliver huffs a laugh, picturing Leo's induction into Ahmed and Carda's very exclusive social club.

"Oh, mate," he tells him. "You are in for a fucking treat. Try not to let them take you to a second location or you'll be shite tomorrow."

Leo smiles, the tentative but pleased kind of someone newly included. They're nearly to the car park when they're intercepted, Nina Clarke racing over in her pinchy-looking stilettos that still leave her a good two heads shorter than either of them.

"Oliver! You are a hard man to track down," she says breathlessly.

"Nina, I'm in this building for hours every day," Oliver reminds her.

"Metaphorically hard," she replies. "But I'm glad I caught you—Royal Charity wants to get something on the books for this quarter."

"Yeah, I'm happy to," he says, all businesslike. "You can have them call my agent. I'm not traveling for any matches right now."

Leo is looking between them, eyes slightly narrowed. Oliver ignores him and starts to inch toward the door, but Nina, either oblivious or just great at her job, goes right on.

"That's what I wanted to talk to you about. They've got a lot of families in right now, they'd like to see if any other players are available to come with you. Are you open to leading something like that?"

Leo pounces faster than he would for an opponent's stray pass.

"What's the charity?" he asks.

Nina takes in the sight of him, young and handsome and earnest, then smiles winningly when she smells blood in the water.

"I should have introduced myself," she says, extending a manicured hand to shake. "I'm Nina Clarke, executive vice president of public relations and sporting media." It's an impressive title, almost certainly with an additional adjective since the last time Oliver saw her. "I work with the team on publicity and charitable opportunities. Mr. Harris partners with the hospital just up in Hampstead. He's been working with them for years. They have housing for family of patients who are in hospital, and we arrange visits with their children—games and reading, the like. It's exciting for them to have guests, especially footballers." She turns her smile on Oliver, then back to Leo with shrewd eyes. "You're just aboard—it could be a chance to place your name, show good face. How do you do in front of cameras?"

"Nina, it's fine," Oliver cuts in. "You know I'm happy to film whatever. One hundred percent at your disposal."

"I'd like to help," Leo says, words overlapping with his own.

"If Harris will have me. I think I'd do okay in front of a camera."

All good, thanks, Oliver imagines replying. *I've got the local family tragedy market covered.*

Nina looks simply delighted.

"That settles it. I'll get both of your agents in the loop tonight." She *click-clack*s back off, leaving them alone.

"Right," Oliver says. "Good charitable lads we are. Have fun at wine night." He makes another attempt at the door.

Leo takes a step closer, near enough for their knees to knock.

"I really do want to help. And to, like, learn. I'm not trying to be a bother," Leo murmurs. This is precisely the kind of collaboration Willem would be dead keen on. Oliver just can't shake the nagging suspicion that if Leo sees him doing this, all his careful silence during trust ball will be for nothing and he'll never be able to keep a secret again.

"I'm glad to have you. But Nina will never let you go now," Oliver says, trying to balance whatever heavy thing is trapped between them.

Leo's nervous expression softens, just as Carda dances up to them with mischief radiating out of every pore.

"*El vino más fino y Leo tan feo,*" he croons, horribly. "*Fiesta, fiesta, que nada molesta!*"

"One of your worst songs ever," Oliver says without hesitation.

"And he doesn't even know what it means," Leo adds. Their reviews don't dampen Carda's mood in the slightest; he simply winks and squires Leo away under his arm, leading him out the door. Oliver wonders absently if he would benefit from learning some actual Spanish.

. . .

His hamstring is hollering at him, a pulsing ache all down his upper thigh. The increased mobility from stretching and treatment and cross-training is coming at a price, along with a reminder that Oliver's recovery is still very much in progress. As soon as he gets home from the Crossing, he hauls several bags of emergency ice from downstairs into the tub and turns the faucet on full blast.

An email dings when he's lowering himself in. The icy water is sluicing over his hip bones and his forearms are shivering with cold and exertion as he grips the marble edge of the tub and carefully, carefully inches downward. Once he's submerged and has caught his breath, he snags his phone from the floor to read.

Nina and their agents have been trading notes for the last few days, and now they've agreed that Leo will come with Oliver to the hospital next month for one of his public visits. They'll shoot a set of photographs to make it all nice and official.

Oliver's had a lot of time to mull it over all week since that strange car ride, and he's decided, begrudgingly, that Willem is right. Leo is neither a beautiful daydream sent to tempt him, nor a fuckheaded upstart intent on ruining his life. He's just a footballer, one who is excellent on the long ball. He's going to be his teammate and, apparently, his friend. That'll have to be that.

Besides, the hospital work is important, possibly the most important thing to him besides football. He always dreads going, seeing himself in the tired kids' faces and the sad-eyed parents, until he gets there, when he loves it—once he can stop posing and shaking hands and sit quietly with one of the children, reading them a book, talking to them seriously, like he wished someone would have when he was there with his dad. If Davies-Villanueva is going to come with Oliver and be part of it, he's got to trust him and be trusted in return. There's no room for rivalries or anger there.

His leg goes blissfully numb as the bathwater turns from frigid to tepid, then to boiling when he tops it off. Between the wisps of steam, he slides down the back of the tub and dunks his head under, letting out a bubbly exhale. Oliver surfaces, wipes his fringe out of his eyes, and, living dangerously, goes for his phone with a dripping hand.

Busy weekend for us, hey? he texts, opening a new chat thread in WhatsApp.

A reply chimes approximately twenty-four minutes later (but who's counting?) while he's sprawled across his bed on his belly, reading *Fever Pitch* for the hundredth time.

How so? No debut 4 me :(Leo's written.

Still got a match to watch tomorrow. Injured guys meeting @ Castlehaven Arms for pints and banter. See you in the morning? Oliver replies.

I'll be the one with green face paint x

We'll be sure to get you a separate table. Oliver spends an inordinate number of minutes debating whether or not to include a kissy-face emoji, if that kind of joking affection is allowable. He sends them to Joe all the time. Eventually, he uses a rose and hits send before he can change his mind.

Saturday, January 14, 2017: Camden FC at Swansea City

MATCHDAY 21

It's an injury-approved walk to Castlehaven Arms, only five minutes up Camden Road into the center of the neighborhood, the cluster of the city where he's always felt most at home. Camden might look different now, more and more so every passing month, but the bones are the same. It's been a long time since people recognized him as Oliver from Camden instead of Oliver from Camden FC, but when he looks closely, Oliver can still find his home in the bricks, among all the familiar sounds and streets. Sometimes he suspects everything in his life is eons away from where things started, no matter what the map says, and that makes him wonder if everything is eons away from where they should be, but then he takes the same route through the same park he's always known, and his feet meet the road as solidly as if they were rooted to the earth.

Camden is playing in the first match of the day, so Oliver lets himself into Conor Bishop's pub before noon, exchanging the cold city air for the smell of beer-damp wood and hot oil. Conor is the dreamiest restaurateur north of the Thames and openly gay to boot, and he never misses an opportunity to flirt with him. Conor seems to think it's a fun game of chicken with a famous footballer, but for Oliver, it's the most reliable action he'll get all season.

Inside it's a fantasy of twenty-first-century England, posh and homey at once, brimming with tartan and black-and-white photos of Conor's extended family at home in Nigeria. Conor is behind the bar like he pulls pints for a living instead of collecting Michelin stars, the sleeves of his waffly shirt pushed back and a tea towel draped over his shoulder to great effect. Oliver feels somewhat the knob wearing double denim and stark-white trainers.

"Don't think you can always just show up before we open, Oliver," Conor says, but he's eyeing him up and down and kicking open the door to the private back room.

"I'll never learn if you never turn me away," Oliver tells him. "You spoil me."

"Someone ought to," he replies in his deep, deep voice, flashing his white teeth, and Oliver flushes so pink he feels the color in his toes. He wants to reply in kind, wants to grope around for the limit just a bit, but before he can, Conor's eyes flit to the door and he nods a greeting.

"Looking for him?" Conor asks, and Oliver turns to find Leo and Woodsy standing at the threshold. He feels like he's been caught doing something incredibly illicit.

"Looking for you, brother!" Woodsy tells Conor cheerily. He hops nimbly onto a barstool and reaches over to smack him on the shoulder. Oliver waves, slightly bewildered, to Leo, beckoning him over.

"Have a good night?" Oliver asks the pair of them; Woodsy nods.

Conor slides two sweet red ales across the counter, the chilled glasses already sweating condensation down the sides, looking so good it doesn't matter that it's still morning. Oliver is going to down his in one enormous glug.

"You're a new face," Conor says to Leo. "Injured too? What do you like to drink?"

Leo has a suspicious scrunch of his mouth where Oliver has come to expect an easy smile.

"Healthy, just getting my sea legs. I'll have what they're having."

Conor, to his credit, is undeterred, reaching under the bar and pulling another pint.

"I hope you teach these lot some manners. I say the Camden boys are always welcome wherever I am, then I usually regret it immediately."

"Oh, shove it," Woodsy declares. "I'm your favorite customer." Conor shakes his head.

"Sorry, Woodsy. Harris is my guy." Oliver feels a pleased rush alongside the feeling, again, that he's been spotted in the middle of something private. Undeterred, Woodsy pivots the conversation as cleanly as he can kickstart a counterattack.

"This is a big day for Davito—you're really home now! Drinking at Castlehaven is as close to hazing as we're allowed to get," he says, knocking each of their glasses together in rapid succession.

"Here's to Leo," Oliver adds. "May you never again know the pain of drinking here on matchday, only the thrill of drinking here after a win."

"And may he never stand on top of my bar and try to start a round of karaoke," Conor chimes in. "As both of you idiots have done before, despite knowing you were risking a lifetime ban."

Finally, Leo cracks a toothless grin.

"I'd have liked to see that," he says, buffing Oliver with one shoulder.

"You're giving him too much credit. It was bloody awful," Woodsy snorts. Conor nods in somber agreement. Oliver feels sabotaged and embarrassed as he faintly recalls tottering along the narrow wooden surface last season, regrettably belting The Smiths, then abruptly remembering nothing else of the rest of the evening.

"Let's talk about something else, shall we?" Oliver tries, turning his attention to the TV mounted above the liquor bottles. "Leo, a pop quiz?"

Right on cue, Woodsy begins slapping his hands rhythmically on the table, chanting "Pop quiz, pop quiz, pop quiz" under his breath. Leo nods, bravely and gravely.

"Tell us everything you know about the strikers," Woodsy says.

"And the midfielders, your new comrades," Oliver tacks on. "Learn anything useful the other day?"

"All right, all right," Leo replies, training his eyes to where the TV is showing Camden's squad warming up in Swansea, each of them looking cold but determined.

"Charles and Gavin," he starts, counting on his fingers and screwing up his face in concentration. "Dynamic duo. I bet they retire soon, but they've got a combined football IQ of, like, a million."

"Generous," Woodsy says. Oliver hushes him and gestures for Leo to continue.

"And then besides Oliver, there's Lukas and Noah and Garcia. Noah is just getting back from being hurt, he won't play today. He invited me to a yoga class with him, which was nice. Lukas is . . . German? And Garcia is from Colombia too, he speaks Spanish the same way my mum does. I like him."

"Lukas *is* German," Oliver agrees. "That's the lot. Who do you think you'll play well with? When the time comes, I mean." He's dead curious for the answer, though he tries to ask it casually.

Leo runs a finger down his glass and ducks his head, put on the spot.

"I think we'd do pretty well, Ollie," Leo says after a beat. Woodsy roars with approval while Oliver's heart turns a somersault in his chest and drops like a cannonball straight through his belly. *Ollie, Ollie, Ollie,* echoes through his head. Conor saves him by delivering three glasses of water, which Oliver gratefully chugs, just to have something to do with his mouth.

"What about the strikers?" he manages, when he feels in control of his voice again.

"Marcos is, uh, not friendly," Leo says matter-of-factly, cutting through the strange tension and making all three of them laugh.

"Do go on," Woodsy snickers, spinning the top of his stool around. Oliver's never met a footballer who wasn't as big a gossip as a schoolgirl, childishly delighted by any exchange of secrets or shit-talking.

"Trevor has the most goals on the team, but Emmanuel has the second-most assists in the entire Prem," Leo continues.

"Black excellence." Woodsy nods sagely, to which Conor offers him a fist bump.

"Then there's Georgie and Finn and that's it. Do I pass?" Leo asks.

"We'll keep you," Oliver says carefully.

In Swansea and on the screen over their heads, Camden is assuming position, a smattering of small green soldiers on a big green expanse. Conor shouts that he's opening the doors, and with their hands full of pint glasses, the three of them slip into the back room for some privacy from the rest of the pub crowd, the revelry and beer drinking settling to a focused quiet as they turn their full attention to the match.

Oliver feels the keen ache of the sidelines—he wishes he could run the length of the pitch a hundred times over, even if he could never have the ball. Maybe the last week of playing around and finding themselves actually worked, because the starting eleven looks fearsome and famished for goals. They're running circles around the hapless Swansea midfield. Emmanuel is moving so quickly he keeps straying offside unexpectedly, slipping past defenders without realizing it.

Camden keeps up a sustained, hard press for twenty-five minutes, chipping away until there's nothing left to do but break through. Alberto Garcia, the best-looking holding midfielder in all of Europe and perhaps the slowest runner on any continent, steps around his opponent almost nonchalantly, just inside the penalty box, and delicately lobs the ball over the keeper and safely into the back of the net.

In the moment of chaotic, flooding giddiness, Oliver casts a fleeting glance at Leo, who's tipsy and looking maybe a touch overwhelmed.

"All right?" he asks, under the pretense of nudging their glasses together before play resumes.

Leo nods and shakes his hair out of his face.

"I'm good, I'm good! God, it's nice to be home. It's so normal, actually. I didn't expect we'd get to go out in public like this."

Oliver takes a deep, satisfying gulp of his drink, letting the carbonation wash all down his body in place of the celebration on the pitch that he's missing.

"Not every week, and not in places where we can't get a room to ourselves, or we'd all get beer guts and be stalked by the fans," Oliver says wistfully. "But when there's something to celebrate or something to need perking up over . . ." Sitting next to each other here, crammed into one booth even though most of the room is empty, Oliver can smell the floral notes of whatever product Leo uses in his hair and can see how fine the gold hoop in his nose is.

"Which are we doing?" Leo asks, startling Oliver out of his observational trance. "Celebrating or perking up?"

"Why not both? Celebrating your arrival and letting it perk us up," Oliver says magnanimously, going for yet another, gratuitous cheers.

Leo's smile crinkles at his eyes, and the two of them spend a long stretch of breaths looking at each other, maybe for the first time, really. For the life of him, Oliver now can't remember why he hated Leo so much, why his arrival announcement sounded like an alarm bell or a death knell. Only the peal of the starting whistle snaps them out of it, drawing their eyes away and up to the screen again. The rest of the match passes joyously, Finn scoring his first goal since his transfer from Eindhoven and Emmanuel closing the door completely even after Swansea pulled one back in the second half. When the ninety minutes are up and the squad is jogging happily offscreen, Oliver is full and warmed, a bit drunk and a lot happy. Woodsy has a Camden scarf tied around his head and Leo has given up his chair to stand behind them both with his arms flung over their shoulders.

"*Increíble,*" Leo pronounces. "*Espectacular.*"

"Olé," Oliver agrees, slumping forward onto the bar. "Now it's bedtime."

"You're wasted, man!" Woodsy hoots. "You can't go out like this."

Oliver waves him off irritably, burrowing deeper into the pillow of his elbow. Of course he's not going out anywhere, he's going to *sleep*.

"I'll walk him home," Leo says. "Let the wind wake him up." That promise is good enough for an annoyingly sober Woodsy, who promptly pays the whole tab and leaves them to it. "Come on, Harris, on your feet."

Oliver cracks open one eye for the sole purpose of being able to glare.

"I'll call a cab. Lemme sleep," he grumbles. There are worse things than being left alone with Conor Bishop.

"My job isn't secure enough to leave you here, Ollie." Leo hauls him up by his collar until he's reluctantly vertical. "Let's go, champ."

Oliver becomes lucid again somewhere along Prince Albert Road, skirting the perimeter of the park, the blurry world revealing some familiar green landscape. He's still on his feet and an investigation of his pockets reveals his phone is on him too. Leo holds up Oliver's keys, jangling them and shaking his head reprovingly.

"Oof," Oliver mutters to the cloudy sky, deciding not to mention his house has a keyless entry. "I think I'm already hungover. We didn't even say goodbye to Con."

"I did," Leo says. "Just wait for tomorrow, Harris, and you'll wish you felt as good as you do now." They keep walking, heading up the path of the water toward Oliver's place, in between the noise of the city and the quiet between them.

Oliver has lived here, somewhere around these blocks, for so long—every building means something to him: a devoted fan's house, or a cranky neighbor, or a restaurant that he loves, the corner store where he used to buy shampoo before he started paying someone to do that for him, the newsstand that bears his picture on the papers every week. He wants to tell Leo what they're passing, to show him around, but the last grip of the alcohol and something like shyness makes his tongue thick. He means to say at least that he can walk himself now, Leo can go, but that he *doesn't* want to do. When they reach the canal bridge, Oliver pauses, scuffing the toe of his shoe into the ground just to have something to do with his limbs. Leo stops too, head turning toward him with a seeking look. Oliver manages a smile and reaches for the keys. For a brief moment they hold the lanyard between them, second-degree touching, and Oliver's heart hammers at the tenuous connection, then Leo lets go and Oliver starts for his door clumsily. When he limps up his landing, he looks back, and Leo is still standing on the bridge, flanked by water on all sides and watching Oliver with the wind in his hair.

• • •

Monday training sounds exuberant, from what Oliver can hear on the hard plastic of the physio table. Everyone, even Willem, is well pleased with the weekend's triumph. Their next two matches are against Burnley and Watford at home—winnable, easily winnable, even. They could be in fifth by the end of the month, close to where Finch is insisting on.

In the changing room, it sounded like the boys had been resoundingly triumphant with the Welsh girls in Swansea on Saturday night as well. The one advantage of not traveling for matches is the reprieve from that aspect of his social life, where Oliver either gallantly offers to be the drunken-teammate minder or otherwise slips out the second nobody is looking, like a thief in the night. The lads tease him for being unlucky (or, sometimes, a cowardly little melt) and accuse him of still being hung up on Maggie, which is convenient enough to be getting on with. It's brain-dead easy to whistle and nod appreciatively when Georgie shows everyone photos of the lingerie models he's seduced, to keep his head down and coast on the inherent straightness a professional footballer projects to the world. Oliver's never getting any to brag about anyway, or at least nothing he'd go telling the team about. What would he even say? *Hey, boyos, don't you like when a guy holds you down by the back of your neck? Like you're a cat being held by its scruff? Isn't that kind of surrender the hottest feeling?* He'll keep that to himself, thanks.

Oliver is pondering that particular routine in the gym, toward the tail end of the session, trying his best to focus on form rather than extension, to feel the way his muscles respond to each movement, something more real than going through the motions, when someone raps the edge of the doorframe behind him to get his attention. Oliver cranes his head to get a good look without ending the pose, then scrambles to his feet when he sees that it's Willem, who's even more imposing when he's upside down.

"Gaffer," Oliver says, half a hello and half a question.

"Don't stop on my account," Willem replies. "I'm only making the rounds."

"Nothing too exciting here. Stretching for now, I was in with Anna earlier."

"Dr. Zhang said you've been an exemplary patient," the manager says. Oliver's mouth pulls into a pleased smile at the mention of Anna's praise and Willem matches it. "Keep on as you are. We're missing you out there."

"Thank you, sir. You lot got on pretty well without me, it looked like," Oliver says, generous from the topical pain medication Anna administered.

"That we did." Willem looks satisfied, close to proud, in a way Oliver can only recognize from de Boer's playing days, the rowdy pleasure from scoring a goal or drawing a penalty. It's infectious. "Sebastian is having them practice spot kicks. Why don't you come up and watch? We'll do a group meeting and then call it a day."

Oliver follows him out up to the pitch, a spring in his step, or rather, limp—two weeks ago, he doubts Willem even knew his way down to this dank corner of the gym, much less would want to come and fetch him from it. Up in the fresh air, the grass is mist-soaked and emerald; the whole squad is bundled in long sleeves and beanies, hopping and jogging to and fro to keep the chill out. They're each taking turns staring Joe down from the penalty spot, trying to beat him with one single, perfectly placed kick. It requires a great amount of physical control and mental stamina, especially with the keeper looking back at you with murder in his eyes.

At the touchline, Oliver and Willem join Sebastian, who gives

Oliver a cautious, friendly nudge with his elbow without taking his eyes off the field. They watch in silence as Finn steps forward but kisses the outside post when he shoots. Leo is up next. Oliver feels an unexpected, queasy knot of nerves as he waits for Joe to set himself so Leo can go, like however their new teammate does will reflect on Oliver, like Oliver really wants him to do well, like he wonders if Leo knows that he's watching, like he can't help noticing the triangle of Leo's shoulders down to his waistline are perfectly proportioned.

Oliver stops worrying the second Leo lines up. His posture stays open and relaxed, like there's no pressure at all, before he unleashes a rocket from his left foot across the goal: the shot is a bull's-eye, too far right for Joe to reach, crisply lodging itself in the back of the netting. Whoever thought he should play defensively was a fucking bellend; Leo was born to score.

"I think we've solved the problem of taking penalties while you're injured, Harris," de Boer says, nodding in approval while the lads whoop appreciatively.

Leo trots back to the end of the line, looking over toward the three of them. Oliver raises one eyebrow. *You know it was good,* he thinks. *You don't need me to tell you.* Leo hears this somehow, at least part of it. His ruddy-brown face pinks up ever so slightly and he shrugs, cheeky. *Can't blame a guy for asking,* Oliver imagines Leo's shoulders replying.

• • •

That evening, at Maggie's—a tiny, chic box in Bermondsey, where he's spent multiple days a week since the moment she signed the lease even though he has to stoop to get through the door—Oliver gets an Instagram notification from LeoDaVi. Maggie is distracted over the stove, deglazing a saucepan of vodka sauce, so he lets himself tap the icon immediately. Leo has tagged him in a photo.

The picture isn't at all what he expected, not a shot from training, nor a snap he doesn't remember from their trip to the pub last weekend. It's an underlit mural on a brick wall, and the swirl of colors reveals a portrait of Oliver himself. It's blocky, somewhat cartoonish, but it takes his breath away. The man in the portrait is standing tall, one foot on a ball, pointing out onto the horizon before a free kick: a cartographer reaching for unmapped land. Somehow the artist has captured the green of his eyes and the determined set of his mouth, the way his hair curls up at the ends over the nape of his neck when it needs a trim. Instead of a pitch, they've painted roses all around Oliver's feet. His body is drawn long-limbed and strong; he looks immovable, maybe even noble. And there, in typewriter black script next to his head, they've tagged the piece *We'll always have Harris,* like he's Humphrey fucking Bogart.

Leo's caption reads *loving life back in london. camden street art > national gallery*. Already, Trevor's commented *we dem BOYZ* and Anthony's left a stream of arm-flexing emojis. Something inexplicable is happening in Oliver's heart; it's being squeezed in a vice, in danger of bursting open. He wants to know who sees him in that golden light, enough to paint it, larger than life on the side of a building. For a split second of insanity he considers that Leo could have done it himself, like the sun he drew on his shoe—but that's impossible. Oliver does wonder how on earth Leo found it, if he sees Oliver the same way the artist did. Some amount of this is visible in his real-life face; Maggie is over his shoulder and stealing a glance at his phone before he can lock the screen.

"Oh!" she gasps. "Where is this?" Oliver hands her the phone so she can see for herself, and she immediately twists into a smile of wicked delight.

"Would you look at that," she says, pinching at the screen to zoom in on the photo. "You've got an admirer. And I *don't* mean the artist." He shrugs and snatches his phone back, embarrassed and gratified and certainly not interested in discussing it. Maggie lets it go and returns to her sauce, but he knows her silence means the discussion is merely postponed, not avoided. Oliver goes back through the last ten, fifteen conversations he's had with her in his mind to try to tabulate how many times he's mentioned Leo and what the ratio of complaints to compliments nets out as.

Maggie waits until he's shoved about twenty tubes of rigatoni into his mouth to pounce on him.

"You should thank him for finding it. And you should try to find out who the painter is so you can buy them a drink. But really, you should thank Leo. That was very sweet of him." The brilliance of Maggie is that she never tells Oliver what to do, only what he *ought* to do, and she always lays it out in such a way that if he doesn't listen it'll reflect poorly on him: the most elegant of traps. Even if he wanted to try to worm his way out of it, his mouth is full and the moment for rebellion will pass before he can swallow.

He really should thank Leo—he gives her a resigned thumbs-up. Oliver doesn't go so far as permitting her to read the text that he crafts over fifteen minutes and a glass of wine, but he does send it before he leaves her place and doesn't wait until right before bed.

Leo writes back just as Oliver is messily unfolding himself from a cab, right leg first to take the weight off his injury.

Too good not to post! I love that kind of thing, Leo says, then: Willem told me after training I'm not in the squad for Saturday, was feeling grim. Went out for a walk to clear my head and ran into you. Nice omen!

Be patient, Oliver tells him, typing one-handed while he

braces himself on the fence post to get up the front stairs. It's coming. If you want, we can train on Saturday instead. Have the crossing to ourselves?

Instantaneously, Leo sends back a praying-hands emoji. When Oliver checks his phone again as he unlocks his front door, there's another reply: That's aces. You're on

• • •

The remainder of the week feels every inch of midseason monotony, and not just from the constant, dull pain in his left thigh. Oliver wakes up, he pounds down a coffee and something caloric, he goes to Camden Crossing, he works himself as close to the bone as he's allowed, finding the midpoint between exertion and agony, then he comes home, he eats again, he crashes into a dreamless sleep. These parts of the winter are always like this. Without a midweek fixture or upcoming travel to break things up, he sinks beneath the waterline of his routine and will only resurface the next time he toes the line at Regent Road.

Saturday does come eventually, though, and Oliver sends the lads his well-wishes before he drives down to the Crossing. Leo is waiting outside, loitering by the doors like he was before his first training session. The tension of that meeting is gone now—Leo is all loose-limbed and casual, leaning up against the brick wall in running shorts and a hoodie.

"You're going to freeze," Oliver tells him as he opens the door. "Why didn't you just go in?"

Leo looks embarrassed.

"I didn't know if this was some kind of secret practice."

"If I was going to try to get you in trouble, I would've been much cleverer about it," Oliver sniffs as they make their way through the hall and down the back stairs to the pitch.

The sun is dipping down under the skyline, drenching the

field in a warm red glow. A few people are lingering at work through the match, their office lights casting a dappled, lantern effect. It's the perfect time and place to play. Regent Road might feel like magic, but Camden Crossing has its own alluring spell on this sort of evening. It reminds Oliver of being five years old, when he could run circles around his parents in the courtyard of Nan and Grandpa's flat for a thousand years without getting tired, back when Dad was just starting to be tired all the time. Leo has a grin on that splits his whole face in two.

"Your call," Leo says to Oliver, tossing the ball he snagged from somewhere over to him.

"What if I said to run laps?" Oliver asks, partly because he's curious and partly, he can't help it, to be mean.

"I'd listen." Without missing a beat, Leo starts jogging away down the sideline. Some kind of topsy-turvy feeling rushes through Oliver's abdomen, his worst instincts almost taking over when he thinks about all the things he could tell him to do.

"I'm kidding, I'm actually kidding," Oliver calls out, regaining control of his senses. "Come back!"

Leo decelerates and loops back toward him, beaming.

"I probably only would've done one," he says. Oliver rolls his eyes and gestures him over.

"Let's just play. But go easy on me, I'm frail."

Leo nudges the ball away from Oliver and to his own feet, arcing it up in a neat swoop and beginning a series of keepie-uppies, each one more elaborate than the last.

"I'm not about to get sent back to Spain for reinjuring you! I'm staying away."

Oliver stalks toward him, gingerly using his right leg to poke the ball free. Leo skips forward and takes it right back, backpedaling until he's a body length away.

"I mean it!" Leo says. "Don't come any closer."

“Remember thirty seconds ago, when you said, ‘Your call’?” Oliver reminds him. “You’re all bluff. I’ll send you some passes, show me a one-touch shot.”

Leo, again, listens to him. It’s an easy rhythm, no different than the game Sebastian made them play a few weeks back. Oliver kicks the ball without force, using his right leg, trying different angles and paces from twenty or so yards out as Leo runs at them full tilt, then sends them on toward goal. It’s a shadow of the real thing without a keeper, but the energy ramps up, Oliver getting trickier with his passes and Leo meeting each of them like they’re at the end of a crucial match. Time slips away from both of them. When you really love football, the game encloses itself around you like a physical thing. It’s self-contained and self-sustained.

Oliver could do this without a trace of boredom until he keels over. It’s a revelation, playing with someone who feels it too. Every new shot is a surprise and delight, every new pass an opportunity to discover something that’s not been done before. He can see every thought Leo’s having on his calf muscles and in the slant of his body; it’s like they’re having a conversation. God, it’s so fucking *fun*.

“How have we never done this before?” Oliver asks. “You’ve got a hell of a left foot.”

“You were always too good for me, Harris,” Leo pants, catching his breath. “It’s taken me this long to catch up.” Then he goes back to running; he moves with an uncannily fierce connection with the ball, accelerating without it ever straying from the inside of his left foot. The movements are so precise as to be almost delicate; combined with his slight frame, he might be dancing, twirling all across a grassy stage. Oliver is an elegant, composed player—but he’s certain he doesn’t look like this when he runs.

It’s been dark for hours when it finally occurs to them to

check the score of the match. Camden's won it, one-nil from a free kick by Emmanuel. Oliver pulls up the larger table of all the day's scores, and there it is: the team is sitting in fifth place. He pumps his fist, euphoric and awash with adrenaline. Standing next to him, panting and sweat-soaked, Leo holds up his phone too, open to a message thread. Sitting there on the screen is a note from Willem.

Let's talk next week. All goes well, you can expect a debut against Watford.

Ashamedly, Oliver's first reaction is a bite of jealousy, a little sting of resentment. But Leo is glowing, he's movie-star handsome, and he just scored a hundred goals that didn't matter because Oliver wanted him to, so he reaches forward, pulling Leo into a rough, unsteady embrace. It's quick and sufficiently manly—Oliver slaps him on the back as he pulls away just to be sure. When he steps back, Leo's smiling even bigger.

"You earned it, mate," Oliver says. "I'll be the first to admit it. I'm excited for you."

Leo scuffs his toes at the ground almost bashfully.

"I'm so happy," he admits. "I've always wanted this, even when I didn't think it would happen." Oliver understands that, remembers the teenage sensation of it: your wildest dream coming true.

"Oh, it's happening all right," he says. "I'll be in the stands yelling at you if you forget." Then Oliver tucks him—his protégé, his teammate—under his arm and leads them off the pitch.

• • •

Ascending to fifth place hits like a shot of adrenaline straight to the heart. The changing room, so frequently sullen since they'd eliminated themselves from any chance for a trophy and started walking around with an anvil over their heads, has suddenly transformed with the pulsating energy of a nightclub. Henri led a mostly naked conga line through the showers on Wednesday, all their bellowing voices bouncing off the tiles in a cacophony, knobs swinging everywhere.

This is the best of it, the greatest feeling there is besides winning a championship, but he'd bet his life on the love the team has for each other in these moments. Leo keeps hanging close to Oliver all week, even over the other Spanish-speakers and Ahmed. Whether he's deciding to try his hand at being shy or just thankful for Oliver's belated half-attempts at mentorship, Leo is always hovering an elbow length away with an eye-squinting smile or a question he probably could've asked anyone. "Davito . . . more like Little Harris," Anthony said on Saturday morning after Leo paused to wait while Oliver tied his shoelaces, and both of them knew better than to argue about it.

By Monday, the normal pre-match loom tamps the energy down a bit, everyone turning their focus to how Camden will beat Watford tomorrow. When Oliver is starting to wind down for the evening, his phone rings.

"Davito?" he answers.

"I can't fucking do this" is the only greeting he gets.

"Hey, hey," Oliver says. "What are you talking about?"

"What if I'm not ready? What if I make a fool of myself? I've waited so long to play for Camden, but now that it's here all I can think is, I might be rubbish at this, actually, and I don't want . . ." Leo trails off, voice choked.

Something sweeps over Oliver and kicks into high gear. He's responding before he can think, almost before he can form the words.

"Leo, everyone from Beckham to Ryan Loxley felt like this before their first Premier League match. It's normal. And you're not rubbish, so take a breath. You've done it before, it's all the same." Down the phone line, he hears only a stuttered inhale. "Take a cab to the Crossing," Oliver says assuredly. "I'll meet you there."

"What?" Leo asks, voice tiny and far away.

"You've gotta run it out. And for fuck's sake, put on something warm." Oliver hangs up and starts for the door, pulling on sneakers and heading for the garage at the fastest speed his hamstring will allow. The Audi careens through the streets like it's in *The Fast and the Furious* and Oliver is grateful, for once, that he owns such a stupid, fancy car.

With his emergency spare key, he unlocks the side entrance at the Crossing and leaves it propped open. They're certainly not the first players to have an existential crisis the night before a match and need to do something about it, but the offices and the changing rooms are empty tonight. Oliver snags his boots and a netted bag of balls off a cart in the kit room and drags them upstairs to the training pitch, flicking on the floodlights and watching the field come to life.

Five minutes later, an uneasy Leo clambers up the stairwell. As requested, he's bundled up, but he's pale and drawn like he's got a fever. Last week Leo had been so cheery when they'd come here and now he looks desolate, a totally different character arriving to the very same scene. Oliver wants to do something daft like smooth his curls off his brow or hold him in his arms. He wishes he could give Leo the kind of impossible physical comfort he always craves for himself.

"There he is," Oliver says instead. "How are we?"

In response, Leo flops gently to the earth and lies spread-eagled, face-down on the grass.

"Mmmph," Leo groans.

Oliver eases himself down next to him and sits cross-legged, brushing one tentative hand across Leo's back to announce himself. His fingertips tingle at the contact.

"My debut was against Kilburn," he says after a moment. "I threw up in a bin at halftime." Leo rolls slightly to his side, exposing half of his face and one curious brown eye. Oliver takes this as a good sign and continues. "I grew up a stone's throw from Regent Road. I was always going to be for Camden even before I started at the academy. It was . . . surreal, to realize I was going to play a role in a match that important. I hated Kilburn so much, I think I wanted to beat them more than I wanted to win. It's not rational. And I was so young. I was a nervous mug. I puked my guts out and then they put me in and I got sent off seven minutes later."

"I didn't know that," Leo says. "Everyone thought you'd lost your mind last month, but you're a damn repeat offender. What the hell did you do?"

"I took Stewart Reed out from behind," Oliver laughs, remembering the sticky spring heat and the copper taste of nerves in his mouth. Beckett, team captain at the time, had tried to placate the ref, to no avail. Oliver had been unrepentant, wearing the green stains to his brand-new white away kit like a badge of honor. "Reckless, stupid boy I was. But I wanted them all to know they couldn't fuck about with me. And they still can't." Even now, he's stubborn and vicious about the rivalry. He and Stewart still can't play nice when they run into each other or both get called up for England. Rovers and Roses are natural enemies, not to be mixed. Oliver trails off and Leo sits with him in silence for a long expanse of breaths, muted city noise filtering from the street down to their secret oasis. "They can't fuck with you either," he says eventually. "You're better than any man on the Watford roster. Just do what you do in training. They'll be wishing for relegation by the time it's over."

Leo chuckles and finally pulls himself up to sitting, stretching his arms up over his head like he's just woken up.

"I'll try not to get booked." Leo has his teasing lilt back in his voice, inching closer to sounding himself again.

"Coward," Oliver tells him. "Come on, we're gonna play." He climbs up, ignoring the persistent thrumming in his left leg and Leo's offered hand. This is more important than the injury. He'll just take it really, really slow. Once they're standing across from each other, Oliver turns to grab a ball, but Leo tugs him back. His hand is warm where it stretches over Oliver's own. His fingers are tingling again.

"Will you come and watch tomorrow?" Leo asks. Oliver almost baits him, almost says, *We'll see,* but he only nods. He can do that, for Leo. Through an unspoken agreement, they ease into passing, gradually increasing their distance across the pitch so they can send loping, floaty balls. They have a good sense of each other, connecting passes faster and faster, starting to put them wider and running them down. Oliver feels steadier on his feet, able to take his own weight and quicken the turnover of his stride for the first time in weeks. He starts to dribble between the passes, closing the gap until they're face-to-face and grappling for possession.

"Go on, then," Oliver pants, voice deep with something like provocation. "Can't you get it off me?" Leo screws his eyes in concentration and shoves him lightly, extending one leg just far enough to push the ball free and run it down. Oliver lets all the exhilaration pour down his body like summer rain and lopes after him. Leo moves confidently, so controlled on the ball, but Oliver is stronger and smarter. He can sense where he's going to move and he gets there each time with the composure to reclaim the territory. Leo is sprightly enough to chase him back, though. They're playing chess and tag simultaneously, going three hundred miles an hour. Oliver nabs it back again and whoops a victorious exclamation, getting a few paces free. He turns to look for Leo, to see how it is for him, then there's a blur at the corner of his left eye and he hits the ground hard, head rattling from the impact and hamstring screaming.

Immediately, Leo is on his knees next to him, stuttering apologies, the ball rolling away uselessly. The tackle was clean—he didn't touch Oliver. He's furious anyway, his whole body smarting and his pride wounded. This was so reckless, so *irresponsible*. What was he playing at, running around injured? And Leo, jumping in studs up like his whole career rested on that tackle? They're going to be in so much trouble. His leg is fucking burning. Oliver has pushed so many boundaries with Leo in just this one month, against his first impression and his better judgment, and now he's lying in the mud as hurt as he was on New Year's Day. He's the one who's made a fool of himself, a damn one.

"Ollie, I'm so sorry," Leo's saying, trying again to help pull him back up to his feet. Oliver doesn't let him and pushes him away instead, both palms flat on his chest and moving with intent, teeth bared in pain and anger. Leo stumbles back at the impact, expression crumpling.

"What were you playing at?" Oliver hisses as he gets his legs under him by himself, unsteady with pain and something like rage. "Kick a man while he's down and maybe you'll get a permanent place in the starting eleven and a nice fucking contract, buy yourself a place in Marylebone? You *absolute* prick."

"Oliver, *no*. It's not like that, you know it's not like that," Leo protests desperately.

"You want a mentor, you want a friend—fuck that, fuck you."

"Don't!" Leo shouts back at him, shoving Oliver in turn, one hard push to his right shoulder, exertion, snot, and the trace of a tear clogging up his face. "You just want an excuse to be mad because I *beat you*. You're so hot and cold with me, and it's not fair. I thought—"

"What did you think?" Oliver asks flatly, cutting him off.

"I thought we were past all that bullshit! I thought you wanted me to do well. And that you meant it when you said we were friends." Leo doesn't even sound angry, but panicked, tearful. "I didn't think we had to be against each other."

The fight hasn't gone out of him yet, but Oliver deflates slightly. They're both red-faced and sweat-damp, standing in each other's space with nowhere to hide. There's some feeling bubbling up inside of Oliver, bigger than he can cope with, but he doesn't know where it's coming from or what it means. Leo's constellations of freckles have collided together where his face is pinched up with emotion, mouth smushed into a tight line. Oliver couldn't tear his eyes away from him if he tried. Unbidden, he reaches out, unsure if he means to push Leo away again or pull him closer, fight him or hold him. As Oliver makes contact, a voice rings out from the building behind them.

"Harris?" They both whip around and away from each other. Sebastian is approaching, crossing the grass with his swift gait, confused and displeased.

"What are you doing here?" Oliver demands.

"My line, Oliver," Sebastian says coolly. "What on earth is going on?" His eyes are flitting between the two of them like he's searching for clues, taking in their mussed clothes and close proximity. Oliver wants to make excuses, wants to get them both out of this conversation and out of danger, but Leo speaks first.

"Sorry, it's my fault," he says, sounding about one meter tall. "I was stressed about tomorrow. Oliver was trying to help." He sounds so unconvincing it's comical.

"I'm sure what would help is a good night's sleep," Sebastian replies, giving Oliver a significant look. "Why don't you get out of here, Davito?"

Leo has no choice but to listen, looking pained, eyes flitting back almost mournfully toward Oliver as he trudges off. Oliver can't stop him, especially with Sebastian glowering in front of him, clearly winding up for the lecture of a lifetime.

"I don't know just what you were thinking—"

"Save it," Oliver snaps. "Willem told me to help him, okay? I'm going home too." He's daring Sebastian to try to stop him, to fine him or report him, but Oliver doesn't care. His world is sparking at the edges like it'll burst into flame with no warning. He has to get out of here, away from whatever just happened.

• • •

Sleep is elusive. Oliver alternately kicks the sheets down and cocoons himself beneath them for hours, until he's finally able to identify where the nagging straitjacket of *wrong* wrapped tight around him is coming from, in addition to the fresh pain in his hamstring. It's guilt, stemming from not just how he's acted but from the increasing sense that he's been lying to himself just as much as everyone else. Oliver's lamented his empty bed on many an endless night, but now, sharing the mattress with the roar of his thoughts, he can't drift off.

When he can't take the lonely darkness anymore, he slips downstairs and starts to rummage through his backpack, where buried at the bottom underneath spare socks and deodorant is the scouting report Willem foisted on him all those weeks ago. Oliver hasn't looked at it since.

He wrangles his DVD player to life and lets the grainy footage of Spanish La Liga matches play out while he sits on the floor directly in front of the TV. It's cut like a series of forbidden daydreams, the camera tracking Leo's every move. Even when he's only subbed in for a moment, it's easy to believe he's one of the most talented guys on the pitch, that the Spanish managers are wasting him, holding him back and missing out on something exquisite whenever they don't let him play. Defenders try to get ahold of him, but Leo is too lithe—having possession doesn't slow him down at all. He dashes past opponents and doles out assists like he's passing out leaflets. It's a highlight reel; Oliver knows Leo rode the bench in Valencia, then at Getafe, then Valencia again. But Oliver can see the truth of it, grainy and dreamlike on the screen: Leonardo Davies-Villanueva is brilliant, and he's beautiful, and he's got something in his left foot that no manager can teach.

There's a roiling in Oliver's stomach that's different from anxiety and less pronounced than remorse; the longer he watches, the harder it impresses itself. Sun-kissed, freckled, bouncy-curled Leo is dancing through his field of vision and his every thought. He loathes him anew for a white-hot moment, before Oliver comes back down to earth. That isn't it at all. He does run hot and cold with Leo. It *isn't* fair. What he's feeling right now, what's been building inside of himself, is beyond any rivalry or camaraderie he's ever had with a teammate or a colleague or a friend. It's bigger than what he gets from flirting with Conor Bishop or soliciting anonymous hookups on the other side of the world.

I'm attracted to him. The thought is fire then bile in Oliver's gut. *I* want *him.*

He's never felt this way about someone real, someone who knows him, close enough to be a temptation and a risk. Every careful, grown-up part of Oliver wants to turn off the TV and run far away from the blast radius of this terrible, dangerous idea. The rest of him is helpless: he keeps thinking, his traitorous mind supplying an endless loop of imagery. Leo, impertinent and shirtless in an ice bath; Leo, plastered all along his side in a blustering pub; Leo, low-voiced and doe-eyed against a pillow of green grass.

"Fuck!" Oliver groans aloud, lustful and miserable. "Fucking hell."

Tuesday, January 31, 2017: Watford at Camden

MATCHDAY 23

Midweek matches bring late kickoffs. Which means Oliver has the whole stupid day stretched in front of him, the first whistle looming hours and hours away. He wants to fuck off completely, sleep for hours or maybe hack off his left leg to avoid telling Anna what he's done to it, but he hasn't been back to Regent Road since the day of his injury and it will surely be noticeable if he doesn't attend, again, today. Part of him wonders how much Leo doesn't want him there, if he could somehow spin his own selfishness into benevolently giving Leo space.

He'd also thought about inviting Maggie, but Oliver hates using her as a crutch, especially in public where people will inevitably speculate about their relationship. It feels particularly rancid to spend the night experiencing acute gay panic about a teammate only for *The Daily Mail* to run a picture of him with his ex-girlfriend, an "effortlessly beautiful girl about town," the very next day.

Every time he checks his phone, he's not sure if he wants time to be passing faster or slower. When five o'clock actually does roll around, Oliver feels paralyzed on the couch. It takes another ten minutes before he can force himself to get moving. As he gets dressed, he feels himself taking pains with his appearance—

reaching for his nicest trousers and the designer jumper with vertical stripes, fussing with a little product in his hair. *You are such an idiot,* he tells himself, viciously, as he smooths an errant strand behind his ear.

Regent Road's staff entrance is tucked along a private side road that winds through the park's mix of wild greenery and manicured garden hedges, then dips to an underground garage beneath the stadium. He heads straight from there for the stands, avoiding the friends and family box where all the wives and girlfriends will watch, and the changing room itself, opting instead for one of the front-row seats that injured or suspended players can reserve. Noah is there too, still benched but arm finally free of his sling, coat buttoned up to his chin.

"Oi oi," Oliver says, and plops down next to him, squirming against the rigid green plastic.

"You cut it a bit late," Noah replies. "No hellos? Didn't show up to kiss Finch's arse beforehand?" Oliver grumbles in response—as long as Finch is thinking about selling Oliver in order to start over without him, there will be precisely no arse-kissing at all—and leaves it at that, swinging his legs up onto the rail in front of them and tipping his head back to take in the crowds above. It is a nice night—comfortably chilly, air buzzing with conversation. A few moments later, the team streams out from the tunnel to warm up, a long line of forest-green shirts moving in concentric circles. Noah lifts his fingers to his mouth and lets out an impressively sharp whistle, drawing the attention of their teammates.

A small band jogs over to the edge of the pitch to greet them, laughing and chatting with Noah, but Oliver clocks the exact second Leo notices him. He's at the fringes of the group, bent down in a wide stretch, drinking in the view of the crowd with wonder. As soon as he sees Oliver, Leo's face darkens and his eyes narrow. In an instant, he composes himself, rises, and turns his back, jogging over to Ahmed and refusing to look in their direction at all. An icy breeze sweeps over Oliver, though he's not sure what else he might have expected. He forces himself to smile and wave to the rest of them, even as his heart pounds with a horrible, sickly feeling.

"Go on, then," Noah yells cheerily. "Do your jobs!"

The squad disperses to alternately settle in the pitch-side dugout or head back down the tunnel and line up as the starters. Leo takes to the bench with no discernible expression on his face, resolutely looking anywhere but behind him. The red-cold backs of his ears look mad, to Oliver. The pre-match pomp and circumstance continues, both teams marching out to the center of the pitch, each of them holding hands with a starry-eyed local child. Watford's kits are a garish shade of yellow, making the lot of them resemble a cluster of lemon sweets. A faction of loyal away fans is chanting away in the east end of the stadium, but most of Regent Road is wearing green and singing The Libertines, invoking tin soldiers and their long, devoted crawl to Camden. The players take their places on the pitch, stretching from the keepers in each goal to the line of strikers in the middle, clustered around the ball. The referee blasts one piercing whistle, and they're off to the races.

It's a strange contest, frantic and physical in places but mostly flaccid in the eighteen-yard-box, where it counts. Camden scores early, one of Matty's gangly, loose legs making contact off a low corner cross and beating the keeper. Oliver can tell it's not to be, though—all the passing lanes and empty patches of grass are amounting to nothing, and Andrew Parker, the burly midfielder on loan to Watford from Derby County, is bodying his way through space and time, Camden's defenders playing tin soldiers in place of the crowd. He scores before the forty-five minutes are up and just keeps running like he doesn't have time to stop.

The halftime break is nervy. Noah chomps away at his fingernails while Oliver taps a drumbeat on his thigh, eyes skyward as if new tactics (or a healthy hamstring) will descend from the heavens and let him fix this. Nothing reveals itself except for Parker, again, streaking down the right wing and walloping another shot that Joe can't reach after sixty-nine minutes.

A handful of moments later, Willem silently signals for a substitution and Oliver spots Leo standing from the bench and shedding an outer layer. The ball goes out of play and one of the linesmen holds up the big neon sign announcing the change: number 8 for number 16. Garcia runs across the pitch to switch places with Leo, who is standing with his toes on the white chalk line that forms the perimeter of the field. They clasp hands momentarily, Garcia putting his mouth to Leo's ear to whisper advice or encouragement. Oliver can't tell if Leo seems nervous or if Oliver just knows that he must be, the big *16* on his back looking like it's weighing him down. Leo crosses himself before he runs toward the midfield, before he takes a leap of faith directly into the Prem.

He is good, no one will deny that. Leo has an impressive debut by nearly every metric. Fast and agile, claiming possession and refusing to cede it, looming dangerously around the attacking third. Until the final whistle, all the commentators will say: Davies-Villanueva made a statement, left his mark for Camden, and announced himself as a contender. For all that he was a nonentity in Spain, de Boer has figured out exactly what to do with him, where to put him on the pitch so that Leo looks lethal and experienced and like he's worth a thirty-million-pound transfer fee.

It doesn't mean anything. There's no match-winning goal, not even one to draw them level. Everyone is frustrated when the time is up, but Leo looks heartbroken. No one ever imagines it is possible for them to lose their first-ever Premier League appearance. Especially not when it's taken as long to happen as it has for Leo.

"Dammit," Noah curses as they shuffle their way toward the garage. "That fucking sucked, eh?" he adds once they're safely away from the crowd. Oliver nods, letting out one low, frustrated whistle between his teeth. "I think I'll hang around and try to cheer them up. You in?"

Oliver shakes his head, pointing to his parking space.

"I'm going home to give myself a lobotomy," he says, ignoring Noah's shouted reply:

"We'll do it for you! Oh, come on, Ollie!"

Sitting in the driver's seat, Oliver doesn't pull away immediately. He wants to get up and go after Noah. He wants to go down and find Joe to commiserate. He wants, badly, to talk with Leo. If he can apologize and set things back to rights between them, maybe he'll never have to confront again what kept him up last night, maybe he'll be forgiven for everything he said and thought yesterday. It's easy to handle an unrequited crush; he has no idea how to cope with this kind of fraught, regretful pining. Typing and erasing and retyping, he finally lands on a simple message. He just wants Leo to know that he was watching and that he saw it all for what it was, that he kept his promise to watch him play.

You couldn't have done anything more. Be proud. Even if you're frustrated too.

For the rest of the night, Oliver lunges at his phone whenever it buzzes or lights up, but there's no reply.

• • •

Oliver is halfway down his street in the morning when someone shouts at the back of his car and smacks his bumper.

"*Hey!* What the hell!"

He slams on the brakes, skidding to an uneven stop and reaching for the door. Before Oliver can get free of his seatbelt, expecting an accident and preparing himself to deliver CPR, Leo is standing there with a brown stain on the cuff of his white pullover sleeve, holding two partly crumpled paper cups and looking affronted.

"Jesus," Oliver says, recalibrating his brain for the scene in front of him and rolling down his window.

"You drove right by me!" Leo sounds incredulous.

"And you just scared me to death, so let's call us square." His heart's still pounding. "What are you *doing*, Leo?"

"I was trying to bring you a coffee," Leo replies archly, holding up one of the offending cups like he's presenting forensic evidence. "I'm being the bigger person." Oliver flicks his eyes up and down Leo's comparatively short frame and wisely decides to keep his mouth shut on that one.

"To be fair, I tried that last night and you ignored me," he points out instead.

"I was still angry last night. But I won't be anymore," Leo says, like it's the simplest thing in the world. "Are *you* still mad at *me*?"

"No," Oliver says immediately. "I just have a great capacity for taking things personally."

Leo's face makes a delicate frown, the bottom turn of his lips reaching one of the freckles on the top of his chin.

"Lucky for you, I don't," Leo mutters. "I don't get you, Harris. Why do you make everything so much harder than you have to?"

Oh, mate, Oliver thinks. *This is not nearly as hard as it could be.* He doesn't say that—he just sticks his hand out the window. The space between Leo's eyebrows condenses in confusion.

"One of those was for me, wasn't it?" Oliver asks. "Hand it over and get in."

"Just like that?" Leo snaps, but his eyes aren't flashing the way they do when he's really, truly upset. "I bring coffee, you give me a ride, and we're buddies again? Aren't you going to apologize too?"

"I can drive away if you'd rather," Oliver challenges. Leo thrusts the cup at him and huffs his way around the car to the passenger side. He takes an excessive amount of time to settle himself, adjusting the seat and fussing with his belt. Oliver ignores him and takes a slurp of the drink—it's a perfect latte, crowned with foam. There's a little football scrawled on the rim of the cardboard sleeve. Leo *ahem*s meaningfully.

"Are you all set? May I move?" Oliver asks, lifting his accent into a posh mockery of itself and trying to make it clear he's only teasing now, not being mean anymore. Leo leans across the space between them and *headbutts* Oliver, an intentional smack of forehead to shoulder. He points at the road ahead of them, and Oliver listens, putting the car in gear, putting himself back on track.

The ride was silent, so he's still nervous as he changes for physio, sneaking glances at Leo's locker, trying to gauge from his peripheral vision if things are fixed, if the glue will hold and everything will stick. Oliver's only taken one sock off when a terrible, foreboding noise floats its way down the hallway.

"Hide and seek, hide and seek," someone who could only be Anthony is chanting, punctuating each word with the booming noise of something hitting a tiled floor.

"What's that?" Leo asks, suddenly cropping up at his shoulder. It would be a good sign he's come to Oliver with such a question, if only the answer wasn't so terrible.

"Oh fuck," Oliver replies. "This is *not* on."

Pandemonium ensues around them, every one of their teammates sprinting for the door, each of them partially undressed in a different way. Ji-Hoon has on a beanie but no shirt. Lukas is pulling Finn by the snood. Emmanuel reaches one hand for the fire alarm, then seems to think better of it and keeps moving.

"Fucking run!" Joe shouts as he and Nick pass Oliver's locker. "Hop on your good leg if you have to!"

"Oliver?" Leo asks again, looking increasingly panicked when the overhead lights flick off.

Anthony materializes in the doorway, wearing only a four-sizes-too-large parka like a cape over his shorts. He's holding an upturned broom in one hand, the source of the noise, and blocking the exit, the very picture of menace.

"Hide and seek," Anthony says again, raising one eyebrow at the stragglers.

"Today?" Oliver asks indignantly. "Are you mental?"

"Some matches we lose, but attitude you choose," the captain retorts mysteriously. "So quit feeling shitty, lickety-splitty." Everyone remaining groans, but Anthony bangs the broom several more times and they force their ways around him and out the door as well. Leo is unmoving next at his side until Oliver grabs his elbow and tows him along while he hobbles on his tender left leg. "Hide and seek! Hide and seek!" Anthony shouts after them, malice and glee in his voice. "Pints if you're strong and sprints if you're weak!"

"Don't quit your day job," Oliver yells back forcefully. "Leo, I swear to God, keep up. Do you have two healthy legs or don't you?"

"Tell me what's happening!" Leo demands, overtaking him but looking back with wide eyes. "We never did this in the academy."

"What it bloody sounds like," Oliver replies, skirting around a suit-wearing, befuddled PR intern and ducking down a side hallway. "Hide-and-seek day, innit?"

"This doesn't answer any of my questions," Leo says.

"Once a year, Anthony makes everyone play hide and seek. He waits until we're all in the worst mood and then springs it on us. You hide in pairs, he looks for us, then everyone has to run sprints based on how early they get found. Winners get free drinks for the rest of the season, everyone is cheery again. Did you even listen to the song?"

"How will *you* do sprints?" Leo asks.

"Seeing as I'm injured, you'd have to run mine for me," Oliver admits.

"Hold your fucking horses," Leo starts.

"Shush!" Oliver whispers, smushing one finger to Leo's lip for emphasis. "He has ears like a bat. No one knows the Crossing better than I do, right? He's not going to find us. Now come on." He keeps up the fastest pace he can manage, winding deeper and further down the labyrinth of cinder block hallways until they reach the basement, where he stuffs the pair of them into the remotest of broom cupboards—where Anthony had filched his props, no doubt, and thus the last place he'd ever think to look. Oliver locks the door from the inside for good measure.

"Isn't that cheating?" Leo asks, his cup runneth over with unnecessary questions.

"Only if we get caught," Oliver replies firmly. "For the *last* time, could you actually shut up? My leg is killing me—budge over, I want to sit on that bucket."

Leo arranges himself in the far corner of the tiny room and glowers over the top of Oliver's head as Oliver eases himself down onto an ancient, upturned paint container and breathes a sigh of relief.

"You know, I didn't ask to play," Leo says angrily. "Or make you run for it. Not the other night. Today neither."

"Ease up. I'm not blaming you," Oliver replies. "I'm only trying to repay you for the coffee with a lot of free booze."

"I also didn't ask you to repay me for anything. I tried to apologize, Oliver. I'm still trying. You're not listening to me at all." Leo's mouth quivers at the first sentence, then sets itself firmly into a line for the second one, like he's gathering steam.

Oliver ducks his head, chin to chest, chastened. He's still running just as hot and cold as Leo accused him of, only now he feels guilty about it, since the hot is running hotter by the second, the longer he looks at Leo and imagines what it might be like to remove the coffee-stained shirt he's still wearing, remembering that he touched his mouth just a moment ago.

"I accept your apology," he says very seriously, forcing himself to meet Leo's dark brown eyes, which are still sparking with annoyance. "And I'm trying, too. I brought you along so you'd win this stupid game, didn't I? Not any of the others."

"You're so sure you'll win, Harris." Leo rolls his eyes now, but his whole demeanor is softening while he does it. He slips down into a crouch, leaving them crammed together on the cupboard floor, back at eye level.

"Sure I am. S'my job to win," Oliver says. He feels a little woozy, so close to Leo without any anger or jealousy behind it. He wants to win at something else, something impermissible. There's not enough oxygen in the cramped room and it's running out faster the more his breathing quickens. Leo is looking at him strangely, like he's waiting for him to say something or do something. He's in Oliver's face now that he's crouched, much closer to him than even the close quarters necessitate. Oliver must be imagining how charged the air feels, because it's too much like what he's been dreaming about these last few days. There's a sheer drop off a sharp cliff and a wide gulf spanning between whatever it is Leo's expecting and all the thoughts lining up in Oliver's head. *I could teach him how to win,* he thinks. *I could teach him a whole lot, if only he wanted to learn.* He wants to get it right, whatever it is he's going to say, but before the words come to him, someone hollers in the distance and Leo claps one hand over Oliver's mouth, hushing them both.

"Harris! Davito!" Anthony is calling. "Stop gloating, you bastards! You've won!"

"See?" Oliver says, vindicated and muffled against Leo's open palm. "Told you so."

Leo rises and sticks out his other hand to help Oliver up. He's still imagining things, he's sure, because it feels like they stand there for a long moment; Oliver is the one to step away first.

Back at his locker, when the real training is over and he's been stretched and observed and poked at by the physios with no concern about the new source of pain in his hamstring, Oliver can't shake the happy idiocy that comes after an adrenaline rush.

"What's gotten into you?" Joe asks, sidling up to him with a strange look on his face. "Quiet and smiling? Are you having a stroke?"

"I'm sure I don't know what you mean, Joseph." He sounds drunk. He feels a little drunk, truthfully, experiencing a sense of relief like it came in a shot glass. "I'm celebrating. I won hide-and-seek day," Oliver insists. Leo picks that moment to join them both and ask if Oliver will drive him home.

"Ah," Joe replies, enlightenment dawning. "And you won with your new friend."

"Who, me?" Leo asks, the corners of his mouth perking up.

"Hush," Oliver says to both of them, all holier-than-thou. "I'm a very happy and friendly person, today being no exception. It is not breaking news when I'm having a laugh." Joe doesn't even pretend not to smirk, but Leo, mindful of their tentative reunion, fights to keep his face mostly neutral.

Oliver can see Sebastian walking toward their group of three, so he quickly escorts them out the door before anyone else can say something to embarrass him, into the relative safety of commuting, where the only risk is his own big mouth and London's traffic.

"It absolutely is news when you're having a laugh, in case you were wondering," Leo tells him when they pull up in front of his apartment building, idling on the cobblestones.

"Cheers. I'll keep that in mind," Oliver shoves him lightly, more to get him out of the car than for what he said, and maybe, a little bit, for the chance to touch him again.

Leo departs but turns back after one step and motions at the window. When Oliver rolls it down for him, Leo sticks his head back in. The air smells crisp and wintry, all the streetlights flickering to life and glistening against the slight dampness that cloaks everything from November to March. *It's a perfect evening*, Oliver thinks.

"If you want to come in early on Thursday," Leo says, running his fingers through his wind-rustled, post-training hair. His cheeks are already pink with cold. "I'd swim some laps with you. So you have company."

"You think you can behave yourself?" Oliver asks. "Won't try to drown me or nothing? It went badly the first time we had a swim together, you'll recall."

"That had much more to do with you than it did with me, if we're being fair about it." Leo rolls his eyes. Oliver has no retort for that, because Leo is unfortunately absolutely correct. "Come on, Ollie. I miss the beach. Don't deny me my pool time."

"Poor Davito. Can't have you going as pale as me, you're right. But I'm not waking up early. We'll do it after your training session, yeah?"

"Whatever you like," says Leo—still very tan, still very handsome—as he smiles in the pleased, half-smug manner of someone who's recently gotten their way. It looks good on him, but Oliver suspects most everything does.

. . .

"Okay, explain this to me, because I'm lost," Maggie says after she drains the last sip of her drink, fairly slamming it back down onto the tablecloth. Oliver reaches for the red wine they're sharing, sloshing the glasses full again and licking a stray drop off his wrist.

"What's there to explain?" he asks tipsily, stretching over the restaurant booth until his back cracks. Wine makes him feel loose and sleepy, a bottle of basking in the sun after an afternoon nap on the beach. The day's easy, pleased mood has carried through the night and magnified with time, until he's sloppy and giggly with it.

"A lot!" Maggie whisper-shrieks, pointing an accusing, ring-adorned finger at him. "You hate the usurper, you reluctantly mentor the newcomer, you bond with your teammate, you fight with your friend, you have a crush, and now . . . what?" As she speaks, she counts the list out on her hand until she's waving an open palm in front of him. "What comes next, Ollie?"

"Nothing comes next, Mags," he says, swirling his drink around to avoid eye contact. "I had a shit end to last year, then I didn't know where I stood with the team, with Willem and his plans. It took a bit of trial and error, and now I do know. Leo and I get along after all. We'll probably fit well together on the pitch too. End of story."

"I don't believe that." Maggie shakes her fringe out of her eyes and grabs for his hands, jerking him forward so he has no choice but to look at her. She sweeps the dining room with a glance, checking to see if they're alone enough, then continues. "Are you really going to just keep pretending nothing is going on? Football as usual, just a bunch of straight teammates having normal, straight feelings for each other?"

They're alone, but the word "pretend" in front of "straight" still makes Oliver wince, popping the balloon of the evening's atmosphere.

"Be quiet," he hisses, then continues in a whisper. The soft, sweet wine feelings have evaporated. "I have to do football as usual, don't you get it? I wouldn't last one second in the changing room if *anyone* knew. The press would crucify me, I would never play again, and my life would be over. No one's ever done this, not at my level, and even anyone who wasn't any good still had their whole lives fucked up when they tried. It's not, like, fun for me to lie about this, Maggie—it kills me. But I have to. People already call me names, and they don't even know. What would they do if they did?"

Her beautiful face falls. She slides across the bench seat and winds her arms around his neck. He tucks his chin over her head: easy, familiar motions.

"You know something?" Maggie says, from the crook of his shoulder. "When you told me, when you *dumped me,* actually, I wasn't even sad for myself. I was the one being broken up with, but all I could think was about how lonely you would be."

"I'm not lonely."

"Aren't you?" she asks, eyes now searching him curiously. "I don't think you're lying, for the record. But I do think you're keeping a secret. Something that keeps you from everyone else."

"It's worth it," Oliver replies. He's thought about it a million times since he was eighteen. It's always worth it, when he does the math. "For now, it's a fair trade. When I'm old and retired, then I can do whatever I want."

"That's the saddest thing I ever heard." She leans back and takes a long pull straight from the bottle, then offers it to him. He follows suit, paws tiredly at his eyes, and rests his forehead in his palms.

"It's honestly not usually that bad." He forces a rueful laugh. "I'm still one of the lads, even if I'm gay. I fit in just fine. It's just, like . . . teammates are especially off-limits." Camden is for football, not for grafting. These are the rules he's got to live by, the ones that got him where he is. It's the only way he can play. And he's only ever wanted to play.

"I doubt Leo thinks so." Maggie hiccups, a playful note creeping back in her voice. "He's obsessed with you."

Oliver scrunches his nose, involuntarily pleased at the idea. Monday night was a lifetime ago, a whole new era of his life devoted to the strange feeling he gets when he looks across the room and clocks the outline of Leo's collarbone, or sees his peach-fuzz earlobes, or smells his clean, grassy sweat. He shakes his head like he's trying to get water out of his ears, snapping himself out of it.

"Come off it. He's—he's who he is," Oliver says, as much to himself as to Maggie. "And I'm a football star. That doesn't mean he's into me."

Maggie smiles dangerously, propping her chin in her hands.

"He's on his way to being a football star too. Take it from someone who used to fancy you," she tells him. "It seems like he might."

She doesn't get it—obviously, a group of often-shirtless men who spend all their time with each other and exchange glorious, sticky hugs in front of thousands of people *seems* gay. But that way lies madness. It's different for the rest of them than it is for Oliver, and if he allows himself to think, even for a second, that it isn't, he won't be able to go back to his normal life again. Oliver would rather snog Prince Harry on the roof of Buckingham Palace than get caught looking at Leo. He's perfected the art of the fully anonymous, pitch-black hookup, but never in his life (not even in the academy, when more than one teammate allowed the other lads to jerk them off because it was the only available orgasm option) has Oliver ever strayed from that. He's supposed to be the beating heart of the team, Willem said—he fucking wouldn't be if everyone knew he was gay and couldn't look him in the eyes anymore. He considers trying to explain this, before deciding he just wants to go to bed instead.

"You can get the last round," he tells her. "As payment for my agony."

Maggie makes a considering expression, then seems to remember she hasn't paid for so much as a wine *gum* since they were twelve years old, and nods in agreement.

Oliver severely regrets that last guzzle of wine by morning, when the fluorescent rectangles of office lights above the exam table are blinding him, head pounding like a nightclub beat. Being injured provides so much more time for midseason drinking than he's used to.

"I have precisely no sympathy for you at all," Anna says after he expresses this, perching on a wheeled stool and brandishing an ultrasound wand at him. "You can stop moaning at any time. Getting drunk on a Wednesday, for God's sake."

"I wouldn't be able to drink on weeknights if you'd fix up my leg, Doc."

"If *I'd* fix it?" she asks, words rising worryingly in pitch. "What if you were to stop running on it, against direct instructions, hm? Don't think I don't know what you were up to." Sebastian is such a fucking rat. Everyone knows he thinks Anna is beautiful—she is!—but it's no excuse to be a tattler.

"The running didn't hurt it," Oliver tries. "It was the tackling."

Mistake, mistake, mayday. Anna shoves his left leg upright and jabs at it with the wand, pressing into the tender tissue of his upper thigh with none of her usual deftness.

"I'm not a miracle worker and I don't like when my advice and my time aren't taken seriously, Oliver." Her tone is clipped, harsher than he's hardly ever heard it. "If you want to spend the rest of the year limping and drinking, be my guest. But I expect this kind of idiocy from Georgie and Henri, not from you. I thought you would take things seriously, after the last year you've had."

Being mentioned alongside two people who have both been invited to appear on *Love Island* is about the same as if Anna had cursed at him or called him a dickhead. He is appropriately chagrined by the comparison.

"You're right," Oliver murmurs, contrition in his voice. "I've been at sea. I'm working on it." There's been a lot swirling around his life and his head since that first week of the year, when he was panicked about his leg and nothing else. The ache that came solely from his hamstring feels far away from the here and now. Anna's still miffed, but she brings her shoulders down from where they were tensely coiled up by her earlobes.

"Then drop an anchor, Oliver. Give me a chance to report some good news to Willem and get your act together," she says, pulling off her rubber gloves and dropping them in the bin with finality. "Leg is moving along fine, in spite of you. Eight weeks maximum, probably less."

Oliver can see the calendar for the rest of the season stretched out in front of him in his mind, everything he's going to have to miss, the international break for England as well. But not the whole campaign. He could be back in time for matches, important ones too—Kilburn, United, maybe Arsenal.

"Would it help if I said I was sorry?" Oliver asks. There's been a lot of that going around recently.

"You know what? I think it would," Anna replies, and she even looks like she doesn't want to kill him.

• • •

When they dive into the pool for their post-training swim, it becomes immediately clear that Leo's experience is much more of the sunbathing and sandcastle-building variety, not swimming laps. He has just about the least efficient stroke Oliver's ever seen, spinning his arms like a windmill but still mostly staying in one place.

"Quit laughing," Leo says, forlorn, while he's catching his breath at the wall. "I'm getting better!"

Oliver is still in stitches—he can't help it. For all of Leo's long, elegant strides on the pitch, right now he resembles nothing so much as a cat in the bath.

"Mate, it's a low bar to clear," Oliver says, trying to keep his voice from wavering with mirth. "How have you made it this far in life without drowning?"

"I'm just out of practice." Leo's tongue is poking out with concentration while he dog-paddles after Oliver.

"You're trying too hard," Oliver says, vaguely conscious of how ironic it is for him to tell anyone that as he treads water next to Leo and tries in vain to adjust his body position, one hand gently smoothing the line of his spine until he's doing something that approximates floating. "Don't fight the water, you're not going to win. You've got to work with it. And you've got to get your face wet eventually."

Leo is embarrassed but intent, kicking away madly like he's driving a getaway car, much more comfortably than he was a moment ago. Oliver chases after him, lungs burning, the water taking all the impact off his left leg and letting him move at the kind of brisk pace he's accustomed to on land. They settle into a nice equilibrium, back and forth like a clock pendulum, surrounded by damp chlorinated air and the echoey sound of water lapping against the pool deck. Oliver loves to swim almost as much as he loves being good at something, and he shows off, just a little, flipping neatly to push off the wall and letting the power of his stroke carry him up the lane.

"I'm Oliver Harris," Leo says, once he's fully given up trying and pulled himself up to sit on the ledge of the pool, catching his breath and watching Oliver finish his workout. "It's nothing personal, I'm just better than everyone at everything. Oh no, there's no need to clap."

"You did suggest this," Oliver reminds him, reaching down to scoop a handful of water and sending it directly toward Leo's head. "Set yourself right up, is what you did."

"It's fun to try new things," Leo sniffs. "You just make everything a competition."

"You have no idea," he says. "Didn't you ever wonder why I'm not allowed at poker night?"

Leo snorts, kicking his own wave of water back at Oliver.

"I've always thought you have, like, the most prickly, old-man vibes—" He laughs at his own description. "Now I realize it's, like, no, he's just pretending to be so nobody realizes he's a fucking madman."

It's not *exactly* what Oliver's pretending, but it's a surprisingly good read. He throws his hands up in defeat, laughing at himself too.

"And you should be glad of it," he warns Leo, taking the offered hand to help him up and out of the pool, shivering at the cold air and their nearly naked touching. "I'm keeping everyone out of trouble." And Oliver means it—he does feel like he could easily get them both into trouble, when he looks at Leo shirtless and wet and laughing. He might have played things a bit differently, that first day in the plunge pool, if he'd known it could be like this.

"You've thoroughly worn me out. And I'm starved. Do you want to come over for some dinner? I've mapped it, mine is technically closer," Leo asks as they walk back toward the locker room. "I, ah, have no food, but I *can* get takeaway."

Oliver hesitates for a moment, running the internal calculus of what the best, most normal answer is.

"When I'm healthy, maybe," he replies. The idea of being in

Leo's home, just the two of them sharing a meal, makes his insides squirm in a way that says, *Crossing a line. You want it too much*. They've spent all day together, more time than the rest of their teammates. If he gets anything more, he'll stop remembering where his limits are. He wants to wear Leo out doing something else besides swimming laps—something he's absolutely forbidden himself from thinking about. "Can't be eating that way without running it off."

"Maybe I'll come to yours another time, then," Leo says easily, pulling his clothes back on over his suit. He has an uncommon ability to process rejection well, by simply breezing right past it without acknowledgment. "You can make us a salad."

Oliver half-laughs, slightly nervous, as he slips away to shower and waves goodbye. He's both relieved and disappointed that Leo doesn't follow him.

Saturday, February 4, 2017: Camden at Chelsea

MATCHDAY 24

From Oliver's vantage point in the visitors' box, the match unfolds as a Greek tragedy, predestined and unavoidable. Camden doesn't look poorly or slow, only hopelessly outmatched. For the first time since November, Willem leaves his spot on the center touchline and paces back and forth, shouting to the back line and jabbing a clipboard full of notes at Sebastian. The best moment they have all match is when de Boer himself stops a pass that's flown out of bounds, flicking it safely down to his feet and trapping the ball under his dress shoes.

It's futile. Three goals to zero, and not close even for a second: a veritable clobbering. When all's said and done, they've dropped to seventh place. Oliver almost expects Finch to burst into the post-match presser and fire them all preemptively. He's not sure any of them would be able to defend themselves.

Most of the squad shuffles off to a clubby cocktail lounge on Camden's High Street in an undignified heap of sweat, cologne, and misery. Oliver joins them, feeling for perhaps the first time in weeks that it might actually be better being sad among friends than alone in his house under an ice pack. Even the forbidden cigarette scent and the slight stickiness on the leather booths don't convince him otherwise. Under the thrumming bass of the

DJ set, Oliver is jammed up along the bar, wedged between Joe and Matty. The two of them have twin hangdog faces and hands wrapped around brimming pints. A better man might be capable of pushing his sleeves to his elbows and bucking them up, but Oliver tends toward being a wallower at the best of times.

"Might have gotten a hand to that second one from Hazard, if I didn't have my head up my arse," Joe mutters into the foam of his drink.

"He wouldn't have been on goal at all if I could've caught up with him," Matty says.

"And then we would've lost two-nil. Same zero points," Oliver points out, and even though he's objectively correct, they wave him away so they can continue their bitching unencumbered by logic. Letting himself drift through the crowd, trying to find another reason to stay and mostly discovering that he's ready to leave, Oliver eventually comes to a stop next to Leo and Ahmed, who has his coat halfway back on and his eyes likewise on the door. Leo's eyes are glassy to match his vodka soda; he isn't going anywhere.

"You want me to take him, Ahmed?" Oliver asks.

"I can take myself," Leo says, but he slurs it. Ahmed plucks the drink out of Leo's hand and passes it to Oliver, who takes one whiff and then swiftly deposits it on a nearby table. Leo doesn't fight it, possibly because he's too pissed to notice the exchange at all.

"Come on, big man," Oliver says, nudging them both toward the exit. "Let's go for a walk, hey?" Leo wrinkles his nose, cranky in the face, but allows himself to be led out to the street. Out on the curb, weaving through the entry line and several hungry looks of recognition from clubgoers, Oliver propels them both out of the messy nightlife sprawl and onto a brick-laden side street.

"You aren't drunk," Leo says, accusatory. He's wearing a rosary that's hanging askew out of his shirt collar. Oliver tucks it back in for him and continues to steer them away from the crowd, one steady hand on Leo's back.

"It's my night to babysit," he replies.

Leo mutters something in Spanish that includes a "no," but when Oliver keeps walking, he follows him, a stride behind.

"I don't need minding," Leo shouts at Oliver's back, sounding knackered and miserable. "I'm allowed to be upset."

Oliver turns to face him but keeps walking backward, the High Street lights twinkling into blurriness.

"You can be upset without being hungover in the morning, mate," he says, with wisdom he doesn't yet possess. Leo is red-faced in the frosty night, so Oliver relents and walks back toward him so he can rub warmth into his shoulders, looking down at his sullen mouth, finding him handsome even under these circumstances. "Let me walk you down to the end of the park, then I'll put you in a cab. Get some fresh air."

"I get plenty of fresh air," Leo snaps. "We work outside." He says it with the conviction of someone ready to pick a fight, but the follow-through evaporates in the air between them and he suddenly half-collapses, going boneless into Oliver's grasp and tipping his head forward into his chest. They stand there—intertwined in an empty alley, the night sky threatening a flurry of midwinter cold—until time seems to stand still and they're two figurines in a snow globe. Oliver isn't sure if he can have this, if he's breaking any rules, but the feeling rattles through him regardless, tingling and much hotter than the February air. He hopes Leo can't feel how his heart is pounding, pushing at the space in between them. "I feel like shit," Leo says eventually, muffled. "I just want to win one. It's so fucking *hard*. And cold."

Anthony would tell him not to whine, Joe would say it takes

ten men and a keeper to win, Willem would say the manager's tactics are at the root of every loss. Oliver's not sure what his line should be.

"I wanted you lot to win too. Maybe it's my fault for being injured, maybe it's Chelsea's fault. Who knows? But I don't think anyone would say it's yours."

Leo lifts his head up from the cocoon of Oliver's jacket lining and frowns at him.

"I don't need a minder, I told you."

"It's the truth," Oliver insists. "You think it's fun to tell you how good you are when I can't play? Don't argue with me."

"I'm not arguing," Leo says tiredly. "I'm moping."

"Oh, Christ. Sorry, mate, don't know how I got those mixed up. Come on."

"You weren't serious? It's bloody freezing."

"Talk to me, then, it'll keep you warm. Step lightly," he adds, when Leo's first attempts at walking are tipsy, diagonal stumbles.

"What do you want to hear?" Leo asks, steadying himself on Oliver's elbow.

"Tell me about your parents," Oliver decides. "The ones who cheered when I got injured."

"It wasn't like that!" Leo says. Oliver hums disbelievingly and Leo pulls insistently on his sleeve, slowing them to another stop and tugging them all the way into the side of the building on the corner, smushed and laughing against the crumbling facade. "*A ver,* let me think." Leo reaches forward to brush the first clinging bits of frost out of Oliver's fringe casually, easily. Oliver is rooted to the spot for one frozen moment, feeling his pulse bleat helplessly out of the veins in his forehead, before he pulls them both upright and several paces down the road.

"I'm listening," Oliver says, but he's not making eye contact anymore.

"My mum is from Medellín, in Colombia. She and her sister

moved to Valencia, looking for work in Spain, like. And my dad was there too, he's capital-*B* British, but he works for HSBC and he was on an international rotation. They met at a bar. Well, she was the bartender. She was studying English under the counter between mixing drinks, and he offered to tutor her."

"Very magnanimous of him," Oliver says, grinning.

"Exactly, like, obviously they fell in love immediately and got married right away. Also, because Mum got pregnant with Rafa, my older brother, anyway," Leo goes on, picking up speed. "I came along too and eventually Dad got promoted, which was super exciting for him, but kind of rough for the rest of us because it meant moving to London, which was, you know, moving *back* for him, moving *away* for us. And there was still a language barrier for Mum, and it's, like, she'd already uprooted her whole life once, she hadn't quite bargained on doing it again, with two children, in English, without her sister."

"How old were you?" Oliver asks.

"I was nine," Leo explains. "I actually think I got off easiest, because I was still little, and I went right into the academy. All Dad had to do was say the Prem is better than La Liga and I packed right up." Oliver can see it perfectly, superimposing a coltish Leonardo onto his own memories of being nine and running pell-mell for the gates of the training grounds, the one place where he could put everything to rights even when the rest of his life swirled between chaos and grief on the hour. "It was worse for Mum and for Rafa, way worse. He took off for college when I was twelve and pretty much the minute his bags were packed, Mum said, 'Me too.' "

"She left?"

"No way. She convinced Dad to go too, didn't she? Hard to argue with 'your beautiful wife, sunny skies, and the sandy shores of the Mediterranean.' Even he doesn't like banking that much. They went back to Valencia together."

"But you stayed?" Oliver likes the feeling of these questions and answers, like he's fitting the corners of a jigsaw puzzle together.

"After much petitioning. I was good enough, then, that they knew I might make it professionally, that I was good in the Premier League way and not in the proud parental way, you know?"

"Ah, so you *are* good in the Premier League way?" Oliver can't resist querying in a singsong.

"You know *precisely* what I mean, sire," Leo parrots back, matching him syllable for syllable. "I remember you, you knew even earlier. You were miles ahead of all of us all through the academy."

"Sometimes I think it's the only thing I've ever known," Oliver admits, emboldened by the distraction of crossing the street and slipping through a loose vehicle gate to enter Regent's Park, the cover of darkness and the emptiness of the park opening up some base honesty in him. Leo follows slowly, darting his eyes for anyone spotting them entering after hours. "They're not going to arrest a Camden player for going into Regent's, mate," Oliver yells at him over his shoulder, blowing their cover entirely. "Hurry it up."

It's properly snowing now, the first and probably only time all season: thick fistfuls of powdered sugar descending in flourishes onto the greenery and feathering the top of Leo's head. They pause, gazes trained upward, arms extending automatically, opening up their bodies for the cold, wet satisfaction of a snowy coat. After a moment, they start to match the statues.

"I love it here," Leo whispers, jaw splayed open to catch a mouthful. "I've just been trying to make it home."

"Did you miss it?" Oliver can't imagine not being here. He's been all around the world to kick a football and he always dreams of the return flight, the one that will bring him back down to earth, to this exact spot. Camden keeps changing, but he doesn't. He still belongs in the memory of it.

"Of course I did," Leo answers. "It's the only place that's ever been *mine*. Like, Camden, the football of it all, I mean. I don't fit anywhere else. Half-English, half-Colombian, not Spanish, kind of Spanish, never really Colombian, not quite British yet. I just want *somewhere* to keep me. You know? To belong somewhere?"

Oliver does know—it hits him like a truck, how much he knows it. He wants to tell Leo that, but before he can, Leo turns away from him and takes off running, ungainly drunken loping that carries him out of sight almost immediately. Oliver follows more slowly, favoring his left leg along the sodden path, only catching up once they're halfway to the boathouse, sidestepping fresh patches of ice and clutching at his thigh, wincing. Leo stops above the edge of the wetland lagoon, bent over his knees, taking long gulps of air.

"I'll tell you what," Oliver says when he finally reaches him. "You run like that after a football match and God knows how many drinks? I think where you might belong is the starting eleven."

"Don't make fun," Leo warns, a bittersweet look on his face.

"I'm being serious. You're grand, you're doing great."

"Maybe it looks that way," Leo mutters. "But I can't make it stick, man. I never thought I'd be back here, in London, wearing this kit, having it be for real. I wanted it so much. Now I just don't want to ruin it, do you know what I mean? I've had this . . . this whole *journey* already and it wasn't right, I was never right for it, the only people who wanted me in Spain were my parents, and they spent the whole time trying to convince me to go back to school. They wanted me to quit, my coaches didn't want to play me more than a few minutes a month, my teammates thought I was bad luck. Eleven men on the pitch, but I was . . . I was all alone." Oliver knows that feeling too, but he can't imagine anyone ever not wanting Leo to play or watch him with the ball. "I don't know why I'm unloading all this on you. I'm blitzed," Leo goes on, like he's waking up and everything he said before was a dream. "Is this how you felt after that time at the pub?"

"I was much more dignified, thanks," Oliver says quietly. "But I don't mind. I find you very interesting." He hazards a step forward, placing them in parallel, and kicks gently at the side of Leo's sunburst-doodled shoe. "You can tell me this stuff."

"Yeah, yeah," Leo says with a wan smile. "So you can do reconnaissance. Assess my threat level."

"You're no threat to me, Davito. Besides, we don't have to be against each other, remember?"

"Yeah, I suppose we don't," he whispers, looking at Oliver curiously, face shining with melted snow. "Two academy lads. Quite a pair."

The wanting in his chest inflates itself and spreads, taking over every limb like a puppet on strings. Oliver could lick the snowflakes off Leo's whole body, trying to tongue up whatever ails him, any loneliness he carries around; he'd be happy to take it and add on to his own, if it meant Leo might look at him like this every once in a while.

"Two roses," Oliver replies, pointing to the faraway edges of Queen Mary's Gardens. When he drops his arm, they're suddenly standing closer, close enough that their fingers brush and their heads jerk away, shrinking from the eye contact but not, somehow, the physical one. Somewhere in the shrubs a round of robins break free from the twigs, awoken by their intrusion, and flit overhead, trilling at the snow. "Come on, then," he murmurs. "I said I'd get you a cab."

Leo trails after him, one pace behind all the way to Ulster Terrace, silent until he's slid into the back of a black cab. Oliver stops to watch him go, but Leo sticks his head out of the window, eyes roving over his face.

"You can start the meter," Oliver tells the cabbie, who does so happily.

"Ollie," Leo says, and it sounds like, *Wait*.

"Yeah?"

"You still owe me dinner," he replies slowly and like he might still be drunk. "A salad. You promised."

"Okay, rabbit," Oliver tells him. "You'll get one. We have Thursday free, before you play Hull City."

Leo nods and closes his eyes, retreating back into the warmth of the car.

"It's a date," he calls back sleepily as the cab pulls away.

It's not, it's absolutely not, Oliver demands himself to think, stamping off back up the street and leaving black holes in the dusting of snow while his heart beats a tattoo. But he thinks that's maybe how dates are supposed to feel: the sensation he's had all night long of looking right at someone's face and seeing their soul instead, like Leo was lit from within, glowing more than he does after running one of Sebastian's dreaded sprint circuits.

• • •

It's barely light out, just one trickling ray of sun slicing the foggy morning open, when Oliver arrives for Wednesday's practice session. He can't sleep when his leg feels this leaden, a rock where his hamstring ought to be, so he lets himself in early and stretches, trying to unravel the strength he knows is somewhere in his muscles.

It isn't pretty—Beckett used to always say that football is as much being at war with your own body as it is with the opponents. Sweat pools at his upper lip and drips into his eyes as he presses deeper into a lunge, quivering with effort. He releases the position, going limply down to the mat. His groan of exertion turns to surprise when he sees Leo halfway through the doorway, gear on.

"Sneak!" Oliver gasps. "Where did you learn to be so quiet?"

Leo lets himself the rest of the way in and perches on the end of the bench press.

"Not from you," he replies. "I could hear your huffing and puffing from my locker. Had to come make sure no one was having a heart attack."

"Fuck off," Oliver tells him.

Leo, bless him, doesn't listen. He just kicks a muscle roller over and watches as Oliver hoists himself up on his palms to gingerly rub the tender spot on the back of his leg, letting gravity press him down into the firm, rubbery foam. He becomes acutely aware of their aloneness, the early hour, and the empty building. Oliver is rocking his body into and then against a tension that somehow burns and relieves at once; now he does wish Leo had fucked off, so he wouldn't be vulnerable, on display and feeling perverted for it.

"Oh, quit pulling faces," Leo tells Oliver, pulling him out of the reverie. He slides off his seat and walks on his knees, tapping him on the leg. "Let me do that."

"All right," Oliver murmurs, not stupid enough to turn down an offer like that. He holds himself still, leg flung out aloft, while Leo handles the roller expertly, pushing it just hard enough to make the help worth the hurt. Oliver's muscles shake from something more than the stretch, but they're quiet for a long while, moving in tandem.

"I meant to say, I'm sorry if I was being weird," Leo says eventually, out of nowhere.

"When, exactly?" Oliver asks, sweetly.

"Ha ha," he replies, no trace of laughter. "I mean when I was drunk and sad."

"Oh, *then*. It's okay, yeah? You're a very nice drunk, at least," Oliver feels himself joking, reaching for a laugh or a smile, but Leo stays resolutely serious, speaking like he's planned what he wanted to say.

"It's not your job to buck me up. I should be able to, what's the word . . . *compartmentalize* better."

"What other job do I have right now, Leo?" Oliver says it lightly, but he means it. Leo shakes his head and starts to turn away, speech delivered; Oliver uses the leg that's stuck out from the top of the roller to nudge him with the flat of his foot, right in the stomach, until Leo falls back from his knees to a splayed kind of seat. "Sit. It's insolent to keep running away from an injured person."

Leo finally laughs, for real this time, making a show of settling in and sitting cross-legged.

"You're not sick of me?"

"Not as of yet," he admits, which is mostly true, and much safer than *Sometimes, but hardly recently, and mostly I can't get enough. I like talking to you, and looking at you, and thinking about you*. "I'm glad you didn't quit football to go back to school. Those poor teachers, Leonardo, they aren't paid enough as it is."

The pleased look transforming into mock outrage is delicious, and Oliver lets himself fall backward from the force of his laughter, sliding off the roller entirely—it's fully worth the payback of getting pelted by every filthy towel from the hamper. That's how Henri and Ji-Hoon find them, breathlessly laughing and throwing shit at each other. They join in without a second thought, which is how all four of them get subjected to the great Respect the Equipment Dressing Down of 2017—that feels worth it as well, even with the laundry duty, for the sight of Leo's bashful expression the whole time they're folding everything.

"All I'm saying is, tomorrow's dinner had better be worth it," Leo says as the lot of them are changing out of their trackies. He has his head halfway into his pullover, muffled by the layer of cotton.

"You're the one who asked for salad. At no point did I offer," Oliver reminds him. "Come to think of it, I don't even really remember inviting you."

"I don't remember you inviting us either," Henri chimes in. "Which is very rude." Ji-Hoon nods solemnly in agreement.

"Absolutely not," Oliver says, in anticipation of their next question. He's disappointed and relieved at the same time, *again*, as an evening alone with Leo slips away from him in real time. "I've been duped into cooking for him, but not the whole grimy lot of you. Do not come over. Do not invite the others. Look me in the eyes, Henri. Look at how serious I'm being."

Warning delivered or not, he doesn't trust Henri as far as he can throw him. Sometimes you have to take matters into your own hands, which he does by calling the French restaurant in Marylebone that's in a converted church and has a ridiculous tasting menu. When it comes down to it, Oliver's willing to take out a loan if it means he can avoid hosting. He's not above bribery either. He asks the hostess who answers the phone about booking the private dining room for tomorrow, tone edging toward pleading. She huffs down the line in a way that suggests she's going to enjoy telling him no, so he goes for broke before she can.

"Sorry, I know it's in poor taste to call so last-minute, and in poorer taste to name-drop, but I'm hoping you could help me out. My name's Oliver Harris—"

"*The* Oliver Harris?" she cuts in, sounding disbelieving.

"I—well, yeah," he says lamely. "I mean, if you're thinking of the footballer, then yes, that's me. I'm, er, him." The only thing more pathetic than using your celebrity to your advantage is being self-aware while you do it.

"Then I think we can make some room for you, of course," she tells him. Suddenly her voice has a lump of sugar stirred into it. "You said this was a party of five?"

She's true to her word and does make room for them at half past seven, smiling brightly as she escorts Ji-Hoon, Leo, Henri, Joe, and Oliver to the back room, where a handwritten sign reading *Welcome, Camden FC* is placed on the table amid the floral centerpiece.

Her hair is full and glossy, she has a cheeky, white-toothed smile, a very readily flirtatious sense of humor, and her hand lingers at Oliver's elbow when she takes his coat. In other words: trouble. Oliver's gay; he's not blind—only a fool or a homosexual would take in her attentiveness and her pretty black dress and turn it away, and Nicola did not raise a moron. They have a waistcoat-wearing server as well, but the hostess keeps checking back in on them, appearing like a beautiful phantom in the arched doorframe to ask if they want another bottle of wine or tell them the chef wanted to send over an appetizer, with his compliments of course.

It happens all the time, the dawning look of recognition that comes paired with something darker than desirous, like they'd devour Oliver if they could. Some men get off on it; a warm bed can make the dark, cold hours of winter training worth it, it can stave off the sting of a manager's criticism when someone beautiful worships your body, tongue-first. Oliver supposes he's not sure what he's missing, since his chief goal when he's hooking up with someone, even more than the orgasm, is to keep things pitch-dark and not be recognized.

When she appears again over dessert, bearing a carafe of coffee, Ji-Hoon turns his brightest smile on her and she blushes when he says, "Aren't you a sight for sore eyes." Still, she turns her attention back to Oliver, hesitating over his cup, waiting for him to indicate one way or the other that he's received the silent invitation to ask for her number, to stay for one more round of drinks, just the two of them. He thanks her while staring resolutely at the scuff on the back of his dessert spoon. She leaves, deflated, and as soon as she's out of earshot, Henri whips his napkin at Oliver's head.

"Are you stupid?" Henri hisses. "Even *you* couldn't possibly be this choosy."

"I'm not pulling at *dinner,*" Oliver replies, deciding to go for obstinate rather than oblivious. "That would be rude."

"You are not pulling ever! Rejecting every woman in the city of London and leaving them heartbroken, swearing off men forever, that's what's rude. Who are we supposed to go out with?" Henri sighs. "Look at Jiji! Now he cannot ever win her over. You're going to make him feel *douleur*."

Ji-Hoon assumes a hangdog face, right on cue. They've had this exact conversation before, Oliver is certain.

"Oh, leave him be," Joe says, having the time of his life. "Ollie's married to Camden. He's just being faithful."

"Well, the least Camden could do is give him a free pass while he's injured," Ji-Hoon says fairly. The four of them keep up the good-natured bickering, Oliver's unforgivable lack of sexual follow-through mostly forgotten, but he has a strange twinge of nerves in his stomach that's from something other than the late-night coffee. It feels off to him that Leo had observed the whole interaction silently, so very out of character for him, almost judgmental.

"Sorry, mate," Oliver says to Leo as they wind their way back to the restaurant entrance. "The night got away from us. I hope you enjoyed the salad, at least."

"More the merrier," Leo says, smiling, but it doesn't reach his eyes. "I still think you owe me one, though."

• • •

Regent Road has a cloud of forbidding air settled over it as the fans trickle in before the match against Hull City. Oliver doesn't blame them: they've not exactly been on a streak of form that inspires confidence. As he hangs his coat in the team box, James Finch beckons him over. It's the first Oliver's seen of him since Willem told him about the conditions of his hiring, and it makes Oliver feel almost violent to see the big boss now, holding court with his model of a wife and their son in a full kit, knowing he'd ax them all without a second thought.

"Oliver!" Finch says companionably, smiling as if they're the best of chums. "There's a good lad. Have you met Jenny? And Junior?"

"I've had the pleasure, yes." Oliver fashions his face into a smile and crouches down to the kid's level, mostly to avoid getting sucked deeper into the conversation. "When will we see you out there, huh, Jamie?"

"Not soon enough!" Finch booms on his behalf. "And when will we get *you* back, Harris? I must say, they look like they're missing you." It's somehow both a compliment and a threat.

"Just as soon as they let me, boss," he promises as he extricates himself, making a beeline for his seat.

He's getting sick of the sidelines—he's *been* sick of them, but now more than ever. By every metric, Camden should be ready to smash Hull City. The beauty and the blasphemy of football, though, is that it doesn't care about the metrics. Every statistic evaporates over the green of the pitch, and it's anyone's game to lose or to win, if they're only strong enough to run it down and take it. Camden isn't strong enough. Frankly, they look a bit shit. Oliver's teeth are achy from grinding them when he holds back a curse.

The first half is muddy and unlucky, full of bad bounces, over-hit shots, and underhit passes. Willem motions for Leo to come in right when play resumes, along with Noah. The two of them come out sprinting, changing the pace of play completely. *That's it,* Oliver thinks, watching Leo shove back when one of the defenders grabs for his shirt. He keeps playing scrappy, skirting the edge of nasty. Beckett used to always say that football isn't a gentleman's game, it's for artists and ruffians, and all the better if you can play at both. Leo certainly can; it pays off in the dying stages of the match. Anthony slides in hard to keep one of Hull City's forwards out of Joe's box, and Woodsy chases down the loose ball, hoofing it forward in Leo's general direction. That's enough to be going on with; Leo takes off after it, whacking through a smear of opposing kits and bodying his way into the penalty box. He pokes a shot with his weak foot, sending the ball right and the keeper to the left, and there it is, right in the back of the net.

"Go on, then!" Oliver roars, jumping to his feet and clapping, even smacking a high five to James Junior's little palm. "Get after it, Davito!"

Down on the field, Leo runs toward the home dugout, waving madly up toward the stands.

"There we are," Finch says at the referee's whistle, like he had anything to do with it. "Look at him go! I knew I kept him around for a reason. I tell you, Harris, it'll be quite a nice return on investment with you two in midfield. I didn't pay a pound for either one of you!"

Oliver is pleased enough to shrug good-naturedly in reply. He doesn't sit back down, sliding his way out of the row and back toward the box so he can make his way down to the dressing room.

He's surprised the whole stadium isn't shaking from the cacophony downstairs, where the lads are having the time of their lives. You should never take for granted how a win feels, even a narrow one. Even one you didn't play in. Oliver accepts the smelly hugs and fist bumps, gives Willem his best respectful nod, and weaves his way through the revelry over to Leo and claps him on the shoulder.

"Hey, big man," he says. "Welcome home."

"Hi" is all Leo says back, beaming ear to ear, sweaty and glowing.

"How'd it feel? Like you imagined?"

"It was uglier than I thought it would be. But it was perfect."

"You just keep at it, you'll get your wonder goal," Oliver tells him. Before he can think better of it, he ruffles Leo's hair, mussing the curls even further. Leo doesn't shake him off, still smiling, warm and damp under the palm of his hand.

"Are we going out, then?" Georgie, the idiot, asks the room at large, which currently includes Willem. Oliver thinks it's a sign of great maturity that he slips out before the bloodbath rather than hanging around to watch and laugh.

• • •

The rest of the month is a strange blip in the league schedule, a listless ten days without matches. Oliver always forgets how much time is structured around those ninety minutes until he feels lost in their absence. He's lost in something else, too, this strange hunger that gnaws in his gut every time he looks at Leo, an insatiable feeling he has no idea how to quiet.

There's a clip on the club's Instagram, filling in for the lack of match content with clips from training, the squad goofing off between drills. Oliver was there when it was filmed, tossing medicine balls just a few yards over, but he can't stop pulling up the video on his phone anyway, helplessly charmed by it. On his phone's screen, Leo sings into an orange plastic cone, the kind that Sebastian marks the practice with, acting like it's a megaphone. Every time one of their teammates takes their turn at shooting practice, Leo picks a tune for them and shrieks it terribly.

"Banshee! Harpy!" Georgie shouts from out of frame.

"He's incorrigible," Noah whispers to the camera, ducking his face in front of the viewfinder, on his way back to join the back of the line.

"Work work work work work work," Leo trills, undeterred. "Shoot your shot, Georgito!" The camera zooms, capturing the glint in Leo's eyes and the bouncy, shining swoops of his hair. Exertion looks good on him. The tired sheen of a difficult training session is missing, leaving only the sweet, heady endorphins showing on his face. Oliver rewinds the clip over and over, watching Leo smile, watching him bop up and down to an inaudible beat, watching him in his element, teasing and laughing until it's his turn to shoot, still smiling as he kicks the ball hard and high, sailing into the goal with such force it nearly takes off the ceiling of netting. Maybe it's the way he dances or the way he plays football or the way he looks like he belongs there—it's certainly not his singing voice—but Oliver is intoxicated. He watches one more time before bed, then dreams about it for good measure.

You're expected at 8! Nina has texted buoyantly, the next morning. See you then!

He's attended a hundred of these charity events in his young life, particularly photoshoot-y ones, smiling or displaying a practiced seriousness, dressed in Camden gear or designer jeans, never feeling anything less than just as handsome as he *knows* he is. Oliver's got no use for false modesty; it's his job to believe that what his body is capable of is worth millions of pounds and infinite spectacle. It's when he's supposed to bring in his personality that trouble arises, when people want something more from him than he can give on the pitch. Harris the footballer isn't meant to be shy, or anxious, or snappish, only charismatic and golden and for all of Camden to consume. Sometimes the hunger other people have for him fills Oliver up, but mostly it's like he can feel them gnawing at his bones. There's always the fear that if someone got a good enough bite, they might taste what's underneath, a mouthful of everything he's keeping secret.

Oliver keeps doing the hospital visits in spite of this, or maybe somehow because of it. He used to have a complex about it, trading on his own pain and the tragedy of other people's lives for money and for his *image,* but it really, truly isn't about that—maybe for Nina, or for the charity, but not for him. Those six months where everyone seemed to realize that his dad was dying but no one wanted to be the one to say it out loud were the longest, most awful period of his life. He would sit at the foot of the hospital bed with his schoolwork and a football and think, over and over, *Is this the last time? Will we see each other again?* He could feel them both, in a childlike way, trying to cram a whole relationship into those last weeks. Dad could barely wheeze through conversations toward the end, but he was always talking to Oliver, listing all the things his son might need to know.

"Ollie, I know you love it," he'd said while they were watching the last Camden match they would ever sit through together. "And you know how proud I am of you, right?"

He'd just been asked to board at the academy, which would mean training full-time and leaving his school. Oliver was afraid of it, of missing Maggie, not living with his mum, no more afternoons in the bookstall, losing any time with his dad. But he wanted it, desperately—he was just discovering how good he could be, where football could take him. And no small part of him wanted to run, all down the length of the pitch, away from all the sadness in this room, the sterile, sick scent of the hospital and the worried glances from his grandparents at the empty till. His life in Camden was slipping away from him, but Camden FC was looming larger and larger, in a way that made Oliver feel like he could keep everything, if only he got his name onto that team sheet.

"But?" he asked Dad, knowing there would be one.

"But my education was the greatest thing I've ever earned. And the only thing I regret is not having more time to use it—to share it with you and Mum. I want you to have that too. I don't want you to have to choose between football and everything else." *What else is there to choose?* Oliver remembers thinking, so helplessly. *Everything else is lost*. But even at nine years old, he'd known he couldn't say that—speaking it aloud would surely break the last spell of life that Dad was carrying with him, and Oliver wasn't ready to say goodbye, not yet, not ever. "Promise me you'll think about it."

"Why do I have to promise?" Oliver felt his voice shaking, tears leaking out the corners of his eyes. Promises were so final, and he was *sick* of everything being final, of everything ending. "You won't even . . ."

And Dad had flinched, and another round of coughing had seized him, and a nurse appeared, and Nan had pulled Oliver from the room, and his father had never talked with him like that again, too weak for more than nods, and three days later he was gone. Oliver isn't sure if he believes in heaven—he'd like to imagine Dad can see him and Nicola, how well they've done, how much they miss him still—but he's a little afraid of whether his father would think it was all worth it: what he gave to Camden compared to what he's gotten in return.

"Ollie?" someone says, and his reverie is broken—he's standing outside the double doors to the big building in Hampstead where the hospital's family apartments are. Leo is standing there, too, looking concerned.

"Hi," Oliver replies, voice full of cotton. "Good morning."

"You okay?" Leo asks quietly, touching Oliver's elbow, and even so soon out of his trance, the contact makes his heart leap.

"I'm okay," he says, and finds it's not a lie. "I'm glad you're here. Let's do this."

Once they're inside, the visit passes in a blur, like always, but Oliver holds on to snatches of it: The boy who has clearly been briefed on their arrival and is waiting for Oliver with a stack of Paddington books that's taller than he is. Leo drawing in exquisite detail, upon request from a previously sullen preteen, a snowman made out of footballs, who can also fly. And Nina asking a little girl whose mother is in surgery if she likes football and her delicate little nod. *Who's your favorite player?* She whispers back, *Oliver,* like it's a secret, and Leo, standing next to them, suddenly gives her a conspiratorial smile and ducks down to her level. *Mine too*.

It feels so good and right to be there, more than ever before, so much that Oliver braves the walk across the way, toward the main campus, much too close to where Dad died, to meet Nicola as her night shift lets off and offer her a ride home. He manages to return her smile when she sees him; returning her embrace is as easy as anything.

"Do you want to go to lunch?" he asks. "To the market?"

The old bookstall sells vintage license plates now, which is incurably lame, but Camden Market is still the best place in the world to acquire both arepas and leather jackets, within ten feet of each other. The idea of crowding onto a picnic bench with Nicola and twelve other lunchgoers sounds like exactly what he wants to be doing. They'll probably run into someone they know—someone they *really* know, who looks at Oliver and sees a kid from the neighborhood, not a press photo.

"I can't think of anything better," his mother tells him, and the warm sparkle in her eyes reflects back onto him like a perfect mirror.

• • •

The warmth in Oliver's gut holds him over during the last few weeks of winter, until Camden plays Liverpool on the final day of February, a cold and sunny Tuesday at Anfield that he watches alone on his sofa.

Camden has a good showing; Oliver feels truly and vilely horny when Leo starts the match and then assists Emmanuel to open up the scoresheet not even ten minutes later. Leo is just so *fit,* running himself ragged in that Camden green. Oliver wants to serve him up a hundred perfect passes as a present and also bite him right on the jugular, to stake his claim. He's drawn out of his slack-jawed imaginings by Liverpool scoring twice in quick succession, erasing the deficit and creating one of their own. The team is shocked, the wind knocked out of them, and though they shore up the defense and don't concede again, they can't quite manage to get one back. For all they started strong and hungry, coming off the win against Hull City, they're right back in the trenches: zero points, sixth place. Oliver wishes he could kick something, *anything,* it wouldn't even have to be a ball.

Then, four days later, he turns twenty-seven years old. It sneaks up on him like a mugger in a dark alley. He feels ancient. He's not a breakout sensation anymore. He's well and truly a man, in a new, uncharted era of his life and his career. The lads apparently convinced Conor Bishop to let them have full run of one of his cocktail emporiums for the evening, with an open bar and an exorbitant tip both paid in advance, but Oliver doesn't much rate partying anymore; he's more in the mood to stay home and cheat on his nutrition plan with ice cream.

When Saturday evening arrives, as he's thinking about all the ways he could still bail his way out, the doorbell rings long and shrill. Joe is standing at the landing with a magnum of champagne in one hand and a horrible gold party hat in the other.

Oliver cracks the door just a sliver and sticks half of his face to the opening.

"I'm terribly sorry, but you have the wrong house."

Joe wedges his foot in the doorframe and kicks it open. He looks despairingly at Oliver's joggers, then thrusts the bottle at him.

"Don't be a twit," he says. "We planned you a whole party."

"I'm getting melancholy in my old age, man. Don't make me drink to it, I'm begging you."

Joe pushes him toward the stairs and starts to crowd him up toward the second floor.

"For a handsome, rich professional athlete, mate, you are about the saddest sack I've ever met. If you don't go put on a nice shirt and some real trousers, I will personally submit a transfer request in your name to Kilburn. Get moving."

Oliver knows he's beaten. He can't explain what's eating away at him to Joe, either. Camden's been reliably dodgy, a chronic underperformer, the whole of his life. Injuries happen to the lot of them. There's no world where he can say, *Cheers, bruv, thanks for the party, it's just that I'm gay, actually, and I can't stop thinking about kissing the new lad. It's all a bit much for me, so I'd like to stay in and have a weep about it. Hope you understand*. He's going to have to put on an outfit and go make an arse out of himself in public.

Joe demands to approve Oliver's clothing choices, then ignores his ideas in favor of badgering him into exactly what he thinks Oliver should wear: the cream-colored shirt that's cut like a pajama top and trimmed with satin, plus a sturdy pair of black denim, cuffed at the ankle to reveal his most pristine Reeboks.

"We could just stay in and play dress-up all night," Oliver pleads, trying to fend off Joe's attack with a comb. "I'll try on my whole wardrobe, I swear."

Joe gives up on the hair-brushing campaign and delivers Oliver a flute of bubbly instead. Oliver gamely takes a swig and then puts on a brave face, or rather, grimaces.

"I already know what your clothes look like," Joe tells him, as if that should be obvious. "Now do me a favor and say thank you for calling us a cab and not letting Anthony start a donation campaign for a party bus."

"Fucking hell," Oliver shudders, the idea unbearable in every way. Camden FC is already tweeting *Happy Birthday, Harris!* what feels like every hour; the last thing he wants is to also broadcast his rapid aging in an enclosed space with all of his coworkers. "Thank you, Joe," he tacks on dolefully.

Party bus or no, the rest of the team brings the revelry that Oliver can't summon within himself, all boozy laughter and mostly terrible dance moves. There's been someone at his side all night, either one of the lads plying him with gin and tonic or one of the beautiful, miniskirted women they've summoned for the occasion trying their luck at engaging him. Oliver's smiling for another selfie, hand fluttering uselessly in the vicinity of a pretty girl's waist without making contact, when Conor makes an appearance, effortlessly greeting her with a kiss on the cheek that signals a dismissal and Oliver with a handshake that signals something else entirely.

"The man himself," Conor says. "Happy birthday, brother."

"Thanks for having us," Oliver tells him sincerely.

"Oh, it's a pleasure. You lot never blink at an all-inclusive." Conor grins wolfishly, which makes his own stomach flip. Oliver's the celebrity, but Conor is way too cool for him anyway, dressed in a loose batik-printed silk button-down over a turtleneck, carrying the whole thing off like a cover model. Oliver swallows the lump in his throat and tries to decide where the safest place to look is. "You know," Conor says, meeting his eyes despite Oliver's best efforts, "I'm glad I made the invite list to this little soiree."

"Come on, mate," he laughs. "You're the host!"

"I mean, I've been wanting to tell you something, preferably when gratuity has already been taken care of." His voice has slipped into full baritone, a low rumble that makes Oliver's toes prickle. "I don't know what your deal is, Harris," he continues. "Far be it from me to assume. But I want it on the record, just between you and me, that I'm not just playing around. I can be discreet."

Oliver is hard-pressed to think of another time someone has ever said anything so sexy to him. He's halfway to another kind of hard, too. He feels caught out, but he's luxuriating in the throes of being seen. It would be so easy to take Conor up on it, to not confirm anything in words, only with his body. They could trust each other; they could make each other feel good without ever being at risk. He can certainly be discreet himself. There's a vision of them alone skirting the edges of his imagination, where the light stays on so he can see Conor's face. It's tantalizing. They're standing far too close together now, bodies angled toward each other in confession. Before Oliver can find the words to tell him he'll take it under advisement, that Conor hasn't misread the room, their party of two gets broken up by a crush of bodies, as his teammates arrive bearing a tray of flaming shots that are sloshing precariously and obviously meant to stand in for birthday candles.

"You have to take them all," Joe shouts. "Come on, Harris, your song's on."

"Oi, not until you put them out," Oliver protests in vain as he gets dragged into the center of the room, looking helplessly back toward Conor as he disappears behind a *Staff Only* door. Oliver could follow him and get everything he's dreamed of—probably more—but he stays. "This isn't even my song," he sniffs when he hears something about taking pills in Ibiza.

"It is tonight," someone declares from the edges of the crowd, grabbing for Oliver and spinning him in a solicitous, unsteady circle under an outstretched arm. When he emerges, stooping to fit himself under the arc of a biceps, Oliver can see that it's Leo. The sight of him unclenches something in Oliver's gut and he reaches for the tray and throws back a shot—mercifully extinguished before they could hurt anyone—as the whole team closes around them, bobbing up and down in unison, encircling like they're playing man in the middle, and his chest burns both from the alcohol and from whatever it was that drove him to drink it.

"You having a good night, then?" Leo yells over the sound of the singer lamenting that you don't ever want to step off a roller coaster and be all alone.

"I feel proper wizened, to be honest," Oliver admits, despite himself. He's on the roller coaster still, he's not alone at all.

"You look just fine for an old man," Leo says earnestly, twisting to the synths.

"Couldn't you play nice for once? On my birthday?"

Leo shakes his head, eyes glimmering.

"Not in my nature," he tells Oliver matter-of-factly. "You should know by now."

And Oliver does know—he's watched Leo skip by any number of defenders with his tongue out, taunting them, daring them to foul him. Leo is a regular ankle-biter, a right menace when he wants to be. Oliver just hadn't realized it carried over this way, that nightclubs are just as much a field of play as Regent Road is. He snags another shot off the rapidly emptying tray, holding it out to Leo like an offering, but he doesn't take it from his hand, just raises one eyebrow and pulls Oliver a step closer by the elbow. When Leo opens his mouth, a lit-up feeling flares between them, like the shot is on fire again, and Oliver cradles Leo's chin in one palm and pours the liquor in himself. Leo's throat works once, twice, as he swallows, then he signals for another one and the team hollers back in approval, Oliver's heart roaring just as loudly.

The drumbeat is still shimmering in time with the flashing lights, casting otherworldly slants of shadow in a way that makes him understand why people love clubbing so much. Two feet away, Woodsy has Matty on his shoulders, while Garcia and Carda are engaging in a drunken bout of gay chicken, grinding theatrically for a flock of girls who giggle and egg them on. It's the rare night where teammates are better than grafting boots, where no one thinks it's strange they're all dancing with each other instead of the girls. They could be anywhere, be anyone, so Oliver gives up fighting it and suppresses the pain in his leg, just for one song, so he can keep dancing and glut himself on the feeling of being near Leo. He's sweating pure grain alcohol, tipsy enough from the drinks and from Conor fucking Bishop to stay very close to Leo. No one could begrudge Oliver this, especially not at his own party.

Leo has a better sense of rhythm than he does—which he might have guessed from how many times he watched that stupid video of him singing into the orange cone—and now Oliver is just trying to keep up. He's breathing out of his mouth, sucking for air and getting lost in the streak of red glitter on Leo's cheekbone, the remnants of a kiss that someone else gave him. Leo's lips are moving, forming words that are lost to the speaker's thump. Oliver leans in, cupping his mouth to Leo's ear, fingers buried in the soft-ending strands of his hair.

"What?" he asks.

"I said now *you're* trying too hard," Leo says. Somehow Oliver can now hear him at a whisper. Their faces are nearly touching. A pair of hands he can't see are tugging on Oliver's belt loop. "Why don't you just feel it?"

It's so filthy, bordering on absurd, how the words hit him, engulfing each of his senses one by one. Leo is sweaty and panting like he's been after a hundred laps around the training ground, but when Oliver looks at him now, he can only see the same vision Conor conjured for him earlier, with Leo's body in its place, the form he's coming to know so well. Obviously he didn't sweat out all of the alcohol, because it's sloshing around in his stomach, heavier than mercury. Of course he feels it—too much, more than anything.

He wants to laugh it off, to dance around it, and he starts to, looking for another body to make contact with, but the crowd shifts again, the walls closing in on them, and as the next chorus hits in the drunken darkness, Leo steadies Oliver with one hand on the small of his back, holding him even closer than before. Their hips are moving back and forth together now, finally in sync, the same give-and-take as passing a ball.

"Like this," Leo says, pleased but garbled, and Oliver wants to ask him, *Do you like this? Is that what you mean? Can* you *feel it?* But the song and the moment seem to float away from him before he can.

Saturday, March 11, 2017: Camden at West Bromwich Albion

MATCHDAY 27

Will we be seeing you on the coach?

Oliver groans. Willem is addicted to sending ransom-note WhatsApps, asking questions that clearly have only one right answer. He just did seventy-five minutes of core-strengthening exercises and he's too sweaty to play mind games.

I'd be happy to come to the match if you'd like, boss, he writes back, as he knows he's meant to. There hasn't been a match since Liverpool—just the long days of cross-training and watching Leo out of the corner of his eye, feeling strangely bashful whenever anyone on the squad starts dancing—but the slate of competition is picking up again.

Wonderful. Wheels up at 11:30.

It takes just under three hours to get from London to the Midlands, but that doesn't stop them all from rolling up to the team coach packed as if they're being shipped off to war indefinitely. Every single luxury neck pillow and portable gaming system on the market are represented. Oliver distributes the requisite hand clasps and makes his way toward the back of the coach, climbing over Joe to take his spot by the window. Last time he was at Mum's flat, Oliver filched a weathered copy of *Pride and Prejudice*—he has to read every line of dialogue twice to comprehend it, even though *they're speaking English,* but he's determined to make it through, if only so he can tell Maggie that he did and feel smug about it. Besides, it's kind of romantic, all the old-fashioned little gestures adding up until they turn into love.

Thirty minutes outside the city, Leo flops into the open row in front of them, then climbs up to sit on his knees and sticks his face between the headrests. *Like this,* Oliver remembers, for the millionth time.

"Whatcha doing?" Leo asks. Joe has his eyes closed and his earbuds in; it's a question for Oliver.

"It's a book, mate," Oliver says. "There are words on the paper. If you read them in sequence, it tells a story."

Leo is unfazed by this. It's a great relief to Oliver that his horrible crush hasn't stopped him from taking the absolute piss out of Leo at every opportunity, and that Leo seems to actually kind of like it now.

"Whoa, dude," Leo replies, all American stoner. "Who's pride and who's prejudice?" Oliver rolls his eyes and doesn't reply, trying to focus on a passage about the Bennets meeting Bingley at a ball—the dancing kind, not footy. He gets about ten words further before Leo interrupts again, waving his hand in front of the page and blocking it. "I never pegged you for a literary type, if I'm honest," he says.

"We all left school at sixteen and now we get hit in the head with balls for a living," Oliver snipes back. "Forgive me for trying to develop some sort of an intellectual life while my brain cell count is still normal. Besides, Harris men have been peddling books for generations. We weren't all raised by bankers."

Leo rolls his eyes, but when Joe goes back a few rows to talk about keeper things with Nick, Leo inserts himself into the vacant seat and starts to read over his shoulder. He's too quick, though, and keeps trying to turn the page before Oliver finishes. Eventually, Leo gives up, and before they're in West Bromwich, his head has lolled onto Oliver's shoulder and he's dozing, making snuffling noises into the collar of his sweater. Oliver sits stock-still, staring at the same paragraph, afraid to move, drinking in Leo's warm breath as it washes over his collarbone and spreads all down his body.

• • •

The match is *awful,* simply out-of-this-world embarrassing. Oliver can take it against Chelsea and the like—he's lost his fair share of matches, but rolling over and showing their bellies to West Brom (West Brom!) is a bridge too far. He knows there's going to be footage of him in the stands shouting and looking murderous, which will be bad for morale and makes him feel like a bit of a wanker, but he couldn't help it. They were just so bad, slow and bumbling. Even Leo and Finn, running faster than Oliver ever could, even if he was healthy, were chasing shadows for an hour and a half.

While he's winding his way through the unfamiliar concrete labyrinth of the stadium, aiming for the visitors' locker room, he sees Terence Morgan, of all people, waiting for the elevator in a navy waistcoat and tapping away at his phone.

"Hey, gaffer," Oliver says to England's National Team manager, his other, non-Willem boss. "Fancy meeting you here."

Terry smiles in that paternal way he has, neat mustache crinkling, as if he'd known precisely when and where he'd be running into you but is chuffed it worked out anyway.

"Oliver Harris, there he is. You better be rehabbing like you've not ever rehabbed before, mate. They're missing you—so am I."

Oliver expects to be pleased at the praise, and on some level he is, but mostly he wishes Camden would play the way he knows they could, champions of some alternate-reality Premier League.

"Ah, you know how it is. Just when you think you can't take it anymore, you turn around and win one that changes the rest of the season," Oliver says, trying to mean it. Terry reaches over and taps him on the biceps companionably, then the elevator finally dings and they go their separate ways.

The mood in the dressing room is bleak and stale. Charles's jaw is so tight it might actually snap; Joe is hiding with a towel over his head. Willem sits on the edge of a table by a whiteboard, flicking through his leather notebook with pursed lips. Oliver moves to perch on the wooden ledge sticking out from Woodsy's locker and tries to be invisible. After a spell, Willem snaps his notebook closed. *If he can talk us out of this one,* Oliver thinks, *maybe he is brilliant*.

"You were rubbish, gentlemen" is what their manager says instead. A low snort rattles through the room. "It happens sometimes. That's what makes the wins special. Unfortunately, we've had more than our fair share of it going around recently. It's not indicative of the talent in this room, which makes it worse. I don't feel entitled to any victories—I know we have to earn them. But I think we're capable of much better than where the league table says we belong. I wouldn't be here if I didn't think so." Oliver looks down at his feet, thinking about the buzzing sound an MRI machine makes and how much money Camden would get for selling him. "The blame falls partly on me. Clearly there's something I haven't been able to tap into," Willem continues, and God, he seems tired. "Some of you will go away for the international break, and I wish you luck with your countries. The rest of you will be working your absolute hardest in training. We have barely sixty days left in the season. Get your heads right."

He stands to leave; Oliver has the strange urge to clap or to cheer, anything to break the awful, resigned silence. Sebastian follows him, stopping by Leo's locker and pointing toward the door. Then it hits him: *Oh. That's why Terry's here. Leo is going to get called up to play for England.*

His pride doesn't feel wounded—honestly, a midwinter set of friendlies isn't much to envy. And as he mulls it over, the idea of Leo playing for England as well as Camden, standing next to him in the only other kit that matters, becomes tempting. Oliver wonders if he'll say yes. Making it as a professional footballer is one kind of pipe dream; being selected to represent a national team is something else entirely. His agent told him once that fewer than ten percent of players with full-time professional contracts ever wear their country's kit—he said it so Oliver would understand the magnitude of what was being offered to him. Oliver wants Leo to have that honor, too, to know what it feels like to look at your name on that shirt. Then he wonders if he might be waiting for a call from Spain instead? Once you play for any international team at the senior level, that's it, for life—forget what your passports say. To play for England, or to choose not to, would be a very public declaration of loyalties.

When Leo slinks back into the room several minutes later, gobsmacked, Oliver makes a beeline down the row of lockers and grabs him by the elbow.

"What did you say?" Oliver asks, desperate to know.

"Oi, wizard!" Leo whispers back, eyebrows up in his hairline. "How on earth do you already know? Did he ask for your blessing?"

"Educated guess," Oliver replies. "Stop dodging."

Leo huffs a laugh and swats at him. "Give us a minute to think. It's a big decision."

"I think you should do it. Don't stop the momentum you've got right now."

"How do you know Spain isn't asking too? Or Colombia?" Leo asks.

"You'd've told me," Oliver says quietly, realizing it's true as it comes out of his mouth. Leo's eyes soften like he knows it too. He starts to step away, but Oliver waves toward the room behind them. *Tell them,* he mouths. Leo nods, smiling now as it sets in. You only get this kind of call once in your career, if you're lucky enough to get it at all. It's special.

"Hey!" Leo shouts. "Guess who just had an interesting conversation with Terence Morgan?"

The room explodes—everyone is cheering and reaching over for hugs and arm slaps. Oliver clocks a few traces of disappointment, but few and far between. There's little doubt the team rates Leo as a player and a friend, and no doubt at all that he's made the case to earn it. Willem first subbed him in less than two months ago and he's already completed the most passes of any Camden player this season, breaking another one of Oliver's records. And they're all hungry for some good news.

Anthony drifts over from his locker to stand next to Oliver, snapping at him with the wet end of a ratty towel.

"Jealous?" Anthony asks.

Oliver shrugs. "Not like I could take a spot right now anyways. I'm happy for him."

"Very diplomatic," Anthony says, goading.

"Shove off," Oliver laughs. "He goes out there and charms Terry now, I get better, then the England midfield is coming up Camden. It's good news."

"*I* know that. I also know if I tried to tell it to you, you'd knock my teeth in." Anthony has a shit-eating grin on.

Oliver hates him, but his retort dies in his mouth when he hears Carda talking across the room, holding court in his tiny underwear:

"My question is this: How is it that you are not getting any, Davito?"

Leo, red as a beetroot, tells him to shut up, then something else in Spanish that sounds ugly.

"I'm serious!" Carda presses on. "We might be a nightmare, but you're the talk of the whole damn league. For the rest of our sakes, *hombre,* please do not waste this moment. Or at least send some of the girls my way."

"It's insane to me," Ahmed weighs in. "You should see this man operate. When we were in the academy, there was a nonstop stream of birds in his DMs, like *mad,* I'm telling you. He was converting one hundred percent of the time too. Made it look easy."

Oliver feels ill. He's rooted to the floor, watching the interaction unblinkingly. *That's the game, isn't it,* he thinks. *Goals get the girls.* All this time he's been reimagining one song's worth of a moment, but Leo probably took someone else home. That's how it's supposed to be. Oliver is the fool for dreaming, even a little bit, about it going differently.

"Don't be gross," Leo says, pushing Carda down from his wide-legged stance up on the bench.

"Sex is a natural part of life, my sweet," Carda replies, "sweet" sounding like *thweet*.

"I don't want to talk about this with all of you, thanks!" Leo's tone still hints at joking, but it's rising in pitch. "I've been focused on my game, on the *season,* which I happen to think is slightly more important than girls, unlike some of you."

"Yes, you're very noble," Carda says. "But if someone snuck herself in here in a laundry cart and begged you for it, would you say no?" He shimmies his shoulders at Leo suggestively, running one finger down his chest and trying to flick at his nipple. Everyone is watching now, half-laughing and half-listening.

"I'd call security," Leo says defiantly, throwing up his fingers in a vee when the lads start to boo.

"You are as bad as Harris," Henri pronounces, tragedy in his voice. Oliver doesn't even think to protest; the locker room suddenly sounds tinny and far away while he processes Leo's vehement devotion to celibacy.

• • •

When do you leave? Oliver texts, after they've trudged back to London and gone their separate ways, allowing the gremlin in his brain to ask for what it wants, which is for Leo to come over and be near him, all the time, even if he knows better.

Wednesday morn x, Leo replies immediately, even the short text radiating giddiness.

Free Tuesday? I can cook something warm. No salad

No salad???

Special occasion.

I'll be there. With an alarm set so I don't forget to pack.

Oliver has figured out the mentorship thing. He's aces at it, actually. Friendship, unspeakable romantic urges—those he's less sure about. But his mum, not to mention Anthony, would box his ears if he didn't show Leo that he's proud of him, that getting called up for England is the rarest, most incredible thing. Plenty of people never make it to that level, even if they play in the proper position at a good club for their whole career. Leo has just now hit his stride; he's already unstoppable.

When Leo comes around a few days later, showing up right as sundown hits, clad in a soft wine-colored jumper and holding a matching bottle to boot, Oliver has committed to roasting a chicken and is feeling not a little embarrassed about the evening's obvious, tangible effort.

"It smells so good in here," Leo says, passing off the bottle into Oliver's waiting hands and following his nose toward the kitchen. The wine label has been scribbled all over, covered in

Leo's particular brand of permanent-marker doodles. "Have you been holding out on me?"

"You're the one who brought his own vintage" is all Oliver says, brandishing the wine as he trails after him. He suspects he'll keep the bottle forever, even when it's empty.

"Only the best," Leo replies distractedly. He's stopped in the small hall off the landing, taking in the array of pictures on the wall. He touches one hesitant pointer finger to the edge of a frame, lingering on the clipping from the *New York Times*. It consists of a slightly faded photo of Oliver as a spotty teen in a crimson England kit, suspended jubilantly in midair after a goal, hovering immortal over a block of newsprint.

"'Can This Teenager Save English Football? He's Not so Sure They Need Rescuing,'" Leo reads aloud. "You're really bloody famous, you know that?" It suggests a joke, revenge for the teasing Leo gets from him, but there's a quaver in his voice tilting toward awestruck, like he's just remembering that Oliver the person and Harris the midfielder are one and the same.

"Fat lot of good that headline did," Oliver admits, turning Leo's shoulders away from the picture to set him straight. "I'm not a poster boy anymore and I don't have any trophies to show for it either. It's your turn to save England now, mate."

Leo consents to follow him to the breakfast bar, but he rolls his eyes as he does it.

"Don't let Charles hear you say that," he says darkly.

Oliver looks up from the ribbons of carrot peels he's resumed scraping into the bin. Leo's top half is sprawled over the marble counter, weight on his elbows, chin in his palms. The slant of his eyebrows is a dead giveaway.

"Hey," Oliver murmurs, coming around to his side of the room and leaning lightly against Leo's side. "None of that."

"Some of that," Leo replies, tone going sharp. "He's never going to accuse *you* of not really being English."

"Did he say something?" Oliver asks immediately, preparing for war at the thought of someone—let alone one of their teammates—ruining this moment for Leo out of bitterness or jealousy.

"I know he thinks it." Leo lets his arms slide out from under him, head resting on the stone surface. Oliver hazards the gentlest poke at his forehead, which makes the corners of Leo's mouth quirk up.

"Listen: I've been playing with Charles, or against him, since I was a sprog. I'd trust him in a knife fight, but he's an idiot. You came through the academy! You fought like hell to end up back here. We're not a team that gets a lot of calls from Terence Morgan, you know? You're a Camden lad and you're a credit to us. End of story."

Leo sighs and turns his neck so they're face-to-face. He glowers, cutely, then pokes Oliver back in his own forehead.

"I know they asked first," he says slowly. "But I wouldn't have said yes if this wasn't home. I know I can't take it back."

"Of course not."

"It's mad complicated, like I said before. When you look at me, you see Colombia, you hear Spain. But I've got as much fucking right as any of you. More, maybe, if I'm good enough."

There's a hardness, a resolve, revealing itself in Leo, who's usually so smooth around the edges when he's not playing football. Oliver thinks he might do anything to protect him from whatever is causing it—but he also thinks the look in his eyes right now, the determined, match-winning-goal one, is impossibly attractive.

"When I look at you," Oliver says, carefully, "I see a lot of future headlines. No matter what kit you're wearing. Besides, there's nothing more English than committing to a lost cause."

Leo sweeps upright and reaches across the distance between them, squeezing Oliver's shoulder with one solid touch.

"You give good pep talks. And you have a very nice house."

This means the conversation is over, Oliver surmises. The compliment is still nice.

"I've already started cooking," he tells Leo, standing up fully and moving back toward the oven. "There's no need to butter me up."

• • •

"I mean it," Leo says later, while he's absently picking remnants of roasted potato and crispy shards of onion out of the casserole dish and popping them directly into his mouth. He'd offered to help clean up, but Oliver didn't realize he meant by being a literal hoover. "This is a grown-up home. An adult lives here."

Oliver laughs and feels the beginning of a blush bloom on his cheeks—he somehow wants to preen and not take credit simultaneously.

"Cheers, mate," he replies. "It's hard to settle into a rental, I think. When you buy something, you'll make it your own and become a proper host."

"It's more than that," Leo says thoughtfully, fiddling with one of the cabinet knobs. "You have good taste. It's not, like, boyish."

Oliver pushes down the little prickly feeling that suggests his manhood is being questioned in favor of the pleased one that Leo seems to like him that way.

"That'll be Maggie," he admits, in the interest of fairness. "She told all the decorators what to do before I even finished the paperwork."

Leo doesn't respond immediately, reapplying himself to the leftovers and munching for a moment.

"Maggie's your ex?"

Oliver nods, eyes on the tea towel. It's convenient that everyone in his life usually knows this by default, which saves him from having to explain the precise nature of their relationship and directly lie about the breakup. He feels under scrutiny about it now.

"It doesn't bother you, to live somewhere where she picked everything out?" Leo asks, still not looking at him.

"She's not that kind of ex," Oliver hedges. "I hadn't really ever thought about it that way." Leo's eyes snap up and he gives him a look that says, *I'm not buying it*. But he doesn't press, only shrugs and finally gives up on picking the plates clean. "I can make something else, since I've obviously starved you," Oliver says. "Growing boy."

That gets a laugh out of Leo, even if it comes with an eye roll.

"I'll stop, I'll stop," Leo says. "Forgive me for fighting food waste."

"I swear I have some contraband sweets around here somewhere. Give us a minute, I'll hunt for chocolate." Oliver knows exactly where the chocolate is: third shelf of the pantry, right-hand side, in a basket hidden under the muesli. He gives himself a break anyway, stepping inside the oversized cupboard and poking around the bins and boxes, quashing the feeling that he was put on the spot and gave the wrong answer a moment ago. They're friends, real friends, but he can't tell Leo the truth about this one. He especially can't tell *him*. It would be so obvious on his face—how Oliver feels, what he wants—if those walls were ever breached, even for a second.

He steps back into the kitchen with half a Dairy Milk and nearly drops it. *Speak of the devil*, he thinks, wretchedly.

"I let myself in," Maggie says. She's standing just at the top of the entryway, carrying a cardboard box that reaches up to her chin. Oliver sneaks a glance over at Leo and finds the knowing look he expected, cut with something darker, almost angry.

"We were just talking about you," Oliver says, regretting it instantly. "Is that—"

"It's the piece I set aside for your mum," she replies, holding it outstretched. Oliver steps forward to take it and promptly lowers it to the ground, feeling idiotic.

"Doorbell not working?" he asks. Maggie's eyes are huge and trepidatious. "Come here a second." With that, he swiftly deposits them both back into the pantry and yanks the door shut after them. He can see the joke forming on her lips. "If you say one thing about a closet, I'm going to kill you."

"Jesus, Ollie! I'm not going to say anything! You know I wouldn't tell."

"What do you mean?" Oliver asks, confused.

"If anyone was going to find out, aren't you glad it's me? I can't believe you didn't say anything!"

"Say anything about *what*? We're just having dinner!" he snaps.

"Oh, sure," Maggie replies, throwing her hands up in exasperation. "I always look like *The Sun* caught me skinny-dipping in the canal when someone finds me having my casual friend over for a normal dinner."

"Mags, I'll do anything you want for the rest of our lives, if you'll just be *silent,*" he pleads. "You and I are friends, not together. Me and Leo are friends too. Everyone is mates, yeah? No one has feelings for anybody. But ah, fuck, don't say anything about feelings at all. Please do not make this weird."

"Ollie!" she snaps, as close to a yell as a whisper can get. "You are the one making this weird! If you don't want him to know what's going on, why are you afraid he'll think we're together?" Oliver shakes his head, but she whips her right hand out and slaps it over his mouth before he can respond, gagging him. "Don't answer that. We both know why."

He tries in vain to free himself by licking at her palm, but she holds firm.

"Breathe through your nose," she advises. "I'm going to leave now and I won't say another word. Try not to have an aneurysm." She leaves Oliver dumbstruck and the door swinging on its hinges behind her, walking past Leo with only a nod goodbye. Oliver is too stunned to move until the sound of her footsteps and the sight of her plaid trench coat recede down the front stairwell.

His spirit is floating somewhere around the ceiling, looking down helplessly while his body is in motion and stepping back into the kitchen, though it looks all wrong—he's not certain he's ever been here before. Leo is standing just where Oliver left him, leaning against the island, but now his arms are tightly crossed over his abdomen. His easy face, handsome and readable, has gone tight.

"Hey," Oliver says to announce his return, since Leo's eyes are locked to the floor. "I'm sorry about that. She should've knocked."

"Well, I guess she's not that kind of ex," Leo bites out.

"Whoa, easy—" Oliver starts to say.

"'Don't want him to know what's going on.' 'We both know why,'" he quotes, cutting Oliver off midsentence. His tone is dripping with antagonism, his lip curled up almost like a snarl. "You do talk your shit, don't you? All this time, I thought—"

"Mate, when you eavesdrop, you don't always hear what you think you do," Oliver says frantically, but Leo takes a step toward him that feels threatening.

"We're supposed to be friends. You keep doing this to me, and I can't— Friends don't lie, Ollie."

"I'm not lying to you," Oliver murmurs, retreating a pace backward, stunned by the acid in Leo's tone.

"You fucking are," he replies, voice cracking. "I should've taken you at your word on that first day and spared myself the trouble."

Oliver is rent in two, panic and pain mingling. In all his worst anxieties about how Leo would react to this, it hadn't felt quite so terrible. If he walks out the door, before Oliver knows what else he heard, before he's had a chance to explain, he'll never recover.

"Leo, please. It's not— I'm not trying to deceive you. This is something, it's so personal. No one knows, no one on the team."

"I don't even know what you're *talking* about," Leo fairly shouts. "Can you actually just give me a straight answer?"

Oliver laughs, a stunned gut-punch noise, not an ounce of humor in it. There's no *straight* answer to be had.

"I never wanted you to be in this position," Oliver whispers bitterly. "I've always been so careful, I promise you. You can trust me. I won't . . . I won't do anything stupid."

Their eyes meet and Oliver's breath comes in shallow waves when he sees it click on Leo's face, epiphany writ in the O of his mouth.

"So you *are* gay?" Leo asks, so quietly it's almost to himself. But Oliver hears it and now it's in the room with them, impossible to put off or ignore.

"Mate, listen—" he says, good as a confession.

"Is there something wrong with me?" Leo asks, like he didn't hear him at all. He's turned himself away, but the anger is gone in his voice. Oliver risks a step forward and reaches for his elbow, completely bewildered by this reaction. Leo resists for a split second, arm tense in his grasp. When Oliver pulls, so they're facing each other again, he's agonized, eyes shiny with tears.

"Hey, hey," Oliver tries, but Leo pushes him away: palm to his chest, the same way he'd defend himself after a tackle, the same way Oliver had when they'd played that horrible, fateful scrimmage at Camden Crossing.

"Is it?" Leo accuses. "You like blokes, just not me? You'd rather I was Conor Bishop?"

Oh. Maggie, damn her, was right. It wasn't hero worship, or Willem, that kept drawing them to each other; it was this all along.

"Leo," Oliver says, calculating his words. He'd never even bothered to fantasize about getting the chance to say them. "Please. I've been killing myself trying not to cross every line I've ever drawn for myself. It's not other blokes that I want, okay?" He's getting the next sentence ready, the chance to reiterate that he won't ruin this, that the conversation they're having right now will go to their graves. The words don't make it out, because he's suddenly been walked backward right into the wall, and Leo has the collar of Oliver's sweater balled up in each hand.

And then they're kissing. Oliver is being kissed.

The first go-round, their teeth clack together, then their noses slot into place and it's sublime. Oliver's not a monk, he's a grown man and an occasional underwear model, but he didn't know it could feel like this. He finds Leo's hip bones with his fingertips, sliding beneath his belt loops and pulling with intent. Someone is making gasping sounds with each breath, maybe both of them. Leo goes up to his tiptoes and grabs for the soft curl of hair at the back of Oliver's neck. He's panting into Oliver's open mouth, and he tastes sweet, even though they never got to the chocolate after all. The tentative brush of Leo's tongue and the velvet of his skin, muscled but soft to the touch under Oliver's hands, root him to the spot; he couldn't move even if he wanted to, which he doesn't—he only wants to do this for the rest of his life.

It occurs to Oliver to open his eyes, to remember every second of this. He's about to, when Leo's phone begins to blare a shrill series of beeps and vibrations. *Packing alarm,* Oliver realizes, stricken. *He's going away to play for England tomorrow.* The force of the noise wrenches them apart: Oliver boneless against the wall and Leo a few steps away.

"Oh," Leo whispers, and Oliver's eyes snap to his. "I have to go." That's all he says, out the door before his next blink, the doorframe rattling with the force of his exit. Oliver is left knock-kneed, buffeted by the remnants of the best first kiss he wasn't supposed to have and the keenness of its absence.

Wednesday, March 15, 2017

INTERNATIONAL BREAK

Sometimes you just have to settle in and make yourself comfortable at rock bottom. Nothing to be done for it.

When Oliver was eighteen, when it was futile to pretend, at least to himself, any longer, he came up with a paradoxical set of rules. *Don't tell anyone, except you have to tell Maggie. Don't look at anyone, but if you do, don't look at footballers. Don't think about it, unless you have to*. All he's done since January is think. And now he's done a damn sight more than tell or look: he's confessed and he's acted on it, with another Rose. He has to look at Leo across the pitch every day until Willem or Finch says otherwise, for work, for Camden, for a shitload of cash, and now whenever he does it, he won't be thinking about midfield formations or shots on goal, he'll only be remembering the hottest thing that's ever happened to him. It would be simpler if kissing Leo had been stumbling or awkward, easy to classify as a mistake. Instead, it was incredible and thrilling. It's going to linger in Oliver's bones and haunt him forever.

Somehow, at some point, he convinced himself that there was no guilt in hiding, only practicality. *But why would you need to confess something you aren't ashamed of?* he wonders, full to the brim with self-loathing. He doesn't want to feel shame. There's no embarrassment in him, no thought of being weaker for it, only the nauseating sensation of keeping up a lie. When Oliver thinks about people finding out that he's gay, that he likes men, his fight-or-flight kicks in. It doesn't feel safe. He has to keep the disparate pieces where they belong, or his life is going to come crashing down around him—like it is right now. When he lost his father, football was the only thing that felt right. But with every passing day, Camden—the home and the football club—looks less recognizable to him. The one thing he knows how to keep is who he is, who Oliver Harris is *meant* to be. And he's meant to be a footballer, staid and straight. He was supposed to support Leo and teach him, not antagonize him and fantasize about him and spoil things between the two of them before they'd ever shared a pitch. He's still injured and for sale, Willem is still on the brink of getting fired, and all Oliver has done in months is pick fights he can't win.

• • •

No matter how depressed you might be and no matter how justified said depression is, *Thou shalt not be late to practice.* Show up on time or suffer the consequences. Anthony has a particularly harsh rule in place: three grand if you're tardy, with interest accruing every fifteen minutes until you show up. It's not even about the cash (though the money will be donated to charitable causes at the end of the season)—the public shaming is the worst of it.

All told, sleeping through five alarms and waking up at half past nine on Friday will probably cost Oliver nearly ten thousand pounds. He takes the stairs two at a time, half-dressed and wholly stressed, landing gingerly on his injured leg. He heaves himself through the entry doors eight minutes later, but he was not expecting Willem to be prowling the front hall, holding a porcelain cup and saucer. Oliver actually doesn't even clock his presence until he's a few steps beyond him.

"Training begins at nine o'clock, Mr. Harris," Willem says reproachfully, over the rim of his mug.

"Jesus H," Oliver swears, wrenching his head behind him. "Er, I—sorry, sir, didn't see you."

"Evidently," Willem replies, sounding as peevish as Oliver has ever heard him. "Why don't you and I have a cup of tea in my office, seeing as the rest of the team has already gotten started?"

It is quite deliberately not a question: classic Willem. Oliver follows him up the stairs, feeling for all he's worth that the ghosts of Camden Football Club past are physically frog-marching him into the manager's office. While Willem busies himself with pouring another cup of—frankly, oversteeped-looking, stupid Dutchman—breakfast tea, Oliver stares resolutely at the rug, nudging the woven flower pattern with the toe of his shoe like his life depends on it. He waits for a lecture or a series of leading questions, but Willem leaves them in silence for a good long while.

"It's not like you to be tardy," de Boer says eventually, raising one eyebrow up into a parenthetical arch. "The others might start getting ideas."

Oliver groans, scrubbing at his eyelids with his knuckles.

"I am sorry, Willem, genuinely. Overslept, innit."

"You look awful."

Even though Willem's right, it's not nice to say. Oliver can't bring himself to raise his gaze and confirm how out of sorts he looks, so he continues studying the floor. Willem doesn't push him, but eventually the weight of the quiet is unbearable, reminding him irresistibly of the stretch of drawn-curtain hours he's spent with his own thoughts over the last two days.

"Did Sebastian ever tell you that we—ah, me and Leo—were

training together after hours?" Oliver asks, retching the words out involuntarily.

"He did."

"But you didn't punish us?"

"I thought that might be counterproductive. Would you have kept helping him if Sebastian shouted at you for it?"

"What if I'd been out there sabotaging him?" Now that Oliver's started this line of questioning, he can't seem to stop.

Willem doesn't laugh, taking the question on its face.

"If I thought you were capable of that, I'd send you to Brighton tomorrow on a loan and never look back," he says firmly. "Oliver, permit me to ask the question this time: did something happen between you and Leonardo?"

Oliver scuffs at the rug even more diligently. It's a perfectly fair question, which makes him feel even more woefully unprepared to answer. Especially about the definitions of "something" and "between."

"I'm not trying to get shipped off," he begins. "I'd be wasted on the seaside. But I don't know if I was cut out to be a mentor, honestly. I reckon Davito would agree with me."

Willem cocks his head and gives him a curious look, then pauses, leaving room for him to continue. But Oliver, leaden with a deathbed confession, will go no further. He takes a gulp from his teacup instead to buy time.

"What makes you say that?" *Why don't you ask* him, Oliver wants to reply, snappish thoughts pushing out at his temples. He doesn't want Willem to ask Leo, though; he doesn't want anyone to ask Leo anything about him ever again. He shrugs instead, keeping his attention fixed on the tea. Willem, of course, is no stranger to filling silences. "Well, for what it's worth, you're off the mark on this one, Harris. From my point of view, it's clear that you and Leo will be well matched in the midfield. I brought him here from Spain because of it." Oliver can't help the tight shake of his head, the visceral reaction to being called any kind of a match with Leo now. "Mentor or not," Willem insists, "he's here to play with you. And he's done brilliantly. He has you to thank for this opportunity. And you'll have him to thank when you're healthy and have someone who can keep up with you out there," he continues, leaning back slightly as his chair creaks in protest.

"Time will tell, I suppose," Oliver manages, choking on the words. Maybe Leo will play so beautifully for England that Valencia realizes what they sent away, regrets it, and puts in a billion-pound bid. Perhaps Oliver and Leo will never speak again except across opposite ends of an international friendly, all of France safely separating them.

Something like concern breaks out in wrinkles all over Willem's forehead, but Oliver is spent. De Boer lets him leave without another word, but everything said and unsaid follows Oliver around for the rest of the day like he's dragging it around in a suitcase. Even his truncated version of the workout feels like it's being pulled out of him against his will, until his legs are jelly and his arms quiver with exertion. He's still wobbly-legged when Anna comes into the appointment room that afternoon, putting on her reading glasses and picking up a clipboard full of medical charts.

"Heard you were late to training," she says without looking up.

"I had a meeting," he lies unconvincingly. "What do those say?" He gestures feebly for the papers, trying to snatch them out of her hands without sitting up from the exam table.

"Nothing you would understand, I'm afraid," she replies, brushing him off with ease and keeping her eyes on the papers. She takes her time with it and by now Oliver knows better than to interrupt, settling in for the long haul of her analysis. Eventually, she hands him a printout.

"What do you see?"

Even when he presses his nose all the way to the paper, his eyes can't follow the pattern of muscle and bone that makes up his leg.

"Nothing," he admits, thinking he's proven her right.

"Exactly." She's smiling at him for the first time this calendar year. "The muscle reknit itself very neatly. Well done."

It's not as if Oliver had anything to do with it, but he's flushed with pride anyway.

"So I'm cured?" he asks in a whisper, not sure if he deserves it.

"You're *healed*. This part of your leg is vulnerable now—it's likely to strain itself more easily than it would before. You have to listen to it, stop when it tells you, and keep it strong. No shirking exercises, no late appearances. Best behavior."

"Best behavior on the pitch, though. That's what you're saying?" He's already up and on his feet before Anna finishes nodding. Oliver knows better than to hug her, but he briefly bows like he's presenting himself to royalty. She waves him out of the room, laughing, as he wills his tired, *healthy* legs to carry him as fast as they can back upstairs to the manager's office.

Bursting in unannounced is probably not the highlight of his career to date, but it's almost worth it for the twin looks of shock on Sebastian's and Willem's faces.

"Harris," Sebastian starts. "We're in a meeti—"

"I've got medical clearance," Oliver says over him, grinning like a madman.

"From Dr. Zhang?" Willem cuts in, half-expecting a trick. Oliver nods furiously, newly energized, wondering if there's anyone left in the locker room to scrimmage with him. "Now *that's* something to think about." Willem has taken on the dreamy quality of someone having a brilliant idea. He hands Sebastian a notebook without taking his eyes off Oliver, sizing him up. "Downstairs, yes? Let us have a look at you."

It's an incredible relief to hear a request from his manager that Oliver can oblige, that he feels ready to take on. He doesn't even reply; he trusts the other two men are following him outside with the same pull in their chests that every footballer gets, the pang that drives you forward even when your body wants to rest. Oliver is through with resting, with worrying and waiting. He's ready to play.

Down on the practice pitch, he hits the ground running, following the many-months-forbidden siren song. It's a curious sensation, to get reacquainted with your own body, like he's catching up with an old friend after a long trip away. Oliver can see the game the same as ever, knowing intuitively where the ball will go when Sebastian kicks it to him and how he should follow, weaving through a maze of cones, but he can't quite get his limbs to move where he needs them. A slight sense of frustration is fluttering in his abdomen. It wasn't supposed to be like this; being able to play again was supposed to fix everything. When he knicks the side netting with a shot and yelps in disappointment, Willem waves it off.

"It'll take me a beat," Oliver concedes, panting. "I'll get it together, I swear. Give us a second."

"Don't play the martyr," de Boer says easily. "You look excellent. I admire your sense of self-improvement, however."

Oliver kicks divots from the grass bashfully, if not slightly disbelievingly.

"How much closer does this put us?" he asks the pair of coaches. "Up to fourth—can we do it?"

"And what would you know about fourth?" Sebastian asks, narrowing his eyes.

"Hush," Willem says. "He's aware of our terms."

"You told him?"

"In confidence, yes. Oliver needed to understand the stakes. Where he goes, the rest of the squad will follow."

Oliver is shocked and slightly smug at this; he's nothing if not a teacher's pet, even when it's Willem. He vows to himself to be worthy of the manager's faith and to give some of it back in return, as much as he can muster.

"Seriously, though," Oliver tries again. "Level with me. Can we do it?"

Willem sizes him up, eyes flicking up and down his body appraisingly, then points one finger toward Sebastian, who promptly whips another ball toward Oliver's midsection. Oliver takes one step back, rotating a hairsbreadth so he can meet it with his foot at the right angle, a firm, volleyed shot from midair. The ball sails into the goal, landing with a *whoosh*.

"That'll be up to you, Harris," Willem announces. "But I don't mind our chances."

• • •

Oliver doesn't even clock England's match as it happens, too caught up in the warring emotions of dread and exhilaration, trapped between his newfound freedom and the anxiety that keeps slowing him up. The international team must be halfway back from Germany by the time it occurs to him to check and to learn that Leo drew a penalty kick five minutes into his debut for his country, which Kane swiftly converted into the match-tying goal. He's returning to London a conquering hero with a new phase of his career unlocked: a serious, international talent. Oliver wonders bitterly how much Finch will try to sell *him* for.

Training is a mere matter of hours away, when the full squad will be back and Oliver will have to take the pitch with Leo properly for the first time, acting like nothing's wrong, like his entire life hasn't been a tangle of self-loathing and self-discovery since Leo showed up from Spain, like Oliver's first match back from the worst injury of his career isn't hurtling toward him, an unstoppable force. He can't stop thinking about Leo, and not in a hot way. That whole night feels unreal and far away: such a tender, tentative brush of domesticity giving way to the acrid taste of an argument, the kiss that was and wasn't. If the memory wasn't jaggedly carved right into his heart, Oliver might wonder if he made the whole thing up. He's feinted his way around a thousand defenders in his day, ball at his feet and eyes on the goal, but he isn't confident enough to play this one off. Which is why he's punching the buzzer for Leo's flat late in the evening, ringing the bell impatiently even though he's the one who showed up unannounced.

"Oliver?" Leo's voice is garbled by the intercom, but Oliver can hear how he says it: half a question and half a sigh.

"It's bloody freezing," Oliver lies. "Are you going to let me up or not?"

Leo doesn't reply, but the door unlocks itself noisily, so Oliver pounces for the handle and storms into the lobby before either of them can change their minds. In the sordid recesses of his imagination, Oliver has wondered about what it might be like to go to Leo's flat, to slip upstairs alone late at night. He imagined he would be nervous, but not like this, not this crushing, ominous feeling. The entrance to number 67 is pointedly ajar.

Leo is in the foyer, in pajamas and tight-lipped, between fear and hope. He heard Oliver on the intercom and he was the one to unlock the doors, but Leo looks at him strangely anyway, like he might be dreaming.

"Oliver," he says again, raising one shaking hand to touch Oliver's elbow. His eyes are half-lidded like someone about to be kissed. Oliver has to stop him now, or he never will. Propelled by the same adrenaline that carried him through the building, he cuts Leo's words off and shakes his arm off as well, for good measure.

"Listen to me," Oliver says. "I'm not here for a heart-to-heart.

I just want to make sure things aren't going to be fucked up at training tomorrow. We can be normal, yeah?"

Leo suddenly snorts and turns on his heel so he's facing away from him, pinching at the bridge of his nose like he's in pain.

"*Normal,*" Leo replies, newly and dangerously quiet. "You're thinking about training?"

"Of course I am!" The words fall out of Oliver's mouth before he even thinks them. He's *supposed* to be thinking about training; all the thoughts about Leo are the unwanted aberrations. "You jumped me and then full tilt ran out of my house like a burglar. I have to make sure, don't I?"

"Sorry, Harris," Leo says, in a tough-guy kind of voice—last-name basis now, two people who have never had their tongues in each other's mouths. "I never thought it would get that far."

"Just how far did you think it would fucking get?" Oliver demands. Now they're facing each other again and Leo has an ironic almost-smile on his face, both baffled and baffling in equal measure.

"I mean, consciously? Nowhere at all," Leo tells him. His eyes flutter closed as he makes a rough, exhausted noise. "Stupid Ahmed, he was right: it's so easy with women. I've never had to even think about it. That's simpler, but it doesn't mean I've not always fancied blokes too. Celebrity crushes, like. Which is more or less what you were to me, even in the academy, really, until a couple months ago." He shakes his head at himself, tugging at his hair with one hand. "I didn't ever think about acting on it, obviously. And I've never, *ever* looked at any teammates. But I just kept thinking maybe you wanted me to. To look at you."

Oliver is guilty as charged. Of course he wanted him to look. He was preening for it, for Leo's friendship and affection and attention, since the very first day. Even when Oliver played at antagonism, he wanted the full weight of Leo's focus, wanted to be at the center of his gaze, any direction he looked. All year, he's wanted Leo to think of Camden, of London, of England, in terms of Oliver. He still wants that, even as any possibility of it recedes from view. Oliver forces the grown-up words out of his mouth, rather than the ones he wants.

"I should never have put you in that position," Oliver says. "I'm older. Supposed to be wiser. I was *supposed* to help you. That's what I was trying to say, when I told you I was being careful. We're teammates. We have to play together. Whatever I want is less important than that."

"Whatever you want?" Oliver shakes his head, pushing the hopefulness in Leo's tone right out of his mind. If he clenches his jaw hard enough, he might feel nothing at all. "Okay, I get it," Leo says, voice hollow. "It was my idea anyway. I misread things."

"We don't have to talk about it ever again," Oliver says, like he wasn't the one who brought it up, like he didn't *absolutely* ask for it, in a thousand ways, meaning each of them entirely. Leo hasn't misread fuck all. "We can just go to training tomorrow and that will be that."

Oliver turns to go; he's said his piece and when he closes the door behind him it will be done with forever. Leo follows him out. He's on him before Oliver quite realizes what's about to happen. *God,* does Leo move quick when he's going in for a kiss. It's stunning that he knows what Leo's like when he's kissing. This one is shorter, one firm press and two more little ones peppered to the sides of his mouth, then the two of them are apart again, wide-eyed on the threshold.

"Sorry, I—I just wanted to know if it would feel the same a second time," Leo whispers. Oliver wants to reach for him, consequences be damned—if he could just get into his arms again, it might all make sense, but the space between them is thick, impassable once more. He wonders what the verdict is, though he can't seem to make his voice work so he can ask. For what it's worth, it felt about the same to him: so good it's obliterating.

Oliver takes one step backward, completely into the hallway. Leo's mouth twists but he doesn't say a word. Their eyes stay locked as Leo steps back too and releases the door, looking at each other all the way until it shuts between them. They've got training tomorrow: it's time for him to go home.

• • •

Oliver is finally taking the pitch. It's laid out before him, calling him home—it's better than last week, when he was testing his limits alone and finding them lower than he wanted. Now he's on display, in the sort of way that makes him feel powerful instead of scrutinized. He's shoulder to shoulder with Joe, jogging past Finn and Trevor, on and on until the rest of the world gives way to a sea of green.

He knows Leo is there too. Oliver can see him climbing up the stairs and starting his stretches from the periphery of his vision. But if he keeps him at the edges, it's almost normal, almost as if nothing ever happened between them at all. *Almost.*

Willem is sideline-surveilling, tongue poking at his upper lip, head nodding in time with their strides. He waves one of the equipment managers over to a ball bag and then the whole squad is only visible through a hailstorm of passes.

Ahmed wallops one too hard, ball sailing high and fast. It's heading out of reach, in the vague direction of poor Sebastian's ballsack, until Oliver gets his legs under him and two paces free of the group, reveling in the extension he can flex out of his left hamstring. He reaches out and is rewarded with the sexiest contact, nestling the ball in the cradle of his ankle and bringing it down to earth with incredible gentleness. It only took a second, but everyone clocked it anyway. Now they're all hurrahing and shouting, enveloping him in a circle and gleefully whacking Oliver on the back in celebration.

Everyone whoops and shouts: Harris is back, *oh baby,* let's fucking *go*. Harris is back, Harris is back. The city of London is reverberating with it, from Enfield all the way down to Croydon. His own name has rarely sounded so sweet in other people's mouths. Oliver knows it was good—and when he sneaks a glance, he can see that Leo does too.

The rest of the session is less eventful, but it is illuminating. There's only so much you can gather from observation alone. You really get the measure of a man once you're playing with him. Oliver remembers the night of training after hours, when he felt Leo's joy and strength fitting their edges perfectly around his own. There's more to learn in a scrappy match or difficult drill when there's someone actively trying to stop you. Oliver gets frustrated on the pitch all the time, but it builds like water coming to a boil until it bursts out of him when he's alone, a scream into a towel or a thrown water bottle on the sidelines. Leo, though: he's never impolite, but he will groan or curse when he fucks up, jogging it off before he gets back in line to run the drill again. He's got a self-awareness of his level of play that Oliver certainly didn't have three years ago and an ability to self-express Oliver lacks even now. It's infuriating and it's enviable, though Leo probably learned it from riding the bench and wanting more. Once Oliver starts paying attention to him, it's nigh-impossible to look away. Willem had it right from the jump, he wasn't talking any shit: Leo is sensational and he's sensational for Camden. He fits into the midfield like a glove and even though Oliver can't look him in the eye, he can find Leo with every pass. There's so much potential simmering below the surface, Oliver half-expects Camden Crossing to be ripped in two by an earthquake.

After he blows the closing whistle, Willem lobs a water bottle at Oliver, who splashes it gratefully over his sweaty head. The manager approaches once Oliver is done shaking the water out of his hair and offers his hand to shake.

"Like I never left, hey?" Oliver says, casting the rod to fish for a compliment. Willem obliges with a smile up to his eyes and pumps their arms one more time.

"Better, even. Now we know what we were missing."

"Ah, gaffer," Oliver demurs, even as he's thrilled down to his toes. "You'll make me blush."

"You won't object to an appearance at the presser?" Willem asks in that way he has—a question answering itself.

Oliver nods; why not? Once he settles himself into the rigid podium chair, he remembers why not. Press conferences are intolerable: the kind of dick-measuring contests where he's never once felt like he came out on top, even if he's scored three times. Oliver clears his throat uselessly into the microphone and looks out into the sea of reporters, every forehead glistening under the fluorescents, every iPhone held in his direction and recording.

"Mr. Harris," someone asks—the older reporter from the *Evening Standard,* he thinks. "To the casual observer, it might seem that the team's place in the table belies the talent on the pitch. Other clubs certainly take fixtures at Regent Road quite seriously, but the upper middle of the table seems to be the—pardon me—*standard* for Camden. Do you think your return might be some kind of catalyst for the rest of the season?"

Oliver swallows every foul word he knows and shrugs, pretending none of this ever occurred to him before.

"A catalyst? Truthfully, you never want to need a turning point," he begins, carefully. "But I do think you're right that we could be quite a lot better. The team is hungry, you can feel that in the room. There's a lot to get out of this season yet. I want to win every match, I want to play my best football. I've spent the last couple of months just raring to go, to get back out there and see what we can do."

"But do you think results will improve now that you're healthy?" the reporter presses.

All the soundbites Oliver knows how to say are dust in his mouth.

"Mate, if I didn't think that, I'd have no business having this job. But every other player in this league thinks so too, to a man. Ask them and they'll tell you—" He points toward the locker room where his teammates are, challenging. "Every time any of us gets on the pitch, we think we could make all the difference. What matters is who's actually right, on the day."

Oliver immediately regrets speaking so frankly, bracing himself to walk it back, to apologize to Willem later, but the coaching staff is huddled in the corner nodding. All the other questions are a cakewalk after that, just simple pleasantries he's trotted out before a million other fixtures. The rhythm of it even feels good in a strange way, because he knows it means he's going to play. In two days, he'll be at Regent Road and he'll look up to the stands with a ball at his feet—he'll be where he belongs.

Sunday, April 2, 2017: Manchester City at Camden

MATCHDAY 28

Oliver is back where he belongs and he's got his fucking work cut out for him. Agüero, tricky bastard, scored twice in the first fifteen minutes of the second half, eliminating the advantage of an early goal from Trevor and putting Camden squarely behind.

He spent forty-five minutes sitting patiently and respecting Willem's judgment, but now there's barely any time left and Oliver is still on the bench, looking hungrily at the pitch and feeling its pull in all of his extremities. Finally, *finally,* Sebastian jerks his head at him and points to the sideline.

"Two minutes," he orders. "Get your sea legs."

Oliver doesn't need asking twice, flinging himself out of his seat and leaping into a jog that's practically a sprint. True to his word, exactly one hundred and twenty seconds later, Willem beckons him over to the center touchline. Oliver tosses his jacket to one of the training staff and braces himself. The air drips with spring sweat and competition. He's in another dimension, one he's been missing, desperately trying to access, for months. When he crouches into a squat and launches himself back up, stretching his disused legs for battle, he half-expects the jump to carry him into the sky and above the stadium. Gravity is a small thing compared to Regent Road.

There's a great roar in the stands when the linesman shows the number 6.

"Olliееееееее," Matty bellows, thwacking his fist into his palm. "Let's fucking do this!" The crowd takes him up on it, shouting an echoey refrain of "Ollie, Ollie, Ollie" until the Ollie in question feels a little poorly with the sound of it.

Lukas and Garcia are in the midfield with Leo, leaving room for Oliver to step into the center and try to direct the flow of play from there. He needs to conduct the orchestra, find a pattern of movement that will put the ball in the net, but he's waylaid by the way Leo is looking at him: deer in the headlamp, anger and admiration and anxiety all muddled. Oliver wants to yell at him, *Not right now. Can't we just do this first? Isn't that what we agreed on?* There's no time or space for anything besides the rest of the ninety minutes and the ball that Joe is about to hurl out of the penalty box and back into play.

Time moves differently pitchside. Somehow, he'd almost forgotten. The first handful of minutes where he's just trying to make sense of things pass in the blink of an eye and he knows the ten minutes left in the match will go the same unless he can get his mind around things. But if you can see the play correctly, every second is its own era, enough time to make things go the way you want them to, the magic of Regent Road giving you the time and space to make something of yourself. When it locks into place, when Oliver spots how City's right back is limping slightly, short on his passes into the midfield, a jolt of electricity rockets through his limbs. He takes off, running out of position and trusting Garcia to hold the line. It happens again, his opponent just one step out of place, but it's enough for Oliver to intercept the ball, and now he's in possession, moving toward the goal with nothing on his mind except getting the scoreline level.

Emmanuel is there too, matching him stride for stride. Oliver kicks to him and keeps on running. He's not as fit as he'd like to be, not moving at the rate he knows he can reach, but it's enough, because the return pass lands right where it should, one soft bounce in front of his left foot. Oliver knows what to do with it: the one thing he truly knows how to do. He strikes it hard and clean, high into the corner. It's a goal, *his goal,* his first of the year.

He accepts the hugs and the hair ruffles, takes the chance to grab Emmanuel by the face and yell "Thank you, thank you!" at him, but then he wrangles the group back toward their own half. Oliver said it in the presser and he meant it: he wants to win every single match. There's only so many left.

Eight minutes later, he thinks he can actually make it happen. Leo is faster than the man marking him; Oliver suspects if he sends the ball long, across the pitch, Leo will beat the defender there without triggering offside. He doesn't turn his head at the first shout, but when Oliver yells again: "Oi, number 16," like he means business, Leo meets Oliver's eyeline reluctantly. He waves Leo on and starts after him. The cross is there, Oliver could have placed it with both hands, pushpin perfect. But Leo dives for it, thinking he's further behind the pass than he actually is, and the ball makes contact with his shin rather than his foot. It dribbles harmlessly onto goal, where the keeper collapses on top of it and smothers the play.

Dammit, Oliver thinks, backpedaling toward a defensive position and watching Leo pound the pitch with one closed fist as he climbs up to do the same. The ref is confirming the time on his watch with a sense of finality. It's a draw, one they clawed back, but it feels like a loss all the same. Oliver breathes deeply, steadying himself after the exertion, and reminds himself to applaud up to the stands and say thank you to the supporters. When they finally trickle off the pitch, Oliver passes Willem, who graces him with a nod and a cuff to the back of the neck.

Not every reception is so friendly. Oliver takes his time getting to the showers—unpacking every second of play with Joe, breathing through the sticky adrenaline comedown between chugs of a raspberry-flavored Lucozade. When he finally does go to rinse off, Leo is alone in the room, face directly under the showerhead like he's trying to drown himself. Oliver freezes and moves to quietly back out of the doorway, at least to grab someone and make them be a buffer, but Leo has already looked over, halfway to sneering.

"Don't be shy on my account," Leo says, but his voice is quavering. "We can be normal, yeah?" Oliver knows Leo is parroting his own words, but they sound venomous coming out of his mouth.

"Leo—" he starts, trying to buy enough time to figure out if this is about Oliver, or the match, or both.

"I don't want your pep talk," Leo cuts him off, stepping out of the water and scooping wet hair out of his eyes. The last time things were normal between them, he'd said Oliver gave good pep talks. "I'm a grown-up, okay? I know I fucked it, so I don't need to hear how it's fine and you're not mad or whatever."

Right. So it's both, Oliver thinks.

"Would it help if I was mad?" he asks, only half-joking. Leo's upper lip curls furiously, a cat gearing up to yowl. "You fucked it, the defense fucked it, Agüero fucked it for us. It takes twenty-two men to win or lose, so don't flatter yourself all powerful."

"Easy for you to say," Leo shouts, voice careening around the tiled room. "When you come on with twenty minutes left and change the whole landscape! It's different for you, Harris. *Everything* is. It always has been."

"You're winding me up, mate. I'm not going to apologize to you for scoring or for trying to set you up for one," Oliver tells him flatly. It is different for him than for Leo; it's fucking worse. "So if you're looking for that, go talk to someone else."

"I didn't want to talk to you at all. You—you followed me in here."

There's just a whiff of a threat in that, about why Oliver would want to follow anyone into the showers. And the worst part is that Leo's not wrong; Oliver wishes he could touch his naked body, even now, get hands slippery with soapsuds and desire.

"To take a shower? Leo, come on," he whispers. "I thought we might be excited, actually. For finally getting to play together."

"Was it like you dreamed?" Leo replies, dripping with sarcasm.

"No, it kind of sucked," he admits. "Because you wouldn't *look* at me. And even then, I gave you a perfect ball. It made me want to do it over and over until we can get it right."

"Yeah, okay." Leo doesn't seem like he's going to yell anymore, but now he does look exhausted, old for his years. "Let's get it right, then, out there on the pitch." He sidles out, sidestepping Oliver in an obvious way that avoids all contact, leaving him to trail behind, still covered in sweat, more tired than before.

"Lovers' spat?" Henri asks jovially when they reemerge.

"Could you, just once, shut *up*?" Oliver hisses, stung by the word "lover" as much as anything else. "Jesus!"

Henri looks stricken and does in fact shut up, which makes Oliver feel worse. Willem spares them both by standing up at the front of the room, clutching a whiteboard marker like it's a dagger.

"Are we ready to debrief?" he asks, and of course they all nod in unison. Oliver keeps his gaze fixed firmly in front of him and nowhere near the corner of the locker room marked with number 16. Willem slaps his free hand against the board once, more of an outburst than he's ever shown. Then their coach rounds on them, jabbing the pen accusingly. But he freezes and for once says nothing at all, sweeping off with his coattails floating out behind him like a vampire's cape. It's hard to believe Oliver ever considered Willem removed, ambivalent. He's as desperate as any of them now. Sebastian looks chagrined as he follows him out of the room. The squad is silent to a man, a gauntlet flung down and shattered among them.

• • •

It's not as if things between Oliver and Leo could reasonably stay so tense—you're only allowed one shouting match in the showers per season, or human resources will get involved. Oliver privately suspects they only got away with it because Willem decided to one-up them afterward. But it's a hell of an anticlimax to go back to training the rest of the week and gamely hold the door for Leo like there isn't a soap's worth of melodrama swirling between them. They're only doing a mediocre job of it, unfortunately. All the chemistry Oliver knows is there, can feel in the tingle on his lips when he's alone, has evaporated. He feels compelled to be careful around Leo now, on and off the pitch. He's hyperaware of Leo's presence, but he can no longer find him for a pass, can't mark him properly during scrimmages. Joe keeps shooting Oliver searching looks, whereas Sebastian has adopted a sideline perma-frown. The looks he gets from Leo are worse: heat and disdain swirled together. He's daring Oliver to want him still and when he does, when he can't help it, Leo hates him for it.

Have I fucked it entirely? Maggie writes over text. Maybe she has, but not any worse than he did for himself. He can't blame her for anything. He can't quite talk about it either.

You've never done anything wrong in your life, Mags, is all Oliver says back before he puts his phone on Do Not Disturb.

Sunday in North London arrives despite itself, gloom in the air misting down in fat wet clouds. Willem, even after all the damning evidence from a week of training, puts Oliver on the starting list. He's barely excited, only shivery under his training jacket. He makes small talk in the tunnel and greets Arsenal's English players with a quick hug and backslap, then retreats to the back of the line to stand in Joe's steady shadow until it's time to play.

No respite, however, arrives from football, even as Oliver prayed fervently during halftime for *something, anything* to break the deadlock on the scoresheet and in his heart. He's got his pace back, running faster and further than he has in ages, but nothing goes through. Anthony choreographed the back line perfectly, hardly letting any Arsenal shirts within spitting distance of Joe's net, but they flailed in the midfield. Leo's shadow was everywhere and Oliver hunted for it frantically, threading passes to no one. He rings the post with a free kick in stoppage time and collapses to the ground in defeat after, sodden and miserable.

The rain and sweat are all mingled on Joe's cheeks like teardrop tracks, as tired and sad as Oliver knows the whole lot of them feel. They drift toward each other, meeting at the edge of the eighteen-yard box for a futile embrace. There's only so much comfort you can offer when you're in need of it yourself. Anthony joins them, patting Oliver on the hip and depositing Joe under one arm for safekeeping. Slowly, the other eight Camden shirts engulf them, the private ritual of whoever's on the pitch when the final whistle blows. Ji-Hoon and Trevor blanket Oliver on either side; he lets his head fall on Trevor's tall shoulder, grateful to let someone else take the weight off him for a brief moment.

"A point is a point," Anthony tells the group, once the sniffly silence starts to chafe. "Let's be better next time."

The circle starts to dissipate amid nods of encouragement,

but Leo is the first one out of the ring, banging into Oliver's side as he strides off. He tries to catch Leo's sleeve—he's not entirely sure what he'll do when he gets it, but the grown-up thing to do, the veteran playmaker's responsibility, is to play it cool. Leo jerks his arm free of him without turning around, so he misses the chance. Oliver stands there a beat longer, smarting with rejection and feeling moronic, until Joe nudges him onward, giving him a sympathetic look that only makes Oliver feel more daft.

Two draws in two weeks, two points that could have been six, two matches they didn't win or lose but prickle like defeat regardless. Seventh place feels closer to relegation than the Champions League. Oliver has never in his life been so relieved to be called for random drug testing, sparing him from having to put a brave face on for the media.

When he slouches to the visitors' locker room after his urine is pronounced clean, Willem is waiting by his locker in a way that suggests he would've been better off giving a tell-all interview.

"Davies," the manager says, the second Oliver sits down. "With me."

Davies-Villanueva. Use his whole name, Oliver thinks defensively, before he remembers Leo doesn't need or want his defense anymore. Leo joins the pair of them at Oliver's locker, visibly reluctant as he crosses the room, and sits at the very edge of the bench, body angled away, only visible in profile. *We can't go on like this.*

"You can't go on like this!" Willem says. He's a mind reader, and he's right, of course. Oliver's shoulders collapse with the shame of it. Slumped as he is, he keeps his head up and prepares to be lectured, Leo bristling next to him, fists clenched and likely the rest of him too. Willem is stern above them, but he does them the kindness of speaking softly, to the two of them only. "I have very little use for a duo in the midfield who won't look at each other. And I won't be made to look a dunce for having banked on this particular pairing."

Leo's whole body is crackling with contrarianism, only a hairsbreadth from answering back.

"Save it," Oliver risks muttering out of the side of his mouth. It's not worth it. Leo responds by turning his body even further away from him, as if another ninety degrees will deafen Oliver's voice. Willem goes scarlet.

"This is *precisely* what I mean."

"We're doing what we can on the pitch, sir," Leo says, the last bit tacked on like a four-letter word.

"And off it?" Willem asks. Their silence hangs in the air, as good as confession. "Then I'd consider doing a damn sight more if I were you, Leonardo, or someone will be getting reacquainted with the bench," he continues icily. "And I don't think you'll like which one of you it is."

The two of them stiffen. Oliver is not sure who the jab is meant to punish more. In January it would have been the height of pleasure to hear Willem say aloud, in proximity to the rest of the squad, that someone who can't play with Harris will of course not be a starter, not factor into the team sheet. Now it's torturous. For all the hurts he and Leo have dealt each other in such a short time, this one is sharpest. Inexplicably, Oliver's mind flashes back to that night on the training ground when Leo tackled him and everything began to well and truly turn to shit. Oliver had really been playing, even though he knew better, running like the league was on the line, and it had been so fucking fun—being near Leo as much as the football.

They were supposed to give each other the midfield and save each other's careers, supposed to make something out of this stupid, wretched season. What did Oliver say that last night they were alone? *We're teammates. We have to play together. Whatever I want is less important than that*. And look where it's gotten them.

"We're sorry," Oliver says, daring to speak for both of them. "We'll get it sorted."

"See that you do," Willem says, his tone evening out. Oliver turns, wanting to tell Leo he's sorry too, but he's already halfway up, fleeing the scene.

Monday, April 17, 2017: Camden at Middlesbrough

MATCHDAY 30

Riverside Stadium is aptly named—the whole giant structure thrown down right on a riverbank, nothing but gray water and grayer car park as far as Oliver can see. Middlesbrough moved up from the second division at the start of the season; he wonders if they feel as disoriented by Anfield and Old Trafford as he does by arriving here, somewhere he's never been before, looking out over a pitch that's new to him. He might be more used to it if Camden had ever qualified for the Champions League or hadn't crashed out of every other tournament, but here it is. Mediocre teams have mediocre schedules.

April is passing three days at a time, every sunrise too cloudy to distinguish itself. Camden FC's YouTube channel shows Oliver sprinting and smiling during training, standing within spitting distance of Leo without bursting into flame, otherwise he wouldn't believe it possible. *We'll get it sorted. See that you do:* Willem's directive rings in his head like the chimes of an old clock. Oliver's not sure if he has got it sorted at all, which means he probably hasn't.

But Willem is starting them both, numbers 6 and 16 in the midfield again; it feels more like a test than a vote of confidence. Oliver threw out a paper earlier in the week when he saw a sports-section headline ask, IS DE BOER STILL BETTING WISELY ON HARRIS AND COMPANY? *What's the alternative?* he'd thought grimly. *Getting five miles out of Charles and Gavin before one of them keels over?*

Willem had reamed them good, sterner than he's ever gotten in front of the team before, worse than the week before Christmas when a bottle-service girl from a nightclub posted a picture of Marcos and Georgie fully caressing one tit each. Oliver knows why this makes Willem so incandescent: he went and got his hopes pinned on the two of them, whereas no one in their right mind, not even a Dutchman, would put his eggs in the Marcos and Georgie basket. De Boer isn't really mad after all; he's only disappointed, which is even worse.

Oliver's got the better end of the stick as well, because he earned his spot in the midfield while Willem was still in business school and because he knows about Finch's fourth-place ultimatum. Leo, on the other hand, is on tenterhooks and probably also a tightrope. *It's a damn shame,* he thinks. Camden's number 16 has player of the year written all over him, all the more surprising considering he's had less than half a season to make his case. Willem could change the course of Leo's life and Leo could change the course of Willem's, if they got the rhythm right. Together, they'd probably both change the course of Oliver's life as well, no problem, but that's all beside the point.

What Oliver really thinks is a waste is that Leo's relationship with their coach is souring. You never forget the first-team manager who gives you your best shot, who teaches you to be a man as well as a midfielder, the kind of mentorship you can't take for granted and still find yourself thanking five years and multiple contracts later.

Leo should be Willem's favorite, by all rights. He's got the talent, which is a given, but Willem plucked him out of obscurity only to find that Leo is wise for his years and brimming with natural charisma, a rookie and a captain rolled into one. Oliver feels guilty that Willem told off the both of them, but even worse that he was upset with Leo, worst of all that Leo answered back with anger he should have directed at Oliver.

He's been daydreaming on the floor of the visitors' locker room, somewhere between meditating and stretching, when Anthony snaps his fingers in front of his blank face. Oliver looks up at him, scowling, but Anthony only sits down and bumps their elbows together. In that captain's way of his, the fleeting touch says more than any speech. Oliver hears it word for word in his flat Mancunian vowels: *Not just you out there. Might as well make the best of it.*

"Thanks, mate," Oliver says softly.

"I didn't do anything," Anthony replies, but he lifts one eyebrow like he knows he did.

From the floor, Oliver overhears what the rest of the room is talking about: transfers.

"Gotta be Munich," Georgie says, cracking his neck on each side. "I'm definitely hotter than any German guy."

"Hey, now," Lukas replies warningly.

"No waaaaaay," Carda butts in, rubbing his fingers together. "Somewhere with that sweet oil money. Diverse portfolio." Oliver feels the beginnings of permanent wrinkles etch themselves into his forehead.

"Not Barcelona? Tiki-taka and beach weather?" asks Henri.

"You're all being narrow-minded," Gavin says. "In my experience, the club matters less than how big of a man you are there. You fools'd be better off at Burnley."

Now Oliver's heart is beating out of his Adam's apple. Camden isn't some stopover team, some farmers' league joke. It's *home,* if not for all of them, then certainly for him and the thousands of fans who buy tickets and kits. Oliver Harris would be a big man anywhere: even after this mess of a year, he could walk into any starting eleven on any team in the world, which is more than any of his teammates can say, and *he* wants to be *here*. He wants to win here too. Regent Road is hallowed ground, worthy of respect. It's the only place he's ever wanted anything. Oliver won't let it be taken for granted.

"Well," Oliver interjects, just a degree louder than his regular speaking voice, willing it not to shake. "If anyone's curious, I'd pick Camden, and that's where we all happen to be, so *maybe,* let's go fucking play like it, shall we?"

The room goes silent, part ashamed for getting caught acting out-of-bounds and part annoyed at Oliver for daring to say it. Anthony is smirking approvingly. From the rookies' corner, Leo pulls out one earbud and stands, facing the door.

"Oliver's right," Leo says firmly. Oliver himself is shocked at the sound of it. Even at their very best, he's not sure Leo ever said he was right about anything.

"You heard the lads," Anthony pronounces, like that settles everything—and to be fair, he's the captain, so it sort of does. "Arses up, it's time to play, off you go."

And oh, how they play. Oliver feels like he's trampolining off the grass with every stride, running laps and loops around every red shirt that tries to catch him. Downing, one of the center backs, comes in hard for a tackle at one point, but Oliver skips over his legs and deftly pushes a little sideways pass to Garcia.

"Fuck me, Harris," Downing groans from beneath him, grass-stained and dazed. "Give us a break."

"Pick up the pace, hey?" Oliver laughs back, not waiting for an answer before he jogs off, not so much a man as a perpetual motion machine. Something just shook itself loose in him, and apparently in all of Camden Football Club. They're sharp, moving the ball up and down the field like it's nothing to them.

Oliver scores early and the team follows suit, knocking back two more goals before halftime. In the waning minutes of the match, he draws a foul, letting a defender walk himself into a trap by pulling his shirt in the penalty box, and the referee points for a spot kick. Oliver's tired, and happy, and they're going to win no matter what. When Anthony tosses him the ball so he can take the shot, Oliver gestures to Leo, whose eyes go big and suspicious like he suspects trickery.

"Okay with you if he takes it, captain?" Oliver asks.

"You're diabolical, you are," Anthony says, grinning. "Let's show them how deep the roster goes, yeah? Davito, you're up."

Leo glares when Oliver passes the ball to him.

"You don't have to patronize me," he says out of the side of his mouth.

"Believe you me, I wouldn't dare," Oliver says. "Willem wanted you to take them when I was hurt, you know. You just never got a chance. Why don't you remind him what you've got?"

Leo doesn't reply, but he does take the ball and step up to the painted spot on the field. When the whistle goes, he takes the kick just as confidently as he does in training, putting Camden ahead four goals to nil, and suddenly Leo seems to forget that he's furious at everyone; he flashes a peace sign and a dazzling smile to his onrushing teammates, even proffering a clenched fist for Oliver to bump and a small nod that looks like it means *Thank you*. When their knuckles slot together, Oliver wonders if any of the thousands of people looking down at the pitch detect the frisson of energy that passes between the two of them, or if it's just for him to feel.

Willem has both arms raised joyously, clapping his hands above his head, and suddenly it seems that's all he's been doing for days. They keep scoring, wherever they go.

Mid-spring warmth wisps down to meet them at Camden Crossing, casting sunlight over every training session and following them to their matches. They dispatch Tottenham with no difficulty at all. Four days later against Leicester City, Oliver scores what the pundits are screeching must be, has to be, the goal of the year, a dainty curlicue run past two defenders and a chip over the keeper to boot. It stuns him as much as anyone, how good it feels, how wonderful it looks. When his teammates catch him the crush of hugs buckles his knees, sends Oliver over into a happy heap on the grass. Leo pulls him back to his feet by his collar, and Oliver is too happy to even remember the last time Leo had his fist in his shirt. He looks up to the tiny dots of people in the crowd at Regent Road, over to the family box where Nicola is watching, back to Willem and Sebastian on the bench, and feels like he could laugh or cry or scream, some combination of all three.

From way back in the opposite penalty box, Joe cups his gloves around his mouth into a megaphone and shouts: "I'll drink to that, you magnificent bastard!" Who's Oliver to deny him? Which is how the whole victorious gaggle of them end up in a nightclub not even two hours later, drunk on exhaustion and probably the alcohol as well.

The girl at the door who led them to a massive leather booth under a velvet rope offered Georgie a costume sailor's hat and he bent down to receive it like he was getting knighted. Everyone around them is tipsy and happy, go-go boots and feather boas flung about. Oliver has no taste for champagne, only narrowly avoiding having it doused over his head by Ji-Hoon and Ahmed, so he slips out with designs for the bar, letting the bass line carry him through the room, as light on his feet as he is in his football boots. The dance floor is a kaleidoscope of lit-up tiles, resembling nothing so much as a giant Twister mat. He's tempted to stay and dance, remembering the booze-soaked night of his birthday when he could feel every drumbeat coming out of his own chest, the rhythm stronger than the tear in his hamstring.

Oliver's cocktail is ruined halfway through the first ginny sip when someone says his name. He's braced for an autograph or a selfie, but when he turns around, he finds it's not a fan at all. Ryan Loxley and Stewart Reed, Kilburn's prodigal and wholly mediocre sons, are leering at him, clad in filmy silk button-down shirts fit to burst and reeking of cologne. *Jesus H,* Oliver thinks, not for the first time in his life. *Being straight seems like so much more trouble than it's worth.*

"Fancy seeing you here, rosy," Stewart says, spitting the last word out and then clunking his pint glass down on the bar, sloshing beer everywhere. "Celebrating your mighty win? Would have been more impressive to beat Leicester last year, of course, but still, good on you."

"Always a treat, gentlemen," Oliver says, still sober enough to want to get out of there before he does something foolish. It wasn't just that first match as a teenager where he got himself sent off—Harris and Reed have reliably nearly come to blows twice a year since then, during every contest between Camden and Kilburn. Loxley might be too thick in the head to actually hate properly, but Oliver does his best. Before he can take his leave, he spots stupid, stupid Leo down the bar, taking speculative steps in their direction. Oliver shakes his head tersely, trying to warn him off, but it's too late. Leo has no business being a professional athlete with that sense of timing.

"Lads," Leo says tentatively when he arrives at the tense little clump, reaching out one hand to shake. "How are we?"

"We've not met," Loxley says dumbly. "You're the new one."

"We can skip the pleasantries," Stewart replies, ignoring Leo's hand. "I'm sure Harris has a busy night planned, what with being a ponce and having absolutely no game at all."

It's not outwardly homophobic, no one's said any hard slurs this time, but Oliver knows well enough what he means. He's well-groomed, son of an Oxford graduate, prettily handsome, and he never has a girlfriend, never pulls on a night out. He's always been this way. Stewart doesn't even think he's actually gay, he just thinks he's soft, and that's enough for him. It's all so pathetic.

"That's the difference between you and me, though, isn't it, Stew?" Oliver asks, voice going deep and dangerous as he sets his own drink down carefully, marking the territory. He can be as tough as the Rovers think they are—tougher than any of them know. "I don't think about your sex life at all, and the only time in your life you've ever started for England, I just happened to be injured."

Stewart makes to lunge at him. Oliver wishes he would, wants to feel blood in his teeth and draw some of his own. Cooler heads prevail; Loxley has Stewart by the collar and Leo has stepped between them, drawing his chest out and up to lessen the difference in their heights.

"Fuck off," Stewart says, shrugging Loxley off with one arm and jabbing one indignant finger into Leo's sternum with the other. "Both of you."

"Gladly," Leo replies cooly, picking up Oliver's drink and turning crisply on his heel. Oliver laughs at the sight of him, breaking up fights in nightclubs, stealing drinks, then acting above it all after. He offers the others his laziest, most sarcastic salute and trails after Leo, nothing but a fish on a line.

They're halfway across the floor, weaving through knots of dancing couples and shrieking hen-dos, when Leo rounds on him.

"What were you thinking, picking fights in public?" Leo shouts over the disco tune din. "Do you *like* being shouted at?"

"Look who's talking. Snapped at our coach lately?"

Considering the matter settled, Oliver tries to reclaim his drink, but Leo holds it out of reach, then takes a long guzzle, narrowing his eyes at him.

"You just let them think all that stuff about you," he says quietly, so low Oliver has to step closer and drop down into Leo's space to hear him.

"So you *are* speaking to me again," Oliver replies, unable to keep the hurt out of his voice. Leo shoves at his elbow, silently prompting the question again. "Okay, okay. Think what stuff?" Oliver can't be bothered at what the sight of them must look like, heads together and standing still in a crowded club. Leo's eyes are melted fudge, looking right at him for the first time in ages.

"Like, you're a nancy boy, you have no game, you can't get girls. Why do you let them?"

"I *can't* get girls," he laughs feebly.

Leo frowns and shakes his head. "You know you could if you wanted. Or you could let everyone think you still had Maggie. Why don't you?"

Someone jostles behind him, Oliver follows the rhythm of the crowd and moves one step closer, steadying his balance with one hand at Leo's hip, just like they were at Oliver's birthday party. Leo's eyes flash downward for one fraction of a heartbeat, and Oliver thinks he might stop him, might step away, but he only looks back up, the question still lingering between them.

"I'm not threatened by it. Why should I be? I know what's real." Oliver's not keeping secrets for the Stewart Reeds of the world and he's not interested in telling extra lies for their benefit. Whatever their idea of being a big man is, they can keep it.

"What's real . . ." Leo murmurs, gaze glassy. "And what is that?"

Oliver can't help it; he hazards a glance around the room. They're alone and not alone, ensconced in nightlife's liminal space. No one is looking at them. He could plant one right on Leo's mouth and it wouldn't make a single headline.

"You'd know better than Maggie would" is all he says. Drunk

on the feeling, he taps Leo's jaw lightly with a closed fist, two pretend punches. Leo's brown eyes are a sea of black now, his whole face a gulp. If Oliver stays, he'll make an idiot of himself. He leaves Leo on the dance floor with the rest of his drink and Oliver's whole heart beating bloody and useless in his palm.

• • •

They can't stay away from each other for long. Training is all well and good, but Oliver can sense Willem's watchful eye, searching for some proof they can play together, while the pair of them wait for a signal that they've passed his test. There's only a sliver of days between playing Leicester and facing Manchester United at home. Oliver is still slightly out of practice, still exhausted every night and every morning, but he's got a pilot light of energy in his chest that's driving him forward relentlessly.

The night before the United match, he stays late after his massage and shoots free kicks alone, drilling a whole pile of balls toward the top right corner until they're sailing into the netting on repeat, goal after goal after goal. Oliver thinks he'll stop after ten in a row, but then it's twenty, then thirty. He's gearing up for the twenty-fourth when someone whistles sharply, and when he turns it feels only natural that it should be Leo waiting for him, barefoot and drowning in a hoodie.

"I didn't even know we had this many," Leo says, kicking a loose ball over to Oliver.

"Brought 'em from home," he jokes, kicking it back.

It also feels natural for them to start orbiting each other, two planets around the same little rubber sun, passing it between them.

"You're kind of intense," Leo says after a spell, bouncing the ball off his knees on repeat. "Anyone ever told you that? Makes the lot of us look like slackers."

"Well, not the whole lot of you," Oliver says fairly, accepting the return pass and indulging in a few keepie-uppies, luxuriating in moving his body and the ball in perfect synchronicity. "You're here too, hey?"

Leo drifts in close and bodychecks him lightly, just enough to throw Oliver off-balance and claim the ball back for himself.

"I like playing with you," Leo says quietly, passing back to Oliver once more. "I've always wanted to. Nothing else has quite come close to that first time, the day of the Burnley match."

Oliver wants to tell him to not be silly, that a kickabout with no audience and no opponents can't compare to the real thing. But he remembers it too, as intimate as anything he's ever felt in his life. If he were Willem, he'd be seething at them as well, for squandering it.

Leo no longer fits a neat classification of feeling in Oliver's head, hasn't for weeks or maybe even months. If there's a word for the mixture of lust and curiosity and occasional antagonism that Leo elicits in him, it's probably in German, and Oliver doesn't know it. All he knows is that he has a primal awareness of him, feels his presence in every room, during any match. Sometimes it drives him mad, but right now, when he knows he could blindfold himself and still play exactly the same, finding the passes with his heart rather than his eyes, he wouldn't trade it for anything. Every tiny move they make balances each other out, creating a perfect equilibrium in the midfield, and it twists around them both, all through the grass, like a thread of fate, leaving them tangled up and better than they started. The way they play together is preternatural, the way they see each other too. Camden could win a championship off this. Oliver could lose himself in it. And the longer it goes on, the more he suspects that the sensation he gets on the pitch when they're together is inextricably linked to the one in his gut when he thinks about kissing Leo, that he can't feel one without the other.

Oliver scoops the ball off Leo with an obvious, gentle foul, holding him in place by the hip so he can get after it, careful not to step on his bare toes, and whips the ball into the goal from twenty yards out.

"Oh, so we're done, then?" Leo laughs. Oliver responds by going to ground, flopping happily to the soft earth and looking up at the pinkening sky.

Leo follows him, gingerly taking a seat beside him. He's still for a moment, then with a furtive look on his face he scoots a tad closer to Oliver, putting them into each other's personal space. They're quiet for a stretch; Oliver knows how much there is to be said between the two of them, but he can't bring himself to break the peaceful spell.

"It's been kind of shite, hasn't it?" Leo says eventually. He's craning his neck up toward the sky, his whole body arcing with it.

"It's been getting better," Oliver says, feeling guilty for his part in it. Leo shrugs, noncommittal.

"Maybe, yeah," Leo hedges. "I miss you, still."

"I'm right here," Oliver says softly, meaning it and still knowing he's not telling the whole truth.

Leo shakes his head.

"You're not, though. Not really. I get it, Ollie, I swear I don't blame you. It's just . . . After Willem first called, while I was packing my bags, my mum told me that she sometimes wishes I was worse at football, because she thinks that would make me happier. She said if I were any worse, I'd give it up, accept the bad luck, and move on. I'm afraid she might be right." Leo has his mouth crooked into a rueful half-smile. Oliver isn't sure what to say, because he could never be happy without football; he learned how to be happy without his dad and without ever telling the truth about himself, but he's never managed to imagine feeling it without football. And now he's afraid, too, that he'll never be happy—even with football—if he isn't playing it with

Leo. "I thought I'd never be happy unless I was great at this. And finally, I'm great. I can prove it was all worth it. After all this time. I know I'm not as good as you are, but I'm better than I ever dreamed I could be. I love playing for Camden, and getting to put on an England shirt, but it's still so fucking hollow. It's not what I want, or at least not enough of it. I could be better, I know I could, I could even be happy, I think . . . but we can't. Or we won't, you don't want to—"

This time Oliver is the one to cut Leo off, stemming the flow of stumbling words by sitting up and grabbing Leo by the face, kissing him like he's just discovered the act of it. They *can*. All Oliver has ever done in his whole life is run laps around what he really wants. In this moment, he can't bring himself to sentence Leo to the same. Leo deserves so much more than this, on the pitch tomorrow and on the practice pitch right now, from Oliver. The kiss goes on for one glorious, perfect minute—the warm feel of it driving him near mad with desire, mad enough to forget where he is and how foolish it is to be doing this, until Leo's hands move from the nape of his neck to his collarbone, pushing him away.

"What are you doing, Harris?" Leo asks, breathless, doing a scrambly little crabwalk to put a body length between them.

"I want to," Oliver admits, reaching across the space between them so he can palm the slight span of Leo's hip bone, bunching it up into his hand. He wants to touch more of him, all of him. "You have to know that I do. I think about it all the time. I thought it would kill me, the wanting, how much I want you."

"Yeah," Leo protests. "I want you too, Harris, if you hadn't noticed. But you said we had to be normal. And we're at the *Crossing*."

"No one's here," Oliver says, willing it to be true while he still has the nerve to say what he needs to. He always asks whoever's on duty at security to turn off the field cameras when he stays late, anyway, so he can practice by himself without anyone watching, even from far away. The one time he didn't, there was a crowd of people around the monitor when he was on his way out, and he felt like a caged lion at the zoo. Oliver's not keen to find out what they'd think of this particular highlight reel. "It's just you and me, and we can—it's okay. You were right. I was wrong. Don't you like the sound of that?"

"Say it again," Leo breathes, like he's just daring to believe it.

"Don't test your luck," Oliver warns him, tipping Leo's chin up so he can brush their mouths together again, a sip of a kiss that deepens the longer it goes on, neither one pulling away this time, until they're clutching at each other, alone in the great green expanse of Camden Crossing.

Sunday, April 30, 2017: Manchester United at Camden

MATCHDAY 33

Gun to his head, Oliver couldn't tell you how he got home last night or what he did once he got there. He can only remember what it was like to kiss Leo, the force of it bowling them over until they were sprawled across the practice pitch like it was a picnic on Hampstead Heath. They kept laughing, at God knows what, giggling just from laying eyes on each other, lost in the wonderful lunacy of feeling truly, unchangeably happy. At one point Oliver rolled onto his back and took Leo with him until he was posed above him on his elbows, quite literally joined at the hips. They'd kissed that way forever, luxuriously unhurried, getting the lay of the land, then suddenly it did feel hurried, it felt *urgent*.

"*Ah,*" Oliver gasped, newly and acutely aware of his earlobes—more tenderly sensitive than any muscle he's ever strained in training—and Leo had one of them between his teeth, sucking and stinging. He could feel the hard line of an erection bumping against Leo's thigh and he chased the friction, the sweet drag and rasp of it.

"Oh, I want—" Leo said, or started to say, thumbing over Oliver's jawline; then, as if all at once, the sun sank fully and the floodlights kicked on, reality coming with it; they'd pushed apart like they half-expected Sebastian to appear again and catch them at it, saying quick goodbyes and taking off before it became unacceptably late to be out the night before a match. When they'd parted in the stairwell, though, Leo for the door and Oliver for the showers, their fingertips met and brushed in a tiny acknowledgment, and in that touch Oliver felt all his worries assuaged, safe in some unspoken confirmation of their camaraderie and friendship and something else, something new and bigger than either of them.

"See you tomorrow, then?" Leo had called from the doorway, half of him already in the hall.

"I'll be wearing green," Oliver said back, privately pleased with how deadpan it sounded, even over the roar in his eardrums and the rapid thrum of his pulse.

• • •

So, somehow, he'd left the Crossing and time enough passed that now it's Sunday and Oliver is in the dressing room tightening his laces so they can go off and play Manchester United. Everything feels like background noise until he's warming up pitchside, Regent Road refusing to be outdone by even the handsomest of distractions. Even when said distraction is ten feet away, prettier than a Christmas present, wrapped up in Camden colors and stretching, low and lithe, with Ahmed. Oliver gets to play with him today, with nothing to come between them, only the ball and the goal and eleven red shirts. He's the luckiest man south of Edinburgh. Leo comes up behind him and snags him by both shoulders on their way back to the tunnel, shaking him slightly.

"Step lightly, Harris," Leo warns, gripping him tight. "Slippery, innit."

Oliver allows himself to be led, marching soldierly to their places in line. When they pass Willem, their coach gives them both a strange look, the kind that suggests he suspects he's been duped but isn't altogether displeased with the result. Oliver goes mental for a second imagining the manager's reaction to learning exactly how much relationship-mending his prize midfielders have engaged in recently.

The Red Devils don't seem to care for the great Harris–Davies-Villanueva reconciliation; however, nor are they bothered by Georgie opening the scoring after fifteen minutes. For a team supposedly in even worse shambles than Camden, they aren't going quietly, and they score twice to prove it. At halftime they all brace for shouting or for the slant of reproach in de Boer's eyebrows, but Willem bounds into the changing room after them with the energy of a much younger man.

"Only the scoreline counts," he tells them. "But I don't expect it to stay as it is. We're pressing high and they don't have the energy to hold it off. Play against yourselves now, gentlemen. Do not let up, trust that the opportunity will come, and for God's sakes"—he points accusingly, but not unkindly, at the clump of strikers—"put your shots on target. The energy is fantastic out there. Don't you know how lucky we are? Give the fans what they're cheering for."

As lectures go, it's remarkably effective. They listen to Willem, keeping up the pressure even when it doesn't pay off at first, and after twenty minutes Camden finally cracks the defense. Leo and Matty are exchanging lateral passes in their own half of the pitch, unthreatening as you like, when Leo takes off galloping and is almost into the opposing penalty box before anyone sees him coming. He drops a neat little pass to Emmanuel, who has a look at goal, all the United players scrambling for a block, before outwitting the lot of them and sending it across to Trevor, who buries it one touch, no problem. Tie fucking game.

Oliver remembers what Willem said when they played another team from Manchester and had a point to show for it. That's not the result they need, nor the one they should want.

Oliver doesn't want to draw. He said it the day he came back from injury, in that insipid press conference: there's not much left to this season, but he isn't counting Camden out. He wants to win. That's what he's thinking about, half-formed ideas all he can afford while this is still underway, but he clings to them like a talisman when they get into stoppage time and he receives the ball from Garcia. Oliver sidesteps the man marking him and keeps possession, nothing to sneeze at, thank you, and keeps on running. He knows that Leo is with him, able to keep up with Oliver's thoughts and his pace. He trusts in it, all the way to the center backs, who converge on him, but not before he slips the ball away to Leo. He's set the other man free and clear, he knows, but he keeps up a sprint in case of a deflection. To his surprise, the ball returns to his own feet, making Oliver the one unmarked in front of the goal. On instinct more than strategy, he takes a shot with his first touch, then there's that *whoosh*ing sound, the one that only happens when the ball hits the netting and the world explodes.

Suddenly he's looking up at the sky rather than toward the keeper, catapulted horizontally from the change in velocity after trying to stop his body from running. It only takes a second for Leo to materialize above him, grinning like a madman, hair sticking in every direction out of his headband. Oliver takes his hand gladly, staggering upright and hugging him tightly—only briefly, but hard enough to make it count.

"You dunce," Oliver says, voice smushed into a nest of curls. "That one was supposed to be for you."

"Owed you one," Leo insists.

Distantly, the referee is bleating a sharp whistle and the United squad disperses listlessly, muttering accusations, while the rest of Camden's players run to join them. Oliver keeps one arm thrown casually over Leo's shoulders as they receive them, gathering in a great tangle of an embrace.

Above them in the stands, the throng of the crowd is singing, belting out a footy rendition of The Beatles in two choruses, conducted by a balding, brilliantly mustachioed fan in the front row.

"Haaaaarris, yeah that's our lad. Took a bad score and made it better," one half bellows, before the other kicks in.

"Na, na, na, nananana, nananana, HARRIS!"

All of Regent Road is shaking with it, thousands of people jumping in unison, all the gruff tone-deaf voices blending into something primal and operatic. Oliver is no stranger to songs in the stands, both as insults and as praise, home and away, but he's struck dumb by it anyway, the near-religious feeling of a crowd of people doing something so big. He could win a hundred more matches and not feel like he deserves this, the devotion and the fervor filling up the Camden air. This is what makes him who he is, this place and the great, booming sound of it. One hundred years from now, Camden will probably be a single giant shopping center owned by someone who's never been to London, but if the fans keep on singing, Oliver is certain he could find his way home.

"The Beatles supported Liverpool," Oliver says manfully, but he's scrubbing at his cheekbone to wipe away the unexpected flood of tears.

"Not today they don't," Anthony tells him firmly as they start the journey toward Willem waiting by the bench. "Up the Roses!"

There's an additional round of hugs when they get to the substitutes, everyone coming to meet them at the touchline.

"Arsenal lost too," Carda shouts, waving someone's phone delightedly. "We're up to fourth!"

Fourth. That magic number where Willem doesn't get fired and Oliver doesn't get sent packing. It's not first, but it might as well be for how good it feels to get there. Sebastian goes to shake his hand en route back to the locker room, but Oliver can't do business as usual, not when he's so happy, so he goes in for a hug, lifting the trainer right off the ground in celebration and maybe in a long-overdue apology.

"Well done," Sebastian wheezes once he's been set back down, gobsmacked. Oliver feels a little sheepish, but it gets washed away immediately when he's pulled into the next tide of celebrations.

• • •

Twenty minutes later, he gets caught up in something else entirely. Leo is fresh out of the shower, half-dressed, face scrubbed pink and clean, and when he reaches up to towel his head, the swooping arc of his pelvis disappearing into his waistband is just too much for Oliver to bear. He has to be alone with him or his heart will give out. When he approaches, Leo grins wolfishly, showing all his teeth.

"Na, na, na, nananana," he trills up at Oliver, bobbing his head amiably.

"Yeah, yeah," Oliver says, willing to forgive any amount of ribbing under the present circumstances, if he can only get to the point. "Give you a ride?"

He very purposely does not say "ride home." Leo seems to note the phrasing of this as well, shocked, and then pleased, and then anxious in three quick blinks.

"Yeah, all right, then," he replies, dusting his fingernails off on the lining of his towel like Oliver's just asked him how his day is going. "Give us a minute, I'll put on a shirt."

Waste of time, Oliver thinks, wickedly. *It's coming back off.*

His bravado dries up when he takes the right turn instead of left coming out of the stadium, announcing to the traffic and to Leo in the passenger seat beside him that they're headed north, away from Marylebone. Leo clears his throat, looking down and saying nothing. Oliver simultaneously longs to offer him an out and dreads the idea of him taking it. *No pressure,* he wants to assure him, even as he cracks under the weight of it, the thought of what they might be about to do rattling him inside and out.

As they cross the little bridge over the canal, Oliver's house coming into view, Leo inhales sharply as the situation finally makes itself unequivocally clear. Oliver pulls over the second he hears that, swerving toward the curb, but when he shuts the car off and turns to face Leo, he's already unbuckled and reaching for the door, stepping out onto the street and not looking back at the driver's seat.

It's not where Oliver had planned to actually park for the evening, but he follows Leo's lead, tiptoeing on his own street corner, fumbling with the keys. In any imaginings he's ever allowed about bringing someone home, having someone in his actual house, he's always played it much more suave. When the front door shuts behind them, Oliver is sweating more than he did in the match, damp and nervy with it.

"Make yourself at h—" he starts, trying to put them back to baseline, but the sentence doesn't get out, since Leo has, maybe even predictably at this point, launched himself at him. "Mmmph," Oliver gets out, wrenching himself free from the kiss. Leo is quaking in front of him like a spooked horse; he palms Leo's sweet, soft head, trying to gentle him and also wanting, more than anything, to keep touching him. "Easy, tiger. We don't have anywhere to be. Let's take it slow."

Leo shakes his head, dislodging Oliver's hand, and comes up on the balls of his feet, smacking one more kiss to his shocked mouth.

"I don't want to go slow," Leo tells him matter-of-factly. "I know you, Harris. I give you time to think and you might change your mind again, which would, frankly, kill me dead."

"Oh, perish the thought," Oliver murmurs, laying his palm over Leo's heart to check it's still beating, thinking, *Hey, now that's closer to suave.*

Leo raises his eyebrows challengingly, so he dives back in, slower in pace but deeper in intent this time. They find that same rhythm Oliver's felt with a ball between them sometimes, both anticipatory and reciprocal. Their breaths are slow and gasps between each other's mouths. The smooth backs of Leo's teeth are slick under Oliver's tongue and he chases the taste and the feeling, swallowing every perfect noise that comes out of Leo. It's unlike any kiss between them that's come before, must be unlike any kiss between anyone in the history of time, really, for how good it feels to Oliver. He's distantly aware of them both grasping and pulling, trying to get closer, trying to put this feeling in every one of their limbs.

It occurs to Oliver that the only thing that could be better than this is doing it horizontally. Carefully, so it doesn't disrupt anything, because he doesn't want to stop, not for anything, he starts to guide them toward the stairs, leading Leo backward. A few steps up, he realizes Leo is taller than him like this. He leans into it, straining on his tiptoes to keep the kiss how he wants it: brazen and admittedly kind of sloppy. Leo pulls away, taking three tries to get fully clear because Oliver follows through over and over, chasing him down like a counterattack.

"Where do you think you're going?" he breathes into Leo's waiting, open mouth.

"To your bed, Oliver," Leo replies. "If you'll have me." Then he takes off running like he did that night in the park after losing to Chelsea, scrambling up the stairs a million miles an hour. Oliver wants him, madly, immediately, and now the only thing between himself and getting him is the time it takes to catch up.

Leo freezes on the landing, looking down the hallway at the cluster of doors, and Oliver overtakes him, yanking them up to the third level by the elbow. He pulls them both through the doorframe to his bedroom, one little leap of faith, then keeps going all the way across the room until he's pushed Leo flat on his back at the edge of the mattress. When Oliver strips off his sweater, Leo's eyes go glassy, tracing the lines of his body with blown pupils.

"My word, man," Leo says, making a vile wolf-whistling noise.

"Give it a rest," Oliver begs. "You've seen it all before."

"Not like this, I haven't," Leo says fairly, running his fingertips across Oliver's waistline carefully, like he's not quite sure how to touch him, but when Oliver presses into it Leo grabs for him with both hands, pulling him up and over, guiding lower until Oliver is cradling his body over Leo's. He responds in kind, one hand under the curve of Leo's ass, pulling his hips off the mattress and toward his own, the other braced on the firm muscle of Leo's bicep. They're kissing again, Oliver losing track of the number he started cataloging in his head in March, as they rapidly approach triple digits. The air is thick with the sensation, trickling like honey all down his body, bordering on an intensity that makes him unsure if he should move toward it or lean away.

Oliver can't, or won't, go anywhere: Leo has him firmly by the back of the thighs, notching them together at the hinges. He slips one finger around the outline of Leo's lips, mapping the cartography of his mouth, and when Leo tongues at his knuckle Oliver sputters out a groan, feeling it in strange, unconnected parts of his body.

"Are we going to do this?" Leo asks.

"What, exactly, do you think is happening right now?" Oliver laughs.

"I mean the rest of it."

Oliver's body is moving of its own accord now, following

Leo's steady, rhythmic heartbeat. He wants to do this right, he wants to make it good, make it worth it, but he's bricking it, terrified as soon as his brain has half a second to catch up with itself.

"Have you ever?" he manages to ask.

"No. I'm a virgin," Leo says, but the punchline is ruined by blending into the rounded edges of a moan when Oliver circles his hips again. "I've had sex, Oliver," he clarifies, more seriously. Leo's eyes are closed, but Oliver gets the sense he's rolling them anyway.

"With another man?"

"It doesn't *matter,* can you please get on with it," Leo demands.

"Not even in the academy? No handies with the lads?" Oliver presses, encircling his own hand around Leo lightly now, just to get the feel of him through his trackies. An image sparks to life in his mind, erotic but unwelcome, a possessive streak surging at the idea that anyone else might have touched Leo like this.

"Fuck," Leo replies, arching parenthetically, throwing his whole body after it. "No, never. Did you? That's so hot."

"It wasn't," Oliver laughs, only a little ruefully. "I couldn't very well have a convenient hookup just to get off during a long tournament away from the girlfriends, no homo like. First because of Maggie, then because the stakes were too high. Someone might have noticed how much I liked it, and then where would we be?"

"Right here, probably," Leo says, clutching at the back of Oliver's neck, pulling him close and kissing him hard.

"Why didn't you?" Oliver asks, words spilling into Leo's mouth. "Weren't you curious?"

"Of course I was. But it's like you said, someone might have realized that it would always mean something different to me than it did to any of them." Leo is right; this feels so very different than anything Oliver's ever done before. His breath catches between every kiss, pulse racing faster than after any sprint he's ever run. "But I've thought about it, I've thought about it a lot."

"What did you think about?"

"This," Leo says, fishing for the elastic scrunch of Oliver's waistband and squeezing his fist. Oliver's thought about it too; it feels even better than he imagined.

"Oh," he murmurs dumbly, mostly to keep from whimpering at the feeling of Leo touching his dick, doing so with intent. "How do you like it?" He means it to be teasing and sexy; it comes out needy.

"I like *you,*" Leo sighs, answering him honestly, and that's all the questions Oliver can bear to ask before bringing their mouths back together. Through some unspoken agreement, they flip themselves around until Oliver's lying flat, Leo sprawled atop him, still kissing. After another long moment, Leo pulls back slightly, looking down at him inquiringly and rubbing the tip of his nose along the bridge of Oliver's. "You're all bumpy," he laughs. "Your nose is crooked, I never noticed before."

"I broke it on a post going for a header. Dumb teenager, I was. Ruined my modeling career."

"Nah, it's cute," Leo says, dropping a kiss right on top of the cute nose in question. "Makes you look dangerous."

"I'm very tame," Oliver says seriously, massaging at the traces of softness around Leo's hips. "You're safe with me."

"I'm counting on it," Leo whispers back; suddenly he slithers downward, slipping deep under the duvet until he's level with Oliver's hips. He looks perfect in this light, skin tan and warm against Oliver's thighs, lips parted with wanting, then all of a sudden parted with something else, as he descends upon him.

"Fuck," Oliver gasps stupidly. "Oh fuck."

Leo looks up at him from under his lashes—Oliver can feel the flutter of them against his pelvis when Leo blinks and just that feeling is as intense as any blowjob he's ever had before.

"I'm going to get you off," Leo says, pulling away with a wet pop. "And it's going to be really good." He's just as competitive here as anywhere else; it's the sexiest thing that's ever happened to Oliver, taking the top spot from five minutes ago when Leo touched his dick for the first time.

"I want you to. I want you so bad, Leo, please," Oliver lets himself tell him, just once. Leo doesn't answer or make him repeat himself, only obliges everything Oliver's ever wanted. Leo's lack of experience is subsumed by sheer enthusiasm; it's all Oliver can do to stay mostly still and not embarrass himself by opening his mouth again.

Oliver desperately wants to be gentlemanly, to take what he's being given, but Leo reaches for more and plucks it out of him as easily as unbuttoning a shirt, placing Oliver's hands in his hair, sighing softly with his mouth full when Oliver tangles his fingers in it, and then kneading his own fingertips against the soft rounds of Oliver's arse, tugging him against Leo's waiting tongue again and again.

"Leo," he says again, while his brain repeats it on a loop, in time with the movements of his hips: *Leo, Leo, Leo, Leo*. "Please, God, take your fucking clothes off."

His own pants never got out from around his ankles and Leo's still fully dressed, all cotton wrinkles and mussed curls. If Oliver doesn't see his dick, right now, his entire life will have been for nothing. Leo retreats, albeit reluctantly, toward the edge of the bed, kneeling like he's waiting for communion. He peels off his shirt, pulling by the collar—for all he's seen it done by hundreds of men after hundreds of matches in his life, Oliver's never truly appreciated before just how sexy it is when someone does that, one fell swoop to reveal the body underneath. And what Leo's revealed is just like he's dreamed it, just like he pretended he didn't know it would be, after months of blink-long glances in the locker room. Oliver's barely gotten to take it in, all the brown skin of his belly and the sparse, dark curls of hair on his chest, when Leo shimmies out of his own trackies, suddenly as naked as Oliver, and just as hard.

"Well? Are you satisfied?" Leo asks, and he sounds like he might be joking and also like he means it very, very much.

"Come here," Oliver replies, and they're already moving, crashing into each other.

It's all a blur after that, a flipbook of feelings, he's careening forward toward the inevitable end and already he's trying to remember it all, cataloging the pleasure, to make sure it will keep for later. Maybe it will never happen again, maybe it has never happened before, but it is happening now, this moment between them. It means anything, everything, and when Oliver knows he's about to come he closes his eyes, but Leo stops touching him, waiting a torturous, century-long second, until Oliver blinks and blinks and looks at Leo again, and when it's over he can only think that Leo's seen him, Leo is the only person who has ever seen him, the only person who's ever really been allowed to look.

• • •

Oliver wakes up with an elbow in his sternum and a chin on his jugular. Leo is stuck to his torso like a barnacle on a barge, naked and warm with sleep and very clingy. The day-after-match soreness is compounding with the weight of another body on top of him, but it still feels good. Leo only snuffles a snore when Oliver shifts beneath him, more to settle in than to dislodge.

Willem, clearly suffering from a kind of crazy-eyed fourth-place frenzy, mandated morning yoga as a team instead of an off day, which means they do need to get up. *They* need to get up.

What a strange sensation. Oliver has never had anyone linger in his bed like this before, not in any sterile vacation hotel room and certainly not here. It's somehow more vulnerable, more inescapably intimate than anything they've done to date, to wake up holding Leo, to see and be seen in the veil of sleep. He doesn't want it to end; he's instinctively afraid of what might happen when it does.

They've been rivals and comrades and friends. Leo was his reluctant pupil and then a target of both ire and desire, and now it seems like they've become something else to each other entirely. *Lovers,* Oliver thinks, in the privacy of his own head where there's no need to be embarrassed about it. It was both of their first times at something last night.

"Are you up?" Leo asks a few minutes later, startling Oliver by being awake.

"No," he whispers back, trying to prolong this in-bed feeling.

Leo snorts and pushes up on one elbow, freeing Oliver from being at the bottom of the cuddle and exposing his face, rumpled sheet lines imprinted on his cheek.

"Bit early to start lying to me, Harris," Leo tells him somberly. "I don't know how you expect this to work."

Eventually, and probably the sooner the better, they're going to have a grown-up conversation where they define what "this" and "work" mean in this context, but Oliver can't do it now. Considering it makes him panic and he doesn't want to, not while the cutest boy in London—as Maggie once rightly called Leo—is here with him. There's a look on Leo's face, an unexpected combination of heat and good humor, the same face he made last night when Oliver finally got his hands on him, when Oliver made him come.

"Let's see if I can't change your mind," Oliver says to Leo, instead of any of the cautious, warning things he should. "Come here, handsome." There's no training today, just stretching: Oliver suspects he won't get a chance like this again anytime soon, and he's aching for it, so he snakes one hand free from their entwined bodies and fumbles for the spare nightstand, digging through the drawer until he finds a crinkle of foil and the outline of a bottle. When Oliver offers him the square, golden packet, Leo bursts out laughing, which is not quite the reaction he had been hoping for. "Well, go on, then," he sniffs. "You're not getting any without it."

"Why do you even have these?" Leo asks, far too joyously, waving the condom between two pinched fingers.

"Search me," Oliver admits. "Plausible deniability? Check the date on it, honestly."

"We're good."

"*You're* good."

"Me?" Leo squeaks, all laughter disappearing. "I'm going to?"

"I assume you know how to fuck someone," Oliver tells him. "And I assure you, I know how to get fucked." It's been so long since he let himself have this and Oliver is ravenous for it, to be held in that suspension, full and hungry for more at once. He wants Leo inside of him, he wants to feel it all.

Leo seems to forget his nerves in the face of that mental image, rolling Oliver over and climbing astride, condom momentarily lost in the sheets while he pins Oliver's wrists above his head and kisses him again. Leo follows the trail of goose pimples down Oliver's neck and toward his stomach, brushing his chin over his abdomen until he's tonguing at the edge of Oliver's tattoo, rose petals framing Leo's face.

"You're so . . ." Leo trails off, sighing a barely-there laugh. "You're just like I thought you'd be."

"I hope that's a good thing?" Oliver says, watching a blush

bloom all over his own naked body. He wants it, still, more and more every second, but he's not a little frightened of it, too, with the daylight streaming in from his bedroom windows.

"It's perfect," Leo whispers, reaching down, at last, to retrieve the little bottle. "It's better than that—it's actually happening."

"It is," Oliver agrees. "It's all for you."

It is *actually happening,* he thinks as Leo rolls them over and hovers over Oliver's back, lips brushing where his shoulder blade reaches his spine. *Because I don't know if we can take it back now.*

• • •

A secret can be sexy, is what Oliver thinks later, looking across the room full of lads in downward dog. Even the unsexy, utilitarian pieces of Leo's body are tantalizing to him—just now, as Leo pulls his socks up over the little bones in his ankle in between stretches, all Oliver can think about is getting his mouth on him, on whatever part he can reach. It aches so good, Oliver can feel the pang of it in the back of his teeth. He's feverish with whatever they've unlocked within each other. He knows Leo is sick with it too, because when yoga is done, he looks neither Zen nor rested, but God, he *does* look flexible. They shouldn't have arrived together, they shouldn't leave together again, for the second day in a row, but Oliver can't say no to Leo when he trails after him. He's weak, he's horny, he's bordering on reckless. He drives them both home.

Up in the kitchen, Leo raids Oliver's pantry like he's the one who pays for groceries, scarfing down organic pine nuts that were originally meant for cooking, not nibbling. Affection has made him a weak man: Oliver only takes a fistful for himself and kisses one of Leo's bulging cheeks.

"You have a whole *room* full of snacks," Leo says, replacing the bag and going back in for some chocolate, but he wipes his oily hand on a tea towel before touching anything else, which is very considerate of him. "This is going to be the best part of dating you."

"Dating" hits Oliver like an emergency siren. Is that what they're doing? He has no frame of reference for what any of this means, not with his *teammate,* not with Leo. Somehow Oliver is both greedy for the idea and sweaty with nausea when he pictures it. This is the kind of thing that's better blown up earlier, day-one achy instead of year-two brokenhearted. He'd rather go back and spend another lifetime yearning for something he can't have than finally get what he wants and lose it all anyway—Leo, his career, his reputation, take your pick.

"It's complicated," Oliver says lamely, belatedly, trying to shake off the images of transfer windows and tabloid journos staking out the canal bridge. "What we're doing. What to call it."

Leo sets the chocolate bar down on the counter very deliberately, like he's lost his taste for it, and gives Oliver a withering look.

"Seeing someone else, are you?"

"I'm not *seeing* anyone." Oliver feels himself clinging desperately to the last vestiges of a onetime thing. All the good reasons for staying quiet are sounding incredibly loud now that Leo is clothed and no longer kissing him. The secret doesn't feel so sexy anymore. "We just have to be actually fucking careful about this. Famous people get papped getting the mail. We're under a spotlight."

"I'm barely famous, Ollie. One friendly for England isn't going to count, in the long run. But you're the real deal. You're worth a lot of money," Leo says. There's something unhappy forming in the crinkle between his eyebrows.

"It's not about *money*." Oliver feels the words that will explain himself slipping away. It sounds so self-important when he says it out loud, like James Finch is talking through him, but inside everything feels urgent and dangerous and all-consuming. "It's the *attention*. People will notice, Leo. If you're with me, if we're out together. There's no way people won't see what we're doing."

"Right, well, I promise I won't plant one on you at Regent Road, if that's what you're worried about," Leo says tetchily.

We could do a lot less and people would still be able to tell, he thinks. *Every time I look at you, it must be all over my fucking face.*

"Look, I've had a lot of time to think about this, the limits of my situation," Oliver says, reaching for Leo's shoulder and feeling bereft when Leo shakes his hand off. He couldn't even make it a day without ruining everything. At this rate, Leo will be playing second division in Romania by tomorrow and Oliver will probably break his ankle trying to lace his boots. They don't even need anyone else to give them ultimatums or threats; Oliver can spoil Camden's season and his entire life just fine on his own. "I made my peace with it. It's football now and gay someday, or gay now and no football, ever again."

And it has to be football; that's what he picked, all those years ago.

"Then we don't have to call it anything," Leo replies evenly. "Or, you know, it doesn't have to be serious. We can hook up, no strings. Nothing more. Just tell me now if that's what we're doing, would you? I don't want to play any games. If I have to start pretending something about myself, then I don't want to pretend anything with you."

It is exactly what Oliver was pushing Leo to agree to: something noncommittal and nonchalant. He's a hypocrite; he hates hearing it.

"It's not pretending," Oliver says, somewhere between defeated and defensive. "I want to be careful so I can keep doing this, not because I don't want it."

"Sure, Ollie," Leo says quietly. It doesn't sound like he believes him. "You make the rules."

The length of the room between them, the site of their first kiss and their, well, not quite *first* fight, is too much. He just wants to be close to Leo, as close as he's allowed, for as long as he can manage. "Come on, then," he says. "Let's go get something else to eat."

"In public?" Leo asks, half-joking, half-exhausted. "Won't that be suspicious?"

"I'd like to have dinner with you," Oliver says. "The rules are for everyone else, not for how you deserve to be treated. I want you to know that. Besides, won't it be hot? When the waitress tries to hit on me again, but you know I'm thinking about you fucking me?"

He offers Leo his arm just to make his intentions certain. He can be chivalrous when they're alone, in his kitchen. Leo smacks the crook of Oliver's elbow down to his side, a little harder than necessary, but he puts one hand in Oliver's back pocket and keeps it there as they walk out, bumping into each other all down the stairwell.

• • •

They're model citizens for the next two days, two bosom buddies who live in separate houses. And if Oliver organized an outing to play pool at the pub tonight, picking the spot that's just one street over from his place and not owned by Conor Bishop, *that's* just because he's a great teammate. Altruistic, even.

Being able to spend the evening with Leo without arousing any suspicion was supposed to be a bonus, but now that they're crowded into a booth, Oliver wonders if it was a terrible mistake. Something else is arousing, is the problem. Have billiards always been so phallic? Sticks and balls, et cetera. Under the neon beer signs, Joe interrupts his indecent thoughts and passes Oliver a cue with one hand, pulling him to his feet with the other, sparing him some torment and introducing a new method of it. Oliver isn't even any good at pool. He's got coordinated feet, no hand-eye to speak of.

"This was a stupid idea," Oliver grouses.

"It was *your* stupid idea, though, wasn't it," Joe replies sweetly. "Put your phone away!" Oliver manages to ignore him until Joe brings in reinforcements, Trevor joining him in pinning both of Oliver's arms to his sides and marching him over to the sea of cheap felt. "Riddle me this," Joe goes on, laughing. "You are *always* glued to that thing, but never once have you responded to any message in a timely manner. I had to change you as my emergency contact!"

"It's a power play," Anthony adds sagely. "He thinks his time is more valuable than ours."

"Joe, you changed your emergency contact to your *wife*," Oliver says defensively.

"He shouldn't have had to!" Finn says.

"Oh, come off it," Leo says casually from the booth, looking down at his own phone. "Oliver texts back."

Joe's face quirks into one of amused betrayal.

"So there is someone else!" He points at Oliver with the menacing end of a cue. "And here you told me I was your number one."

"He said that to me too," Trevor sighs.

Oliver squirms, the only one in the uncomfortable middle of a gay joke. Well, maybe not the only one, because of Leo, who is just now pink as boiled prawn and busying himself with shredding the corners of a damp coaster to ribbons, avoiding everyone's eyes. Oliver brandishes his own cue and initiates a fencing match with Joe to distract the lads into placing their bets rather than continuing the conversation, which, surprising no one, works like a fucking charm. He's so busy poking blue circles of chalk onto the back of Finn's sweater, he doesn't even notice they're one man short until Leo texts him from the loo.

Didn't realize I was such an exception

Leo is an exception to every rule he's ever set. Oliver wants to go kick the toilet door in and say, *Duh*. Instead, he stomps off to the bar for a refill on water—being responsible is not all it's cracked up to be; when this season is over, he's going to become ninety percent piña colada—where he can look at his screen in peace.

who's this? he writes stubbornly on his way back to the table.

I think you know. Oliver feels sparks down from his abdomen to the tops of his thighs. And between them. He knows, all right—the idea of it is so thrilling he barely notices the follow-up text. what are you wearing?

cheeky. come have a look, because I'm not going to sext you

like hell you aren't. tell me what you want to do to me.

There's so much he wants to do to Leo, none of it safe to type in public. Oliver can barely remember to breathe, much less heckle his pool opponents.

strangulation. He fucks up another shot, nearly missing the cue ball entirely, then clarifies. but not in a sexy way

kind of in a sexy way

Leo now seems to be having the best time of all of them, smiling devilishly down at his phone while Oliver shoots the worst round of billiards in Camden FC's history. Joe is begging him to stop embarrassing them, to focus, but Oliver's hands are clammy and useless, unless they're touching Leo.

maybe so. but we live ten minutes apart, there's no need for a text trail

you made the rules for scheduling, Leo replies.

The glass of water is going down like a shot of tequila. And if they don't leave, right now, all his careful years of subterfuge will go down like the *Titanic*. Oliver puts out a distress signal:

I'm changing them. consider yourself irresistible and get out of here

Leo responds with a single smirking emoji, which hasn't always seemed so coquettish to Oliver as it does now. When he looks up, Oliver can see the live Leo making a big show of begging off, suddenly knackered while he shrugs into his denim jacket. Maybe he's more like DiCaprio than Messi after all. Oliver forces himself to wait six whole minutes before he follows him.

He must have misread the room somehow; Oliver's front steps are markedly empty when he comes jogging up the lane, ready to carry Leo over the threshold like a blushing bride and then follow said blush all the way down his body. They're supposed to be careful, yes, on account of the neighbors, but he didn't quite intend for Leo to hide in the shrubbery.

??? Oliver texts, only slightly miffed that his grand entrance has gone awry.

His phone rings immediately.

"Where are you?" Leo asks.

"Standing in front of my front door, actually. Where are you?"

"*Your* door? Oliver!"

"Don't 'Oliver' me! I live around the corner from the pub!" he objects.

"Exactly. Where it would be very easy to be seen," Leo says, like he's talking to someone incredibly slow. "I told the front desk my teammate would be coming by to drop off scouting reports and everything."

Well, he's got him there.

"Ten minutes, all right? I'm getting in the car right now."

"I'll give you eight," Leo tells him archly as he hangs up on Oliver.

It takes him closer to fifteen, what with the parking and hoping the doorman doesn't clock the fact that he's showing up without any trace of a scouting tape. In the mirrored doors of the elevator, Oliver's fringe is askew like an old paintbrush, the green in his eyes almost entirely overtaken by black. He looks rabid, starving. Thinking about what's going to happen, what's waiting for him upstairs, turns the whole metal box on its axis until his feet are resting comfortably on the ceiling. There are still parts of Leo's body he's never touched, like the crevices behind his knees and the hollow of his belly button. Oliver wants it all—consumingly, dangerously so.

Maybe that's why he goes for the front door assuming it'll be unlocked, like Leo will have read his thoughts and expedited the process for him, bringing them closer to the moment where they'll get to have each other. Maybe that's also why Leo was waiting in the foyer, eyes up to the peephole, to pull it open for him. Whatever it is, they go for the knob simultaneously and the door swings inward with full force, right into Leo's face.

Leo makes a noise like a basset hound, between an *argh* and a howl, somewhat muffled by an ominous *crack*. Oliver was already seeing red with sheer desire, but now his vision is crimson from the steady stream of blood coming from Leo's nose.

"Fuck!" Oliver shrieks, reaching instinctively for Leo's chin, trying to get him upright so the bleeding will slow.

"Ow!" Leo yelps back. "Don't touch it!"

"Sorry, sorry. We've just got to get your head up, to help with the bleeding."

"You're supposed to knock," Leo says thickly, the *p*'s turning to *b*'s like he's underwater.

"I didn't know you were standing right there," Oliver says,

carefully groping across Leo's cheek to feel for his nose as lightly as he can.

"I wanted to surprise you."

"You did that and then some. Well done." Leo hisses when Oliver makes contact but doesn't push him away, screwing his eyes shut and breathing heavily out of his mouth. "Not broken, I don't think," Oliver concludes, gently twisting his nose ring back into place.

"How can you tell?" Leo asks.

"Mum's a nurse. But I'm not, to be fair. I think you've got to go to the hospital and make sure I'm right."

"Will you come with me?"

"I better not," Oliver says reluctantly. The thought of Leo in a hospital makes his stomach turn. "Might look a bit dodgy." Leo frowns as he nods, still covered in red. Oliver hates the incursion of these stupid rules when Leo is hurt, in need of him. For a split second he thinks of calling his mum, then puts that idea right back into a box. "Give me your phone, let me call you a cab," he says instead.

"Dodgy, right. They might ask who hit me," Leo says impatiently, stepping away from Oliver taking out his own phone. "I'll call the car. Don't want it to be under your name. Should I plan on you being here when I get back?"

"Not in range of the door," Oliver says gently. "But here, of course. Got to see our matching nose bumps, hey?"

"Sounds all right when you put it like that," Leo admits, scrunching his face and wincing when the movement reaches his nose. "Okay, okay. See you."

When the door swings shut behind him and he's alone in Leo's flat, allowed past the threshold for the first time, Oliver is overtaken by the urge to snoop, but finds it far less gratifying than what they were supposed to be doing. He's been in flats like this before, the starter place of a young man with cash to burn and a schedule that precludes hanging out at home. It's more charming on Leo than on anyone else.

Oliver follows his curiosity from the kitchen into the bedroom and finds the aftermath of a hasty cleanup. It's silly and slightly endearing to him, that the bed is half-made and there's been a clear effort to stuff some of the strewn-about clothes back into the wardrobe. On the nearly empty spare nightstand there's a waiting glass of water set out like an offering. Oliver can see the two of them together in this room, the way he's starting to picture Leo popping up in every nook and cranny of his own house, making himself comfortable. He likes the impossible image of it, despite knowing better. Wherever they end up after this season, in Oliver's imagination they might still be right here, in a flat in Marylebone.

When he turns back toward the main room, Oliver's eye catches on the top of the low wooden dresser. Sitting next to a clump of cologne bottles and sketchbooks and headbands, a pool ball is nestled among the chaos. It could only have come from the pub, could only have come from tonight—when he brings a hand to it, it's still warm to the touch like it was recently in a coat pocket. It's a solid: number 6, painted almost–Camden green. He can also picture Leo lifting this, quietly ruining one of the lads' games of pool, to take a token of the night, one bearing Oliver's number. His heartbeat reaches up past his throat, quickening on the back of his tongue. He's not sure if he was meant to see this, or if it was never meant for him to find.

Leo sends him a picture not long after—Oliver is still sitting on the edge of the bed, thumbing through drawings of skylines and football pitches and handsome faceless figures—he clearly jumped the queue to see a doctor so fast, and in a private room, no less. Leo's got on a bloody grin and some gauze stuffed up one nostril. He looks tired but relieved.

ok, dr. harris, you were right. no break. gotta tell anna for monitoring purposes but not "injured." be back soon

So there won't be any face masks or squad list announcements; Leo can play the next match. Oliver gets to keep him, here in this bed and later on the pitch. How Leo will explain this to Anna is another matter entirely, one Oliver is too exhausted to unpack or even worry about, going right in the box with the abandoned plan to call Nicola.

• • •

Leo and his intact nose are of great use later, when Camden wins again, firmly lodged in fourth place and with another assist for Harris in the referee's book. Even after all the running, Oliver feels alight with the spring air. It isn't until he's half back into his clothes that he remembers his plans for the evening and the associated, somewhat morbid occasion for them. It brings the mood down slightly.

No one is going out: the schedule has reached the end of season, the warm-weather fever pitch where they can't drink beer and can only just catch their breath before it's time to play again. They're driving to Stoke-on-Trent tomorrow evening to face Stoke City on Wednesday—Oliver can only keep track because he updates his Google calendar obsessively and because Sebastian and Willem spend every spare minute hammering tactical updates at them, sending scouting videos practically faster than they can be produced.

"I'm having dinner with my mum," Oliver says out of one side of his mouth to Leo, loitering above his locker casually. "I'll see you in Stoke?"

Leo nods and replies even more quietly, a tiny whispered "Miss you." Oliver doesn't say anything back, because if he does, he won't be able to stop himself from admitting he'll miss him too. Only once he pulls up in front of the flat on his bike, muscles finally relaxing, does he fish out his phone to send a single text: save me a seat on the coach.

Nicola is waiting at the front steps, waving and grinning. Dad's birthday is usually a somber affair, quiet but for the scraping of cutlery on the dishes. But a good football result could always hold back the well of grief for himself; it's a welcome relief to see it might work on Mum as well, under the right circumstances.

She pulls the roast out of the oven before Oliver's even out of his coat, fussing over the trimmings and refusing any help. She wipes her hands on the tea towel sticking out of her pocket and turns him by the shoulders to face her.

"Come on, then," she says, cupping one cheek in each palm. "Let's have a look at you, triumphant one."

"Same as ever, Mum," he replies, stooping slightly to kiss her forehead.

"Hmm," she hums. "You look right as rain. Very healthy. Some nice color on you."

He feels the warm glow of pride at her assessment. They move toward the dining nook; he offers her a wineglass and proffers his own pint of water to clink.

"To Dad?" Oliver asks and she smiles in a sort of faraway manner as they touch the glass rims together. Nicola seats herself at the head of the table in an elegant unfolding of limbs, taking a swallow of wine and beginning to serve them both. Oliver watches her carefully, taking in the pepper of gray in her plush fringe, the wedding band on a gold chain kissing the stitched edge of her collar. She looks nice in her civvies, hair down and scrubs off. "Mum?" he asks around a mouthful of peas, before he can lose his courage.

"Ollie?"

"When did you know—like, when were you sure that it wasn't just a crush, with Dad? That it was real?"

The words spill out in a jumble and he immediately feels guilty for raising it now. But it's Dad's birthday, and he is his namesake, and he walks around with his face on his own every day, and he misses him, and he never knew him at all. He wants to know when they chose each other, the other Oliver and Nicola. He knows the basics, the movie-premise version of events: Nicola Baird sat next to Oliver Harris in the library during a rainy primary school lunch break and they started a conversation that never stopped. They lived in each other's pockets, friends, then family, then lovers. Nicola waited for Oliver when he left London to go to Oxford, and he came back to her, working the family bookstall while she finished nursing college, staying on even longer to account for the newly arrived Oliver, longer still when he was too sick to work anywhere else, right up until he stopped working at all.

When Dad was admitted to the hospital, Nicola was almost done with a specialized nursing license in the next building over, and she wasn't working in the cancer ward, but she reviewed all of his treatment plans anyway, discussed every avenue with his doctors. Oliver spent most of that time with his grandparents, haunting the bookstall, or underfoot at the hospital, learning medical terms he was too young for. The end of the story doesn't feel right to Oliver, and it never will, but it stays the same: Dad gone. The bookstall out of business within two years, caught between a recession and the first wave of gentrification in Camden. His grandparents, ill and frail and aging rapidly, one after the other, then gone too, before Oliver made his debut. Oliver alone in the academy, but not too alone, clinging to his football and to Maggie. Nicola working, always working.

It takes her a long time to answer—like she's thinking about all those things too.

"What makes you ask, darling?" Her eyes are shining, her

voice is low. He feels guilty, prone with sorrow, but not any less curious.

"I met someone, I think," he starts, courage not stretching quite far enough to say *who* or *where*. "But it's not . . . not like I expected." That much is certainly true.

She gives him another watery smile, looking not a little shocked to hear it.

"That's wonderful, wonderful news—for God's sake," she says, suddenly dabbing at her eyes with the old cloth napkin on her lap. "Leaky as an old roof, the state of me." Oliver laughs, half-crying himself. He wants her to ask for more details. He wishes he'd never brought it up. "I wouldn't trade that feeling for anything, those early days, when every choice is laden with love," she sighs. "Your dad was such a romantic, he could make sharing the water bill feel like Austen wrote it."

"He was?" Oliver asks tentatively, thinking of reading *Pride and Prejudice* with Leo on their way to the Midlands.

"Oh, terribly so. He wanted such a courtship. It moved so slow I wasn't even convinced he really liked me until he told me how much he missed me at Oxford."

"How did you find out for sure?"

Nicola takes a careful mouthful of carrot, chewing slowly.

"Well, he came back," she says softly. "He could have stayed on, found graduate funding and tried to write. But he wanted to help your grandparents, and he wanted to be with me. When he finished his degree, he said we should get a flat together and it was my turn to focus on school. I was so shocked! Straight to living together. Uni instead of marriage. What a scandal," she says. Oliver is hanging on every word, drinking in the images of them as he's seen in old photos, terrible haircuts and healthy, handsome faces. He has a thousand more questions bubbling up inside him, but he doesn't want to risk stopping her from going on. He's not sure they've ever talked like this before, as Nicola the wife and Oliver the son. It's always been the nurse and the footballer, no ghosts to speak of. It was safer that way, almost like it never happened. "I think it made me nervous how much I wanted to say yes. I didn't want to tie him down, I was afraid he'd feel trapped. Everyone gave him quite a bit of trouble for leaving, for going to Oxford. They thought he was up himself, with his literary salons and his big degree. But he was just smart, he loved learning. He wanted to read everything. I didn't want him to come back to prove anything, I wanted to be sure it was for me. So I told him I'd go to school wherever I first got an offer, and if it was London he had a deal." It's pragmatic, such a grown-up and feminist sensibility. It's so *Nicola,* every inch the mother he knows. "But he was so happy when Royal Free came calling. I knew he loved me then. I told him, 'What are the odds?' and we moved right in, engaged a year later. I didn't admit it until later, but University Hospital in Southampton accepted me a week earlier."

"What?" Oliver gasps, shocked into laughter. "Seriously?"

"When I got the letter, I was so disappointed!" She has such a pleasant laugh, giggling like a schoolgirl. Nicola is flushed with wine and reminiscence; Oliver feels like he's getting gossip he isn't quite supposed to know. "I knew then, what I really wanted, for me, was to be where he was. So I decided to hedge my bets . . . I just wanted to be on his team. I wanted us to choose to live our life together. To choose our life in Camden."

"Team" thumps and echoes, soft in Oliver's ears like his own heartbeat. Who wouldn't want that? Even if it scares you, even if it's a risk. Maybe especially then.

"If you knew then that it would mean you'd be alone now, would you do it again? You don't have to tell me, I mean—I just—" He has to know, even if he doesn't have a right to. Was it all worth it to her? If he lost something like Dad, would he survive it? Nicola did, somehow, but she's always been stronger than everyone else.

"It's all right, Ollie," she tells him, staring him down with the same green eyes as his. "You're allowed to be curious, my love. I'm happy to tell you. It was hard to learn to do everything all over again, without his company. I'd be up half the night crying and then at two in the morning I'd make a cake for you to have after school, just to keep my hands busy. I'm sure everyone thought I was raving. But we had each other. We weren't alone. And you were so strong. I remember thinking, sometimes, *Who's taking care of who?*"

"I mostly remember football, to be honest," Oliver admits, shamefaced. "I just wanted to go to the academy. The more I ran, the less sad I was."

"You were just a wee thing," she murmurs. "I thought it was too much pressure, all that football right after the funeral. And I knew your dad didn't want you to. I was afraid to betray him, his memory." Oliver feels choked and guilty. He was afraid of that too. "But the academy offered room and board with your scholarship, and more than anything, more than school, I wanted you to have a stable place." Oliver sits bolt upright, nearly knocking his water glass over. He didn't know that's why he got to stay, to keep playing football instead of grieving. "Everything felt like it was falling apart. We had some benefits, but I was terrified of making ends meet. Your grandparents wanted to help us, but they couldn't. Then your youth manager, Alec, such a nice man, he came over here in person. You were upstairs with schoolwork and I wanted to send him away, I was so ashamed of the mess, but he asked for just a minute of my time." Oliver can picture it perfectly, Alec in his tracksuit and his graying beard, those horrible nine-year-old days where, alone in his room, he counted the hours between training sessions and heard Nicola pacing all through the night. "He was so sorry to bother us, he only wanted to tell me it would be worth it. He promised to look after you. He said you had such a bright future with Camden. He said he thought you might be less lonely with a group of friends to play with every day. I felt he really cared for you. My little star . . ."

"I didn't know about that," Oliver murmurs. "I always thought I was so lucky you let me stay, like I'd gotten away with something." The man he became, football star with a big bad secret, all traces back to that year, when he started at the academy, gaining a new life to make up for the ruins of the old one. Oliver retreated into football because he couldn't get hurt on the pitch, not even when he was fouled or injured. Not *really* hurt, not in the same way he and Mum were, not in the way Dad was by the end. Looking back at it now, at the small version of himself in Camden green, he wonders if he's still on the practice pitch, if he ever left at all, or if he's been running drills alone after dark the whole span of his life. Maybe Leo was the first one to ever find him there and ask what he was up to. Even now, he's not sure of the answer.

"Oliver," Nicola says, taking both of his big hands in hers.

"I am lucky, Mum," he tells her. "Lucky to have you. And to have had Dad. You both did so well by me."

She squeezes hard and he squeezes back. In the compressed air between their palms he can feel Dad's presence, holding them both together through time and space. He wonders what the other Oliver would think of him now: his hair cut and his house and his pace on the ball. He wonders what Dad might think of Leonardo Davies-Villanueva.

"He'd be so proud," Mum whispers, answering his silent question. "He would have been *thrilled* that he was wrong. You playing for England, the pride of Camden—you could have held it over him forever. He loved you, Ollie, more than anything. He'd have given anything to watch you grow up."

"I can feel him with me," he says back, just as quiet. He can see his father on the touchline, watching all the many matches he's played in. He wants to go to him, even though it's impossible. "There's so much I want to tell him."

Nicola blinks the last of her tears away and nods insistently, shaking their joined hands in tune with it.

"He would have wanted to hear it all. And you know he would want to know every detail about all your love life. That's why I have to be nosy now, in his memory, you see. So who is it? Tell me everything!"

Her excitement slips over his skin like water, choking and drowning him. The voice in his head, the one who is beginning to sound suspiciously similar to Willem, asks: *Why have you never told Nicola?*

If she didn't know, Oliver replies bitterly, *then at least no one else has to be as secret-keeping and duplicitous as I feel, yeah?* It's something for him to deal with alone; he's not asking anyone to lie but Maggie, sweet Maggie, who's always been just what he needs her to be even when he can't be anything for her in return. And Leo. His Leo, who has stars in his eyes and no temperament for shame.

Nicola observes his silence, his lack of enthusiasm for the change in subject.

"Well," she says briskly but not unkindly. "Anyone who caught your eye must be rather striking." She rises from the table and touches his shoulder on her way to load the dishwasher, leaving him silent but feeling like a liar anyway. Nicola spoke so carefully, not a gendered pronoun in sight, no use of "pretty" or "beautiful," though Leo is of course both of those things. It would be so simple to tell her, even to allude to it. The opening is right there, a door swinging on its hinges. He can't do it. Mum doesn't press him, just lets him follow with the glasses, wondering why he's such a coward. When the kitchen's clean and he says good night, Oliver reaches for her so he can give her a hug, breathe in the particular washing powder and antiseptic scent, something comforting in his memory and in the here and now.

"I'll come to the Everton match, shall I?" she asks in the foyer.

"If you wanted, you could come to the derby instead—you'd be an away fan, at Kilburn, but I could get you a nice seat, we have a block in the away stand. No Rovers allowed."

"The great battle of North London," she says in a somber voice. "I haven't been in ages. Oh, there's nothing quite like it. I'll be there with bells on."

Oliver kisses her cheek and gives her one more hug, a nice tight squeeze, just because he can. Then he pedals away, he takes himself south of Regent's Park, bumping down the cobblestones all the way to Maggie's door, whacking the buzzer until he can hear footfalls on the stairs. She answers in her dressing gown, peeved and wreathed with cigarette smoke. He waves it away from them irritably, but when it clears, the hardness in her jaw makes him almost miss the stench.

"If you've shown up with bad news, please go home. I was in the bath."

"I meant to stop for flowers," Oliver says dumbly. "To bring you a bouquet, like."

"Ollie," she replies, sighing so heavily it shakes her shoulders, her beautiful features wan in the single flickering entryway light. "That's not your job. You're going to give my other suitors the wrong idea."

He probably deserves that.

"It's my privilege," he tells her, meaning it truly. "I wanted to tell you I'm sorry for being such a dickhead, and I wanted to do it in person, so you could slap me if you wanted."

"Ollie," she says again, but it's nicer this time. "You're always playing the martyr. It's fine! You're in the thick of it in a way I could never understand. I just wish you wouldn't shut everyone out over it. You make everything seem so lonely."

"I'm not lonely. Truly, Maggie, I swear to God."

Her face changes in an instant, exhaustion swirling into a rich tapestry of gossip and glee.

With Leo? she mouths. He nods assent and she squeals, throwing her arms around his neck and continuing to let out a high-pitch frequency. "You told him?"

"He . . . guessed," Oliver admits. "And it took a beat to, ah, sort things between us. But now it's good. I think it is, anyway. Complicated. I don't really know what I'm doing, I'm not sure I've ever felt like this before."

"Gee, thanks," she says. He grips her elbows, beseeching, and she forgives him with a returning squeeze.

"I don't know how to get anything *done,*" he admits, finally, for the first time. "I think about him all the time."

"You're supposed to, babes," Maggie assures him. "When you're with someone who makes you happy. He does, doesn't he?" He nods again, feeling the smile turn up at the corners of his mouth. He's never been happy before, not if this is what it feels like. "Oh, Oliver! You're growing up. I need to know everything. Do you want to come in, then?"

She takes his arm and tugs conspiratorially, the same way she's done since they wore primary school uniforms and gaps in their teeth.

"Honestly, I'm knackered. I need to sleep hard. I don't think I could talk about it even if I was awake. It's so much. I keep waiting for it to all fall apart."

"You're pessimistic when you're tired. It won't fall apart if you don't keep expecting it to," she scolds, but then rises on her tiptoes to kiss him gently on the cheek, one hand gripping his shoulder for balance so she can whisper in his ear. "You've always been the most important man in my life. It's about time you found the most important man in yours."

• • •

In the yellow hallway light of the hotel in Stoke-on-Trent, the most important man in Oliver's life is standing furtively outside his door, five rooms down from his own. Oliver leans against the doorframe, poking his head out to meet him. Leo's pajamas almost match the horrible hotel carpeting.

"Yes?" Oliver asks, casual as anything.

"Do you have an extra phone charger? I forgot mine," Leo replies loudly, standing at attention and beaming with pride at his ruse. Oliver rolls his eyes as he lets him in.

"Look at you go, James Bond. Cover story of the century, very sneaky." He kisses Leo lightly, just to say hello. Leo keeps hold of Oliver's waistband when he steps back. "I'm not going to let you fuck me," Oliver says definitively. "They call it *isolation* for a reason. With only goals to ponder, absence makes the heart grow fonder, and all that."

That's why Alec used to tell them they weren't allowed to text girls after midnight. It feels very grown-up to lecture someone else with it now, particularly a someone who he's very much attracted to.

"Wow, pervert," Leo replies. "Who said anything about sex? I just wanted to have a cuddle."

Oliver doesn't believe that for a second. He knows what it's been like, between them, recently: physically, the chemistry is a ceaseless revelation. Matching their steps stride for stride during training is as good as foreplay. When they're alone together, all bets are off. Since that blessed evening of the United match, Oliver has seen his bedroom from a hundred different angles he didn't even know existed before. Case in point, Leo is currently palming him on each flank, pawing, ravenous, at his hip bones.

"Jesuuuuus Christ." Oliver lets out a low whistle. Leo is a Renaissance painting, more intricate than the triptych of earthly delights Maggie once spent a whole month yammering on about. He wants him desperately, but he can't have him right now, not in a hotel before an away game, when the season still has its claws in them. Oliver can't bring himself to send him away, though.

There's so little time left, just a handful of matches—he's not sure how many more moments like this they'll have together before Finch discards them or they inevitably discard each other. Leo doesn't understand just how likely it is they'll look back on this as the end of something, but maybe he deserves to.

So when they've clambered into bed and Oliver has tucked the comforter up to their chins, sliding down the mattress enough to make them equal in height, he broaches the silence.

"Can I tell you something?"

Leo breaks the parentheses of their embrace, craning his neck backward so their gazes connect in the semidarkness.

"Shit, that's ominous," Leo whispers back.

Wednesday, May 10, 2017: Camden at Stoke City

MATCHDAY 35

The red lines on the alarm clock indicate it's just after midnight and *well* after when they should have been asleep, but instead they've been sitting upright and cross-legged for over an hour, poring over the league table and talking through the upcoming fixtures. Oliver might have known that telling Leo they've got a Champions League–shaped guillotine hovering over their heads wouldn't go down without further discussion.

"And you're sure Finch wasn't bluffing?" Leo asks for about the eighth time.

"I only know what Willem told me," Oliver repeats patiently. "But he looked spooked."

"Why fourth place? We could play in the Europa League with fifth. Why not start there?"

Oliver slumps back against the pillows and shrugs, rubbing at his scalp tiredly. Leo has a faint line on his cheek and the sleep-rumpled hair of someone Oliver would love to be spooning.

"Haven't the foggiest. I think when you're rich enough, the only things you can get off on are ultimatums."

"Be serious, Ollie!" Leo says. "They're going to sell you—they'll sack Willem."

"No one's sacked yet," Oliver insists. "All we have to do is keep winning. We're in fourth now and there's less than a month left. Four matches. Just stay where we are."

"But you're nervous," Leo accuses. "You're telling me this because you're afraid."

He probably deserves that, but it isn't true. Not in the way Leo thinks. He's not afraid of losing—Camden players have to get used to that early on. Oliver *is* afraid of being sent away and losing Camden. He's afraid that he's not sure what will happen even if they stay in fourth place and get another season. What will he and Leo be to each other once the league table resets? How long will that next season last, if anyone finds out about them?

"I'm not afraid. It's just . . ." He pauses, grasping for words that feel true. "I want you to understand the stakes." He wants Leo to know how precious these last matches are. He wants them to play together, as well as they can, for as long as they can.

Leo's eyes soften in the dim bedside light. Tentatively, he scooches back up the mattress and lies down facing him, then reaches out to smush his pointer finger against Oliver's lips. Oliver softly kisses his fingertip.

"You don't have to believe me. But *I* think we can do it," Leo whispers. Oliver wonders if he's talking about more than one thing. He hopes he's right.

• • •

Once, when he was properly little, probably too young to be expected to behave, his dad took him to the Proms. The music wasn't his favorite, with no words to follow along, but both Olivers had sat silent and rapt while they clocked the way every performer moved in tune with each other. That's what they're doing now. They're making some kind of music, conducted by Willem and accompanied by some power bigger than themselves. The midfield is afire, twin flames leaving scorch marks up and down the stadium. Even though the match is tied for a solid forty-five minutes, the Stoke fans draw a collective inhale of panic whenever numbers 6 or 16 take possession. Oliver can't imagine anything in the world better than this, discovering that the only feeling he likes as well as opening the scoreline himself is cementing a win by assisting Leo.

It's a gift he's giving himself, to see the pocket of space and move to it, stepping in time with his heartbeat, ball at his feet, then over to Leo with one surgical pass. Leo doesn't need any help with it once he's got it, that's for sure. The second it's in the back of the net, Leo reverses, sprinting back toward the team, toward Oliver. Oliver opens his arms to him and gets more than he bargained for, Leo leaping at him like a man possessed, sending him staggering backward with a heavy armload of boy.

"You brilliant fuck!" Leo shouts in Oliver's face, their foreheads stuck together. "I bloody love you!"

The words ring for a moment in Oliver's ears, but he insists to himself that they don't matter: everyone loves the person who sets them up for a goal like that. It's not the first time he's heard it from a teammate on the pitch; if he plays well enough, it might not be the only time he'll hear it today. He holds Leo instinctively, spinning them around deliriously like a sweaty, less-coordinated Fred Astaire while Leo anchors himself to Oliver's waist by crossing his legs and holding on tight.

There are twenty-five minutes left to run lengths of the long green lawn, but he never truly leaves the sixty-fifth minute, despite his best efforts. It's the heat of the moment, of the match, that's getting to Leo, making him say things that sound dangerous and different to Oliver than they would to anyone else. He keeps reminding himself: *It was about football,* while *Love you, love you, I bloody love you* plays in his head on repeat. Oliver talks a lot of shite in the media scrum after the final whistle, telling all the reporters how dedicated Camden FC is to the rest of the season, how pleased the squad is with their performance today, while his mind wanders, unbidden, back to the same words.

Leo, as the winning goal scorer, was also summoned for media duty, leaving them in a nearly empty locker room once they're finally turned loose. When Anthony steps into the hallway to call his wife, they're fully alone, just for a minute. Leo hasn't gone to shower yet, still sodden with sweat and stinking of it. He's sitting on the bench in front of Oliver's locker like he belongs there, so handsome in his kit. It was tailor-made to look good on him, as if he's been wearing it a lot longer than one season. Smelly or not, Oliver wants to knot his hand in Leo's collar and keep them leashed to each other. *He said he loves me,* he thinks, dazed at the memory. *He said he bloody loves me. Why did he say that?*

"What made you pick 16, anyway?" Oliver asks, to give himself something to do other than ask any of the real questions he has, tracing the smooth outline of the numbers on the back of Leo's shirt with one fingertip.

"Number 6 was taken," Leo tells him, all cheek and flirtation, flushing prettier than Camden's rose crest and looking back at Oliver with winner's eyes. When their gazes meet, though, something dark flickers over his face. Leo casts his eyes downward, then toward the door, then back at his feet. He's gnawing on his lower lip. "Oliver, listen, earlier, I was being stupid, the goal, you know—it was an amazing pass. But I didn't mean—"

"Of course not, mate," Oliver interjects breezily, at his most lad-like. Obviously, Leo didn't mean to say it. He didn't mean it at all. Oliver knows this. He only wishes Leo hadn't bothered to remind him of how ridiculous the notion is. Especially not in the locker room, where anyone could walk in. "It was a good shot, too."

He reflexively checks the doorframe again to be sure they're alone, Anthony still saying his own sweet nothings in the other room, so he can swoop down and kiss Leo's forehead, trying to finish everything he's saying with the brush of lips. From the frosted windowpane on the locker room door, they might be only huddled and whispering, offering each other congratulations. Oliver gives himself just one second anyway, to be safe, then pulls himself away.

He doesn't pull away later, when they've thrown their bags down in the hallway and gotten into bed, grinding against each other lazily in the way that could maybe lead to sex or just straight to sleep, somehow equally satisfying. Just when Oliver thinks the needle might be tipping toward sleep, Leo ratchets things up, pulling their faces close and licking at Oliver's jaw, then suddenly sitting upright with the same pace he brings to the midfield, coming up out of the pivot to start a driving run toward a goal.

Leo is looking down at Oliver through a haze, more of a silhouette than a man, but in the dark of his eyes there's something lit like a flame, a candle that won't burn out, tipping itself over and starting an inferno.

"Ollie," Leo whispers. He takes Oliver's hand and brings it to his cock, and Oliver loves the feel of him in his fist, like silk over stone. He twists his wrist, faster then faster still, and Leo twitches into it, following the motion with his whole body. Oliver wants to feel him everywhere, wants him inside and out. It's mad, only ten days since they started playing a far more dangerous game than football, but whatever they've said in words is being taken over by what they're saying with their bodies, earlier on the pitch and again right now. Something is slotting into place, like it's exactly what's supposed to be between them. They first met when he was in the downswing of his life and Leo was clawing his way upward, toward something, toward Oliver, toward Camden. Now they're meeting in the middle.

"I know," Oliver says, belatedly. He *does* know, how it feels, what it means. He dislodges Leo gently, turning over to his stomach and slithering downward, pausing to rest his forehead in the flat strip of skin at the edge of his forearm, kissing Leo's rib cage, imagining he can reach all the way to his heart with his mouth.

"Oh," Leo sighs, voice cooing then humming wordlessly. Oliver persists, licking a fat stripe across his chest and following through with his teeth, wondering if he'll leave a mark, if the dressing room will tease Leo for it tomorrow, only the two of them knowing just where it came from, just how it felt for him to receive it. Leo strains upward, body contorting itself for more contact. Oliver could drown in the feeling of knowing that Leo wants him like this, so much, all his own desires mirrored onto that gorgeous body, that handsome face. "Come on, Ollie," he says, so breathless it's like he's just run for a whole other match. "Are you gonna?"

Oliver breathes in the sound and the scent from where Leo's chest meets his underarm, clean sweat and expensive soap, closing his eyes to intensify all the other senses.

"Yeah, darling, yes," Oliver says. "I'm gonna let you in. Come here."

"Uh-uh," Leo gasps, straining against his embrace, bobbing at the waist in search of a return to Oliver's palm.

"No? You don't want it?" Oliver asks, feeling just how much Leo wants it, hard and insistent against his hand.

"I want you," he says.

"You've got me," Oliver promises.

"I want you to fuck me," Leo clarifies, throwing the arm Oliver isn't nestled against over his eyes, like he's overwhelmed in the same way Oliver is. Earlier he would've said no, it's too soon, don't say anything you don't mean, not again. Now, he can't think of anything he's ever wanted more, except for maybe on that first night when Leo kissed his shoulder blade as his body gave way to the impending stimulation.

"Okay, sweetheart," Oliver says, endearments spilling out of him. "Let me look at you, then, yeah?" Leo emerges from the crook of his elbow and blinks at him like he's staring into the sun. Oliver brushes one stray lock of hair off his forehead and watches the resulting brightness in Leo's eyes; his smile drives him wild, beyond reason or rationality. He turns Leo over, onto his elbows with half his face in the pillow, and when he tugs on his ankles, bringing him down the bed, Leo laughs so happily that Oliver is tempted to stop the whole affair and redevote his attention to causing that sound and getting to hear it.

"I thought you wanted to look at me," Leo says, muffled into the sheets.

"Trust me," Oliver replies, splaying his fingers across his sacrum, mesmerized by the shape of his big hand on the small of Leo's back, holding him perfectly in place without using any of his weight. "I'm looking. You look so good, Leo."

He keeps looking better, when he's pinioned between the sheets and Oliver's fingers, crooked just so, and then approximately four hundred heartbeats later, when he pushes in, one hand over Leo's shoulder and his lips behind his ear, Oliver is doing more than looking, making a noise like he's been shot and feeling the embarrassing, irrepressible pinch of tears in the bridge of his nose. *This is it,* he thinks, through the haze enveloping them both, fog rolling in over London and only covering one building on Regent's Park Road. *This is the happiest I'm ever going to be.*

"Oh, wow," Leo says helplessly, almost laughing on the exhale. "So that's what it's like."

"Getting fucked?" Oliver asks, rolling once on his haunches and seeing pops of light at the corners of his eyes.

"Getting fucked by *you,*" Leo moans. "Keep going, don't you dare stop."

Being inside Leo is the hottest, tightest feeling he's ever known; it's so visceral it's almost painful. Every thrust makes his legs shake. Leo clenches against him once, driving himself downward against Oliver and pushing his own cock into Oliver's waiting hand, and the slick heat feedback loop makes them both gasp.

"Stop that," Oliver says. "It's going to all be over if you keep it up."

"I *can't,*" Leo laughs. "It's too good. Give it to me, Harris, I know you can."

He could never back down from a challenge like that, and Oliver wants to give Leo everything; he's delighted to know that he can, that he's the only one who could, and that it's his privilege to do so. *God,* he loves fucking him, he loves the things they can do together with their bodies, what they can give each other when they move in tandem, just like they do when they're wearing Camden green. It's perfect and Oliver wouldn't change a single second of it, not even the fact that it ends after five minutes.

• • •

Leo's side of the bed is empty and unmade when Oliver finally becomes conscious, taking advantage of the rare off day by sleeping so late that by the time he wakes he's groggy and somehow exhausted all over again. When he goes to rub the sleep from his eyes, there's a sticky note stuck to his forehead. Someone, presumably the artist he keeps sleeping with, has drawn on the little neon paper an extremely unflattering portrait of what Oliver looks like while he's sleeping, including a cartoon speech bubble indicating snoring. There's also a ransom note reading *Make coffee first thing.* Stumbling downstairs in pursuit of the demanded coffee and maybe a kiss, Oliver spots Leo from the stairwell window, outside in the garden.

He's barefoot, wearing one of Oliver's old shirts, holding his phone to his ear with one hand and absentmindedly juggling a football with one foot. Oliver can see the morning dew clinging to every surface, can practically smell it, late spring and damp grass.

He makes two cappuccinos and seeks out another window, settling into the bench seat and keeping his eyes outside. Even from behind, he can sense Leo's smile from the way he's gesturing his free hand in time with the words, punctuating his sentences with each bounce of the football. Even when he's not in motion, his athleticism is undeniable; Oliver is struck by the differences in their bodies, compatible but dissimilar. Leo's frame is slight, but he's firmly built regardless: his leg muscles are larger than Oliver's, the center of gravity lower in his hips. Sometimes when Oliver looks at him, especially like this, especially when there's grass and a ball in focus, he wonders if he's actually gay or straight or nothing at all, maybe something else entirely: sexually obsessed with football. He wants to tackle Leo, wrestle him to the ground, and kiss him all at once. He's jealous of the strength in his body even as he wants to show off his own longevity, the lithe stamina in his height. How much of an overlap is there between desire and competitiveness, anyway? Is there a word for feeling both?

When Leo turns back toward the house and catches him snooping, he gives him an anxious look, like *he's* the one who was caught at something. Oliver holds up the second mug in explanation and Leo waves him down toward the garden reluctantly, as if Oliver needs inviting anywhere in his own house.

On the patio, Leo reaches for his coffee and greets Oliver with one sharp tug to the earlobe. Oliver saw it coming and tried to dodge, but Leo can be treacherously speedy, a tricky fucker when he wants to be, which is often.

"I got your note," Oliver says, rubbing at his ear. "Who was that?"

"My mum," Leo replies, licking a stripe of cappuccino foam out of his fuzzy morning mustache and rattling on. "That woman gets more done before noon than I do all week. You call your parents to brag about your incredible ascension as a professional athlete, and you know what they say in response?" Oliver nods, familiar with this feeling—Nicola's usually saved two or three lives before he's laced up his boots. "Dad says, 'You looked wonderful out there! Must run in the family, we've just run down to Patacona and done some laps in the sea.' "

Oliver can't help but laugh, vaguely picturing the parents that Leo described donning matching jogging shoes and running right into the Mediterranean, but Leo looks nervous still.

"You want to run to the coast, then?" Oliver teases, gently, hoping he can put them both in the same morning mood. "The Thames will put you in the sea eventually. Might make it back before the Sunderland match."

"Right, let's go, then. If you're game," Leo replies distractedly, until Oliver actually starts running for the back gate. This works: he can hear Leo in pursuit, so he relents and allows himself to be caught, a fair trade for Leo winding his arms around his waist from behind, tethering them back to chest. He lays one gentle kiss between Oliver's shoulder blades. "Let's stay here instead," he says.

"Hmm? And do what?" Oliver spins in the embrace, adding his own arms to the mix, so they're face-to-face and holding on to each other.

"Use the massage gun," Leo replies honestly. Oliver pushes him without force, sending him backward toward the house. As they approach the door, the question that's prickling at Oliver spills out, the one he's not sure he really wants the answer to.

"Did you talk about us? With your parents?"

Leo freezes on the top step and replies without looking at him.

"What is there to say? Have you told *your* mum how much you like my cock?"

"Jesus, easy," Oliver says.

"You don't have to keep testing me, Ollie. I told you I didn't mean it." Leo gives him a dark look under the stained-glass transom window.

"I wasn't trying to—I was just asking," Oliver sputters.

"You weren't," Leo says. "I get it, okay? I've got a lot to lose too, Ollie. Maybe more than you do. I'm not established, I'm not in demand. But it's hard for me to accept that the only way to have a football career is to lie. I told you I didn't want to pretend anything." He pauses, looking at Oliver like he's hoping for some kind of guidance or reassurance that he can go on. Oliver touches Leo's wrist softly, with the pads of his fingers, feeling for a pulse, and waits for more. "I mean . . . did you not ever think about just going for it? Telling a reporter and making it your thing?"

Leo said "your" but Oliver knows he meant "our." This is the question at the crux of everything, the one that will still need answering if next season ever arrives. Oliver considers it for a lingering, tiring moment. He can't stop thinking about the Southampton player calling him a faggot.

"Sometimes, yes. When I was young and foolish, when I thought I was more talented than anyone could ever afford to lose. But I'm nobody's boy-wonder anymore. I've tried to be and there's a losing record. I guess I've just never felt like it would help anyone more than it would hurt," he admits. He still feels this way, maybe more than before. It wouldn't just be him getting hurt, not anymore. It would be Leo, and Leo's right: he's got more to lose. Even in the worst-case scenario, Oliver can imagine the third-rate American club that pretends not to care about his sexuality because they just want to *finally* beat the other team from Ohio. He can't picture anyone making that kind of call for someone with half a season under his belt. Leo has so much potential, he's finally playing at the level he deserves to—Oliver can't be the one who takes it from him. He couldn't live with himself.

"I never even got to be a boy-wonder," Leo murmurs. "I'm just a boy-wasn't. But it has to be *someone,* sometime." Oliver shrugs uselessly, withdrawing from their connected hands and looking down at his own as if he could read his palms, before giving Leo a plaintive look. *Please don't,* he thinks, sending it telepathically. *Please let's not do this now.*

"It would kill me, if this defines your career, or fucks your chance to play in the Prem. I'm the older teammate, I seduced you, I'm gay. *You* could meet a girl someday. I don't want to condemn you to my fate. It would be a lonely fucking locker room, Leo. If we were in one at all. What would we even say?"

Leo shakes his head, brows furrowed.

"We'd say what it is! Or what it could be, I suppose. You make it sound like we've done something wrong. It's not a *condemnation,* Oliver. It's who we are. I've known I was, I don't know, queer, for a long time, so don't lecture me." Leo falters, voice shaking, then steps backward slightly, scrubbing at his eyelids angrily. "Ollie, I'd still be this way even if you pied me off right now. I don't want to meet a girl. I want you. Don't you want me?"

"I've told you," Oliver starts, intending to mollify, but Leo moves toward him like he didn't hear at all.

He kisses Oliver just like he did last night: wholly and wildly. It's so good, every time. If Oliver was strong enough, he'd push him away and keep on arguing; he's done it before. He can't now. He wants Leo too, he wants him too much. Oliver thought they'd solved this, or maybe that they'd decided there was nothing to solve, but he misread the play entirely, the attacking forward unmarked in the penalty box and him several paces behind, desperate and useless. He doesn't know what to do, but he knows he needs to do it tenderly, with the greatest of care. One last kiss, then he pulls back, but he keeps Leo's face between his palms, looking down at him so their foreheads bump, so they can only see each other.

"I want you," he insists, totally superfluously. Of course he wants him. "I don't know how not to. You make me feel—Leo, you make me crazy. It's everything else I don't know about that makes me unsure. Can you be patient with me? For now? Until we know . . . until the football is figured out."

Leo looks like maybe he'd like to forget football entirely and figure it all out right now, possibly with his fists. Oliver has the horrible sensation of disappointing him spreading like pinpricks down his limbs, the forgotten feeling he thought he'd cast off months ago.

"You're right," Leo concedes, closing his eyes tiredly but, crucially, not pulling away. "Of course you are. I'm sorry. I can wait."

Oliver blinks furiously to stem the threat of tears. He wishes he knew what Leo was waiting for; he wishes he could give it to him.

"I'm sorry too. I don't want to disappoint you."

Leo looks at him again and presses his thumb into Oliver's chin, tipping it down slightly so he can brush their lips together, more of a reassurance than a kiss. Oliver sags into the embrace; Leo holds him up.

"You're not. You're exactly who I want you to be," Leo laughs, shaking his head. "That's the fucking problem."

Oliver comes up for air, mostly so he can look at Leo again, and manages a watery smile.

"God, I'm fucking beat. You're worse than an away game, you are," he says. "Can we go back to bed?"

"Sofa," Leo replies. "Come on, make us another coffee."

Later, when the coffee's been drunk and Leo is snoring despite it, face in the sectional and feet in Oliver's lap, toes blocking half of the book Oliver can't seem to focus on, he counts Leo's exhales and thinks about how precious everything feels when it's balanced on a knife's edge, one heartbeat away from oblivion. Oliver wishes he could crawl down the sofa and join Leo in dreamland, where the laws of gravity don't apply, but he stays awake instead, keeping watch over him.

. . .

Camden's winning streak ends abruptly against Sunderland, only darkness falling at what they call the Stadium of Light. It hardly seems to matter that they're still in fourth place for how hard it hits Oliver; he'd somehow forgotten the feeling of losing, the helpless, guilty tang of it, all metallic in the back of his teeth. Every visitors' locker room looks the same, but somehow this one feels especially unwelcoming, gray-tinged and cold-tiled. Willem will give them a speech now, as a matter of course, and they'll have to unravel his metaphors and try to make something useful of them, translated into Sebastian's diagrams. Oliver is not sure if he has the stones to sit through it tonight.

Perhaps de Boer doesn't either, because he enters the room as unobtrusively as Oliver has ever seen him do anything. Willem takes a seat on the bench next to Joe, where he'd usually keep his feet at the front of the room, patting the keeper's knee sympathetically and telling him something quietly that actually wrings a wry chuckle out of Joe's sad, silent vigil under locker number 1.

The break from routine is a spectacle, enough so that the squad is at attention when Willem speaks louder, for all to hear.

"I told my two children, back in November, that I was going to accept a job here in London. My daughter Sophie yelled at me like I've never been yelled at before. Do you know what she said?" The room is silent, still dangerously close to sullen. None of them are quite in the mood to discuss Willem's family. Oliver is straining all the muscles in his face to keep his expression blank and all the muscles in his hands to keep from reaching for Leo, three seats to his left. "She said: I can't believe you'd rather get your shit rocked by Swansea City in the middle of nowhere in the freezing rain than go to the World Cup with the Oranje. I can't believe you'd leave us for some piece of rubbish team and not even ask what we think," he explains, over the rising tide of titters. "It's the only time in her life she's ever told me she hated me."

Everyone is bristling at the accusation. Willem doesn't seem to register it, like he's back in Amsterdam relitigating this choice with his family. Oliver has a sudden surge of sadness for Willem, who took this job under Finch's conditions and received resentment from the team in exchange, from Oliver especially.

"I've carried that around with me all season," Willem says, still monologuing to a difficult audience. "Was it hubris to think I could change our results this season? Am I not the father and husband my family deserves? This game can put a man on a lonely road. We play for our clubs and our countries, but we shoulder this responsibility we feel inside of us alone. It's that part of us that enabled you to get to this place, to this pinnacle of the sport, in the first place. It brought us here and it holds us apart from each other at once." The manager takes a rasping breath as if he wasn't quite expecting to confess all of this until now that it's flowing out of him against his will. Oliver finds he's been holding his breath without meaning to. "But we have to walk it together now. We have, this year, and we've been brilliant. So we go again. I want you to take in this match, what you did right and what you did wrong, and learn from it. We're in fourth place. That's where I've been told we must be for this project to be considered a success. I won't get another shot at it if we don't maintain this position. And I'm telling you now: I want another shot."

The dour quiet is transforming, crystallizing into something sharper and more defined. The magic number is in the room with them now, the truth of unspoken expectations finally put to words, but it's hardly the point. There's a rallying cry building up in all of them, awakened by some forgotten instinct. The win streak might as well still be intact. Oliver knows, clearly and all through his limbs, that they're going to beat Finch's odds.

• • •

On the plane home, Oliver crouches in the aisle next to Leo's seat, where he is not quite pouting but in the vicinity of it, pensive bordering on sore loser. Oliver wouldn't admit it, of course, but even that is attractive on Leo, the refusal to limply accept defeat sitting plain on his face, in the tightness of his jaw and the downward slant of his eyebrows.

"Shite match, good speech, hey?" Oliver offers, when Leo doesn't deign to greet him. He gives him a *look,* one that says, *Leave. Me. Alone.* Oliver ignores this and shuffles forward on his knees, settling his elbows into the hard plastic armrest. "You're very cute when you're angry," he says, as quietly as he possibly can. "You go on and brood, I'm no worse off for it. Just be ready to go again, okay?"

The drive to win, the competitiveness that vibrates in his bones and powers his lengthy strides, lives somewhere in Leo's body too. Oliver knows where to look for it and it makes him feel less alone. He always thought that his sexuality and the footballer in him, two core pillars of his being, were diametrically opposed. Now he's starting to think he can't have one without the other, that no one except Leo could look at him and see the sum of all the parts.

Leo's gaze goes from murderous to sheepish, then soft and sweet as custard. He slips his fingers around the zipper of Oliver's jacket and gives it a tug. Oliver can feel the affection come through the metal zip and layers of fabric. True to his word, he goes back to his seat and lets Leo do his thing, but if he leaves a part of himself holding vigil over seat 5A, that's between him and the flight attendant.

The coach rolls its way from Heathrow back to Camden Crossing and deposits them, exhausted and wound tightly, on the midnight concrete. Trevor is the one to eventually suggest they go inside to review the match, which leads to a pell-mell cluster of folding chairs and crossed legs around one of the conference room television sets. Finn manages to connect his phone to the screen and Sebastian's team has kept up the pace of sending footage as fast as the team can produce it on the pitch.

In the green light of the grass on the screen, Leo's dark curls look especially shiny. Oliver wants to bury his nose in them and let his mind go blissfully blank, but he contents himself with taking advantage of the dark office by reading Leo's feverish note-taking over his shoulder and toeing at his ankle bone repeatedly without anyone noticing. Leo's handwriting is rubbish, serial-killer style, but the notes are solid.

With twenty-two minutes left in the replay, Willem passes by the windowed far wall, holding what can only be a pack of cigarettes, which is very interesting indeed. They all look up in unison, the manager guilty, then pleased, when he sees the lot of them. Oliver gives him a toothless smile, just one quirk of the mouth. Willem doesn't interrupt or intervene, just nods smartly and continues on his way, so they can all get back to work.

"You think he'd let us bum a few?" Matty asks in a whisper.

"I'll tape your mouth shut," Anthony warns.

Leo looks less petulant when the replay ends, more likely to fall asleep on Oliver's shoulder. No one bats an eye when Oliver stuffs him through his passenger door.

"Still with us?" Oliver asks gently as they pull out of the Crossing.

"Mmmph. Tired. Are we going to yours?"

"If you like."

"I like." Leo sounds barely conscious, but Oliver needs him to listen while he says what he couldn't put words to on the plane.

"I don't like losing any more than you, all right?" he says. "But every match since I've come back—every match I've played with you, Leo—they meant everything to me. I wouldn't trade them, even the ones that were awful. You're so, so good. Better than I was at your age. I mean it." He takes one shuddery gulp of air, eyes prickling, streetlights flickering, letting all the tension out of his body and into the front seat of the Audi, between them.

"You're talking like this is the end of something," Leo says, shell-shocked and missing the point entirely.

"I'm trying to tell you that if it is, you're the best partner I ever had in the midfield."

"In the midfield . . ." Leo trails off. "And what about everywhere else?"

"Maybe everywhere else is less important," Oliver says firmly. "I want you to have the career you deserve, wherever it takes you. To be able to do it on your own, after this."

Leo is quiet, suspiciously so, for so long that Oliver finally dares to look at him to make sure he hasn't actually fallen asleep. When he does, Leo is shaking his head. Oliver wants to push, to ask what he's thinking, but he can't. All he can do is look down Regent's Park Road, stretching before him as solidly as ever, like it might take them all the way to the end of the season.

• • •

Everton, they of the stupid elephant mascot, are proving as solid as the pavement on Regent's Park, lumbering like a parade of their namesakes through Regent Road.

Oliver knows he's back to full fitness—the statistics and Anna's hamstring exams don't lie—but his limbs are leaden. The opposing squad's got their own version of Leo: a Spanish midfielder with sharp eyes and a stride that turns over lightning quick. He's faster than Oliver, skipping around him in the center of the pitch. Every time Oliver manages to advance into the attacking half, he's rewarded with a heavy shove to his midsection from one of the defenders, each one of them shaped like a thick column of bricks. Most of his energy is going into not entering the disciplinary notebook. The scoreline remains deadlocked.

Leo is taking a different tack, to put it tactfully. He's not necessarily provoking shithousery, but he's not exactly engaging in gentlemanly sportsmanship either. There's a glimmer in his eyes inviting mischief, a dare offered up to their opponents. It's, frankly, not dissimilar to the kinds of looks he's been giving Oliver the last few days: a challenge to push at the limit, to cross the line between what is and what's to come. Against Everton what's to come can only be some kind of violence. It bubbles over just as soon as the thought occurs to Oliver.

Number 25 reaches for the back of Leo's shirt, yanking him backward and away from the space he needs to receive a pass. Leo reacts instinctively, limbs independent from his brain, throwing an elbow back and making sharp contact with the other player's rib cage. In the next heartbeat, Leo's been shoved face-first toward the ground, the ball trickling, forgotten, across the damp grass as every green and blue shirt from both ends of the pitch converge on the scene. Oliver gets there first, just in time to hear some rapid Spanish being lobbed between the pair of them, Leo whipping himself back onto his feet, covered in dirt and foaming at the mouth with rage. Oliver is still monolingual, but even he knows, or can at least guess at, a rough translation of *qué maricón de mierda,* which is what the defender has pronounced that Leo is. Oliver thought having slurs thrown at himself made him crazy—foul-tempered and violent—but this is another level; he could fuck someone up, really hurt someone, for talking that way about Leo. There's a lot of that going around, apparently; Leo shouts back, something too fast for Oliver to catch, and the instant it's out of his mouth, his opponent is winding up to land a punch, ready to accept a red card in his haste to knock out Leo's teeth.

Oliver is there in the nick of time, stepping between them and absorbing the closed fist at his shoulder, staggering backward at the force of it but saving Leo's cheekbone from the impact. It gives Oliver the excuse he needs to puff up at the chest, holding himself broadly and clenching his fingers into a ball, ready to get in a blow of his own. The referee has other ideas, as do all their teammates, who are arriving en masse, shouting and shoving until there's a twenty-two-man horde at the edge of the sideline, tempers aflare like a forest fire.

There's a bright red card in the ref's hand already, held up to the sky with a flourish, his other hand pointing menacingly at the man from Everton, who throws up his own hands in defeat and exits without ceremony, not even bothering to protest. Oliver shouts when he pulls another card, this one yellow, gesturing at Leo.

"He got fouled!" Oliver hollers, unsure if he's arguing as a vice captain or for Leo specifically. "You can't book him for not getting punched."

"Harris, I'll book him for those elbows, and you'll thank me he's still on the pitch," the referee replies coldly, palms facing out, a demand for return to order that every footballer knows is a last warning.

Anthony has one sleeve of Oliver's kit in his hands, Leo has the other, and he's being pulled backward, back toward the match.

"Sodding fuck." He can't help himself. "Bullshit."

"Come *on,* Ollie," Anthony says. "Back to it. Channel that rage somewhere productive, would you?"

"And you!" Oliver snaps, ignoring his captain and whirling around on Leo. "What are you playing at, picking fights? What did you say to him?"

Leo shrugs innocently, fruitlessly wiping at some of the mud he's accumulated on his shirt.

"I just asked if that didn't make it worse, that his mum still likes it so much."

Anthony bellows, a big belly laugh in the middle of the damn match. He's still chortling, shaking his head, as he jogs his way over to the back line, resetting Camden's formation.

"Jesus Christ," Oliver says, not only at how impressively foul that is, but at the idea that Leo might ever fuck anyone's mother.

"Don't worry," Leo reassures him. "It was before we met." Then he, rather cheerily, gives Oliver a businesslike slap on his left arse cheek and gets back to work, backpedaling toward his place at the left of the midfield. It figures that Leo would score the game winner, eighty minutes in, like he planned it all along and was just biding his time for maximum effect. Trevor curled in a keen shot, rolling hard and fast toward the net, and Leo finds it with his left foot before the keeper gets anywhere close, guiding it through to the target.

He's the reigning prince of Regent Road, mop-headed and

gorgeous, blowing kisses to the fans, who receive them like tangible things, cupping them to their cheeks rapturously. Oliver half-worries he'll get possessive or jealous, but the only feeling he can put a name to, besides the swirl of lactic acid turning to ache in his calves, is pride. Everyone should adore him, be in awe of Leo's particular pitchside charisma, the way Leo meets the wave of the game's rhythm and flips it inside out, crashing onto an opposite shore.

When the final whistle blows, they have precisely five minutes to stand before the crowd and drink in the victory. Then they'll have to truck back inside and start thinking about Sunday's derby. Oliver personally usually approaches Kilburn matches in terms of inflicting maximum embarrassment with as little consequential violence as possible; the stakes are more nuanced this time, requiring a more formed strategy than the base, primal hatred that fuels him when he thinks about Stewart Reed and company.

Leo loops back from performing a complicated handshake with Ahmed to where Oliver is giving Trevor a mighty hug. Leo ducks his head shamefacedly.

"Trev," Leo says, joining the embrace briefly. "I owe you one, mate. Your shot was probably going in anyway, but I just wanted to make absolutely sure. I didn't mean to poach."

Trevor scoops Leo up like he weighs nothing at all, throwing him over his shoulder like a sack of potatoes.

"You little shite," Trevor bellows, laughing. "Mooch! Thief!" The rest of the squad takes the cue to teasingly heckle Leo, booing and tossing their discarded, smelly kits at him as they pass by. Trevor puts him back down, but squires him under one arm for the walk back. "Nah, you're golden, Davito," he tells him magnanimously. "You want to win so much it's inspiring. Frightening, too. Harris has enough of the scary eyes for both of you, okay?"

"Ah, I've just learned from the best," Leo says, smiling sweetly in Oliver's general direction from under Trevor's bicep.

Willem sticks his head into the showers, a disembodied face through the thick puffs of steam, and congratulates them in one breath and informs them their presence is requested at Camden Crossing forthwith in the next, signifying the celebrations are to be fully on hold until after the derby. It suits Oliver just fine, because Camden Crossing has the canteen, and the canteen has chocolate milk, plus that one old squishy leather sofa, which under the right circumstances he could absolutely fall asleep in sitting upright.

At the meeting, Oliver gets his preferred seat next to Joe and somehow manages to stay awake, Leo sitting on the sofa arm he claimed for himself way back in January, at his first training session, back when Oliver didn't know the difference between a crush and a nemesis. Everyone is slowly starting to disperse; when most of them have, Oliver takes the stairs to Willem's office, half on a whim.

There are a cluster of de Boers inside: two pretty teens who are perfect matches for Willem in looks, alongside another, older woman who's holding the manager's hand. Oliver sticks his hand out to shake and is suddenly gripped by the fear he'll be expected to dispense cheek kisses, which shocks and frightens his English sensibilities, before he's saved by a warm, firm grip from Willem's wife, and a series of giggles and whispers exchanged between the two sisters.

"Girls," their mother and father say in unison. The girls adopt identical, serious expressions, though their eyes shimmer with identical mirth. All four of them are well matched—cashmere clad, honey blond, and beautiful.

"I'm Ilse," Willem's wife introduces herself. "Our daughters, Katja and Sophie."

"Oliver," he says, indicating to himself stupidly, as if they might have been confused. "I've heard a lot about the three of you. It's nice to meet—"

He's cut off by the renewed teenage giggles, Katja and Sophie clutching at each other and shaking with it. Willem gives them another sharp look and they sober themselves, one of them nudging the other forward.

"We've heard a lot about you too," Katja-or-Sophie says, which makes Oliver decidedly nervous. What has Willem to say about Camden, about London, about him?

Before he can ask, Ilse lays one elegant hand on her husband's arm.

"We should go soon, if we want to see the house."

"Too right you are," Willem says briskly. "Girls, go on with your mother. I just have one email to send, I promise. If I speed, I'll beat you there."

The three of them shake their heads together, disbelieving but forgiving, like they've heard it before. Ilse swoops upon Oliver and gives him a series of dreaded kisses that he actually doesn't mind too badly when it comes down to it. Sophie and Katja shyly offer him a simultaneous hug—he takes it gladly.

The three of them leave Oliver halfway in the doorframe, unsure if he should stay while Willem sends the email or follow them at a respectful distance.

"Close the door, would you?" Willem asks, answering the silent question. Oliver slides into the old chair across from the desk, a perfect mirror of nearly every conversation he and his coach have ever shared. "They're touring Cambridge and Oxford," he says, pointing his chin out toward the hall his daughters are walking down. "And Ilse wants to buy a house. We're all hoping to be based in England next year." It's weighted, the understanding of the cost it took to get the de Boer family to this point, together, and the chance that it might not come to fruition after everything. Six months ago, it would've been unthinkable to him, but now he's sure that what Camden needs is for Willem to return next season. "But those are just an old man's wishes. What's on your mind, Oliver?"

"I honestly can't remember," Oliver laughs, mostly at the idea of Willem thinking he's old. "Just checking in, really." Willem smiles, leaning his cheek into one hand, propped up on the desk by his elbow. Irresistibly, Oliver pictures his father, the blurry, nine-year-old memory he has of him. The mention of Oxford and the look on Willem's face when he talks about the twins lead him right to it. Willem is a father the same way he's a manager: strictness and indulgence mixed, high expectations you cherish instead of resent. It's nice, nicer than Oliver ever thought it would be, to look at someone and think of his own father. He was just a sprog when he started thinking, with his whole heart, that his team was his family, but this is another dimension entirely.

"Well, meeting you will have made their day," Willem replies, blue eyes darkening gray. "Soph has got quite a crush on you, and I don't think it's just about your football."

"Ah, gaffer," Oliver says, mortified. "You don't have to worry about that with me." Willem gives Oliver a sharp, strange look, protracted and contemplative; he has the sickening sense his protestations might say more than he meant them to. Before Willem can reply, Oliver stands, scratching at the back of his neck. "I'll let you get to your email, sir."

"Very good work today, Harris," Willem replies evenly.

• • •

The house is not unoccupied when Oliver arrives, which would worry him, except there's only one burglar who would stop to turn on Frank Sinatra while he's ransacking the place.

"You're doing that wrong," Oliver tells Leo, who is in trackies and putting plates in the dishwasher backward. He sets his phone and his keys down and starts to help. "Did I know you were coming over? Please tell me you didn't break a window."

"Power of observation," Leo replies distractedly. "Your passkey is not secure."

Oliver gives up on the dishes, sighing and crowding Leo front-first into the counter so he can slip his arms around him, pressing them back to chest and nuzzling into the soft skin where neck meets shoulder, but Leo is still and unmoved beneath him.

"Not feeling it?" Oliver asks. There's a first time for everything, he supposes.

"I need to tell you something," Leo says. He's holding on to a plate like he might break it.

"Yeah?" Oliver prods. "Go on, then."

"He was right," Leo says. "Number 25 was. I am a *maricón. De mierda,* too. A real piece of shit. And we almost lost today—I really thought for a second we might."

"Davito," Oliver says. Leo had played it so cool out on the pitch, so much better than Oliver did when it happened to him, but it was an act, he can see that now. Of course it was. "That guy was out of order, you know he was. And we won because of you."

"That's not what I mean." Leo wriggles free and turns to face Oliver, then changes his mind and moves across the kitchen island. "Please, just let me say this."

"Okay," Oliver says cautiously. "I'm listening."

"I am actually in love with you." Leo's cheeks are red and his eyes are dark. He's looking at Oliver like no one ever has. He's saying beautiful, insane things. "I wasn't chatting shit when I said it before. You are . . . Oliver, I love you, I can't help it. I've been—since I got back here, since the moment I saw you again—I've been falling in love with you. Even when you were being *such* an arsehole to me. I wanted you anyway. I thought I wanted to be you, when we were younger, in the academy, but now I know, I just want to play with you, to be with you, be by your side. You drive me absolutely mad. I keep waiting for it all to be a dream. And I—I can't wait anymore. It's not casual for me, and it never has been. I want to win tomorrow, and I want to stay here, because Camden is my home, and you're more Camden than anything. But even if we don't finish fourth, I'll still want you. I had to tell you that before the derby. While I still have a chance." Oliver can feel the weight of the words like a pressure around his windpipe, just as breathtaking. He wants to say, *Don't, stop* or maybe *Don't stop,* but he can't speak. "Say something," Leo says.

He was stoic before, but he's begging now. Oliver wants to give Leo what he needs, he wants to give Leo everything, but he doesn't know how. And suddenly on the tabletop next to them Oliver's phone is buzzing and displaying a picture of Anthony. He fumbles for the screen despite himself, trying not to look at Leo's face, which is now looking resolutely downward.

"Just give us a second," he pleads before answering the call. "Captain?"

"Ollie boy," Anthony greets him tiredly, sounding about a century old.

"What's wrong?" he asks, anxiety spiking. Leo's head perks up slightly, like a dog smelling danger. Leo starts to step away, toward the door, until Oliver catches his sleeve in his hand. *Please,* he mouths. Leo doesn't respond, but he stops moving, looking downward, away from Oliver, and screwing his eyes shut.

"My bum knee." Anthony doesn't need to say anything else—Oliver knows immediately. It's bad news and it's not likely to be fixable. Anthony wouldn't call him like this, after a match, right before another, more important one, unless he needed help. "Anna says I won't play next year if I don't stop now. I might not anyway." There's resignation in his tone; he knew this was coming as well as the medical staff. "Our season's not done, but mine is."

"Hell" is all Oliver can manage at first. "Anthony, I'm so sorry."

"I don't need you to be sorry, you prick. I need you to be captain. Can you do that for me?"

It's in the job description of vice captain to fill in when the armband needs somewhere to rest, but this is heavier than a usual substitution. It's the last match, their last chance, it's a derby, it's fucking *Kilburn*. Everything is on the line now and the Rovers are across it. He remembers, again, the Manchester City draw, his first game of the year, the match where he played with Leo for the first time and ruined everything by pretending he didn't feel what he felt, when Willem listed all those names to frighten the team, but instead it woke them right the fuck up, which was probably his plan all along. Oliver has to do this. The rest of it has to wait. He can't be whoever Leo was just talking to; he has to be the captain, has to belong to Camden alone, not to Leo, not even to himself. He has to answer Anthony now; he doesn't have the right words for anyone else.

"Of course I'll do it," Oliver says into the phone, but he's looking at Leo's stricken face while he says it.

"You don't really have a choice," Anthony says, half-joking. "But I'm glad you see it that way."

"How do you figure this shakes out?"

Maybe he's captain for now; he still needs Anthony, steady back-line Anthony Moss, to help him make sense of the world around him.

"There's three ways out of this mess," he says. "Maybe we stay in fourth, no harm done. Possibly we could drop to fifth or sixth. Mathematically, we could end up in third. It all depends on how Chelsea and United play."

The trick of that is that all the matches will start at the same time, as is tradition with the final schedule of the season. Camden won't know the scoreline they need, because it will be determined in real time, while they're going scorched-earth mortal combat against Kilburn.

"We'll say a prayer at halftime. Then we'll fucking win," Oliver says into the phone, willing himself to believe it as simply as he's said it. Leo has finally looked up from the floor and now he's staring at Oliver with his jaw clenched. He's fiddling with the rosary under his shirt and nodding like he's trying to believe it too.

"You might need to give a bit longer of a speech than that, Ollie," Anthony replies gruffly. "Listen, I have kids to put to bed. I'll be with you from the bench, okay?"

Anthony hangs up without letting him say goodbye and Oliver takes the phone down from his ear slowly, almost disbelievingly.

"I'm sorry," he mumbles to Leo. "I don't know what to—"

"You don't have to, Ollie," Leo whispers back, the words punched out of him. "I understand. I could hear. This week, it's for football. You've gotta be the captain."

"But—" he starts.

"It's okay," Leo insists, slowly and deliberately. It must be, because he's touching Oliver, one tentative hand at his waist. "Please don't say anything else. Just—let me stay?"

Oliver couldn't send him away even if he wanted to. He nods and pulls at Leo's wrist until he's back in close and Oliver can get his arms around him, for however long he's still allowed to.

Sunday, May 21, 2017: Camden at Kilburn

MATCHDAY 38

The coach trundles its way through traffic, stopping and starting for the whole section of the city that separates Camden and Grange Park, home of the Kilburn Rovers and thirty-two thousand of their most devoted supporters. The further they get from Camden Market, the more the neighborhood changes, dark green giving way to burnt orange, the footpath crowds growing ever thicker and more antagonistic. June is looming: the Premier League season has carried itself through every kind of weather and now, as it arrives at its end, it's coated with high stakes and high temperatures, the sun beating down in a way that leaves everyone drunk faster than they expected, angrier faster still. From the tinted window, Oliver can see the throngs of fans following the same road to the stadium, promenading down the warpath in perfect rhythm. Every time their coach overtakes a new group, the mob mobilizes, stopping to jeer and shriek and throw things. The chants they lob at them are impressively varied and universally profane, surprising even Oliver, who thought he'd heard them all.

"Good God," Finn says, cupping his ear to the windowpane. "I think that one's to the tune of 'Claire de lune.' "

"They're always creative," Noah admits, not unimpressed,

watching the great iron structure of Grange Park grow larger and larger in front of them.

The din extinguishes itself, thankfully, once they're underground and changing into their kits. All the crisp visitors' white starts to replace their suit jackets and pleated trousers, until they've swapped one uniform for another. Oliver tries his absolute hardest to shut out the roar of his own thoughts while Willem points an uncapped marker at squad lists and various formation drawings, but his head is somewhere in the atmosphere, looking down on derby-day London and trying to make sense of it. Joe drifts from locker number 1 to number 6 so they can sit next to each other, knocking their knees the same as always, beating a familiar tattoo between their bodies.

Willem gives them the gift of silence, leaving the room twenty minutes before it's time to assemble for warmups.

"They're going to keep shouting at you," the manager calls back to them from the hallway. "Enjoy the quiet while it lasts."

All of them start to turn inward the same way Oliver is, engaging in the intricate rituals of preparation, somewhere between superstitious and spiritual: lace the left boot first, comb your hair off your face, try to believe in God, but only until you're sure he's heard you.

Anthony would normally be preparing to give a pre-match speech, but he's silent, still in his suit. Oliver looks over at him once, twice, for some kind of confirmation or maybe encouragement, but all Anthony does is meet his gaze with an unblinking stare, inclining his head once like a benediction.

When Sebastian yells "Five minutes!" from the next room, Oliver knows it's now or never, maybe the last time he'll ever wear Camden colors, the final afternoon he'll spend with this group of people, playing football together. He can't bring himself to look at Leo, dressed for his first-ever derby, or he'll lose his head completely.

"Listen," Oliver says, clearing his throat and standing on shaky legs. His teammates obey, turning toward him, all eyes on the captain's armband, but he's lost for all the words he practiced in the shower last night. "Garcia, you have to stay low and cover the center—without Anthony, they're going to try to press the full backs first, so you'll shore it up and then they won't be prepared if Woodsy or Matty move things up from the flanks." He meant to be inspiring, a leader of men, but his pulse is thrumming a thousand beats a minute, the tactics spilling out of him as easy as breathing, the only things he knows how to say. "And, Trev, stay close to me—I'll play end to end, but I don't want us exposed in the pivot, because we've given Garcia enough to do." He tries to start again, but he stammers, looking wildly at each of them, trying in vain to commit their faces to his memory perfectly. "Lads, I just . . ." Oliver trails off. "You know what we have to do, don't you?"

Lukas, sitting to his immediate right, reaches out and grips Oliver's calf muscle, holding on for dear life.

"I hear you, captain," Georgie says in a serious baritone, the gravest tone he's ever used, and everyone nods and whistles in agreement. Someone starts a drumbeat of feet on the tile, clacking away with their boots until any words that might occur to Oliver would be drowned out anyway.

"You're ready?" he asks, knowing the answer in his heart. Oliver doesn't need to say anything more: they knew what his speech would be, they know what he means, and they've already heard him a thousand times before. "Then let's go do this."

Pitchside, the light is blinding and the noise is deafening. Warming up is like trying to perform surgery in a sensory deprivation chamber. It awakens something primal in Oliver, the sheer competitiveness that's at the core of him, his desire to win even overtaking his desire to play. He's not scared of Rovers, but they sure ought to be frightened of him. When he meets Stewart Reed at the center of the pitch with the referees to shake hands, he's looking at him through narrow, dark tunnel vision.

"They're just letting anyone wear the armband over there?" Stewart says out of the corner of his mouth, eyes narrowed as he tries to crush Oliver's fingers under his knuckles. Oliver is surprised to find himself unfazed, seeing Stewart and only feeling a sort of amused pity at the state of him. Kilburn will do their damn best to thwart them, and there's every chance they will, but it's impossible for them to overtake Camden in the standings—for all the rivalry, the meaning of the derby aflame around him, Oliver knows they've already won something, and he transmits it through his grasp to Stewart's damp palm.

Kilburn wins the coin toss and then the first good spell on the ball. Oliver was right that they'd push hard down the middle, trying to throw Camden off-balance without Anthony anchoring the back line, but Ji-Hoon keeps running them down, sending Loxley rolling about the grass and calling for a foul more than once. Oliver keeps to his own word, playing the whole length of the pitch, tackling and attacking in equal measure. After twenty-five minutes, Camden goes up two goals. Still, it's a tight match, and it goes back and forth, back and forth, gritty and stroppy and long. The team is buzzing at halftime, but in an exhausted way. There's something to be said for needing to maintain versus hoping to disrupt; when they return to the field, Kilburn is salivating and whooping, buoyed by the screams in the stands, and Camden is stooped and sweaty, guzzling from their water bottles.

"How are the other scores?" Oliver asks in between dumping the tepid leftover water over his head, trying to cool down enough to reset his heart rate.

"You don't want to know," Sebastian replies. "United is up and Liverpool is down. Chelsea put three past them."

"Christ alive," Matty swears from Sebastian's other side. "They couldn't make it easy on us, could they?"

"We're up ourselves," Leo says stubbornly, pausing from adjusting his shin guards obsessively to look up and glower at them. He's been playing hesitantly, without his usual verve, chewed up and spat back out by the rivalry and the quarter meter his roving counterpart has on him in height. "Can we go get this done?"

"It's the derby, Davito," Matty explains, paler by the second, waving his arms around at the palpable hostility in the atmosphere. "And two-nil is the most dangerous lead in football."

He's prophetic in that way, dooming them all. All of Oliver's disdain for Kilburn dries up in the hot sun when they start throwing him around like they mean business. The match is unfolding fast and furious around him, rapidly slipping out of his control, before he's suddenly gasping for air in the intervening seconds between the referee calling for a corner kick and Stewart Reed setting himself up at the far end of the stadium to take it. Stewart's already got one, so did Loxley, and when the ball reenters their orbit the scoreline is three to two, Kilburn in the lead, Karim Ahmadi heading it home. It's the seventy-fifth minute and they've given up the lead and then some, all their plans and Oliver's attempts at speechmaking ground to dust.

Oliver doesn't have a choice, so he keeps running; Willem is tracking him from the sidelines, yelling, impossibly audible over the din: "*Do not let up, do* not *give up—Harris, do you hear me?*" Oliver wants to listen to him so badly his heart might give out from trying.

When the linesman holds up a number 7, so much stoppage time—they've been fouling each other with such frequency it feels like the match stops every minute—Oliver is so tired that a huge, weak part of him wants to ignore Willem now. But he can't, because he can't stop thinking about his debut, muddled with the way Leo looked at halftime, how the feeling of his first derby enveloped him then tossed him to the bench with a red card to his name. He felt so small and so lonely, all those bright lights blinding him. As Oliver forces himself to a sprint, digging into the well of stamina he's honed his whole life, moving back up the pitch now, following Garcia's metronome rhythm, he can see it all.

He feels every person he's ever loved and every minute he's ever played inside of him, holding him up like a puppet on strings. His dad, somewhere, he hopes, his mum in the away stand cursing like a sailor, Maggie chiseling a block of marble with Sky Sports blasting in the background, Joe behind him, omnipresent in the net, and fucking Willem, part of every move Oliver makes with a football now, even when he's not welcome, presiding over his life, and Leo. Of course Leo, who he wants to share everything with—this especially—regardless of whether they win or lose. Willem was wrong after all. Nothing can hold them apart from each other, not any longer. This is all Oliver's got, for the next seven minutes, for the rest of forever, this is what he has to offer: his left foot and his heart. He wants Leo to have them. He loves him, he has all along. He should have said it a thousand times already, but he's going to prove it now.

Everyone is with him as he moves up the pitch. Oliver wants to win for them. Reflected in their eyes he can see the kind of man they believe him to be looking back at him like a mirror, wearing an armband, one that reads *Camden FC*. He's going to become who he's meant to, and he's going to thrash the Kilburn Rovers right into the fucking sod. Garcia passes to Oliver and he takes off again, ducking and weaving, vaguely aware that he's dribbled right through Diego Ojeda's legs, the crowd groaning at the sight of it, seeing the penalty box appear, stepping into it, still in possession, staring the keeper down, ready to shoot, ready to put them back at level ground, ready to score.

It doesn't happen like it should—nothing ever goes to plan, certainly not in football.

Someone's tackled him, body colliding right into his lower half, tangling Oliver's legs and forcing him into an overextension, then down to the ground, tumbling until he skids to a stop, sprawled inelegantly like a chalk drawing of a corpse. There's a familiar, devastating pain coming from his left thigh. He can already see the beginnings of a bruise dotted above his ankle, a perfect recreation of the studs in Max Wheatley's boots.

He's dizzy with pain, head rattled and the stadium warping at the edges. Wheatley is gesturing to the ball defensively, Stewart appearing at his side to plead their case to the ref, while Emmanuel yells on Oliver's behalf, out of view.

"It's a penalty, Mr. Reed," the referee is saying calmly. "Don't play stupid. Clear goal-scoring opportunity. I'm not going to send him off, all right? So you take that and calm down."

There's still spitting and cursing happening from both sides somewhere above him, but the world has narrowed itself down to the sharp hurt and to Leo's familiar, beloved hands, reaching for Oliver's shoulders and pulling him up to sitting, crouched over him protectively.

"Ollie," Leo whispers miserably. "Please be okay, you're okay, you're okay."

"Hey, you," Oliver replies dazedly. "You teach Wheatley how to tackle like that?"

"Don't," he hiccups. "Come on, you've got to get up."

"Leo," Oliver says, taking his face in his hands, all the game's urgency evaporating, overtaken by the need to explain this to him, cupping his palms around velveteen red cheeks, skin to skin. "I've got to go see Anna. I can't take this penalty."

"Don't *say* that," Leo replies, clutching at Oliver's wrists and holding them in place. "There's no time, there's no substitutions—come on, we have to do this."

"I know," Oliver says. "*You* have to do this, okay? Can you do it for me, for us?" He knows, as solidly as he's ever known anything, that this is what Willem would want, what Anthony would do in this position. He also knows what Leo can do on the pitch—what he *will* do—for Camden.

"No, I fucking can't," Leo hisses, voice rising anxiously, shaking his head, their entwined bodies moving with the motion. "I can't, Oliver. Ask someone else, I'm not ready." Leo pulls away, starting to stand, but Oliver tugs him back down to his knees, pressing their foreheads together. He feels like he's already been given pain medication, all woozy and drunkenly insistent.

"It's for you," Oliver whispers, bringing his lips in close to seal them in secret for one brief moment. He can't help himself, he kisses Leo's face, the side of his nose, the curve of his cheek, just above his mouth, once, twice, then again. "It's all for you, Leo. You are ready. I love you."

"You what," Leo breathes, speaking directly into Oliver's mouth.

"You heard me," he replies stupidly. His leg fucking hurts. "I love you. It's supposed to be you."

"Oliver, I swear," Leo starts, but the others are arriving, breaking the spell between them, reaching for Oliver to lift him up.

"I've got you," Garcia and Ji-Hoon say in unison, fashioning their bodies into crutches on either side of Oliver. He'll allow them to make him get up now, he's said his piece. Leo follows them, still shaking his head, terrified.

"Sebastian is coming," Garcia adds. "We're going to walk you to him and he'll get you off to Anna."

"I want to watch," Oliver says stubbornly, hopping on one leg. "And Leo needs to take the penalty." Over his head, their teammates are nodding, no fear in any of their eyes; Leo hasn't missed a spot kick in training since March and he's the damn breakout of the season, he's played his heart out this year, better than Oliver has. "Jiji," he says weakly. "Take this and make him take the kick, please."

Sebastian has arrived, red-faced, and they're handing him over, as Oliver holds out the captain's armband.

"Davito, you're up. Come on," Ji-Hoon says confidently as he accepts the little strip of cloth, stepping into captaincy like he's channeling Anthony's spirit. He pulls Leo into a brief embrace, shaking him gently by the neck like he's physically knocking sense into him. "It's just like practice. You've got it, you're going to smash it."

Sebastian hauls Oliver the whole way to the bench, even his right foot barely touching the ground, neck twisted to keep an eye on the proceedings while the Kilburn defenders and Camden's squad assemble themselves in a messy clump. Leo has deigned to listen to the rest of the squad, if not to Oliver, and is now carefully placing the ball for a penalty kick while the keeper hops madly from one foot to the other, arms extended to his full, gargantuan wingspan.

"Doctor, Oliver," Sebastian is saying, tugging on his sleeve as if to continue on to the dressing room. "Come on."

"No way," he replies, shrugging him off, balancing on one leg, shielding his eyes from the sun and watching, still watching, unblinkingly. "It's almost over." For once in his life, Sebastian doesn't argue, only puts an arm back around Oliver's waist to steady him. Willem is a few paces to their left, hands clasped together almost in prayer, surveying the scene silently. Oliver sticks his free arm back behind him without turning and Anthony appears, like Oliver hoped he would, to join their trio and also help hold him up. "I couldn't even make it ninety minutes," Oliver says quietly.

"You did enough, Ollie," Anthony tells him, both of them still looking straight ahead.

The whistle blows, Leo moving in slow motion, his left leg thrown gracefully behind him, winding up to unleash the power of his body onto the goal. There's a collective inhale, thirty thousand strong, as the shot progresses, then an exhale, split unevenly between relief and grief, when the keeper snags it between his fingertips, holding the ball tight to his chest.

Willem ducks his head into his shirt collar, eyes scrunched tight, as Sebastian abruptly releases Oliver and stomps back toward the bench, pinching his nose in concentration. Oliver is strangely calm, all the tension in his body released, close to laughter, shoulders shaking uncontrollably.

"Keeper's off his line," Oliver whispers to no one in particular, though everyone in earshot looks at him askance. "They're going to retake it."

Sure enough, the referee is waving away the jubilant Rovers, saying the keeper moved too early, and gesturing Leo back to the spot, pointing repeatedly at the ball and shaking his head as Stewart Reed shouts at him, ugly mug twisted with rage and disbelief.

"Wizard," Sebastian says quietly, staring at Oliver in shock.

"He's going to make this one" is all Oliver says back, more sure of it than he's ever been of anything. Leo is petrified in the spotlight, jaw tight and mouth half-open, looking between the ball and the goal as if he's not sure they're real, then turning his head toward the visiting team on the touchline. Oliver isn't sure if he can see him clearly, hear him at all, but he takes one wobbling, achy step forward and calls out to him, just as he did during Leo's first training session, five months and a lifetime ago. "Just one more, Leo! Take us home!"

Their teammates, standing from the bench or encircled behind Leo on the pitch, all chime in, clapping and hollering as he sets himself once more. It's more of a mind game than a physical one now, the mental fortitude required to deduce where the second shot will go or how to put it on target again. Oliver remains sanguine, watching the wonderful lines of Leo's body take shape. He's cheeky to the last, stuttering his steps when the whistle goes and he advances forward, before taking exactly the same shot as before: hard, low, left. Without the false start, it's no contest at all.

Oliver catapults himself, one-legged, onto Anthony before anyone else seems to register they've scored—Leo's scored—Camden has tied the match. When it hits them all, Anthony takes off running, Oliver still hanging on to his back, flanked by every reserve and the coaching staff, racing full tilt across the field toward Leo, who has slid forward on his knees with his arms thrown skyward, the dictionary definition of triumph, the rest of Camden FC sprinting in his wake.

Kilburn is fit to be tied, screaming for more time, but seven minutes has come and gone, the match is over, the clock stopping and the scoreboard reading three and three. All the draws that killed Oliver this season, the ones he considers losses, are dust in the wind compared to this feeling, the sweet sensation that's almost better than victory for how closely they snatched it from the jaws of defeat. *Fourth place,* he thinks. *Not too fucking shabby. Davies-Villanueva with the penalty.* He loves the sound of it, even only in his own head.

Oliver hasn't even gotten to Joe, much less Leo, for congratulations. He's still hobbling out of an unexpected, tight, full-body embrace from Marcos when Woodsy lets out a roar, snatching a phone out of one of the physio's hands.

"United lost! They bottled it!" A good chunk of the squad half-climbs over each other to get to him and get a look, squinting at the tiny screen while Woodsy's shaking hands pull up the highlights.

"God, they're shite, aren't they?" Joe says, then hollers to the whole team: "They fucked it! United lost!"

They're still in a huddle as Woodsy searches again, this time for the Chelsea-Liverpool contest. "Four-three," Woodsy breathes. "Liverpool came back. They beat Chelsea."

Someone shrieks while someone else makes a grab for the phone; Oliver has slumped right to the ground as if he's been reinjured *again*, seeing stars. It's impossible, it's bedlam, but it has to be true, or else he wouldn't feel this way, like he's being reborn. He would've given anything to be fourth; he hadn't bothered to dream about third. The sun is slipping under the edges of the ironwork, coating them all in brilliant pink light, and all the screams in the stands have died out, Rovers unwoven.

"Dear God, we've killed Harris," Finn is saying, hoisting him back up by his armpits. "Come here, you idiot. It's good news. Third place!"

"I know, I know," Oliver repeats, stumbling on his exhausted legs, salt water dripping off his nose. "I just can't believe it. Davito? Where's Leo?" Finn hands him over, Joe pulling Leo to them, depositing 6 and 16 into each other's arms. Leo smells rank and his hair is collecting blades of grass like the beginning of a bird's nest. Oliver has never loved something so dearly as he does right then, never looked at anything and known it was his and perfect and for keeps. He pulls some greenery out of Leo's headband and bundles him into his chest, squeezing tight. "I told you. It was for you," he tells him.

"If you didn't mean it," Leo says, muffled, into the crest of Oliver's kit, "don't tell me until later."

Oliver is no longer weeping the delicate, manful joy of a winner; he's unleashed a biblical flood from his eyeballs and his nose, wailing into Leo's head and making him even filthier than he already was. He wants to tell him how proud he is, how much it means to be with him now, but anything additional in his heart would probably literally kill him, and he's not even had a party about this yet.

"I meant it" is all he says.

Leo wriggles himself free and gleefully socks Oliver in the shoulder, once, twice, thrice, and it hurts and it feels so good.

"You are a madman," Leo laughs, eyes damp. "And you need to go to the doctor."

• • •

In the end, Oliver didn't even make it out to celebrate; by the time Anna had finished looking over his leg he was ready to drop dead from sheer sensory overload. From the exam table, he'd seen a suspicious champagne stain on her sweater, which set him to giggling uncontrollably, even after she swatted him with her stethoscope.

"It'll be okay. No recurrence of the tear at all, you just gave it a good strain. Well, Wheatley did," Anna said. "Nothing to worry about, Oliver. Take two weeks of vacation before you start your unhinged summer running plans. I won't tell Willem."

Leo, on the other hand, did make it out for at least one round of antiseptic-strength vodka sodas, because Oliver can smell it on him when there's a midnight knock on his front door.

"What happened to my passkey not being secure?" Oliver asks, tucking his hands into the top of the doorframe and leaning against the side, showing off just a little, all stretched out in nothing but pajama pants, putting himself on display.

"Things were different then," Leo replies. "I was sober. Are you going to let me in?"

"What's in it for me?"

"Let me show you," Leo says, but he hardly needs to, because Oliver doesn't want to playact anymore and is pulling him in by the collar, grinning.

For a moment it's just like that first night, kissing in the foyer, and it feels good in the same way it always does, Leo smudging his top lip with the tip of his tongue, Oliver pressing into the gentle rasp of Leo's stubble against his cheek.

"There's so much I want to say to you," Leo whispers, up on his tiptoes, into Oliver's ear like he's telling a secret. They're giving their weight to each other and swaying with it, holding each other up. "But I don't think I can do it in English. I'm . . . well, Garcia was pouring my drinks."

"It'll keep," Oliver says, intimately familiar with what that means, but Leo buries his face in Oliver, hooking his chin over his shoulder and holding on tight, and keeps talking.

"*Siempre quiero estar aquí, contigo,*" he says quietly, muffled into the warm skin over Oliver's scapula. Oliver can't understand what he's saying, but the words sound so sweet. "*Cuando me tocas, es diferente a todo lo que conocía antes. Te quiero. Sigo amándote más.*"

Me too, he thinks. *Whatever you feel, I feel it too*. Oliver wraps his arms around his waist and Leo follows his line of thinking instinctively, letting himself be lifted and twining his legs around Oliver's hips. Anna said not to run, she never said Oliver couldn't lift anything, so he carries Leo up the first flight of stairs.

He presses them against the wall in the hallway, halfway to the sitting room, but as far as Oliver can go without having Leo. Flush together like this, he can feel every inch of Leo, all of their similarities mirrored against each other, muscle for muscle. He wants to stay like this forever, or at least until it's time to play football with him again.

Leo turns around, palms flat to the wall, hips angled outward, like he's offering himself, and Oliver wants to look at him, but maybe not quite as much as he wants to touch him, plastered along his back and kissing Leo's neck. Leo fumbles for his jeans and Oliver follows suit, slipping out of his pajamas and palming himself once, then tucking his leg between Leo's, pushing into the hot, warm skin between his thighs.

"Ah," Leo groans, touching himself in time with Oliver's rhythm. "God, I don't want to wait. Please, I want to feel you come."

That's about all it takes, hearing the low rumble of desire in Leo's voice, knowing that Oliver's pleasure makes Leo feel good. He gasps and gives himself over to it, riding the hard, pulsating sensation until he's spent with it. Beneath him, Leo moves for a moment more, then whimpers and goes still.

"Every time we've done this," Leo says, panting, "I thought it would be the last one. Maybe someday I'll get used to it, but— I just kept hoping it was real."

"It was, Leo," Oliver tells him, squeezing one hand at his hip. He leans forward and kisses the first part of Leo he can reach: the side of his temple. "It is real."

Everything is still so very real in the morning, miraculously so. Leo followed him into the shower, naked and smiley, and Oliver's been luxuriating in the steamy feeling of holding his damp body up against the tiled wall. He ignores a persistent buzz of his phone on the countertop, dedicating all his focus to tonguing at Leo's collarbone and feeling the resounding, gratifying tremors along his upper thigh in response. All the congratulations and schemes for day drinking can wait until he's done with this, the single most urgent thing in the universe.

Another ring joins the echoes, Leo's phone lighting up as if in response to Oliver's. Leo looks distracted from his kissing, looking over his shoulder to try to spot the screen.

"I'm doing some of my best work here," Oliver sighs.

"They both keep ringing!" Leo protests. "We're going to miss the party."

"*This* is the party," Oliver sighs, but releases Leo so he can tiptoe, dripping water everywhere, to the edge of the bath mat and check on the missed calls. "Huh. It's my agent."

"Mine too," Leo says. "Think they want us to sign lifetime contracts?"

Oliver rolls his eyes and hits return call.

"Hello?" a harried voice answers. "Oliver? Hold on a second, let me patch in the others."

"The others?" he asks, but the line turns to jazzy hold music. Next to him, Leo's phone vibrates once more and he makes to pick up his own call.

"*Diga?*" Leo says to whoever's on the line, while he gives Oliver one confused purse of his lips.

"I have Nina Clarke, Willem de Boer, and James Finch," Leo's agent says over speakerphone. "Hold for Oliver Harris and team."

"Oliver?" the first voice says over his own phone. "We have the whole group now."

"Hi," he replies nervously, taking one reflexive step away from Leo so the acoustic feedback doesn't give them away. "What can we—I, I mean—do for you?"

"Well," Nina says, sounding exhausted. "I'm sure you've seen the news. We're sorry to bother you with this today, but after talking with your management and leadership at Camden, we do think it might be necessary to make a statement, just to head things off before there's any more speculation or press."

"The news?" Leo breaks in, shaking water out of his ear like he's misheard her.

"Have you not seen?" a tinny, faraway-sounding version of Willem asks. "Leonardo, Google yourself and call us back on this line."

"Harris, you too," Finch's thundering voice adds.

Then there's a *click*.

"What's gotten into them, you think?" Leo asks. Oliver shrugs, too nervous to speak, flinging pants at Leo and taking the stairs two at a time, hopping to avoid his still-sore left leg.

He mashes at remote buttons until it turns on Sky Sports News, standing arms akimbo directly in front of the television, heart racing as the images make sense of themselves, nausea roiling when he starts listening. A charcoal-suited pundit he vaguely recognizes is sitting lazily in a high-backed chair, giving a righteous lecture. Floating next to his head is a picture of Oliver himself, on the ground in his away kit, forehead to forehead with Leo.

"Listen, this is *just* outrageous. Anyone who knows a thing about football knows that Camden FC and Oliver Harris are one and the same," the man is saying. "He's just gotten them to their best finish in his lifetime, after a campaign many people counted them out of last year. This is the biggest moment of his career! His return to form! He's the captain with Anthony Moss out, but he can't take the penalty. So what he needs to do here is prepare a teammate for the biggest moment of *his* career. Harris is bucking him up. He's being a leader. And now what? Both of these men are going to have to taint this moment, this season, by issuing some kind of . . . statement about their sexuality! It takes away from the results, for me. It's disrespectful."

"But you have to admit, it does look a bit strange," another man across the panel is saying, pointing to the photo assertively. "And there were photos late last night, I don't know if you saw—"

"Disrespectful, if you ask me," the first one repeats, belligerent. "Off the mark entirely. Nothing gay about it. Wrong to suggest there is. I won't comment on any of the other rumors."

The image in question blows out, filling the whole screen. The picture looks so private, so out of place, Oliver would almost be shocked, if he hadn't experienced it for himself yesterday. The way they're looking at each other—it's too much, it's so unbearably intimate. Oliver is holding Leo's face in his hands while Leo clutches at him, then the image shifts and Oliver's mouth is on Leo's face, he's kissing him, they're almost kissing each other. It's markedly different than even those loose boundaries of affection the pitch will permit. Somehow, everything they feel is captured in the pixels, real and visible.

Oliver slams the off button and hurls the remote, venomously, out the nearest open window and into the garden, satisfied by the plastic crunching noises of something shattering and breaking beyond repair. For good measure, he goes to have a kick at the couch as well, but when he turns around, Leo is teetering at the bottom of the stairwell, deadly pale and completely silent. All the violence in Oliver's body drains out, puddling on the rug.

"Hey, hey," Oliver says, stepping toward him and opening his arms. "I'm sorry, that was childish of me. Are you all right?"

Leo only shakes his head tightly, biting his lip and squashing his eyes closed. Oliver tentatively holds Leo by the hip bone, suddenly unsure what's allowed, what can be seen, even here in this room where they've been so easily, happily intimate. He wonders, distantly, frightened, if anyone can see them now. Then his own phone buzzes *again,* making him wish he'd thrown it instead.

"What?" Oliver answers through gritted teeth, uncaring who's on the other end.

"Oliver," Nina says, "I'm sorry. I know this must be difficult for you."

It is difficult, but not in the way she thinks. Oliver is so outraged he could spit at everyone's reaction to this, especially his own.

"What can I do for you all?" he replies.

"It's just me," she says tiredly. "I told the others you both might be more comfortable if you weren't facing the half–Spanish Inquisition. Leo's here too." Oliver looks at Leo, who is indeed holding his phone an arm's length from his head like it might bite, and thinks, *You have no idea*. "If you'll let me put on my comms hat," Nina is saying, "I think what might make the most sense here is if the team issues a statement swiftly. We want to keep the two of you out of it as best we can, let the club protect you both from the brunt of it. Basically, my thinking is in line with what a lot of the media are already saying: it's inappropriate speculation and it's off the mark. Footballers are allowed to be close on the pitch without anyone asking if there's an underlying sexual nature behind it. Does that resonate with you?"

Oliver is nauseous again, phantom alcohol from the celebrations he missed turning to bile and threatening to make a reappearance. Nina is right, it is inappropriate, only because it's no one's business, not because it's insulting to wonder if someone might be gay. He and Leo can play together and celebrate together without it being vulgar, without it being sexual, but there's nothing vulgar about their sexuality. The statement makes it sound like they're denying the remotest possibility of queerness, like the idea of it is offensive, like it never even occurred to anyone at Camden FC that it might actually be true. Oliver has no idea how to express any of this without coming out over speakerphone, and he feels guilty and wrong-footed that still, even now, he's not sure if he wants to, if it would be possible to survive the experience. He chances a second glance at Leo, who is edging away from him, further into the living room, his lower lip quivering like he wants to argue or cry, or both.

"Let me think about it. Can you set up a meeting in person? This afternoon? Same group from earlier?" Oliver speaks quickly, not even bothering to wonder if it's okay to speak for both of them, if that's how it sounds to Nina or to Leo.

"Of course, Oliver, look out for an email from me. And, genuinely, I'm so—"

He never learns what she's so; he hangs up so he can take a deep, shuddering breath, letting out the tiniest of cries. Anger and terror fistfight in his diaphragm, leaving worse bruises than anything Kilburn caused yesterday. The twin urges of self-protection and discontent are at war within him. His instinct says *Deny, deny, deny,* but he hates the idea of propping up the homophobia simmering in that statement, of agreeing with those stupid, has-been bellends on his television. All Oliver wants is to know what Leo feels, where his head is at, but when he looks at Leo he can't get a read, the back of his neck is inscrutable, the rest of his body nearly catatonic with worry.

"I feel so naive," Leo whispers, pulling Oliver out of his head back into the room with him. "When I asked if you ever wanted to go for it . . . Ollie, I had no idea it would feel like this." It does feel like that. Oliver can hear the chants now, every away stadium yelling: *Men go down in Camden Town.* "I'll do whatever you think is right," Leo goes on. "I'm sorry, I didn't understand before what you were afraid of. What people would say. You were right."

But Oliver knows he was wrong, or at least he isn't right any longer. He can't tell this lie, the explicit one, said aloud through a mouthpiece.

"I have to go," Oliver says, glancing down at his phone again and texting furiously. "Nina is going to send a time for the meeting. I'll see you there, okay?"

"Wait, Ollie, please—can we talk about this?" Leo reapproaches him, beseeching, reaching futilely for Oliver's arm, but he's already halfway out the door, reaching for shoes he'll have to put on in the street. "Please don't go."

"It's going to be okay. See you shortly. Don't worry. And don't look at Twitter again," Oliver says, without looking back.

Anna said to take his vacation, to be careful, but he can't wait. Oliver needs to speak with Willem and he needs to do it now. He does the ride in under six minutes, biking through London faster than he ever has, standing upright on the pedals and practically running his way to Camden Crossing, past the Lock and the Pirate Castle and over the canal.

On the threshold, Oliver freezes. He doesn't want to run headfirst into incident command; he certainly doesn't want to talk to Nina and Finch. His feet carry him to the locker room, for a chance to catch his breath, but when he pushes through the door, he finds what he's looking for.

Willem is standing in the center of the room, surveying the empty metal shelves worriedly. When de Boer turns to him, eyes full of concern and affection, Oliver is gripped by the urge to go to him and ask for a hug. Instead, he starts talking.

"Willem, it's true." His manager starts toward him, reaching out as if to take his hand, but Oliver shakes him off. He has to say it before he loses his nerve, because when he shuts out all the noise in his head, all the reactions to this, one thing crystallizes into a cogent thought: all he wants, still, is to become the man he's meant to be—as a player, as his father's son, and as the person Leo chose. Maybe he'll only be that if he steps forward as the man he already is, the one who knows the only thing he loves enough to not risk giving it up isn't Camden Football Club anymore; it's Leonardo Davies-Villanueva. "It's all true and it's all my fault, it's on me. I came to put in a transfer request. Can you help me? Will you protect him?"

"Oliver, why don't we talk about this," Willem says slowly, like he's negotiating a hostage situation, but not necessarily as if he's been given a great shock.

"I am talking, I am," he spits, shaking with it. "*I did it*—I did what you and Finch asked of me, didn't I? The last time we finished in third place was the same year I was born. Did you know that? More than a quarter fucking century. You said he would sell me if we didn't get to fourth. So here we are. We're *third*. It's actually everything I dreamed it would be, being this good again, playing like I have this spring. If it's the last thing I ever do as a Rose, it will have been worth it, to play with him, to play for you. I love him, Willem, and you were right—we're a match made in heaven, everywhere, not just out there. And I want him to have the world, I want him to be the face of this club. It's his turn now. I don't need any of it, I just need him. So if we can't play here together, I'll go if I have to. You can sell me like you were supposed to. But please, *please,* Willem, don't punish Leo for what I dragged him into."

De Boer doesn't respond, only looks at him seriously and waits for further outbursts, except Oliver is all out of words. He sinks, shaking, onto the nearest bench and rests his forehead in the heel of his hands, taking deep, unsteady breaths. A moment later, he feels Willem settle beside him, then one warm palm is resting between his shoulder blades.

"I'm not going to punish him. Or you. You haven't done anything wrong." Oliver thinks he knew that, except hearing Willem say it feels like a tremendous relief. "Does Leo know you're here?"

"He might," Oliver hedges. "He doesn't know why. He'd try to stop me."

"Someone ought to," Willem tells him matter-of-factly. "I'm out of my depth, Oliver, but I swear to you I'm trying. You got us far better than fourth place, you did what was asked of you. I will not allow you to be shipped off for it."

"You don't have to," Oliver whispers miserably. "You don't owe it to me."

"Maybe not. Maybe a manager doesn't owe his players anything outside of that pitch. But I feel that I owe you something. I owe you this."

"Why?"

"Because you've looked after Camden since you were too

young to know how much was being asked of you. Now someone needs to look after you. I'd like to be the one to do it."

"How?" Oliver can't stop asking one-word questions. His brain is only supplying him single syllables at a time. He thought he'd have to argue more. He thought he was giving everything up so that Leo would never have to, only now Willem is saying Oliver doesn't need to either.

"It's not my place to say. That's for you and Leo to decide," Willem is now rubbing careful circles onto his back.

"But what do you think we should do?"

"Do you know what I would have done, this winter, to get you to come to me for advice? My God, I had no idea what I was getting myself into." Oliver groans and Willem chuckles wryly. "It's easy for me to say, so you might tell me to fuck off, but in life there's no way out but through. If I were you, I would tell the world they saw what they saw, you aren't sorry for it, nor is Leo, and neither is the club."

"Come out with it? Are you having a laugh?" Oliver says, suddenly serious again. "Willem, they'd fucking crucify me. We'd never play again in the fifth division, forget the Champions League."

"Not if we tell the team first and they stand with you. What could they do, relegate all of us?"

"Since when do you fancy yourself a mind reader?" Oliver asks slowly, like he's talking to someone concussed. "You're sure they'll just all conveniently be okay with it? You think everyone will be chuffed for us? Have you heard the way footballers talk in the locker room? About gay people?"

"You're Oliver Harris," Willem says. "They'd stand with you over anything. I told you: where you go, the team will follow."

This takes his head off completely. Oliver bursts into ugly, racking sobs, intermixed with the hysterical laughter of someone whose world is being unmade and reshaped in real time.

He's cried more this year than in the whole of his life put together, even counting the months after they buried his dad. If Willem is wrong, the club is doomed, the whole miracle season wasted. If he is right, Oliver has spent his whole adult life suffering in silence when maybe he didn't have to. He turns to his left and collapses into Willem's steady, waiting arms—already held out for an embrace—and lets it all seep out of him, boneless and held aloft by the strength in the manager's body. They stay that way for a good long while.

Eventually Oliver's voice returns to him and he asks the last nagging question, the one that makes this plan seem foolhardy, even when explained in Willem's authoritative Dutch rumble.

"What good would it do, anyway? Say we keep playing, what changes? Or we get run off and everything is just as homophobic as ever, another nice fat warning for anyone else who ever thinks about coming out?"

The accusation joins them on the bench, wedging itself between Oliver staring at the floor and Willem lighting an illegal cigarette, dutifully smoking it in the opposite direction when Oliver glares at him.

"Would it be terribly cliché for me to talk about Cruyff?" Willem asks.

"Yes," Oliver answers immediately. "Do it anyway."

"He told me a story once, before I signed for Atlético. I wish I could call him now, you know? He would tell you exactly what to do and you would believe him immediately. You'd have no use for me at all." Oliver rolls his eyes and gives Willem his full attention, turning toward his smoky mouth and sitting cross-legged, listening with his whole body. "The way he explained it, when his son was born, he decided to call him Jordi, after the patron saint of Catalonia. Fitting, you know; it was while he played for Barcelona. But in those days, Franco was in power in Spain, and it was illegal to use the local language. At the hospital, they told him, it has to be Jorge, you need to use the Spanish name, that is the law. And Johan insisted, 'My son is from Holland, not Spain, so I'll name him what I like, and his name is Jordi.' And so he was: officially registered as Jordi Cruyff on his Dutch passport."

"So you think we should adopt a kid?" Oliver asks, deadpan, and Willem smacks his knee almost affectionately.

"I *think,*" Willem goes on, pointing the cigarette at Oliver like one of his whiteboard markers during a halftime lecture, "Johan would tell you that it's not your job to fix it all, but it is your gift and your great challenge to keep hold of the spot you've earned, for football, for yourself, for the man you love. He would say there's worth in any attempt to stand in truth, in righteousness. The first Catalan name registered in Barcelona in years, can you imagine? That certainly didn't depose Franco, but no one else could have done what Cruyff did and gotten away with it. Only he had that power. No one else can do this now but the two of you. And that means something. It might mean everything. To me, I think it does."

Oliver thinks it over for another quiet spell, imagining what it would be like to take this secret out of the locked compartment of his heart and wear it on his sleeve, written as plainly as number 6 is on his back. What would it be like to be all the things he already is, at once, none of them swapped in and out?

"If Leo will have me, if he wants to do it, then we should. I don't want to leave, mind you. I was just trying to be noble," he says meekly.

Willem hoots a big laugh, slapping Oliver companionably on the shoulder.

"Oh, he's smart. He'll do what he needs to to keep you. Sometimes I've had half a mind to remind Leonardo that there are nine other players on the pitch, not just you and him."

That makes Oliver blush, roses on his cheeks, because he's

had to remind himself of that too. Maybe if Willem had yelled at them about it, they might never have been photographed looking like they were in love and this conversation would never have happened. Oliver can't bring himself to wish that was the case anymore.

He and Willem must have been sitting there, talking and thinking, for more time than they'd realized. Willem is still smoking when Nina sticks her head in the door and sighs at the sight of them.

"There you are! Willem, honestly, where did you run off to? We've been waiting for ages! And, Oliver, when did you get here? Leo's just arrived. Could you both come with me? Now! And put that cig out, Willem, for God's sake," she snaps when both of them look at her blankly instead of immediately jumping up and following her out the door.

The coterie of people from the morning's conference call are all milling in the hallway, besuited and whispering. Leo stands out and apart, two paces closer to the door in one of Oliver's old baseball caps, the very face of misery. They lock eyes and, before Oliver can speak, Willem emerges behind him and Leo's features go blank, jaw agape. Leo pushes past Nina and their agents—sliding behind Finch without so much as a word—and snatches Oliver's sleeve in his fist, then yanks the pair of them right back into the locker room, kicking the door shut behind them with an air of finality and an audible slam.

"You arse—" Leo starts, but what kind of arse he is Oliver will never know, having flung his arms around Leo's waist and picked him up off the ground, kissing his slack, shocked mouth for all it's worth.

"Leo," Oliver says, once he's put him back to his feet. Now it's Leo's turn to interrupt, with his fist, landing a pretty impressive hook with his nondominant hand, catching Oliver right in the gut and knocking the wind out of him—not an unfamiliar feeling where Leo is concerned, albeit a slightly more painful version.

"Don't kiss me," he says.

"Hey!" Oliver exclaims back. "Don't *hit* me!"

"You deserve it," Leo hisses. "*Hijueputa!* I will not be broken up with through Willem, you fucking coward, so go ahead and say it to my face."

"Listen to me," he insists, catching Leo's clenched hand before it strikes him again. "I'm in love with you. I know I'm slower on the uptake than you are, but I'm here now, I swear. We're not going anywhere, unless you want to, and if you do, then we'll go together. Leo, Leo, Leo—" His name sounds so good, Oliver wants to say it over and over. Instead, he keeps talking. "I'd rather let Wheatley have another go at my hamstring than break up with you, right? I want to do this, I want to do it for real, I want to do it forever. I've never loved anything like I love you, not even football, because it wouldn't be enough anymore, not if we aren't playing together. I want to spend my career and my life with you. I love your stupid nose ring and the sound of your voice when you speak Spanish and your perfect fucking face. You are it for me. On the pitch and everywhere else."

"Ollie," Leo says, voice breaking.

"It's all going to be okay, I swear to you," Oliver says, sliding down to his knees and clutching Leo around the legs, which has the added benefit of leaving him out of range of future punching, just in case. "I told Willem, too. Some of it, at least. But I thought if he sold me, you could stay and they could just blame me, call me a creep or a bad influence."

"No," Leo starts to protest, but Oliver is into the rhythm of it now and he can't shut up.

"He doesn't want me to, though. He wants us to come out, publicly, like. We can stay here, Leo, we can stay at Camden. He said the club will stand with us. He can explain it better than I can. Do you trust me?" Leo nods, blinking rapidly and saying nothing. "Come on, then," Oliver whispers. "I love you."

Leo doesn't reply, but he does pull Oliver back to his feet and kisses him, up on his tiptoes with his arms around Oliver's neck. Then Leo allows himself to be led by the hand out into the hallway, where everyone is diligently ignoring their previous outburst, nodding hello like they've just shown up.

Oliver will probably never remember the conversation that follows, since he only hears it all through the filter of the roar in his ears. But he was right that Willem could explain it best, weaving a tale that leaves him feeling faint, unsure if it actually resembles his life over the last six months or has been embellished for maximum impact. At several points someone asks, "Is that true, Oliver?" or says, "Oh, you poor darling," and Oliver can't say if he even responds. Somehow, they're moving easily into discussing logistics and timing now; no one has yet said Oliver is immoral or going to hell or destroying the stock valuation, even though Finch's face is taut and closed off. Nina is taking notes with a slightly manic smile on her face, reminding them that everyone should arrive for the press conference by noon and saying she'll confirm there's enough space for guests to watch from an adjacent room.

"It's decided, then?" Willem asks, like it's as simple as the lineups for five-a-side. "Oliver and Leo, you're prepared to speak tomorrow?"

"I mean, yes? If that's okay with Leo, of course," Oliver adds, finally finding his voice usable again and only slightly terrified of the answer. When he turns to face Leo, he's looking at him like he hung the moon. "Is it okay?" he asks in a whisper. Leo responds by throwing his body at him, hard, the kind of embrace usually reserved for heroes returning from war. Oliver holds on tight, letting Leo bury his face in his neck.

"Er, sorry," Leo says when he finally pulls away and seems to remember they're in a room with their bosses. "I, well. Willem and Oliver said it all. I want to do the press conference. I want to tell the truth. And the truth is that I'm in love with you, with Ollie."

James Finch, billionaire and incredibly likely Tory voter, surprises them both by finally nodding in agreement.

"What a story this is!" Finch says not quite emphatically, like he's trying to convince himself in real time, talking with exclamation marks included. "Optically, this is the only option. Imagine what the press would say if we didn't keep you. Not to mention, imagine what the table would say next season."

Oliver is not so sure he needs or wants Finch's support, coming so cynically, after this season, but he'll keep taking his paychecks, no problem. Finch releases them and turns back to Nina, asking for media strategy documents, leaving the two of them a pace away from the rest of the group, Leo still holding Oliver about the waist like he couldn't be removed with any amount of force. The business end of the operation is proceeding full speed ahead and they're alone on the train platform. When Oliver nods toward the door and Leo shuffles toward it without letting go, no one tries to stop them.

"I brought my bike," Oliver says, once they're out in the sunshine, still attached at the hip.

"Yeah, I noticed, when you bolted out of the house and I thought you were riding away to go and get me sent back to Spain," Leo tells him blithely.

"You know that's not how it went," he pleads. "Don't tell people that's what happened, please." Leo hums noncommittally, but the purse of his lips suggests he's holding back laughter. "You take a cab," Oliver continues. "And I'll meet you back at mine in a spell?"

"I love you," Leo says again. Oliver is getting the sense that Leo's been trying not to say it for so long, now he can't stop. He feels the same.

"I love you, too."

He heads for the bike rack aimlessly. He could beat Leo home on two wheels, easily, only there's no rush anymore, no urgent need to solve a season of football or a scandal: he's on vacation, he's just another person who lives in Camden. Tomorrow he'll put everything back on the line and tonight he wants to be home with Leo, make him dinner and suck him off like a gentleman, but for the length of the path down into Regent's Park and back home he wants to be alone, so he can test-drive being the version of Oliver Harris who has no secrets. He walks the whole winding path once, twice, again, wheeling his bike along with his headphones in, passing the swaying narrowboats and the burbling fountains, the footbridges and the perfectly clipped hedges and the trickling waterfalls.

Home looks different, almost saturated, like the world has more color or maybe he's just using more of his eyes than he was ever allowed to before. He's well sprung, done a bunk, freedom as sweet as anything he's ever tasted, besides Leo's mouth. The truth is still making itself known within him: the self-protection he'd always cultivated and craved is nothing if it traps Leo, if it holds him prisoner in a separate cell. And if there's a microphone in his face asking Oliver to say he doesn't love him, he couldn't lie, not on pain of death. It's *not* on pain of death, because they're going to continue on as they have been, right after they tell the truth. He's going to wear green next season. He's going to be a Rose. They both will. Oliver could scream, he could call the BBC, he could swim the Channel without taking a breath.

"Oliver," someone is saying from behind him, a sharp inhale. He turns, expecting to need an escape, worrying it might be a photographer. It's not. It's his mother, walking fast and wearing scrubs.

"Mum," he replies. "What are you—"

"I just finished my shift," she explains breathlessly, pulling them off the footpath and onto a bench. She keeps hold of him even after they're seated, eyes searching his face like she's trying to diagnose him. "You share your location with me, on your phone, remember? I've been chasing you all down the park. Ollie, are you okay?"

"I'm alive," he says, half-certain it's true. "God, Mum, I'm sorry."

"What on earth are you sorry for?" She sounds downright snappish now, releasing their joined hands and smoothing a strand of Oliver's rustled hair off his forehead.

"That I didn't tell you!" he replies, feeling like he's explaining the obvious. "That you saw people talking about my sex life on the telly."

"That part wasn't so nice, you're right. But you mustn't be sorry for the rest of it, for who you are. Ollie, you didn't have to tell me anything." Her voice is soft again, almost coaxing. Their knees are angled toward each other and bumping together. Her hand is still in his hair, scratching gently at the nape of his neck, the kind of comforting motion he's gotten from her a million times before.

"So you knew something?" he whispers, putting his head in his hands. He wondered if she might have. "Jesus. Aren't you angry with me for keeping it from you?"

"I didn't *know* anything. I might have suspected." Nicola puts her arms around him. Anyone could walk by and not even know it was him; his mum has wrapped him in both a hug and in a kind of shield. "But I would never have been angry, no matter what. I'll love you the same, Oliver, no matter who you are or who you become."

"I was afraid. If you knew, like, it wouldn't be a secret anymore. And I could only manage it secretly, barely even then. I just felt . . . I thought it had to be like this. We gave up so much, I didn't want to lose football too. I didn't want to lose the only parts of Camden we had left."

"You'll never lose them, Ollie. They're part of us," Nicola says, squeezing him tightly. She's right—all around them, Regent's Park looks the same as it ever has. They could have been here, just like this, at any point in Oliver's life. His dad could have been sitting with them.

"I wish I was telling you differently. On my own terms," he says quietly, voice cracking and muffled into her sleeve. He wishes he was telling Dad.

"You can tell me now, darling," Nicola soothes. "Anything and everything you want to."

So he does.

• • •

Oliver takes one great breath, a steadying, slightly frightened inhale, when he reaches the house. Tomorrow is all well and good, but tonight he needs to text Maggie and prepare her for the inevitable questions people will have for her. He's hoping Leo will help him with a script, but when he opens the front door and calls, "I'm home," he gets two hellos instead of one.

"Oh, for fucking hell," Oliver swears, hobbling up the stairs. "Does no one knock anymore? All year long, everyone has just been letting themselves into people's houses and wreaking havoc. You're supposed to wait until you're invited in!"

Joe and Leo are standing two paces apart in the sitting room, grimacing guiltily.

"May I come in?" Joe asks.

"I tried to hide," Leo adds sheepishly.

"Great job," Oliver tells him.

"Davito." Joe nudges Leo with one elbow. "Could you give us a minute?"

"I'll just go upstairs," Leo says. "If there is an upstairs. How would I know?"

He slips out of the room; Oliver gives him a very tired thumbs-up as he passes. Joe watches the exchange silently, settling himself proprietarily on one of the armchairs and raising his eyebrows at Oliver in an invitation to speak first. Oliver shakes his head, then crosses the room so he can sit cross-legged at Joe's feet, looking up at him expectantly.

"Oh, mate" is all Joe says. "I just came over to check on you," he goes on. "I didn't have any expectations one way or the other. My plan was, like, affirm and support. Open door for anything you wanted to talk about. But obviously I kind of, you know, found out what's what."

Oliver snorts a sad little laugh, shaking his head helplessly.

"And what's that?"

"Oliver," Joe says gravely, resting his hand on Oliver's tousled head like he's giving a priest's blessing. "You stupid bastard." It's not the first time someone's called Oliver that this year. It's been true every time. "Well, you're certainly punching above your weight class, looks-wise."

"Don't I know it," he replies, feeling the heavy weight of Joe's hand on his head, the only thing keeping him from floating away. "I was just hoping no one would tell him that, you know, before I've gotten things locked down."

"I tried, but I don't think you need to worry," Joe soothes him, scratching at Oliver's tired scalp now like he's petting a feral cat. "He's absolutely arse over tit for you."

Oliver tips forward, resting his head on Joe's knees and letting his shoulders shake—again somewhere between laughter and tears—just for a minute.

"I am too. For him. Well, arse over cock, maybe."

"I can tell, brother. How long has it been going on?" It's a credit to Joe that he doesn't even blink at the word "cock." Oliver can't wait to abuse this shamelessly in the future.

"With him? Not that long. For me, though, like, always. But, Joe, listen—I am . . . completely spent, emotionally. I want to talk about this stuff. I don't ever want to keep a secret from you again. But I feel like I'm gonna pass out."

"There's lots of time for us to talk," Joe says evenly, standing to go like it's as easy as that. "There's no rush, Oliver. I'll be here. Starting with tomorrow, hey?"

When Oliver turns back toward the rest of the house, Leo is crouched on the second-floor landing, still making a guilty face. "Sneak," Oliver greets him. "At least I don't have to debrief you."

Leo scampers down and tentatively touches Oliver's wrist with two fingers, halfway to holding hands.

"Well, that went better than I expected," Leo says, totally lacking in remorse for someone who was eavesdropping on a personal conversation. "Not that I expected anything bad from Joe, like. But it's nice. If anyone tries anything next season, he'll pop their Achilles tendon with the power of his mind."

"Don't give him any ideas," Oliver warns, taking Leo's hand properly and interlacing their fingers.

"Hmmm," Leo says, squeezing their knuckles together tightly. "I think we should order two large pizzas and not look at the internet again until July. You in?"

"But what will *you* eat?"

"You are not even a little bit funny," Leo replies, but cheerfully, peppering Oliver's face with kisses, loud, smacking ones. "Get the good stuff, would you? Not Pizza Express."

Oliver has his marching orders: two margherita pizzas and a side of halloumi, panna cotta for dessert, more dairy than the human body should be able to tolerate—they're on vacation.

It's been a spell since he's walked for takeaway, saving his legs for the pitch, and when Oliver reaches the restaurant's red awning, dotted with flower boxes, he sees that the great brick wall over the ceiling up toward the roof is the home of the same mural Leo took a photo of so many months ago, that beautiful portrait of Oliver himself. It's still there now, only it's been recently defaced.

Pizza Express will have to do. Sorry, Leo, he thinks, turning to head back the way he came and immediately bumping right into a teenager who yelps and almost tips over a bucket of paint.

"Sorry, mate, sorry," Oliver says, wishing he'd thought to wear something with a hood or at least put on a hat.

"It's you," the paint holder says, sounding surprised and pleased, rubbing his shirt hem at his glasses' lens to get a better look at Oliver.

"Kind of embarrassing, to be honest. I just fancied a pizza. Though I suppose I might have known something like that might happen," he says, gesturing at the big *F* at the start of the graffiti.

"It's my uncle's place," the kid explains. "He hit the fucker with a broom when he caught him at it."

Oliver can't help but laugh, picturing a mustachioed old man in a sauce-stained apron chasing off the vandal, screaming in Italian.

"It's really beautiful," Oliver tells him sincerely. "Davito—er, Leo—sent it to me, months ago. I'm glad you wanted to keep it up, after all this."

"After all what?" the gangly youth asks, fumbling around his pocket for a cigarette, like it's nothing. "Oh, Harris got us back into the Champions League for the first time in decades, let's tear down his mural because he might like blokes! Who wouldn't fancy Leonardo Davies-Villanueva, after the season he's had? Come off it. I'm going to fix it and then paint him too."

"Well, thank you, then," Oliver stammers, bewildered. "I've

always thought you did a great job on it. Glad I got to tell you in person."

"Cheers, mate. Thank *you* for scoring all those goals." They laugh and Oliver starts to be on his way, waving awkwardly, before the kid calls back to him. "Say, do you, actually?"

"Actually?"

"Fancy blokes. Him, Leo."

"I really, really do." Oliver's voice shakes, but he doesn't lower it.

"Right on, Harris. Good luck next season."

• • •

In the morning, all the cheese they eventually got around to scarfing, after several more phone conversations and many more missed calls, threatens to make a reappearance—Oliver doesn't think he could keep down water, much less coffee. Leo is, predictably, dolloping jam into his yogurt on top of half a bag of muesli like it's nothing. If Oliver offered to cook, Leo could probably put away a dozen eggs, no problem.

"Aren't you nervous?" Oliver asks, straightening Leo's shirt collar for the fifteenth time.

"Of course I am," Leo says, batting him away. "That's why I'm stress eating."

He can't argue with that; Oliver suspects Leo might have had the right idea once they get to the Crossing and his nerves compound with his empty stomach, leaving him feeling faint. They're early, the locker room is barren, but that's almost worse, standing in the front of the room in business casual, waiting for the beginning of the end. It's a small consolation that Leo looks so dashing next to him, as if he's planning on coming out as a high-fashion model rather than a bisexual. Everyone arrives in one jumbled flood only moments later. Charles is missing, Gavin arriving last and all alone.

Oliver can sense his teammates searching his face for answers, but he keeps his head down, making the barest of small talk with Sebastian, who won't stop touching Oliver's elbow like a comforting nag. Eventually, Willem clears his throat and everyone stands at attention like this is a normal training session.

"I appreciate you making time for this, right at the start of vacation," Willem says in that going-on-posh way of his, the one that means he's going to assimilate in England just fine. "I'm going to give Oliver the floor, but I want to say my piece first: Your presence is noticed and we are thankful for it. I expect this same show of commitment and solidarity, publicly, going forward."

He steps back, leaving Oliver center stage. Oliver is not quite sure when it was agreed he would be the mouthpiece instead of charming, charismatic Leo.

"Well, now that the stakes are nice and high," he says uncomfortably, as Willem raises his hands in apology; the room laughs tensely. "Gaffer said it best: it means a lot to me that you're all here. I know you've probably seen the stuff on the telly, online, about me, about Leo, and I know you have a lot of questions."

"What exactly is going on, Ollie?" Trevor asks. "Are you all right, man?"

"I am, Trev, I swear. We all are. The thing is, the media speculation is right. Leo and I are—well, we . . ." Oliver trails off uselessly, wishing everyone could fill in the blanks for themselves, then steels his nerves, reminding himself what the point of all this is, of the life in front of him where he never has to avert his eyes or tell a lie again. "We're . . . involved, romantically, like. We're together. I'm gay. Leo's bisexual, which is different, but for our purposes right now, kind of the same."

The oxygen sucks right out of the room, but no masks drop from the ceiling. Next to him, Leo has gone tense and combative, like he does when he wants to give a defender the excuse to foul him.

"You're . . . together?" Carda asks, pointing between the two of them and looking flabbergasted.

"This isn't something I really wanted to talk about at work," Oliver goes on, ignoring the question and meeting Joe's eyes, trying in vain to look nowhere else. "But since the issue was forced, since those photos caused all these questions—I don't want to lie. I don't think I've done anything that needs to be covered up. This isn't a piece of myself I planned on sharing, it's something I consider private, but the truth is that I'd rather give the Rovers some more material about me than pretend I'm something I'm not. And what I am is in love with Leo. As much as I'm a Rose, a midfielder, a vice captain. We're going to say much the same thing in the press conference later, and I wanted you to know first, because you're my teammates, and you're important to me. I hope that we are important to you too, enough to have your support in this. So, ah, thanks for listening, I guess. That's all I've got to say."

The room erupts, a din of questions and frowns and a handful of smiles, some forced and others huge. Oliver retreats from it, stepping backward and sitting down at his locker lamely, feeling spent. Anthony immediately appears at his side, crouching down and putting a hand on Oliver's knee, holding on tight.

"Did I not literally just tell you I'm fucking Davito?" Oliver mutters out of the corner of his mouth. "Ease up."

Anthony only holds on harder, looking up at Oliver with something between pride and flint on his sun-freckled face. The room is funneling the noise in their direction, looking at the two captains sitting together, demanding answers.

"Shut *up*!" Anthony roars at the pack of them, looking away from Oliver for the first time. "One at a time, you animals, I swear on my mum."

"And if you put one toe out of line, just know, I'm going to actually, literally kill you," Joe adds, a good head taller than everyone else and looking entirely threatening. "So, Finn, why don't you go first."

"I just want to say: you still have to pass to the rest of us," Finn announces to the room matter-of-factly, undeterred by Joe's simmering violence, as Dutch as a windmill, almost like the two of them planned this in advance. Oliver suspects they might have. "You can't play favorites now."

"Why don't you come give me a kiss, Finny," Oliver replies, drunk with honesty, nonplussed and thankful for an initial response he's equipped to respond to. "Then we'll talk."

Finn plays right along, grinning dangerously and stalking toward Oliver, lips puckered and smacking, and he makes to shove Anthony out of the way. Most of the team boos when Oliver shoves Finn off in turn, but Leo whispers, "Phew," and then there's more laughter, sounding real this time, almost like it's a normal day at training, the spell broken, most everyone converging on the pair of them to offer congratulations, to hug them, even. It does break his heart that Charles isn't there. He searches the room for him sadly, then slips to the edges of the crowd, where Gavin is waiting for him.

"What's happened?" Oliver asks.

"I told him not to come," Gavin replies in a low, tight voice. "Not if he couldn't be there for you right. And that I wouldn't play with him until he could be."

Charles and Gavin have been friends longer than Oliver's been alive; they've stood together at touchlines and marriage altars and christening ceremonies—a deeper relationship than Oliver could claim with Leo, when it comes down to it—and Gavin told him not to come. Then he showed up. Oliver feels unmoored by the depth of that; he doesn't have the words for describing it, much less repaying it, being worthy of it. He touches Gavin's shoulder cautiously, then accepts the resulting embrace that the gruff defender yanks him in for, and then, finally, the crush of the rest of the bodies as the team converges on him, holding him down to the floor and keeping him in the room with them.

"Here's to Leo, right?" Matty asks, ruffling Leo's head affably. "Here's to the man who finally bagged Harris! We always thought it wasn't possible, brother."

Leo blushes, looking at Oliver with the same face he made once before, right before he kissed him for the first time, when fear gave way to desire. It feels just as good this time.

Eventually, Sebastian reminds them there's a press conference to give, and they make their way out into the largest conference room, everyone milling about while the stage is set and the reporters line up outside, shoving like they're trying to get on the barricade at a rock and roll show. Other attendees are being shown in by one of Nina's assistants, and suddenly Nicola is there, waving to Maggie and looking assured in a blazer and tall in a pair of pumps. When Oliver calls out to her, she makes a beeline for Leo and envelops him in her arms, then pulls back to give Leo a good look, and suddenly she's crying silently, wiping two little oil-slick spills of mascara off her cheeks. Leo's lower lip quivers and Nicola reaches up, cupping his face in her palms and standing up on her toes to kiss him on the forehead.

"I have really, really been looking forward to meeting you," she whispers. "And I thought you might need a mother's hug."

"You were right," Leo says, blinking away the threat of his own tears. Oliver can hear the room still filling in behind them, the clock ticking somewhere above their heads, but he wants to stay here and watch these two people get to know each other, possibly forever. "Nicola, thank you."

"I know you two have to go—just tell me before you leave, Leo, dear, shall I give your parents a ring? So they can hear the conference?"

"That's really kind of you, Nicola," Leo says, tasting the

name again like he's looking for any excuse to use it. "Our friend Ahmed, he's got them on FaceTime." True to his word, Ahmed is on hand holding Leo's phone out to the room—a blurry, good-looking couple occupying the screen—while keeping himself one foot away from Leo at all times like he might need to play bodyguard.

A whole host of other unexpected people have shown up to quite literally stand in support. In the time they've been with Nicola, the room has fit itself to bursting. The de Boers are huddled in a cluster, Ilse holding Willem's hand and Sophie giving Oliver a worldly shrug, like, *Well, you can't win them all*. Maggie is holding court with half the squad. Alec, the youth manager who came to Nicola after the funeral and saved Oliver's whole life, looking wizened but still in his customary tracksuit, is forming a triangle with Sebastian and Anna, stage-whispering, *We'll talk later,* when Oliver starts toward them.

"This is bedlam," Oliver whispers to Leo. "I feel like I'm in a parallel universe."

"You didn't mention your mum has been absolutely frothing at the mouth for you to bring home a man," Leo replies woozily.

"I think it might be that you're such a catch, honestly."

"Do you think they all really mean it?" Leo asks. "That it's okay? Or are they just feeling guilty?"

"I hope they mean it," Oliver says. "But if they don't, Joe's going to kill them, right? So it's sort of out of our hands."

"Lads," Nina says, appearing between their elbows and smiling encouragingly. "Shall we?"

"You've got it, boss," Oliver tells her. She swats at him cheerfully and guides them into the little hallway that separates the press room from the holding area. Willem is now waiting there, straightening his tie, with Terence Morgan at his side.

"Gaffer?" Oliver asks.

"Yes?" they reply in unison.

"Er, Terry, I mean," Oliver says. "I knew you'd be here, Willem."

The older men laugh, Willem tucking Oliver under one arm and Terence putting Leo under his own in a perfectly choreographed maneuver.

"I'm your manager too," Terence says evenly. "And if I'm going to bring you both to the World Cup next year, I want it to be very clear where I stand on the matter."

World Cup, Leo mouths at Oliver, eyes sparkling. The dark curtain tunnel they're waiting in and the muted noise from next door drape over him like a shock blanket until Oliver's senses ebb away. He remembers imagining the World Cup final, Leo appearing in his dreamscape unexpectedly. Maybe it was a premonition.

"Let them get through this, then we'll talk about national call-ups, shall we?" Willem says to Terence before looking over the pair of them seriously. "Gentlemen, are you ready?"

Oliver shakes himself back to awareness, looking over at Leo to confirm, reveling in the fact that he's allowed to now; he's supposed to. He nods with the same ferocity he brings to the pitch and sticks out his hand defiantly. Oliver takes it tenderly, interlacing their fingers and holding on for dear life. It's not so different from starting a match, really: he just takes one deep breath and steps out, right into the great flashbulb sea of light.

Friday, June 30, 2017: Camden Town, London

42 DAYS UNTIL MATCHDAY 1

The line at the coffee shop had stretched all the way from the till to the door, spilling messily onto the street. Oliver has nowhere to be and the wait would have been worth it regardless, because now he's strolling home and Camden is in full bloom; roses are bursting and ballooning off every planter, coating the air with the smell of a spilled bottle of wine. It's perfect like this, a midsummer morning's dream—Oliver is, too, laden with latte and pastry, a rose himself, down to the red in his cheeks.

Every time someone recognizes Oliver now—somehow even more than before—the whole last month replays in slo-mo in his mind, plotting the distance between point A and here. It's been a whirlwind of publicity, more than he bargained for, pushing at the upper limits of fame. There are new *New York Times* headlines, and party invites, and the scary feeling of going to a concert hand in hand, scarier still when Robbie bloody Williams shouts them out in the audience and the whole arena roars when he says someone ought to make Oliver a knight (he'll pass, thanks), and even after all that there have been the security threats, and keynote speeches, and this new frame around his life that leaves him split open in a way he still doesn't want to take back. Every day of vacation, today's normal, wonderful morning, is so much bigger and better than he dreamed, the line at the till time well spent, being stopped for photos by teenage girls with pink hair instead of their dads.

Oliver still flashes back to the press conference on most days, remembering the primal pull of it cut with levels of anxiety like being hunted for sport, rapidly overtaken by some kind of righteous indignation.

"Do you think your personal life will be the story next season?" a bespectacled journo had asked right at the start, looking at him over his glasses like he was personally disappointed with Oliver's choices. "Will it be a distraction for the team, all this attention on who you're . . . seeing?"

Willem had moved to interrupt, reaching for a table microphone like he was making to throw it, but Oliver had spoken first, before he could talk himself out of it.

"All due respect," he'd replied, meaning it entirely disrespectfully, "I'm Oliver Harris, aren't I? You lot were already writing about my romantic life. This is just par for the course, I should think."

Then he'd shrugged affably and the room exploded, evenly split between follow-up questions from the reporters and suggestive whoops from the Camden squad.

"Take a bow," Leo had whispered from his left, and the photograph of the two of them huddled together, Oliver grinning smugly and Leo smushed along his side, cupping his ear, makes it above the fold in nearly every major newspaper in the world.

Other memories float their way back to him, too, like his actual favorite press conference moment of all time, coming from Ryan Loxley, who announced in Kilburn's respective end-of-season presser that he didn't hate Oliver because he was gay, only because he's a bellend, and he just wants everyone to be clear on that. Woodsy still sends the video clip of it to the team group chat once a day, like clockwork.

Probably the kindest response was the text from Conor Bishop, reading: Glad to know my radar for these things is still in working order. I'm proud to know you.

("Come off it! That guy actually wants you so bad," Leo had exclaimed, craning to look over his shoulder.

"He's just got good taste. You staked your claim pretty clearly," Oliver replied loyally, pulling Leo close and kissing the crown of his head.)

Probably his *least* favorite reaction is still unfolding, in the form of Henri having asked Oliver for Maggie's number, which, apparently, he figured was all well and fair, on account of Oliver not liking women. When she'd first said they were going out for dinner, Oliver felt a sudden urge to acquire weaponry.

("Henri? Really?" he'd asked.

"Listen, Ollie, I went for the right kind of footballer once before—" Maggie had begun saying.

"There is no right kind of footballer!" Oliver yelled back.

"And look where that got me. If I want a handsome Frenchman with a mustache to explain wine vintages to me, that's my right as a woman. Don't piss me off," she'd said, settling the matter.

"I want *you* to be happy, Maggie, but I'm going to kick *his* arse.")

Despite his best attempts at reasoning with her, Maggie is well and truly besotted. Leo, the turncoat, is on her side—they went shopping for sunhats to wear on her impending trip to the South of France, even after Oliver threatened a hunger strike. So, he hasn't yet kicked Henri's stupid *derrière,* but he's going to. On the training ground, where there's plausible deniability. After dark, when there are no witnesses.

He's still deciding what exactly to do about that, just crossing St. Mark's Crescent, when Leo appears up the street, jogging toward him, dressed implausibly in the hideous Hawaiian-print shirt Oliver bought for Joe's stag do, worn open over his shirtless chest, flagging Oliver down like a drunken, queer traffic marshal.

"What on earth happened to you?" Oliver asks as Leo skids to a stop in front of him and snags one of the coffees, gulping and then wagging his burned tongue in pain.

"Come on, you've got to come home."

"Is the house on fire?" He's not entirely joking. Leo is allowed to use the kitchen, but not without supervision.

"There's a great deal, super cheap, on first-class tickets to Medellín," Leo wheezes. "Only one stop, Ollie! My mum is on the phone, she wants us to book now."

"Do we need a deal?" Oliver is now being made a spectacle of, pulled down the street by the hem of his shirt, croissants jostling dangerously in their paper bag. "How much money have you just re-signed for, anyway?"

"It's about the thrill of the thing, Ollie—honestly, don't you know anything?" Leo explains impatiently, picking up the pace. "Would you please come *on*, my grandma insists on picking people up from the airport, but she goes to bed at half past eight. Hurry!"

All the impending vacation chaos unfolds itself in front of him like a road map of disaster: Leo definitely won't be ready to leave for the airport in time, Oliver will inevitably make a fool of himself trying to speak Spanish with Abuela, and by the time they get back to London it will practically be preseason, so they'll show up jet-lagged to the first week of training and Willem will absolutely be able to tell.

Who is he kidding? He can't fucking wait, not for any of it—not if he's doing it with Leo.

ACKNOWLEDGMENTS

I'm very much like Oliver: I love winning. So I am thrilled to report that I hit the absolute jackpot in life, to have so many people on my team who made *Two Left Feet* possible and every draft better.

Wesley, who was my boyfriend when I started writing, and has since been a stellar fiancé and a wonderful husband: I love you madly. Being with you makes every word part of a love story.

My agent, Caroline, who is a dream collaborator and the best person to have in your corner. Knowing you has changed my life and career forever. I owe you and the team at Frances Goldin a debt of gratitude.

My editor, Jesse, and everyone at Ballantine, who have already taught me so much in such a short time. It's a great privilege to have your stewardship in art and in life. I can't wait to do it again.

My beloved friend Shannon, whose watchfulness, care, and affection gave the manuscript sentience like Frankenstein's sickest little monster. Without you, *Two Left Feet* would never have been more than a hundred words of daydreams. Thank you—and Matt and Peach—for being there, always.

Many people sat next to me in comfortable silence (it's not

overrated!) while I tried to untangle this idea after meetings and on trains and in cafés from San Francisco to Brooklyn to London to Barcelona.

The Gregg-Brittons and my new Emblidge-Holley family. My best friends and very best readers, Angelica, Anna, David, Marea, Miriam, Olivia. My colleagues at the *Post* and *The Atlantic.* My comrades in leadership at the Post Guild.

No one has ever been . . . more loved and more lucky . . . to have your support. Camden's winning streaks will always belong to you as much as they do to Oliver and Leo.

TWO LEFT FEET

Kallie Emblidge

A BOOK CLUB GUIDE

A Letter from the Author

Dear Reader,

Have you ever watched a sporting event and felt like you were on the field with the team, because you were *that* invested in the outcome? If you've been there, *Two Left Feet* is for you.

It's okay if you're a lover and not a footballer, though. Have you ever had a first kiss so iconic it changes your life and alters your brain chemistry forever? If you've been *there, Two Left Feet* is also very much for you.

To me, there's nothing more romantic than football, except for the love and community that you inherit as a queer person. And there's nothing more important in football than the special kind of affection that comes from being on the same team. So this story was always grounded in two of the great loves of my life, which have a lot more in common than we give them credit for.

This is my first novel, but it was a long time coming. When I finally put pen to paper, it was always going to be a love story, and it was always going to be about the beautiful game. I got into football when I was young and needed something to believe in; I latched onto La Liga and the Prem like they were a religion. They still are to me.

I like to imagine a world where a future Oliver Harris might come out and go on to play in the World Cup. I can only imagine it because of the many, many talented women who have already done it. Here's to all of them—and here's to you.

Up the roses,
Kallie

The Official *Two Left Feet* Playlist

From the music library of Leonardo Davies-Villanueva

"Once Upon a Poolside" – The National, Sufjan Stevens
"Seventeen Going Under" – Sam Fender
"Wolf Pack" – The Vaccines
"You Get What You Give" – New Radicals
"this must be the place" – dad sports
"What You Know" – Two Door Cinema Club
"Knee Socks" – Arctic Monkeys
"Fame and Fortune" – The Libertines
"Pressure" – The 1975
"Futbol Rock" – CLUBZ, Little Jesus
"I'll Be Your Man" – The Black Keys
"Saturdays" – Twin Shadow, Haim
"Yo x Ti, Tu x Mi" – Rosalía, Ozuna
"Everybody Loves You" – APRE
"Sixteen" – Kayslee Don Collins, Oceans1985
"Tiny Moves" – Bleachers
"Runner" – Alex G

"We're So In Tune" – Kississippi
"White Ferrari" – Frank Ocean
"Free" – Florence and the Machine
"Fine Line" – Harry Styles
"Boyhood" – The Japanese House
"Caution" – The Killers
"Season 2" – Phoenix
"Hey Jude" – The Beatles
"Closer" – The Kooks

Oliver Harris's Guide to London

A thinking man's guide to the best city in the world

Queen Mary's Rose Gardens

Chester Road

Leo ran here after the Chelsea match. I could not keep up.

Marylebone

St. Vincent Street

Leo's neighborhood, but just until I'm ready for him to move in with me.

Camden Market

54-56 Camden Lock Place

Formerly home of the Harris family bookstall.

Daunt Books Marylebone

83-84 Marylebone High Street

A great place to buy books, ever since the stall closed.

The Regent's Park

Prince Albert Road

Regent Road, up the roses!

Castlehaven Arms

At the corner of Delancey Street and Camden High Street

One of Conor's bars. Good beer and better company.

Pizza and Murals

At the corner of A4201 and Arlington Road

Best pizza in the neighborhood. It helps that there's a painting of me and Leo on the side of the building.

Camden Crossing

Near Talacre Town Green

Spent most of my life right here.

My Place

On Regent's Park Road, near St. Mark's Church

Between the park and the canal. The best house in London.

Oliver Harris's Football Reading List

A reading man's guide to the beautiful game

The Glory Game by Hunter Davies
Spend a year embedded with Tottenham Hotspur (they're no Camden, but it's still a perfect read) in the 1970s.

How Soccer Explains the World by Franklin Foer
It's called football, but it really does explain the world!

The Striker and the Clock: On Being in the Game by Georgia Cloepfil
Ninety remarkable essays, one for each minute of a match.

Fever Pitch by Nick Hornby
A classic memoir about the shape of a life happening in between Arsenal matches.

Fear and Loathing in La Liga: Barcelona, Real Madrid, and the World's Greatest Sports Rivalry by Sid Lowe
A clever history on the only derby as intense as Camden vs. Kilburn.

Brilliant Orange: The Neurotic Genius of Dutch Football by David Winner
Important to read to understand why Willem is like *that*.

© ERIKA COLBERTALDO

Kallie Emblidge works for *The Washington Post* and is a co-chair of the paper's union. She lives and writes in New York City. *Two Left Feet* is her debut novel, but she's been a football fan forever.

kallieemblidge.com

Instagram: @kallie.emblidge

Bluesky: @kallieemblidge.bsky.com

ABOUT THE TYPE

This book was set in Sabon, a typeface designed by the well-known German typographer Jan Tschichold (1902–74). Sabon's design is based upon the original letter forms of sixteenth-century French type designer Claude Garamond and was created specifically to be used for three sources: foundry type for hand composition, Linotype, and Monotype. Tschichold named his typeface for the famous Frankfurt typefounder Jacques Sabon (c. 1520–80).